# PRAISE FOR LYNSAY SANDS!

"Intrigue and humor . . . that will make you laugh and turn up the air conditioning. 4½ stars."

—*Romantic Times* on *Always*

"Lynsay Sands (is) . . . talented at creating endearing romps."

—*All About Romance*

"The Key is a happy surprise . . . a whimsical tale that never sacrifices smarts for silliness."

—*The Romance Reader*

"Lynsay Sands's strength lies in creating very light entertainment with elements of comedy."

—*All About Romance*

"Readers are swept up in a delicious, merry and often breath-catching roller coaster ride that will keep them on the edge of their seats and laughing out loud. A true delight!"

—*Romantic Times* on *The Deed*

# BEYOND RESTRAINT

"Hmmm." She peered at him doubtfully. "So, you're a virgin too?"

"Too?" Daniel seemed to sag with relief, apparently pleased by her admission. Then what she had asked sank in, and he frowned. "Nay, I—Only women must refrain until after they are married."

"Ah ha!" she crowed, a bit derisively. "Ladies are the only ones who must restrain themselves! Not men! Now is that not interesting?" she asked. "Who exactly would it be who made up that rule, do ye think? Men, mayhap?"

"Aye, but—"

"Now why do you suppose that is?"

"So they would know that any heirs born of the union are theirs," he answered.

"Oh, *of course*," she sneered. "That *must* be it. It would not be another way to control women. Nay, of course not."

"Well," he smiled slightly. "No doubt they enjoy the fact that it also makes women behave a certain way. But the fact is, a man—even myself—does not wish to leave his family estate and name to someone else's by-blow."

Valoree's eyebrows rose slightly, and then she nodded her head. "I suppose I can understand how that might be an issue in the normal course of things," she admitted, then shrugged. "But nothing about my situation is normal. I am the one with the land and title. I also must produce an heir. And as it is a business deal, whomever I marry will have no rights in the matter of what I do with my body. So . . . "

Stepping closer, she pushed his undone shirt off his shoulders, licking a path from his right nipple up to his neck as she did. Then she pressed her breasts against his chest, kissing him just below the ear, and murmured, "Help me make a baby."

Other *Leisure* books by Lynsay Sands:
ALWAYS
SWEET REVENGE
THE SWITCH
THE KEY
THE DEED

# LADY PIRATE

## LYNSAY SANDS

LEISURE BOOKS     NEW YORK CITY

A LEISURE BOOK®

January 2001

Published by

Dorchester Publishing Co., Inc.
276 Fifth Avenue
New York, NY 10001

ISBN 0-8439-4816-7

The name "Leisure Books" and the stylized "L" with design are trademarks of Dorchester Publishing Co., Inc.

Printed in the United States of America.

Visit us on the web at www.dorchesterpub.com.

# *Prologue*

*The Caribbean—late 1700s*

The water was flat as a looking glass, capturing the moonlight and stars that twinkled down from above and reflecting just enough light that the ship gliding ahead of them appeared black and ghostlike in the darkness.

From her position at the front of the small dugout canoe in which she rode, Valoree motioned, and the men at the oars immediately slowed their rowing. At another signal, the sailors raised their oars out of the water, and the craft slid silently up beside the larger craft.

Immediately those on the left side of the canoe withdrew hooks on long ropes and sent them whistling through the air to catch on the rail above. For a moment they waited, staring breathlessly up the side of the large galleon and holding the lines, allowing their craft to be dragged along by the larger ship's momentum. At last, when a hue and cry failed to arise, all eyes slowly returned to Valoree.

She stared back, knowing these men all saw her as a slender young man—little more than a boy, really. All of them but Henry. He alone knew that their deceased captain's younger brother Valerian, who had served as a cabin boy these last eight years, was really a girl. Of course *he* knew; he'd been the one who had suggested the charade so many years before, when he'd realized that Jeremy—his captain and her brother—intended to keep her aboard a ship full of pirates.

Aye, these men all thought her a lad, young and untried. And yet, they had vowed to follow her. Only a desire for vengeance could make these two dozen men, cutthroats and hooligans all, follow someone they had always looked upon as a green lad, a little brother or son to be coddled and spoiled. And vengeance they would have.

Glancing down into the water, Valoree took in her reflection. Her body was slim—she was lean rather than muscular—and it trembled with anticipation. For a moment she imagined that her eyes were no longer those of the youth who had moved easily among these men, laughing and chatting as she'd gone about her chores. Nay, her eyes now seemed old, hard, bitter with fresh loss. A loss these men shared as well.

Her brother had been a good man and a fair captain, and his ship, the *Valor*, had been the only home most of his crew had known for the last eight years. The men who now accompanied her were the last of that crew. She glanced around at them, then back at her reflection.

Though her shirt was her own, she now wore her brother's breeches, along with his hat and jacket. Jeremy's boarding ax and pike were hooked through the thick belt at her waist, and a brass-barreled flintlock was sticking out of those baggy, too-large pants. The captain's cutlass rested in its sheath where it hung at her side. She had taken his clothing when she had sworn vengeance for his death—and she had not bathed since.

Every inch of her body, every item, every inch of cloth, wood, and metal was covered with its owner's dried blood, as were Valoree's face, hands, and feet. Even her long hair was crusty with the stuff. Though it was normally a vibrant, fiery red—as her brother's had been—it was now streaked through with crimson, marked by the red blood of her brother's death—a reminder of her vow.

Her brother had not died easily. He had not died quickly. He, along with the majority of his men, had died slowly and in torment. And for that, Valoree and the remainder of Jeremy's crew had vowed, these Spaniards would pay.

She glanced toward Skully and nodded. The cadaverous man immediately reached for his tools, and Valoree turned her back as he began to bore holes in the bottom of their craft. She regarded her crew, awaiting their reaction. She did not have long to wait. Skully was still working on the second hole when the last of them turned to her in understanding. In their faces she read approval and a grudging respect. To reassure them of her intent, she half hissed, half whispered, "We take this ship or we die. There is no escape. We fight not only to avenge the deaths of good men, but for our lives."

"For our lives and vengeance," Henry vowed beside her in a hushed tone. His words were immediately taken up by the others.

"Life and vengeance!"

She relaxed somewhat at their acceptance, an odd calm overtaking her as she silently watched Skully finish boring the holes in the bottom of their boat. The holes were relatively small, but even so, by the time he had started on the sixth, the boat was already gathering water and beginning to sink.

As Skully hurriedly returned his tools to his satchel, Valoree drew her brother's cutlass from its sheath. Moving to the side of their slowly sinking ship, she led the men in a stealthy climb up the side of the Spanish galleon. Her bare hands and feet moved surely up the rope until she reached the top, the others close behind. Pausing there, Valoree peered over the side and glared about.

Several men, taking advantage of the night breeze, were sleeping out in the open air of the deck. Valoree glanced toward the helm and smiled grimly upon seeing the helmsman. The man, while still at his post, had nodded off and was now dozing away his shift, senseless. There was no one to give an alarm. The Spaniards would be taken completely by surprise.

Slipping silently over the side, Valoree hunkered low, sticking to the shadows. Her men followed. As the last of them slid to the deck, she gestured silently, dividing them into two groups with one simple wave of her hand, then gesturing for one group to stay above deck, while directing the others toward the dark hole that was the entrance to the cabins. They all began to move at once, separating and moving all over the ship. The men above deck positioned themselves among the sleeping Spaniards, ready to set to work, but waiting the few moments necessary to allow those men slipping through the hole to reach their targets, lest some sound or death cry warn their enemies below.

Leaving the rest of the crew to the others, Valoree moved stealthily toward the helmsman. She had nearly reached him when something startled the man awake.

Drawing a sword, the Spaniard peered blearily at her. She froze, but his gaze found her anyway. Taking in Jeremy's bloody clothes and her red hair flowing about her blood-streaked face, he blinked.

*"Rojo . . . El Capitán Rojo?"*

Valoree stiffened at the words, recognizing the name the Spanish used for her brother. Captain Red, because of his red hair.

*"Regresa del muerto . . . El Rojo,"* the man whispered faintly, then straightened abruptly, shrieking. *"Regresa del muerto. El Rojo!"*

His cry awoke others nearby, and the sleepy-eyed

men turned to gape at her in horror. The helmsman's cry was taken up again and again. *"Regresa del muerto. El Rojo!"*

For a moment, everyone was still. The others she'd brought with her, startled by the shouting, turned to peer at Valoree. She drew back, annoyed, then peered about at the frozen tableau. Her crewmates seemed as transfixed as the Spaniards. With a glance at the nearest of the men, she snapped irritably, "What the devil is he saying, Henry?"

Drawn out of his startled state by the question, the quartermaster relaxed and grimly smiled. Then he shrugged. "He's thinkin' ye're yer own brother, Captain Red. He's thinkin' ye're back from the dead. He's screamin' 'Back-from-the-Dead Red,' " he explained. The cry continued around them.

*"Regresa del muerto. El Rojo!"*

"Back-from-the-Dead Red?" Valoree repeated, then frowned at the terrified Spaniards. "Well, at least they shall know why they die." Raising Jeremy's cutlass, she advanced on the helmsman, but much to her consternation, the man immediately dropped his weapon. For a moment, Valoree was nonplussed, but the sudden chorus of metal against wood drew her attention to the fact that every Spaniard aboard the ship was now giving up his weapon unasked, all dropping them to the deck floor.

"What the devil are they doing?" Valoree cried in dismay. "Are they not going to fight?"

Henry glanced around, then turned to face her. "Well," he drawled, scratching at his ear. "I'm thinkin' they're thinkin' that since ye're a ghost and all, there ain't no sense in afightin' ye. Most like they think we're the rest of the men that were kilt . . . and ye cain't kill someone what's already dead."

*"El Rojo."*

Valoree glanced up at hearing again the helmsman's

15

terrified murmur. The Spaniard was now tugging his pistol free and dropping it on the deck beside his sword. Throughout, he continued mumbling, *"Regresa del muerto. El Rojo."*

Before she could decide on a course of action, a scuffle at the entrance to the cabins drew her attention. Valoree glanced over as the men who had gone below returned, pushing several captives ahead of them. The first was obviously the captain, and he looked angry. He also looked willing to fight, Valoree saw with relief. At least someone would. It was hard to take revenge when the enemy refused to fight. She wouldn't simply kill unarmed men; that was not fair. She was just about to move to confront the Spanish captain when the helmsman spotted his commander. He immediately shrieked, *"El Rojo! Regresa del muerto!"*

The captain started to glance toward the man, but his gaze caught and stayed on Valoree. The whipping wind filled the cloth of Jeremy's jacket, making her appear larger than she was, and she had to fight to keep her bloody red hair from covering her eyes. She pulled Jeremy's hat down further onto her head and glared at the Spaniard with hatred. The man gaped, then murmured, *"El Rojo?"*

*"Sí,"* the helmsman cried. *"El Rojo, regresa del muerto."*

"Shut up!" Valoree said in a growl to the mouthy sailor. She was sick of hearing those words. Stark terror entered the captain's face as well. "Tell him to shut up, Henry," she said hurriedly.

Henry translated the order into Spanish, but the panicked helmsman could not have obeyed had he wished to. He seemed able only to repeat himself over and over. Irritated, Valoree drew Jeremy's flintlock pistol and shot him.

The man dropped to the deck with a shriek, grabbing for the wound in his leg.

As if that were the signal for some preplanned form of action, the Spaniards all made a sudden exodus toward the sides of the ship. Taken by surprise, Valoree and the others could only watch in amazement as the crew of the galleon, as one, cast themselves screaming into shark-infested water.

Cursing under her breath, Valoree stalked to the side of the ship and peered down at the men in the sea below. They were thrashing about in the water, moving in the general direction of the nearest island. "The gunny cowards," she muttered.

"Aye," Henry agreed. He and the rest of the men had moved closer to peer down at their fleeing adversaries.

Slamming a palm down on the rail in frustration, Valoree cursed. "Jumping rather than fighting, can you imagine?"

Henry shook his head. "Spineless Spanish bastards."

Sighing, she frowned at the water below. A moment later, One-Eye let out a dismayed oath. Glancing up, Valoree peered over at where he was pointing. The helmsman was on his feet, and had hopped to the side of the ship. He was now balancing himself precariously on the railing. As she watched in amazement, the man hefted himself over the side of the boat to land with a splash in the water behind his comrades. It seemed that swimming with sharks was more attractive than keeping company with ghosts, even for the wounded man.

"Ye want we should shoot them?" One-Eye asked with little enthusiasm.

Valoree shook her head in disgust. "Leave go. They are not likely to make it to shore. 'Sides, none of them bore the scar." She desired revenge, but there was no pleasure in killing cowards.

The others nodded in agreement. Besides, this was apparently not the ship of their true enemy. One of the

17

few things they had learned from Jeremy, ere he took his last breath, was that the Spaniard who had ordered the torturous deaths of her brother and so many of his men bore a scar in the shape of a question mark on his neck. And the captain of this vessel had borne no such scar.

Sighing, Valoree straightened and turned to survey the Spanish galleon. "Well," she said softly, "it would seem we have a ship."

"Aye," Henry murmured. "That it would."

"Have we enough men to sail it?"

Henry surveyed the small number of their remaining crew. "Aye," he said. "Enough to get to port and pick up more men . . . Captain."

Valoree glanced at him sharply. "Captain?"

He nodded solemnly. "Aye. Of this, the Valor II. I'm thinkin' we've got us a fine captain. Ye've the spirit, the courage, the determination . . . and, better yet, ye've already got yerself a reputation and title." When she looked bewildered, he shrugged. "Ye've already taken yer first ship. If any of those men out there survive their swim, all will hear about their terrifying encounter with Back-from-the-Dead Red."

Valoree rolled her eyes and glanced at the others. All of them were standing about, nodding in agreement. It seemed she had not only stepped into her brother's clothes, but she had also stepped into his command. Back-from-the-Dead Red, indeed. Thanks to a load of superstitious Spaniards, she was now the captain of some of the most bloodthirsty cutthroats it had ever been her misfortune to meet—if she wanted them. She was only nineteen. That was young to be a captain. But then, Jeremy had been only eighteen when she had helped him purchase and outfit the *Valor*. And as for her gender, they already thought her a boy.

Seeing her hesitation, Henry moved closer. "Now, think on it for a minute before ye go making up your mind. Cap'n Red—yer brother Jeremy—he did this only to make some money; then he planned to go claim your family estate, set it to rights, settle down, and start a family."

"Aye, but—"

"But nothing. Now that dream is yours."

Valoree blinked at that. "What mean you, now that dream is mine?" she asked suspiciously.

"I mean, with him gone, ye have to make his dream come true for him. Claim the inheritance, settle down, start a family."

Valoree was silent for a moment, then frowned. "But I do not have the money to—"

"Well, that there is true enough. That was what Jeremy was doin', earnin' the money to claim the estate. It's not been lived in since ye was a wee babe. He said he needed a fair sum to put the place to rights."

"And he had earned it," One-Eye put in bitterly. "More than enough to claim the land and set it to rights. We were all to have homes there," he reminded her. "He promised all of us a cottage and a little plot of land. He—"

"The boy knows all about that, One-Eye," Henry interrupted, silencing the first-mate.

"Aye, I know." Valoree sighed. "But the Spaniards took the riches when they killed Jeremy."

Henry nodded. "Aye. And that means we would have to start over."

"Start over!" Valoree glared at him. "Eight years it took my brother to acquire that money. Do not tell me you now want to waste another eight years."

The man hesitated at that, then cleared his throat. "Well, now, I been thinkin' on that, too. It occurs to me that out there somewhere is a Spanish galleon with yer brother's treasure on it—or someone who knows where it is. If we could just manage to find that—"

"The Spaniard with the scar!" Valoree exclaimed. Henry nodded solemnly.

"We could kill two birds with one stone. We could have revenge and settle down in England all nice and proper, too."

"For life and vengeance," she murmured thoughtfully.

"Aye," the quartermaster agreed. "For our life, and Jeremy's vengeance."

# Chapter One

*Five years later*

"I'm thinkin' pink'd be nice."

"Pink?" Valoree glared at One-Eye as he walked beside her, then glanced toward Skully as he added his thoughts on the subject.

"Redheads don't wear pink. It don't look good."

"Aye, but the captain's in need of some real feminine-type colors to make her look less . . ." Another glare from Valoree made the man hesitate, then murmur diplomatically, "To make her look less captainlike. 'Sides, her hair's kind of a brown-red. It might work."

"Forget it," Valoree snapped. "I am not wearing pink. It's bad enough I have to put on a damn dress. It will not be a pink one."

The two men traversing the dark London streets with her fell silent for a moment; then One-Eye murmured, "Well, what about yellow then? Yellow's real feminine. Maybe—"

"One-Eye," Skully interrupted, then paused in his walking.

"What?" One-Eye asked irritably. He and Valoree paused, too.

"Ain't this the place?"

One-Eye and Valoree both turned to peer up at the building they now stood before. It was small, two levels, squeezed in between two other storefronts. The building's lower windows were dark, but the upper ones were filled with the soft glow of candlelight.

"Aye, this is it. Them lights upstairs is where they live," One-Eye announced unnecessarily.

Nodding, Valoree gestured toward the door and waited. Her two crewmen glanced at each other, shrugged, then charged like two bulls spotting a red cape. Her angry cry of realization was lost in the sound of splintering wood. The door caved in under their combined weight, fragments flying in every direction.

Grimacing, Valoree glanced quickly up and down the street to be sure no one had witnessed the deed then followed the men into the dark interior. Inside, she found the two lying in a tangled heap on the floor.

"You were supposed to knock, you blathering idiots."

"Well, how was we to know?" One-Eye sputtered, jumping to his feet and reaching up to be sure the patch that covered his missing eye was still in place.

"Aye," Skully added, regaining his feet nearly as quickly as his friend, despite his peg leg. "And if that was all ye were wantin', why didn't ye do it yerself?"

"Why, indeed?" Valoree sighed as the sound of feet pounding down the stairs somewhere at the back of the building echoed through the quiet shop. The bright light of a lantern appeared a moment later, and Valoree stepped forward to stop her men from drawing their swords as the man carrying it paused in the entrance to the room. He was dressed in a long nightshirt.

21

For a moment it looked as if the man might swallow
his own tongue as he took in the scene before him,
and Valoree couldn't blame him. His shop was a shambles. Not only was there a great gaping hole where the
door had once stood, but when that door had given
way, Valoree's men had fallen inward, crashing into a
table holding piles of fabric. All of these were now
strewn across the floor. Added to that, the intimidating
presence of three disreputable-looking characters now
filled up the little space there was left in his small shop.
The fellow took all this in, and swayed slightly as if
he might swoon.

The man's reaction was understandable, Valoree
supposed with a wry grimace, her gaze moving over
her men. She herself was small and not very intimidating. She wore a billowing white shirt, black
breeches and waistcoat, boots, and a wide belt. But
One-Eye and Skully more than made up for her, what
with their own dirty, less respectable clothes, Skully's
oft-broken nose and peg leg, and One-Eye's patch.

"There was a bit of a mishap with your knocker,"
she said pleasantly in an effort to calm the man. He
was shaking so hard that the light from his lantern was
wavering, making shadows dance on the wall. One-
Eye gave a guffaw at that, and she turned to glare at
him briefly, then glanced back to the shopkeeper.
Rather than appearing reassured, the man had merely
stepped warily back the way he had come, looking fit
to burst into a run at any moment. And most likely
he'd be screaming for the authorities at the top of his
lungs.

Shifting impatiently, Valoree held out a hand toward
One-Eye, who immediately unhooked the bag that
hung from his belt and dropped it into her hand. She
promptly sent it sailing across the room. The coins in
the bag jangled merrily as they sailed through the air,
and the man's backward motions stopped abruptly.

Nearly dropping his lantern, the shopkeeper reached instinctively to catch the purse.

"I am in need of some dresses," Valoree announced dryly.

The little tailor looked startled at that announcement, then weighed the bag in his hand, eyeing his guests a little less warily. "Ye broke me door."

"My men will fix it."

The man shifted on his feet, a calculating look coming into his eyes. "Decent folk come to me shop during the day; they don't drag a body out of his bed in the middle of the night."

There was a tense silence during which One-Eye reached for his cutlass, but Valoree stopped him with a gesture. Instead, she held a hand out toward Skully. The cadaverous man muttered something about people disrespecting their betters, but he unhooked the bag at his own waist and handed it over. She sent that hurtling toward the greedy shopkeeper as well.

Amazingly enough, the man managed to catch the second bag without losing either the first or the lantern. Holding more gold in his hands than he had probably seen at one time in his life, he nodded accommodatingly. "Ye'll have to be bringing the wench here ye want gowned. Iffen ye don't, I cain't guarantee the dresses'll fit."

"The dresses are for me," Valoree announced grimly.

The shopkeeper froze at that announcement, amazement covering his face. The expression was followed by a sneer, and he began to shake his head.

"Now, that there is another situation altogether. I'll not be dressing a man in—" His words died as One-Eye drew his sword.

Sighing, Valoree caught her crewman's arm as he started forward. "Leave off," she muttered. "You men thought me a man for years, too."

"Aye, but we knew you as a boy. I mean, we thought we did. We just thought you was kind of a fey and delicate type."

Valoree rolled her eyes. She supposed she should be flattered that they had at least thought her fey and delicate.

" 'Sides, we wouldn't have thought that if Henry had told us the truth instead of keeping it all to himself fer so long."

"Henry did what he had to do," Valoree snapped, then drew off the hat she had been wearing low on her brow. Stepping forward so that the light could reach her face, she calmly addressed the shopkeeper. "I am not a man."

Her face had been cast in shadow by the brim of her hat, but was now revealed. As she felt her hair spill down from where it had been piled, Valoree caught the dressmaker leering slightly before he saw the expressions of the men accompanying her. Swallowing any comment, he forced a blank expression to his face and nodded before turning his eyes upward. "Wife! Wife, there's work to be done!"

Valoree turned then to take in Skully and One-Eye with a glance. "Fix that door and—" Her words were cut off in surprise when the gaping hole in question was suddenly filled by a behemoth of a man. He was taller even than Skully, and much wider. There was a kerchief on his bald head, an earring in his ear, and he wore tight tan pants and a billowing white shirt that contrasted with his dark skin. "Bull," Valoree said.

The man's dark eyes swept over the people in the room; then he stepped aside, revealing an old hag he had in tow.

"Yer aunt," the giant rumbled, pushing the reluctant woman forward.

Valoree, One-Eye, and Skully were all silent as they stared at the woman. She looked to be in her fifties.

Her dress was torn and filthy, and her hair was the color of a dirty London street. The woman looked like an aging prostitute. Come to that, she most likely was one. Valoree shook her head grimly, turning on the man holding the creature still with one arm.

"I said someone decent, Bull," she chided.

"This is as decent as it gets at the docks at night," came his answer. "She'll clean up good."

Sighing, Valoree took a step toward the woman, then paused, stepping back as she got a whiff of her. The action didn't go unnoticed by Bull's captive, who immediately drew her shoulders up defiantly. The action touched something in Valoree.

Turning to One-Eye, she held out her hand. A third bag of coins hit her palm. Valoree tossed it across the room to the already weighed-down tailor. None of them were terribly surprised when he managed to catch it without difficulty, though it required some deft readjustments. They had been told the man loved gold better than anything in the world, and it appeared the rumors were true. *Good.* Honestly, those rumors were why Valoree had chosen to use this tailor's services. That and the fact that the man was as crooked as Skully's nose. A man who would take customers who visited in the wee hours of the night, and were accompanied by such a rough lot, would be unlikely to gossip—or at least to be believed.

"The old woman will need dresses as well," Valoree announced. "And a bath."

The shop owner stiffened indignantly. "This ain't no inn."

Skully had more gold out before Valoree could signal. This time she tossed the bag at the man's feet. Cursing, he jumped quickly back, then bent to retrieve it. Straightening then, he raised his head, and bellowed again. "Wife! Get yer arse out of bed! *Now!*"

\* \* \*

Three hours later the shopkeeper's bellows had mellowed to tired sighs as he and his wife finished measuring Valoree for the three gowns upon which she had decided. It had taken some time to deal with the old woman, so they had done that first; dumping her in a tub, scrubbing her to a shining glow, then taking the measurements they needed before dressing her in one of the shopkeeper's wife's old gowns. Valoree was pleased to see she didn't look nearly as cheap cleaned up and in a borrowed gown. In fact, if it weren't for her surly manner, Valoree was sure the woman would be perfect for the role of her aunt. Perhaps she was not a poor choice after all.

"Arms up, please," the shopkeeper's wife instructed, smiling with gentle sympathy at Valoree's impatient frown. "This is the last measurement," the woman added quietly as she drew the tape around her chest.

Valoree sighed in relief. She was exhausted, so tired she felt sure she could sleep for a week, and it wasn't the hour. She was more than used to late nights—it was impossible to run a boat full of pirates without half your nights being late ones. It was this task she'd been busy with that had worn her out. There was nothing so boring to her mind as fussing over gowns and cloaks and just which material went with what. It was all a lot of bother, and a task she would have been more than happy to hand over to One-Eye or Skully . . . if she hadn't feared being stuck in something pink and frilly.

"Very good," the tailor announced with relief as he wrote down the number his wife spoke. He looked tired himself, and was likely eager to have Valoree and her burly companions depart. But before she went, she needed to clear things up.

"I'll need one day gown for each of us by tomorrow. I want the other gowns the day after. The men will return for them. Make sure they are ready by noon."

"Noon tomorrow?" the man squawked at once in horror. "But that is mere hours away! I cannot possibly—"

"You can and you will," Valoree interrupted mildly as she began to walk toward the front of the building.

"You don't understand—" the shopkeeper began, following closely behind her.

"Aye, I do." Valoree paused and turned to glower at him. "I understand that I have paid you well, and that I wish for two of the gowns to be done by noon tomorrow."

"Aye, my lady, but I cannot—"

"Did I not give you enough coins for at least ten times that many garments?"

"Well, aye," he admitted reluctantly.

"Exactly. Now, if you cannot have the gowns done when I wish, I can take my business, and my coins, elsewhere."

The threat got the reaction she'd expected. The shopkeeper took a step back, abject horror on his face. He began to stutter. "N-nay. I-I w-will have them done. I-I w-will hire extra women to sew."

"Good." Turning back, Valoree glanced around the front room of the man's shop. Her sailors were playing cards on the table they'd crashed into when they'd busted the door down. Apparently they had fixed that, too, though she hadn't thought to order it. In addition, all the fabric that had originally rested on it and been strewn on the floor had been gathered and restacked on the table adjacent. The old hag, her soon-to-be aunt, was sound asleep on an old mat in a corner of the room.

Though Valoree briefly wondered how the woman could bear to sleep on the hard wooden floor with only a thin rug for cushioning, she quickly pushed the question aside. The woman had likely slept in worse places—places and situations Valoree did not even care to think about.

Her glance slid from the old woman to Bull, who immediately straightened. Without a word from her, the immense pirate bent to lift Valoree's "aunt" in his arms, then headed for the door.

Skully scooped the cards they'd been playing with into his pocket, then hurried to open the door for his comrade. One-Eye stood too, but moved to Valoree's side. Taking a small but painfully sharp knife from his boot, he slammed it into the counter beside the tailor.

Valoree glanced at the shopkeeper and his wife meaningfully. "One-Eye's leaving that as a gift. And a reminder."

"A reminder?" The shopkeeper was beginning to get the nervous look he'd had when he'd first come downstairs.

"Aye. A reminder not to mention this night. To anyone."

One-Eye smiled widely then, an expression that did not quite reach his one good eye. "Keep it nice and sharp," he said in a menacing growl. "Or keep your tongue from wagging."

The shopkeeper seemed to understand at once; he was nodding vigorously when his wife suddenly piped up with a nervous, "Why?"

"Because I'll be cuttin' your tongues out with it if I hear ye done gone and mentioned us to anyone. Anyone at all."

Valoree almost sighed aloud at his words. One-Eye truly did enjoy his work. And he did it well, too. Too well. With a small gurgle, the shopkeeper's wife went into a full swoon, hitting the floor with a resounding crash.

Shaking her head at One-Eye in reproof, Valoree turned and led the way out. It took them very little time in the empty London streets to find their way back to the ship.

The moment Valoree awoke and stepped out of her cabin into the sunlight, a barrel-chested older man hurried toward her. At his approach, she sighed. *Henry.* Her quartermaster. He had held the position for her brother when Jeremy was captain, and continued to hold it for her. The rank put him right below her, second in command. In some ways, it gave him more power. He was her right hand, and though she was loath to admit it, she doubted she could control the men without him. She had left him in charge of them last night while she had gone in search of a dressmaker, and he'd surely had his hands full trying to prevent anyone from slipping over the side to follow the lure of rum and women that going ashore promised. They had been at sea a long time, and most of the crew were eager for leave. But if anyone knew how to help control these cutthroats, it was Henry.

"Some of the men are wanting to go ashore," the man announced at once, barring her way onto the deck.

"No."

"Ah, now, Cap'n, girl," he wheedled, tucking his thumbs into the front of his belt and rolling back on his heels. "Ye know as well as I that the boys have worked right hard the last few weeks, and they been real patient 'bout goin' ashore, waitin' till you was ready to let them. But I'm thinkin' if ye're awantin' them to stay patient, ye best be lettin' em have a little leave."

Drumming her fingers against her leg, Valoree glanced at the crew gathered on deck. They were all looking pathetically hopeful. She supposed she had kept them aboard long enough. But she'd wanted to avoid trouble, and once the men got some drink into them, they could be a whole passel of that. Still, they

were going to be in port only one more day. If her
appointment with the lawyer hadn't been set for so late
in the afternoon, they would have left already. However, she had not been able to secure an earlier meeting, and none but a handful had been allowed leave
since they had left the Caribbean more than a month
ago. It was no wonder the boys were looking so
hopeful.

Pushing Henry back toward the men, she looked
them over slowly. "No stealing, no brawling, and no
killing. If you break anything, you fix it or pay for it.
And leave all but tavern wenches alone. If I hear of
any of you bothering shopkeepers' daughters, you're
off the ship. Understand?"

She suspected by their eager nods that they would
have agreed to nearly anything to go ashore. Her gaze
moved to the largest of the men, a Scot nearly as large
as Bull, with hair the color of a carrot. "You're in
charge, Jasper. Anyone gets out of line and I'll be after
*your* hide."

She waited until he nodded, then continued. "Leave
enough men behind to guard the ship; let the rest go.
Then switch. Richard." Her second mate stepped
quickly forward. "You decide who goes first."

Henry moved forward to join the group as Richard
began to pick and choose, but Valoree shook her head.
"Not you, Henry."

"Ah, now, Cap'n, girl—"

"I need you." It was all she said, then turned and
headed back belowdecks. It was all she had to say, and
she knew it. Henry's wheedling died at once, and she
heard him follow her to her cabin. He would do whatever she requested without complaint. He always had.
He, Bull, Skully, Pete the Greek, One-Eye, and Richard were the most loyal of her crew. She wouldn't have
been able to manage the men without them, and she
was just as grateful as they were trustworthy.

Stepping into the captain's cabin, Valoree glanced at the dress lying on the small cot built into the wall, then turned to glance at her quartermaster. "Can you drive a carriage, Henry?"

The man's face scrunched up at the question, his doubt obvious. "Well, now, I ain't never had no reason to drive a carriage—but I reckon if Skully can drive one of them things, so can I."

A rare smile briefly touched her lips at that. Skully and Henry were the best of friends, but it was a competitive relationship. They were constantly trying to outdo each other. Shaking her head, Valoree pulled her pistol out of her belt and laid it on the table, then began to shrug out of her vest. "There's no need for you to try if Skully knows how. Take him with you and go rent a carriage and horses. The best you can find. It must be a *quality* carriage," she emphasized. "Then I want you to get clothes for yourself, Bull, Skully, and One-Eye. Make sure they fit."

"What kind of clothes?" Henry asked suspiciously.

"Servant's clothes. Livery."

Henry opened his mouth to refuse, but Valoree forestalled him with one sentence. "I need men I can trust with me, and I can trust you four."

Closing his mouth, Henry nodded and turned toward the door.

"Have the men bring me a bath before you go," Valoree called as the door closed behind him. She wasn't sure he'd heard her until the men brought in an old wooden tub, followed by pail after pail of hot water. Once the tub was full, Valoree slipped quickly out of the rest of her clothes and slipped inside. She bathed herself quickly and a bit impatiently, then started to dress.

Half an hour later she was grateful that she had left herself plenty of time for the task. It wasn't as if Valoree had never worn a gown before, but that had been

31

some thirteen years ago. *And good Lord!* She didn't recall donning a gown to be such a complicated task. There were stockings, and the fussy little garters that held them up; the chemise; the petticoat; the farthingale; the corset—a nasty piece of work, that; the partlet; the kirtle; the overskirt; and finally the bodice and sleeves. *Good Lord!* And with all those clothes on, she was still catching a draft up her skirt! It was indecent to be walking around with nothing covering her nether regions under those damned voluminous skirts. At least, it certainly felt indecent to a girl who had been well trussed up in breeches for thirteen years.

Muttering under her breath, she grabbed her trousers and attempted to pull them back on under her skirt, finding it quite a chore with all the binding upper clothes, and the layer upon layer of lower clothing. Dragging skirt after skirt laboriously upward, she tried to hold them with her chin so that she could don her breeches, but that simply did not work. Giving that up, she dropped to the floor, dragged her skirts up, and tried again. A moment later, panting with the effort, she stuck one foot in one leg of her breeches, then her other foot in the other.

"Next time I'll put these damn things on first," she muttered to herself, dropping flat on her back. Arching her butt off the floor, she proceeded to wiggle, squirm, tug, and pull in an effort to don the damn pants.

"Captain?" One-Eye's voice drifted through the door, followed by a brief tap.

"Hold yer arse!" Valoree roared, rolling onto her side but still struggling with her clothes.

There was a brief silence; then One-Eye spoke again. "Ah, Captain? Are ye all right in there? There's an awful lot of bumping and huffing going on."

"Thank God!" Valoree gasped as her breeches finally pulled into place. Letting her skirts slide back down over her legs, she dropped flat on the floor and tried to catch her breath. A moment later the door opened and One-Eye popped his head in. Valoree gave him a surly look. "I told ye to—"

"Hold me arse. Aye, I heard ye," One-Eye said, peering at her flushed face with concern, then around the empty room. "And I am, see?"

Letting the door slide farther open, he showed her that he had one hand planted firmly on his left arse cheek. Valoree released a weary laugh. That was the beauty of One-Eye. He would follow an order literally, if it would gain him his purpose. She could hardly flog him for entering when she had not said 'don't enter.' He had done as she had ordered, after all.

Seeing her smile, he eased into the room, giving it a more thorough examination. "It sounded like there was a bit of excitement goin' on in here."

"Aye. If you call trying to get into me breeches excitement," Valoree admitted dryly.

One-Eye's hand went to his cutlass, his charming smile replaced with deadly intent in a heartbeat. "Who was it? I'll kill the bastard for ye."

Valoree blinked in confusion at him before understanding struck; then she grabbed one of the boots on the floor nearby and whipped it at him. "It was *me*, ye silly souse!" she roared. The boot slammed into the door. Then she jerked her skirts up, revealing her breeches. "I was trying to get my breeches on!"

One-Eye blinked at that, then relaxed with a grin. "Well, now, it's a sad day when a captain can't even manage to don her—" His voice died as her eyes narrowed grimly on him. He changed the subject. "Ah, well, Henry sent me to—"

"What the hell are you wearing?" Valoree snapped, sitting up on the floor suddenly as she took note that his usual attire—tight breeches, flowing white shirt, and leather vest—was gone. It had been replaced with pink hose, pink knee breeches, and the most God-awful pink waistcoat it had ever been her misfortune to see.

Sighing heavily, One-Eye immediately began to nod in misery. "Livery," he said with disgust. "That's what Henry called it. Said it was all he could find."

"Dear God," she said softly, shaking her head in horrified wonder at the ugliness of the outfit. One would think the pink clothes would make One-Eye look effeminate and dandified, but that was hardly the case. If anything, the fancy dress simply seemed to make him look more disreputable—like a pirate dressed up in the fancy clothes of a servant. Which he was, of course.

"See! I knew you'd see that this was wrong. Shall I just go change back into me own clothes?"

Valoree actually almost nodded at the suggestion, then shook her head with a sigh.

"Nay. You cannot run around London looking like a pirate on the prowl."

"Oh, but—"

"Nay," Valoree repeated firmly. "You'll wear these clothes."

At her tone, One-Eye nodded, though still appearing a bit disgruntled. "Well, I'd best go tell Henry and Skully that ye'll be along directly."

"Wait!" Valoree called as he started to back out. He paused, and she gestured to the object lying by the door. "My boot."

Eyebrows rising, he bent to retrieve the footwear, then moved to hand it to her.

"Nay. Put it on for me," she ordered instead of taking it. She'd had enough trouble putting on the breeches. She could use help lacing up the boots.

One-Eye's eyebrows rose so high, Valoree thought they were going to fly off his forehead. "Do you not think some slippers might be more appropriate?"

"Well, aye, they would. And if I had some, surely

I'd wear them, wouldn't I? But I don't recall stopping by a cobbler's shop, do you?"

The corner of his mouth twisting at her testiness, One-Eye bent to grab the second boot as well, then moved to her feet and knelt there.

Valoree watched him set to work with disinterest, her eyes wandering over Henry's choice of livery. It really was atrocious, and she would guess it was just about killing One-Eye to wear it. The man had always fancied himself a bit of a heartbreaker. He was tall, with dark hair and a swarthy complexion, and was as lean and strong as a captain could want for a first mate. He had all his limbs and, really, other than a small scar or two from injuries gained working the ropes in storms, was still in one piece—other than his missing eye, of course. And the eye patch didn't seem to detract from his attractiveness to the ladies. In truth, whatever port they'd come to, One-Eye had always managed to find many women who found his rugged good looks and maimed face the object of desire.

Valoree didn't share that attraction, herself. From the ages of ten to nineteen, she had been treated like a younger brother by the pirate, with all the harassment and teasing that included. And while she had always known in an objective way that he was a handsome fellow, she had looked on him as another older brother as well. So seeing him now, dressed in Henry's awful choice of pink finery, Valoree could hardly stifle her chuckle. It might do him good to be dressed in such.

"There ye are, Cap'n," One-Eye announced, straightening from his task and getting to his feet. He eyed her with amusement. "I suppose ye'll be needing help up now, too, huh?"

She raised her hand in answer. Reaching down, he grasped her at the wrist instead, waiting until her fingers closed around his own wrist before pulling her to her feet. With that, she left the cabin.

"Ye look real pretty in that gown," One-Eye commented as he followed her across the deck a moment later. "But I never thought I'd see the day that Back-from-the-Dead Red needed help putting his own boots on."

His taunt did not go unnoticed. "One-Eye," she said.

"Aye?"

"Unless ye're wanting to don one of the other two gowns I bought and spend the day in it here with the men, ye'd be best to close yer trap now."

"Aye, Cap'n."


"Ye look real fine in that there getup," Henry said as he helped her out of the dinghy and up onto the dock. Valoree was amused to note that the crusty old salt was blushing, and his voice was gruff.

"Like a real lady. Pretty, too. Never noticed ye lookin' so pretty in breeches."

Valoree found herself embarrassed by the compliment to her looks, whereas a compliment on her skill at swordplay or such had never given her anything but pleasure. Flustered, she waved a hand vaguely in the air as if swatting the words away, then turned to stomp toward the carriage where Skully waited. One-Eye leaped to the dock behind her.

"Well," Henry grunted after her. "Ye're not so much like a lady when ye stomp about like that."

Pausing, Valoree turned to glare at him, then sighed and started to walk again, remembering to keep her steps shorter and less determined. She'd have to remember to keep her bearing more feminine, she thought as she paused by the carriage and peered in through the window. Inside sat Meg, the old prostitute Bull had found to play her aunt and chaperon.

Valoree grimaced at the societal foolishness of forbidding women to travel alone, and threw the door of the carriage open. Ah, well. She would make do. With a quick heave, she clambered into the coach. This woman would serve her purpose. It was only once she was inside that Valoree noticed the other woman's pallor. Left over from her drunken state the night before, no doubt, Valoree thought dryly. She looked sober enough to play her part, though. In fact, today the woman looked so sober that Valoree almost pitied her. Her "aunt" would probably welcome a little hair of the dog that had bitten her.

However, other than obviously suffering the ill effects of overindulgence—her face had a slightly gray cast to it, and the lines around her eyes and the way she was squinting spoke of head pain—"Aunt Meg" looked fine, much better even than Valoree had hoped. Her new gown, black and demure, and her carefully upswept hair gave her a regal air. In fact, if she hadn't known better, Valoree might have sworn the woman was a true lady, rather than the prostitute she knew her to be.

"Ye're ready," Valoree said as she arranged herself in the coach.

One eyebrow arched majestically, and the woman subjected Valoree to the same inspection she herself had just been through. "You're not," came her response.

Valoree blinked, then felt anger wash through her. "What the hell do you mean, I'm not?" she snapped.

"Your hair. A lady would never walk about with her hair all wild about her head like that."

Valoree raised a hand to her head, a frown on her lips. "I—"

"Sit," the woman ordered, gesturing to the carriage seat beside her, and apparently fully expecting to be obeyed. She turned and began to sift through the contents of a small bag on the seat beside her. "I expected as much, which is why I asked your man Henry to collect a couple of things—Aha!" Pulling a brush free of the bag, she turned and smiled triumphantly at Valoree, then frowned at her lack of response. She smacked the empty portion of the bench seat again. "Well, come on!"

Valoree hesitated, then glanced at Henry, who had followed her to the carriage and now stood studying her hair with a frown. "She's right, I guess. Ladies usually have their hair up like hers."

Though annoyed by the fact, Valoree had to admit she herself was completely ignorant of what ladies did or did not do. She had not left the ship more than a handful of times over the past thirteen years. When she was younger, the ports they had usually put in to were not the sort Jeremy and Henry felt she needed to visit. And when she had become Back-from-the-Dead Red, she had remained primarily on the ship to avoid discovery of her identity. All her memories of society were from her very early childhood. She had no idea what ladies were sporting nowadays.

Cursing volubly, she switched to the other seat with a flounce of her skirts. She ignored "Aunt Meg's" reproving look as the woman set to work on her hair.

# Chapter Two

The coach jounced and jostled more than a small ship on the high seas. Harder, too. Valoree grimaced as it crashed over another bump and gingerly raised a hand to her head.

Her discomfort did not go unnoticed. "Are you ill? You look quite pale," the old woman across from her asked with feigned sympathy.

Valoree's eyes snapped to her "aunt." "If I am look-

ing ill, it is because every part of my scalp is on fire."
The woman had swept her hair up in a towering coiffure and piled it on her head. "And by the way, I am
not foolish enough to think that ladies go through that
kind of pain every time they put their hair up—so if
you try another trick like that, I'll have you whipped.
And keep your mouth shut while we are in this meeting. The last thing I need is for this Whister fellow to
figure out you are an old prostitute."

Meg stiffened, then colored at the insult. Valoree felt
a moment's regret, but it was brief. She had too many
worries and too little time to be overly concerned with
anyone's hurt feelings. Her entire crew, and now this
woman, were dependent on her for both a home and a
new way of life. She was feeling the strain. And it
hadn't helped that the woman *had* pulled her hair awfully as she'd tugged it into shape.

"My apologies, my *dear*," Aunt Meg said haughtily,
sounding every inch a noble as the coach finally came
to a lurching halt. "I shall endeavor to remain silent
while at this appointment should it please you. However, I have lived the 'good life' so long, one can never
be sure of not meeting a previous . . . patron. Let us
hope this lawyer of yours is not one of them."

Valoree's eyes widened in horror at the possibility,
and her "aunt" smiled back with quiet malice. Further
conversation was cut off as One-Eye opened the door
of the coach.

"Damn." Valoree cursed under her breath as Meg
exited, then moved quickly to follow the woman, intent on catching her and shoving her back into the
coach. She was not willing to risk Whister's recognizing her. Surely it was doubtful that he had ever solic-
ited her favors, but one never knew. Unfortunately, in
her sudden panic to catch the woman, Valoree used
more speed than care in disembarking, and she managed to trounce on, then tangle her foot in, the folds

of her skirt. She ended by tumbling to the ground outside the coach, her hair falling out of its do and tumbling around her shoulders.

One-Eye blinked his one good eye, then gaped down at her in horror as she tried to struggle to her feet. Henry was a touch more helpful. Leaping from his seat beside the driver, he hurried to assist her.

"What are ye doin', ye silly souse?" he snapped, slapping the other man in the back of the head and knocking the fine new hat he wore askew. He helped Valoree back to her feet. "What were ye gonna do? Leave her lyin' there till the dolphins swam alongside ye?"

"Well . . ." One-Eye straightened his cap and hurried to brush down her skirts in an effort to remove the mud that now clung to them. "How was I to know she was to be needin' help gettin' up? She ain't never needed help gettin' up afore."

"She wasn't a lady before. She was the captain."

"Well, and so she's still the captain now."

"Aye, but she's wearin' a dress. That makes her a lady. And ladies is more delicate and helpless than captains. Just look at how she tumbled out of the coach like a—Ah!"

"That is the blade of my knife you are feelin' at your arse, Henry," Valoree announced coolly, annoyed by his words. "It's a little reminder that dress or no dress I am still your captain. I am *not* helpless. Got that?"

"Got it, Cap'n."

"Aye, sir. Ma'am. Me lady," One-Eye, added.

Grunting in satisfaction, Valoree placed her knife back in the bag she had brought along for just that purpose, and waited as the men straightened on either side of her. "Now. You two shall wait here with the hack. My "aunt" and I shall go in and see Mr. Whister. You will not accost any passerby nor talk at all. You will stand silent and solemn-faced at your posts. If I come out and find either of you behaving at all in any way that is unbefitting of footmen, I shall have you whipped. All right?"

"Righto."

"Aye-aye, Cap'n. Me lady."

"Very good," she muttered, then started up the path to the front door where Meg stood waiting. She knew the men knew her threats were mostly idle—she'd never whipped either of them in all the time they'd sailed together—but she also knew that such threats were the only way to convey the seriousness of the situation.

Aunt Meg apparently saw it differently. "You should not draw your knife in public, *dear*. It is most unbecoming in a lady. Should anyone see—"

"No one saw."

"I did."

"You don't count."

"No, I do not suppose I do," the woman muttered as Valoree reached to tap at the door. After a moment she added, "There is nothing to worry about."

Hand still raised, Valoree glanced at her sharply. "I am not worried."

"I see. Well, your men told me that when you are cranky it is usually because you are worried and refusing to show it."

"My men are a bunch of carpies."

"They care for you very much. And I think you care for them, too."

The comment silenced Valoree for a moment; then a peevish anger overtook her. She tried glaring the other woman down, but the creature was not to be intimidated.

"They are like family to you, are they not?"

Sighing, Valoree swallowed and glanced back at the door. "They are. The only family I have."

41

"And you fear you will fail them," Meg guessed, then rushed on when Valoree started to protest once more. "There is no reason to fear that. I've heard of your difficulties. It matters little if your behavior is not exactly that of a lady. They cannot refuse you your inheritance for that. Besides, you shall see it is not that difficult to play at being a lady. You merely need to say as little as possible and follow my lead."

Before Valoree could comment, the door before them swung open to reveal a solemn-faced servant.

"Lady Valoree Ainsley and her aunt to see Master Whister." Meg made the announcement imperiously, striding uninvited into the entry as if she had every right. Gesturing for Valoree to follow, she turned to the servant to add, "We have an appointment."

"Of course, my lady." Bowing, the servant nodded at Valoree as she entered, then closed the door. "Master Whister is with another client, but he should be only a moment. If you would wait in here?" Turning to a door on his left, he opened it for them, then bowed again as "Aunt" Meg led Valoree past him into the room.

"I shall see to some refreshments for you ladies while you wait," he continued. "If you would care to—" A sudden shout from the room across the hall made him pause and glance toward it nervously, a frown sliding across his face. The expression quickly disappeared, however, and he gave them a sickly sweet smile. "I shall be back directly with those refreshments."

Valoree nodded solemnly to the man, barely waiting for him to withdraw and pull the door closed before hurrying forward. Resting her hand on the doorknob, she leaned her ear to the wood in an effort to listen to the shouting coming from across the hall. Unfortunately, she could hear nothing but Meg's hissing reprimand as the older woman flew across the room to pull her away.

"Please calm down, Lord Thurborne. 'Tis not as bad as all that," Whister soothed.

"Not as bad as all that?" Daniel glared at the man seated across from him. "You tell me that to claim my inheritance from my grandmother—money the Thurborne estates need quite desperately, by the way—I have to . . . to . . . What the hell did you say?" He broke off irritably, reaching across the desk to snatch up the scroll the man had been reading from before he'd interrupted. " 'To give up my dissolute ways, find a bride of noble blood, and beget an heir from her,' " Daniel read grimly, then slammed the parchment down.

"Lady Thurborne, your grandmother, was concerned that you were not taking your title and position seriously. She wished to see you settled and happy."

"Settled and miserable, you mean," Daniel said with a snarl, then stood to pace the smallish room. "I cannot believe she did this. I cannot believe she could even come up with this on her own. Someone must have—" He stilled, anger filling him as he saw the way the other man was suddenly nervously straightening his desk and avoiding looking at him. "*You!*"

Whister jumped slightly in his seat, his gaze guiltily meeting that of the younger man. "Me?"

Daniel's eyes narrowed grimly. "You gave her this idea, didn't you?"

"I-I may have mentioned that a client of mine had made just such a stipulation in his will toward his daughter's inheritance," he admitted unhappily, then looked up with a meek smile. "In fact, the daughter in question is probably awaiting me out in the salon right now, Lord Thurborne. I was not expecting you today and she—"

"Oh, *well*, you should see her at once then, by all means," Daniel said in a snarl, moving toward the door. "I would not mean to be so rude as to intrude on someone else's appointment. I shall just wait until you are finished and then speak to you. Unless there's a stipulation in the will against that, too," he added dryly as he reached and opened the door. Outside, Whister's man was just opening the door across the hall.

"What are you doing? Are you mad? You cannot—"

"Shut up!" Valoree hissed back. "How am I supposed to hear anything with you caterwauling in my ear? I am trying to—Ouch!" The sudden opening of the door made her stumble several steps backward, her hand on the doorknob the only thing that kept her upright as the wooden door crashed into her head.

"Oh, my lady! I am ever so sorry!"

Valoree recognized the butler's voice and even managed a smile, though it was more grimace than anything. As she raised a hand to rub at the sore spot on her skull, she suddenly found herself surrounded by people. Meg had moved quickly to her side, her expression more chiding than concerned. The butler was fluttering helplessly before her, horrified guilt written all over his face for braining her, however unintentionally. She also saw that a second man, much younger, and obviously of the nobility, had crossed the hall to join them. Valoree suspected his was the shouting voice she had been trying to eavesdrop on. That being the case, she supposed she should feel chagrin at being caught. Instead, she felt annoyed. If there was one thing Valoree hated, it was feeling foolish, and the obvious amusement in the man's eyes was making her feel just that.

"I was just coming to inform you that refreshments would not be a moment," the butler said, drawing her gaze again. He was wringing his hands miserably as he eyed her. "I never meant to—Well, I did not expect you to be—Can I get you anything? A cold compress, perhaps?"

"Stop fussing, man," Valoree snapped. Her head was beginning to pound, and mollycoddling would simply make it worse. "It's not the first time I've been knocked about a bit, you know."

The sudden silence that fell gave her the first hint she might have misspoken. With a gulp of dismay, she took in the threesome around her. Meg looked horrified, and the butler and the newcomer looked completely nonplussed.

Sighing, she closed her eyes. Yes, that had most likely been the wrong thing to say. Most ladies probably didn't get knocked about. Ever. And if they did, they certainly didn't admit it. She should have thought before speaking. That was one of the first things she had learned to do as captain of a ship full of pirates. Thinking before speaking could avert all sorts of catastrophes. Why hadn't she done so now? "I must have got knocked harder than I thought," she muttered in disgust.

"Perhaps some brandy?" the butler inquired sympathetically, her words seeming to have shocked him out of his stunned silence.

Valoree shook her head, wincing as pain shot through her skull again. "Never touch the stuff. I'll take some rum, though, if you have any."

"Oh, dear," Meg said with a sort of horror, then managed to force a titter of feigned amusement. "Oh, my dear, you are ever the witty one. You must not joke so, however, for not everyone knows what a prankster you are." Turning to the butler, who relaxed at her words, she added sweetly, "A cold compress will be fine. And a touch of brandy, please."

Nodding, the servant hurried to a sideboard to pour

the brandy, then started back toward Valoree with it, only to pause when "Aunt" Meg met him halfway across the room. "I shall fetch a cold compress," he said as he handed her the snifter, then disappeared through the door.

Valoree watched him go, but was distracted by the newcomer.

"Whatever were you doing at the door?"

Valoree peered at the man with irritation. He was tall and handsome and carried himself as only a member of the nobility could. And she would bet her share of the booty from that French frigate her crew had just taken that he knew exactly what she had been doing. There was no mistaking the glint in his eyes for anything but malicious humor. She supposed he was working off some of the temper his appointment had stirred in him, but she didn't like it. Were they on her ship—

But they weren't on her ship. They were in a parlor. She made a face at the thought and did the only thing she could. She lied.

"I was about to leave the room, obviously." Turning away, she moved toward a chair and sat down. "I was about to go looking for the loo."

A sudden sputtering made Valoree glance abruptly over at Meg. The woman had paused a few steps away. She was clutching the brandy glass with white-knuckled fierceness and looking ready to swoon. Abject horror was the only explanation for her pale, pinched look and the way her mouth was flapping with nothing but insensible sounds emerging.

The newcomer, too, was reacting oddly, blinking at her rather blankly, unable to believe he had heard what he thought he had just heard.

Gathering from all this that ladies did not "go to the loo," Valoree sighed inwardly and offered a bland smile. "Lou. Louis. Our footman. I left my smelling salts in the carriage and I was going to have him fetch them for me. My aunt faints quite easily," she added drolly. Then, putting a hard edge into her voice, she addressed Meg. "Aunt? Is that brandy for me?"

"I—Yes, dear." The woman hurried forward at once, pushing the glass into Valoree's hand and patting her on the back. "Come, my dear. You should rest *silently* and drink this . . . after that knock." Her emphasis was not missed by Valoree.

The butler hurried into the room just as Valoree lifted the snifter of brandy to her lips.

"Here, my lady. This should help," the older man murmured, rushing to her side with a flowered blue bowl filled with water and a fresh cloth. Setting them on the table before her, he watched anxiously as Meg took her glass, set it aside, and took up the cloth to dip it in the water.

"I am ever so sorry about this. All of this. You should not even have had to wait. Yours was the only appointment scheduled for today, but—"

"But I arrived unexpectedly and quite rudely usurped some of your time," the younger man interrupted. "Of course, once I realized that Master Whister had another appointment, I politely took myself off here to allow you your time before I finish with him. He should be along directly."

Valoree accepted that bit of information with interest, then glanced toward Meg as the woman touched her arm.

"Lean your head back," her faux aunt instructed quietly, then laid the cold cloth out flat over her forehead and face so that even her mouth was covered.

If Valoree had suspected that compresses were not generally supposed to cover the mouth as well as everything else, a short burst of laughter from the newcomer assured her she was right. Dragging the cloth away, she sat up to glare at Meg, then glanced toward the newcomer. But before she could give him the dressing-down he deserved, the butler murmured, "Well, then, Master Whister should be ready to see you now. I shall just check to see—"

"No need to check, Hinkle. I am ready."

They all turned to the door at that bluff announcement, and Valoree took in the lawyer with curiosity. He was tall, slender, and distinguished-looking. Too, he had a gentle, reassuring face that seemed to suggest he was trustworthy. He took a moment to survey his guests, then started forward, his smile of greeting turning to a look of concern. "Is everything all right? You are not ill, are you, my lady?"

"Aye. I mean, nay, I am fine," Valoree murmured, rising to her feet as the solicitor paused before her. Turning to Meg with sudden panic, she added, "And this is my aunt." She fell silent then, deciding at that point that she would be more than happy to allow the woman to take over. The lawyer intimidated her. She didn't know why. The other man and the butler hadn't, but this man, gentle-looking though he was, did. She supposed it had something to do with the fact that she had to go through him to get what she wanted, Ainsley Castle. And she knew that cutlasses and flintlocks were not the way to do it this time. She was out of her depth.

Meg stepped in to take over. As Valoree watched, Meg smiled and chatted away, entirely charming as the lawyer ushered them out of the salon and into his office. Once there, the small talk between the two continued briefly before they finally got around to business.

"I received your letter regarding your brother Jeremy's death. I am sorry for your loss," Whister began with suitable solemnity. "I realize he is the last of your close family."

"It was years ago," Valoree murmured, ignoring the pang of loss she felt at the mention of his name.

"Yes. Yes, of course. Well, it was lucky you had

such a lovely and warm aunt who could take over your upbringing and shelter you until now, though. Was it not?" He smiled charmingly at Meg, who actually blushed. Rolling her eyes, Valoree muttered a quiet agreement to that.

"Well." Clearing his throat, he smiled once more at Meg, then looked away before getting to the sticky part. "I need proof of his death, of course. I presume you . . ." The lawyer paused as Valoree suddenly tugged a rolled-up scroll of paper from her sleeve, then removed the ring she had not taken off since the day Jeremy had given it to her. The day he had died. She set both on the desk before him.

Whister read the scroll, a doctor's letter, then examined the family signet ring silently before setting it gently back in the hand Valoree held out. He then settled himself behind his desk once more and began to shuffle through his papers. "Well then, of course you know that Jeremy never really claimed Ainsley. He made an appointment to see me and have ownership transferred from the guardianship into his name, but he never arrived for that appointment."

"Yes, I know." Valoree ignored Meg's startled glance and cleared her throat. "Ainsley was—probably still is—a shambles. Lord Swintun released the servants when he took over and rented the estate out for several years. Until it fell into disrepair."

"Yes." Whister acknowledged gently. "Your brother did write to explain that he would miss our appointment. He did say that the estate had been poorly used by Lord Swintun. He claimed that Ainsley needed extensive work and monetary input to make it liveable and self-sustaining, but that there was not nearly enough money to make the repairs necessary. He had purchased, instead, a small ship and contracted to privateer for the king to earn the funds."

Valoree nodded mutely.

"What I never understood was, why he did not take the money he purchased the ship with and use it to begin the repairs on Ainsley? Surely he might have borrowed upon the estate then."

Valoree felt her hands clench in her lap. She had made that same argument herself. And had Jeremy agreed, he would still be alive. But things had not turned out that way. "My brother was a proud man. He did not want to *borrow*. In fact, Jeremy bought the ship with jewels that were actually left to me," she explained quietly. "He intended to make enough wealth to return both those jewels to me *and* restore Ainsley . . . without involving anyone outside the family. And he succeeded in doing so! Had he not been robbed and killed . . ." Valoree fell silent as her throat constricted with emotion. For a moment she struggled with anger and grief, then, noting the pitying expression on the lawyer's face, she straightened. "But he was killed," she finished gruffly.

Whister immediately began to shuffle his papers again. "Yes. Well, in the end it was fortunate that he hadn't claimed Ainsley . . . since he left no will. As it is, since he died without either producing an heir or claiming his inheritance, we must revert to your father's will. According to that—" He paused briefly, skimming a few lines of the paper he held. Nodding, he said, "According to this, that makes you the heiress. Which, of course, you already know. Else you would not be here."

"Aye," Valoree murmured, shifting uncomfortably. It did not feel right that she was there to collect an inheritance gained through her brother's death. She would rather her brother were alive. Still, things had not turned out that way, and she had to be strong.

"Well, then, on your twenty-fourth birthday . . . Let us see, that would be . . . My goodness, that was almost three months ago."

Valoree nodded solemnly. They would have come sooner, but they'd run into rough weather on their first attempt to head for England. It had been as if the sea itself were trying to prevent her gaining her inheritance. They had been lucky to pull through the storm, but not fortunate enough to escape with their ship undamaged. They'd had to put in to port for a bit to make repairs; then there had been a bit of trouble with illness—several of the crew had come down with a fever of unknown origin. And as Valoree had refused to leave the ill men behind, since they had fought for her for long and well, they had waited until the sailors' illness had run its course.

"Well, then, let me see here." Propping a monocle over one eye, Whister lifted several pages and squinted to read them quickly. "Yes, yes," he murmured after a moment, then set the sheets down and smiled at her sweetly. "It is all very simple and straightforward. All you need to do is have your husband come with you to sign these papers—"

"My husband?" Valoree stared at him blankly.

"Aye. According to the will, your husband must sign—"

"Husband?" Valoree interrupted. "It is not mine, but my husband's?"

Eyebrows rising slightly at the dismay in her voice, the lawyer shifted unhappily. "Well, technically it will go to your heir, but your husband will have charge of it until your son is of age." Seeing that the news did not appear to improve her grim expression one whit, he began straightening his papers nervously. "It is very common. Most men are hesitant to leave such a large estate in the hands of their daughters. Either they leave it to their sons, or—"

"Fine. I shall marry then," Valoree announced calmly, almost to herself. It was little enough trouble to accomplish that deed. She could marry one of her men, for that matter. None of them would be foolish enough to think that they could take control of her inheritance, and if they did . . . Well, they simply wouldn't. They would realize that the rest of her crew would quickly make her a widow should they try it.

Mr. Whister peered from her to her aunt and then back. "Am I to understand that you are not married?"

"Not yet. No."

"I see. Well . . ." Frowning, he began to straighten the papers on his desk, then glanced at her uncertainly. "Your husband has to be of noble birth, you know."

Now Valoree was frowning. "Noble?"

"Aye. I fear that was a stipulation of your father's will as well. A noble of some intelligence, good reputation, and . . . er . . ." He flushed slightly, then muttered, "Capable of fathering a child, of course."

"Fathering a—"

"Lord Ainsley was quite concerned with continuing the family line." Whister was quite pink now. "To prove the . . . er . . . last requirement, you have to be married and either with child or already having had one by your . . . er . . . twenty-fifth birthday."

"By my twenty-fifth—But that is only—Why, it's not much more than nine months away."

"Aye, I know," he admitted apologetically.

"What if she is married but not . . . in the family way by then?" Meg asked as Valoree simply stared.

"Well, then the estate would revert to the next in line. I am not sure who that would be, but I can look it up—"

"That will not be necessary," Valoree told him, getting abruptly to her feet. "Thank you for your time. Good day."

Blinking as she started for the door, Master Whister got abruptly to his feet. He hurried around his desk as Aunt Meg followed Valoree out.

"I am sorry. I did not realize that you were not aware of the stipulation," he apologized miserably as he hurried down the hall behind them.

Nodding silently, Valoree sailed through the entry and out the door, leaving Meg to deal with the man.

Henry leaped from his perch and hurried to open the door of the hack as she approached. Valoree ignored his frown, knowing that he was worried by her stiff demeanor and cold expression. He could wait for an explanation. As she seated herself in the carriage, she turned to see Meg hurriedly exit the house. Valoree raised her eyebrow in question, hoping that something had been said that altered the situation.

The woman shook her head in answer and climbed into the carriage, pulling the door closed behind her.

Valoree rapped on the coach, and, shrugging, Henry climbed back up onto his perch at the back of the coach so that Skully could get the horses in motion. They set off.

The silence in the carriage was heavy. At last Meg spoke, and Valoree was surprised by the concern in the woman's voice. "What will you do now?"

Valoree was silent for a moment, then shrugged. "Return to the ship and set sail." She glanced over, regretful. Bull had promised this woman a place on the estate if she helped them. Now the promise was in vain, despite Meg's having held up her end of the bargain.

Sighing, Valoree spoke. "You may sail with us if you like." It wasn't exactly a cottage on an estate, but it was all Valoree had to offer. "You could help Petey cook," she added, just to let the woman know that her position would be a respectable one.

"Where do you plan on sailing to?"

Valoree frowned and considered briefly before answering, "Back to the Caribbean most like."

The woman shook her head. "Will you not even try?"

Valoree blinked in surprise. "Try what?"

"To find a husband?"

She did not even bother to answer, merely turned her face back to the window and stared at the passing street. It seemed obvious that she had little if any chance of finding a husband, not with the prerequisites her father had left her: find a man, intelligent and nobly born, who would be willing to marry her. That would have been hard enough, but she also had to be with child or have birthed one by her next birthday. No, it was all quite simply impossible. If the "nobly born" part had not been included, well, then, that would have been one thing. But where the devil was Valoree to find a noble who would be willing to both marry her and leave her in charge of her own estate? And where would she find one she was willing to lay down with to beget a child?

Valoree wasn't the timid type. Being raised on a ship full of pirates had seen to that. But she wasn't anywhere near experienced when it came to sex either. She had never even been kissed yet. That was something else that being raised on a ship full of pirates had seen to. Or more specifically, that's what hiding her gender on a ship full of pirates had seen to.

Still and all, she had heard quite a bit of bragging from the men about their exploits. She had even stumbled across one or two of the men with prostitutes they had sneaked aboard-ship over the years. Between those two things, Valoree had a good grasp on what it was all about. As far as she could tell, it all appeared rather awkward and silly to her. All that mushy mashing of mouths, humping, and moaning. It didn't appear very exciting to her. But if the men were to be believed, it felt a whole lot better than it looked. That being the case, Valoree wasn't against trying it out. She just hadn't yet met a man who attracted her in that way. She was rather hoping that she would be lucky enough to find a man like that, though, for she suspected sex was one of those things that could be a chore if there wasn't some attraction involved.

The idea had her so caught up, it took her a moment to realize the carriage had stopped. Glancing about distractedly, she peered at the open door of the hack where Henry stood patiently waiting.

Sighing, she shifted along the seat, then leapt clear of the door, landing in a puddle with a satisfying slap of her boots.

Ignoring Henry's startled and even slightly disapproving look, she turned and strode up the dock, uncaring of how it looked for a woman in a dress to be striding about like a man. This was how she walked: purposeful, commanding, with someplace to go. This was her life.

Pausing at the end of the dock, she waited as Skully and One-Eye hurried to catch up to her. She scowled. They looked ridiculous in the livery. Pale pink simply did not do a thing for Skully's peg leg or One-Eye's patch. Their hair was too long, their faces scruffy and sun burnt. They did not fit in such finery. They looked better and were more comfortable in their worn and ragged pirate garb. Mayhap it was better that they would not be forced into the roles of gentlemen farmers.

"I want you to rally the men, Henry. We leave as soon as the last of them return."

"Leave?" her friend asked in shock. "For where?"

"The Caribbean. I shall not inherit. It looks as if we have a few more years of sailing left before us."

# Chapter Three

Valoree had changed out of her gown and back into her usual dress of breeches and top, yet this time she no longer bothered to bind her breasts. It was the first time she had worn her captain's clothes without doing so. She had been binding her breasts since she'd developed them. Younger brothers and cabin boys did not have breasts, and that was how the crew had thought of her for thirteen years—until now.

Henry had announced to them that she was a girl the afternoon they had sailed into London. It had seemed a good idea at the time. Now that things had gone differently, then they'd planned, Valoree wished he had kept that information to himself. The men had been shocked, of course, and one or two had not taken it well that their captain had turned out to be a girl. Still, they were probably over it by now.

Right, she thought sarcastically, then leaned back in her chair with a sigh and propped her feet up on the table. Grabbing the bottle of rum she had brought to her cabin with her, she took a swig. She was working very hard at emptying it.

Valoree was more than halfway to being sotted when a knock came at the door. Sighing, she started to sit up, then changed her mind and slouched even further in her seat. Surely they had come only to tell her that they had voted someone else captain, anyway. They would hardly keep her now that everyone knew she was a woman, nor could she supply the longed-for home in the country that had been promised years ago when they had all signed on with her brother.

"Enter!" she snapped, then watched calmly as Henry ducked inside. He was followed by One-Eye, Skully, Bull, Petey, Meg, and as many of the rest of the crew as could fit inside the room. She could hear the rest clustered outside the door.

"What?" Valoree asked wearily, then waited for the announcement to come.

The men all turned to Henry. He grimaced at being stuck with the job of speaker, but stepped forward, clearing his throat. "Well, now, ye see, Cap'n, Meg here told us all about what that there Whister feller said."

"Of course she did." She had expected as much.

"Aye. And then One-Eye here and I, we went and rounded up all the men and brought them back."

"As you were ordered to do."

"Aye. And then we . . . er . . . Well, we informed them of what was said."

"I am not surprised."

There was silence for a moment; then One-Eye nudged him. Henry sighed and continued. "Well, the men . . . we all discussed it some, ye see, and then we . . . er . . . We had a vote."

"Here it comes," Valoree murmured to herself. So much for five years of successful piracy.

"And we vote ye marry."

Valoree blinked. "What did you say?"

"He said we voted, you marry," Petey repeated helpfully from his position near the door.

Valoree frowned at the cook's words, then glanced over the rest of the men. Every single one of them was nodding solemnly.

"You voted that I should *marry?*" she murmured with disbelief, unsure whether to laugh or scream. It would almost be easier if they had voted her out of position as captain. Were they mad? Did they not understand things? No, of course they did not, she realized suddenly. They had no concept of what a monstrous undertaking marriage was. Especially in noble circles. Hell, *she* was not even sure of the full details.

Shaking her head, she dropped her booted feet to the floor and calmly stood. "Gentlemen, while I appreciate what is at stake, you do not seem to understand—"

"We understand," One-Eye assured her with a grin. "We understand that you gotta marry to gain Ainsley, so we voted ye get married."

Valoree paused at One-Eye's words, then frowned. "Now, see here. As my crew you can vote on a lot of things—where we sail, whether to take a Spanish ship or not, whether to kill its crew even—but you cannot vote on whether I marry."

"Well, now, that's no' exactly true."

Valoree frowned at that announcement, coming as it was in a Scottish brogue. Jasper stepped forward unfolding several contracts he held. "According to Article six of the contract we all signed upon joining up with you, and I quote, 'Every seaman shall have a vote on such matters as affect the welfare, safety, health, and future of the crew.'" Lowering the contract, the Scot raised his head and smiled at her, an expression revealing a number of missing teeth. "This here affects the whole crew."

Every man present was again nodding in solemn agreement. Even Meg was.

When Valoree merely stared at them, baffled, Henry explained. "To get Ainsley, ye got to marry. Gettin' Ainsley or not affects all of us. It's why we all threw in together—first with Jeremy, then with you."

"Aye," One-Eye agreed, drawing her gaze. "Jeremy

said he would give each of us a cottage at Ainsley where we could settle down."

"Where we could get married," Petey added almost dreamily. "Have a wife."

"And bairns," Jasper put in.

"A garden," Henry added. Everyone turned to stare at him. Straightening his shoulders, he scowled at them defensively. "Jeremy promised me a garden."

"So's you can grow vegetables," Skully added hopefully, but Henry shook his head.

"Flowers."

"Flowers?" They gaped at him, but he shrugged, indifferent to their scorn.

"I'm thinkin' on growing me some roses. I've got a green thumb, don't ye know. Think I'll try me hand at makin' one o' them new roses. I'll call it the Grand Valoree."

Valoree shook her head in disgust and sank back into her seat. Staring at her motley crew, she shook her head again and shrugged. "Fine," she said with feigned indifference. "I shall marry. I suggest you go out and find me a husband. All you need is a nobleman capable of getting me with child. However, I warn you, he has to be willing to let me make all the decisions and run the roost. Otherwise, do you think he'll let me set you all up on his estate? Good luck to you. I shall just wait here for you to accomplish the deed."

Grabbing her bottle of rum once more, she sank back into her seat.

The room was silent for a moment as Valoree studiously ignored her men; then they slowly began to file out.

"Marry," she muttered, raising the rum to her mouth and gulping some of it down before shaking her head. "Me." She was aware of her shortcomings. More than aware. They were all tied up in her past and who she was.

Lynsay Sands

Her parents had both died by the time Valoree was
five—her mother breaking her neck in a fall down the
stairs shortly after Valoree was born, and her father
during a cholera outbreak when she was five. That had
left her and Jeremy. Jeremy had been six years older
than she, a tender eleven years old when they had been
left to fend for themselves.

Well, they hadn't been left entirely to themselves;
there had been Lord Swintun. He had been a neighbor
and their guardian. He had been a kind and tender man
who had been good to them both. Unfortunately, he
had been less kind to their birthright. He'd raped the
land, destroyed the pastures, and generally done his
best to run the place into the ground, milking every
drop of profit out of it that he could—as had been his
right to do as guardian of the inheritance.

Still and all, Valoree had been sorry when he had
died in her tenth year. He truly had been kind and
caring toward her and her brother. He had hired the
best tutors for them, seen to Jeremy's training, and
openly nurtured them both. Then he had died, and they
had been left in the hands of his son, a fellow who'd
had a terrible tendency to leer at Valoree even at that
tender age. It had been most uncomfortable for a while.
Four years later, Jeremy had turned eighteen and taken
Valoree home to Ainsley to reclaim their birthright.

And that had been worse. Neither of them had been
near the estate since their father's death, and what they
found was shocking. The manor house was uninhabit-
able, with not a stick of furniture left. Swintun's son
claimed it had all been stolen and, seeing as selling off
the goods and household articles was not exactly accepted as a right of the guardian, they had believed
him. There had been nothing to do about it by then
anyway, as it was apparent that the furniture had been
gone an awfully long time. The house had obviously
been used as a squat for various passersby, including
animals, birds, rats, and spiders.

Cleaning and refurbishing had been what it needed. That took money, however, and that was something they were sadly short of. In his mismanagement of the land, Swintun had made it almost unrentable. Farmers would not rent land they could not work.

Valoree recalled that Jeremy had taken one stunned look at his inheritance, walked around the destroyed entry and great hall, then moved to the fireplace, removed a small rock there, pulled out a bag, and turned away. He'd walked straight out, mounted his horse, and ridden off.

Knowing he was distressed, and trying to help, Valoree had set her hand determinedly to cleaning up, hoping that she could make a difference. Unfortunately, after the whole day and most of the night cleaning, she had barely made a dent in the ruin that was now their home. She had cried herself to sleep on a bed of rushes in a corner of the great hall, the cleanest space she could find.

That was where Jeremy had found her late that evening when he returned, and that was where he had told her of their change of plans. The bag he had removed from the fireplace had been their mother's jewels. They were to have gone to Valoree. Instead, Jeremy had taken them and bought a ship, and he had hired a quartermaster—Henry. He intended to enter the risky business of privateering. He would attack the king's enemies, take their goods, and split them with the Crown. Then, when he'd made enough, he would return and legally claim his inheritance. It seemed the only way.

Valoree had protested, of course. But when her brother had gone to great pains to assure her of the safety of his undertaking, she had rebelled at Jeremy's next intention: to ask Lord Swintun to continue her guardianship until he returned. She hated and feared the young nobleman, and anything would be better than a sentence of living under his care. If a seafaring life was safe enough for Jeremy, it was safe enough for her. And that was how she'd become a pirate.

Now Valoree knew all there was to know about sailing, and she was quite a hand at battle as well. But that was where her talents lay—not in wifely duties. True, she'd been trained in Latin, English, and German while under the older Swintun's care, and her brother had continued her reading and writing lessons in those languages while he was alive, but those weren't exactly womanly arts.

Even her speech was lacking. Jeremy had made her speak properly while he was alive, but she had slipped somewhat since his death. Especially when she was angry.

She certainly had none of the useful crafts that should be known by women. She was not very good with a needle. She could sew, but her stitches were nowhere near as straight as they could be. She knew next to nothing about running a household, and was as good as useless when it came to tending illness. Her mother had been an expert with healing herbs, Jeremy told her, but had died long before being able to teach Valoree any of what she needed to know. And for such pastimes as dance and music, the years she might have been learning those she had spent sacking galleons in the Caribbean. In short, she was terribly lacking. No nobleman would want her—let alone one who understood her needs.

Her depressing thoughts were brought to a halt by a light tapping at the door. Sighing, she set the almost empty rum bottle on the desk and sat up straight. "Aye."

Henry opened the door and stepped silently inside. This time he was alone. Valoree did not know if that was a bad sign . . . or worse.

Pausing before the desk, the quartermaster eyed her

for a moment, then shifted uncomfortably and cleared his throat. "The men have been talkin' the problem over."

Valoree arched an eyebrow at him. "Which problem would that be?"

"The problem o' findin' ye a husband."

Valoree grimaced. At least it sounded as if her men were being realistic about it, and weren't fooling themselves into pretending it would be an easy task. "And?" she prompted.

"Well, we're thinking that the docks are no place to meet up with some of them there noble fellers. We're thinkin' we need to get you into society."

Valoree nodded at his logic. "How?"

"How?" He frowned. "Well, er . . . I guess we'd have to be gettin' ye some o' them there invites to some of them sorries."

"Soirees," Valoree corrected dryly, then repeated, "How?"

"How?"

"Aye. How? You cannot steal or force those at swordpoint, you know."

"Aye, well. . . ." His lips puckered briefly; then he backed toward the door. Her exceedingly quiet and calm manner seemed to be making him a touch nervous. Perhaps he'd learned over the last thirteen years that when she was calm, it usually preceded a storm. "I'll be getting back to you on that," he ended lamely, backing through the door.

"I am sure you will," Valoree snapped, then returned her attention to her bottle.

"We are here."

Valoree glanced about at the announcement just as the coach came to a halt. Shifting closer to the window, she looked out at the town house they had stopped before, peering at it through a jaded eye. They were about to waste a whole lot of time and coin pursuing the impossible.

This was the answer the men had come up with for getting her "some invites to them sorries." They had determined that she must rent a town house for the "seasoning" and "have one o' them there comin'-up things." *Brilliant. Marvelous.* They were all mad. How did they think renting a town house would get her married? It was not as if the members of the ton were like to be overwhelmed by her grace, charm, and beauty.

The door suddenly opened and Henry appeared, offering a hand to aid her out. Sighing, she caught up her skirts in a bunch, grabbed his hand, and clambered irritably down from the coach. Once on the ground, she released her skirts, giving them a slight shake so they would fall back in place, and glanced at the carriage parked in front of their own. The door to that one opened and a tall, slender, fair-haired man alit somewhat cautiously even as Henry helped Meg down from their own carriage.

"Lady Ainsley?" he asked hopefully as he approached.

Nodding, Valoree automatically offered him her hand to shake.

"Lord Beecham, at your service," he assured her, giving a smile before bending to gallantly kiss her hand.

Eyes widening in dismay as he slobbered over her fingers, Valoree glared briefly at Henry as if to say this was all his fault. Quickly, she drew her hand back to gesture toward Meg as the woman moved forward, eyeing the man with intent interest. "My aunt."

"My lady." The man could do no less than bend to kiss her hand as well now, and Meg appeared as stunned by the act as Valoree had been. Afterward, he straightened and smiled from one woman to the other. "The house is all in order. I had it cleaned as your uncle requested in his note. It has not been used for several months, so it took a bit of doing. I shall send him the bill, of course."

"Of course," Valoree agreed dryly with another pointed glance at Henry. He had written the letter, signing it as her uncle. Women did not perform such transactions. Either their man of affairs did, or a male relative. Henry had thought an uncle, husband to Aunt Meg, of course, might be a good touch—so that it was not thought Valoree was without protection. As for the bill, the town house was the men's idea, so let them pay for it.

"The house is pretty much yours for as long as you need it," Beecham continued, turning to lead them up to the front door. "Just have your uncle write me a note should he wish to stay longer than the six months he has already rented it for."

Nodding mutely, Valoree stepped past him into the house as he opened the door for her. Inside, she stood glancing about the entry as Meg—Aunt Meg, she reminded herself—joined her.

"As you can see, it's just what your uncle requested. Large, top quality, and clean as a whistle." He ran his gloved hand down the banister of the stairs that led to the second floor to prove his point, and Valoree nodded before turning to move into the first room on the left.

"Ah, now, this is the salon, as you can see." Her host hurried to keep up with her, rushing into the room at her heels and nearly running over Aunt Meg in the process.

Valoree was just wondering if she should comment on his rudeness when the woman spoke up for herself. "We can see what the room is, young man," she reproved gently, surprising Valoree. Considering the talent for tartness Meg had displayed over the past couple of days, Valoree had expected a harsher chiding—a nice cutting comment, or an outright verbal slap. Instead, the older woman was smiling at the fellow almost fondly. She's trying to endear us to him because he's a noble, Valoree thought bitterly. She considered the man to see if it was working.

Lord Beecham, realizing what he had done, was now flushing a bright shade almost as pink as the god-awful livery Henry had chosen for Skully and One-Eye. He stuttered out an apology. It was only then that Valoree took notice of his appearance. He wasn't bad-looking, or very old really, perhaps twenty-five or -six. But he was the studious sort, she would guess. After spending the better part of her life in the company of strong, fit pirates, Valoree thought he appeared weak and too skinny. His discomfort now didn't help either. Once his aplomb was gone, it seemed quite impossible for him to regain it. It was almost painful for her to watch as he began to stammer out an offer to give them a further tour of the house. It was Meg who let him off the hook.

"That will not be necessary, my lord. I think we can find our way around now."

"A-aye, of course." He glanced briefly at Meg, but turned to Valoree to speak again. "I . . . Your uncle never asked me to see to servants, so I—"

"That will not be necessary," Aunt Meg answered for her again. "We have people coming later today."

"G-good. I'll just—Oh! I nearly forgot. My mother, Lady Beecham, thought that if you were not too tired from your journey here, you might like to attend a small soiree she is having tonight." His voice trailed away when Valoree stared at him rather blankly; then he began backing out of the room. "Well, nay, of course not. You are probably rather tired. I—"

His words came to an abrupt halt, as did his retreat, when he managed to back himself right into Skully.

The pirate stood in the doorway of the salon, eyeing the surroundings with some disdain.

Jerking around to see what he had backed into, Mr. Beecham paled, his jaw dropping slightly. Valoree supposed he'd never seen the likes of Skully before. Apart from the man's being dressed in pink, Valoree imagined that to anyone who didn't know him, he would look like death itself. His peg leg didn't help.

Chuckling quietly, she waved the pirate out of the room, then took Lord Beecham's arm and led him to the front door. "It is kind of ye—you," she corrected herself quickly. "It is kind of you, Lord Beecham. And you must thank your mother for us."

"And tell her Valoree'll be there," Henry inserted from behind her.

Beecham's eyes widened in amazement at such bold behavior from a servant, and Valoree wheeled, glaring furiously at the older man. But Henry merely glared right back, and a glance at the other men showed the same determined looks on their faces. Grinding her teeth together, she took a deep breath, then turned back to Beecham, forcing a smile. "Of course you must tell her that we would be delighted to attend her soiree."

"You will?" the man asked, craning his neck to peer over her shoulder at Skully, who was grunting in approval of her concession.

"Aye, of course." Opening the door, she smiled at him cheerfully, then urged him through it. "Thank you again for all your trouble, my lord, in attending to all of this for us."

"Oh, well, my lady, it is my pleasure," he began modestly.

"Aye. Well, you do it well. Good day to you," she said cheerfully. With that, she closed the door on his smiling face and turned to glare narrowly at her men.

"See that! Got us an invite already!" Henry crowed, ignoring her obvious displeasure.

Snorting in disgust, Valoree moved away from the door and led the way back into the salon, where Meg was staring out the window into the street. "You got lucky," she snapped irritably, dropping into a chair and casually hooking one leg over the arm of it. "Lady Beecham is probably the only person in this whole town who would make an impulsive gesture like that, and you happened to rent the house from her son."

"Nay." Skully shook his head.

"Nay what?" Valoree asked with a sigh.

"I'd bet all my shares of the booty from that last Spanish galleon we took that his mother ain't never e'en heard o' ye," the tall man said, bringing a frown to her face.

"She—"

"Not she. He." When Valoree merely stared at him blankly, he shook his head and explained. "The boy. Are ye blind, Val? He was sniffing about ye like ye were a bitch in heat."

Meg snapped with outrage from the window. "You will leave that kind of talk out in the street, if you please. Lady Valoree already has a tendency to slip up without your bandying such foulness about."

Skully flushed bright red at the set-down, but Valoree went from pink, to red, to white. She didn't know whether to defend Skully, snipe at the woman, or agree with her. True, the "bitch in heat" remark had been a touch vulgar, even for Skully. She supposed that was why he wasn't snapping back at her himself. That or he was just as shocked by the starch in her words as Valoree was. The words seemed exactly what a "lady" would say, and—*good God*—the woman had actually sounded the part.

"Were you ever onstage, Meg?" she asked at last.

Ignoring the question, the woman turned to regard her. "Skully is right, though, for all that his sentiment could use rephrasing. Lady Beecham surely did not extend the offer. She does not have the heart to think of it."

"How would you know?"

Shrugging, Meg turned back to the window. "Everyone in London has heard of Lady Beecham and her mean-spirited, snobbish ways."

Valoree stared at her for a moment longer, then glanced toward the doorway of the salon as the front door of the town house opened and closed. Bull and One-Eye wandered into the room a moment later.

"Mighty fine digs," One-Eye commented, glancing about the room. "We stayin'?"

"Aye," Henry announced, drawing himself up and facing Valoree as if expecting an argument. "We're stayin'."

When Valoree merely shrugged, he continued. "We'll be needing some more things from the ship, though. Some more men to act as servants. And Petey."

"Petey?" One-Eye raised his eyebrow. "Who's gonna cook for the men if we bring Petey out here?"

"They can fend for themselves for a bit."

"We shall need the gowns," Meg interjected. "In fact, if you expect her to attract a husband, she will need several more gowns."

"More gowns?" One-Eye gaped at the woman. "Why? She's already got three of them."

"One evening gown and two day gowns will not do," Meg informed them primly. "She shall need at least a dozen of each."

"A dozen!" Valoree looked no more pleased by that announcement than the men. "Why the hell would I need a dozen dresses? There's only the one of me."

"A dozen to start with," Meg repeated firmly.

"Now just a minute—" Henry began, but Meg cut him off.

"She is seeking marriage. She must make as good

an impression as she can. She cannot be seen twice in the same gown, else she will be thought to be too poor to be able to afford the proper accoutrements and therefore less desirable as a mate. Believe me, Valoree needs all the help she can get. She has none of the social graces considered necessary in a wife in this day and age. She has grown up and spent her life around a bunch of rum-guzzling, tobacco-spitting, foul-mouthed pirates and it shows. Just look at her."

Silence followed as the men glanced guiltily at Valoree. She sat pretty much sideways in the chair, legs splayed, one thrown over the chair's cushioned arm, and the other upon the floor. Her skirt was hitched up to reveal the boots and breeches she wore beneath. The men groaned as one at the sight, knowing that every word Meg said was true.

"Well, maybe if *someone* had told us that she was a girl." One-Eye glared at Henry as he spoke. "Maybe then we would have done some things different."

"What?" Valoree asked dryly. "Like mutiny?"

"Nay," he snapped, affronted. "Like maybe throwin' some of them there grace lessons in along with the sword handling and fisticuffs."

"Oh, aye," she said with a sneer, but was suddenly uncomfortable under their censuring eyes as they took in the way she was sitting. For the first time in her life she felt quite inadequate. She was the captain. She led some of the most ruthless, notorious pirates in the land, and they followed her orders. Yet she suddenly felt like an ignorant, uneducated child. And she didn't like it.

Slamming both her booted feet flat on the floor, Valoree stood and glared around the room. "Well, I'll be leaving all this decision making up to you to 'vote' on. Me, I'm going to go take a nap."

\*     \*     \*

She didn't sleep; she sat in the window seat in the bedchamber she had chosen and stared out at the passing people. Valoree had never seen so many people in one spot in her life. London was just bustling with activity. It was also overcrowded, and noisy, and it stank. She missed the open sea: the breeze in her hair and salty spray on her face. She missed the sound of the men singing their shanties into the wind as they worked. She missed her cabin with its constant rolling sensation, and the safety she felt there. And more than any of those things, she missed the feeling of being in charge, of deciding what to do, and where to go, and what should happen next in her life. It seemed that her life had somehow gotten out of control, and she didn't much like that.

Trying not to think of such things, she watched through the window as the men left together in the carriage. Some time later, she saw Henry return alone on foot, a young boy following with several packages. Shortly after that, the carriage returned with Skully and One-Eye on the driver's seat, and Bull riding atop, seated on towering stacks of goods. When the coach had rolled to a stop in front of the town house, its door popped open and several more members of her crew piled out. She watched mutely as Bull began to hand down sacks of flour, salt, sugar, and other miscellaneous goods from his perch, accepting unhappily that her men expected a lengthy endeavor and obviously intended to stick it out.

Once the last of the culinary goods were removed, the men turned to unpacking the last two items, a pair of chests—a small coffer, no doubt stuffed full of the coins they planned to spend on this foolish enterprise, and a larger chest. She recognized the latter as the container she had stuffed her gowns into when they had been delivered. Moments later she heard the men banging their way down the hall toward her room.

Sighing, she stood and moved to the door, pulling it open and stepping aside for Henry to enter. He was followed by One-Eye and Skully and the clothes chest. Setting the chest on the floor, they straightened, grinning from ear to ear.

"Yer gowns is here," Henry announced with determined cheer. "Ye'd best get ready."

"For what?" she asked, bringing frowns to each man's face.

"For the sortie tonight."

"Soiree," Valoree corrected, then shook her head. "Haven't you noticed any of the women passing by the house?"

There was a hesitation as the men exchanged glances; then Henry shook his head. "What of them?"

"They are all wearing heavy white gook on their faces, then some sort of red stuff on their cheeks and lips, and thick black stuff on their eyes."

"She is right." They all turned to glance at Meg, who stood in the door to the room surveying them all. "The fashion has become to wear thick makeup on your face, lips, and to even wear kohl on your eyes." Her gaze went to Valoree. "I take it you have none of that?"

Valoree shook her head, though she was not overly disappointed at the fact. Maybe this would be a way out.

"Well . . ." Henry frowned. "We'll get her some of that on the morrow. But she'll just have to do without tonight. Every shop will be closed by now."

"You cannot really imagine that you can take her to the Beecham soiree without it?" Meg exclaimed in dismay.

Henry frowned at her. "Course we can. Who knows when the next invite will come iffen she don't show up tonight?"

"Well, if you insist on her going tonight without it,

I will not be involved." Turning on her heel, the woman marched out of the room.

"What do you think?" One-Eye asked, and Henry scowled.

"We don't have no makeup for tonight, but we don't have no invites for tomorrow. That's what I think."

"Hmmmm." One-Eye made a face. "Maybe Petey can come up with something. He's got lots o' white stuff in the kitchens. Red stuff, too."

Henry brightened at once at the suggestion. "Aye. Go tell him to see what he can do."

Valoree sighed. It seemed there was no escape.

# *Chapter Four*

A buzz going around the ballroom drew Daniel's attention from John Beecham's liturgy on the importance of wise investments and renting unused properties.

Beecham was like that. Money was his main priority in life, a stricture he'd had pounded into his head by his father, who, disappointed in love, had settled for a loveless marriage and instead had poured his energies into the art of increasing his wealth. Riches, the older Beecham had often said while he lived, were never known to betray a man.

The philosophy was rather vulgar as far as the members of the ton were concerned. For them, money was to be spent, not earned, and if it *was* earned, one should never be so crass as to discuss it. Beecham's obsession with it was the reason he was considered beneath the majority of the ton. And yet, the amount of wealth his family had was the reason no one missed one of their balls.

Thoughts of Beecham fled Daniel's mind as the murmuring began. Turning, he let his eyes follow the direction everyone seemed to be looking in, to the doorway of the ballroom. They immediately widened on the young woman standing there. She was tall and slender, wearing a simple gown of midnight blue and an expression of dismay on her face as she took in the gathering.

It took him a moment to recognize her as the woman from Whister's salon, and then all he felt was disappointment of a sort. He had thought her attractive at the lawyer's office; she'd had a sun-kissed face and natural beauty. Now she sported the death's-mask white face that was so popular, with red cheeks drawn on. Her hair had flowed down her back naturally then, but was now looped and tied and knotted atop her head. Well, sort of. Actually, it looked to be unraveling somewhat and sliding down her face. That was the reason everyone was abuzz, he supposed. Most of the nobility cropped their hair and wore wigs, but this woman's brilliant red hair was obviously all her own—and if he was not mistaken, it had been arranged using nautical knots. He couldn't be sure of that, though, for it was already escaping its confines.

"Lady Ainsely," Beecham murmured nearby, drawing Daniel's startled gaze.

"Did you say Ainsley?" Whister had never mentioned her name.

"Yes. She and her aunt rented my cousin's town house for the season," Beecham explained.

"Her aunt, hmm?" Daniel glanced back toward the woman. "That is not her aunt with her. Who is that fellow?"

*　　*　　*

"This is a *small* soiree?" Henry whispered in disbelief.

Sighing, Valoree glanced at the man sympathetically. He was all dressed up in the poofy—as he described them—clothes of a nobleman. He was "Uncle" Henry tonight, thanks to "Aunt" Meg having cozied herself up to a bottle of rum while the men were busy solving all the problems that attending this "little party" had presented. Rum, of all things! And after she'd made such a stink about Valoree drinking it.

Still, Valoree herself was much more uncomfortable than Henry, especially with her hair. Henry had tried to wake Meg to dress it, but the woman had been well sauced and beyond waking, so the sailor had seen to the task himself, snapping and cussing the whole while. At last Valoree had suggested he fix it up in nautical knots—she didn't know the first thing about style or fashion, and really couldn't care less, anyway—and after half an hour of his tugging at her hair and swearing, she had suggested he try something he knew. At least if he tied her long tresses up in knots on her head, they would stay. So she'd thought.

Her coiffure had looked good when he had finished the task, or at least all the men had said so. But the ride in the carriage had been quite jostling, and all the bouncing and bobbing around in the airless hack had loosened the knots. She could feel the heavy tresses sliding slowly to one side of her head and was positive the whole mess would come tumbling down at any second.

"Oh, just a moment." Henry reached out to brush something from her cheek with one finger. Valoree forgot her hair and scowled. Her face was even worse.

"There's just this piece . . ." Henry frowned. "A raspberry seed, I think."

Valoree grimaced. Pete had come up with some sort of white gooey substance to slather on her face as makeup, but had apparently not been able to come up with something for red cheeks and lips. One-Eye had returned from the kitchens with a bowful of raspberries, announcing they would do the trick. . . . And they had, she supposed, though she could have done without the men smooshing them on her cheeks and squeezing and rubbing them on her lips. She could also have done without the hour of picking at her face to remove the seeds afterward. Apparently they hadn't gotten quite all of them.

Her eyes dropped to his hand as he pulled it away from her cheek. A seed surrounded by white and pink gook stuck to the end of his pink-stained finger. She shook her head in disgust. "I suppose you've messed up my face, now."

"Nay, nay," he said quickly, surely realizing that she might use it as a chance to escape. However, his frown as he peered at her was less than reassuring.

Valoree eyed him briefly, then gestured to his hands. "Try to keep those out of sight. Those stains are— What the devil are you frowning at?"

His eyes shot to hers nervously. "Oh, nothing."

He'd answered too quickly, she decided, scowling at him suspiciously. "You'd best tell me. You know I don't like surprises."

"It's nothing," her quartermaster repeated, then wrinkled his nose. "It's only that your face appears to be cracking somewhat in the spots that it's drying."

"What!"

"Don't!" he cried, but it was too late; her hands had already risen instinctively to her face. She pulled her fingers away covered with the muck Pete had made as substitute makeup.

"Now you've done it," he muttered, and reached out with his finger again to pat and smooth her face. "Stand still."

Valoree tried to do as he asked, forcing herself to remain still, but she couldn't withhold the question that was now on the tip of her tongue. "How can my face be cracking when it's still wet?"

"It's drying around the edges," he informed her, a frown of concentration on his face as he worked at hers. "And on your bosom. That's where it's crack—" He paused, cursing when she glanced down to see that, indeed, the muck they had insisted on spreading on her neck and bosom, where it wasn't covered by the dress, was now dry and beginning to crack and flake.

"Now look what you made me do. You've a streak where my finger was. I told ye to stand still," Henry chided, using a finger at her chin to force her face up so he could repair this new damage. "I don't know how I got talked into this," he grumbled as he worked. "Wearing a monkey suit and playing lady's maid—"

"You?" Valoree scoffed. "You and the men are the ones who voted to marry me off. Don't whine now about what it takes to do so. 'Sides, if you want something to whine over, you should try wearing this damn dress. It's about as comfortable as an iron maiden."

"Well, at least you aren't wearing these damn ribbons everywhere. I look ridiculous."

"Aye, you do," she agreed with her first real smile in what felt like days. Her gaze slid over him, taking in the white breeches and shirt under a lime green waistcoat, with lime green and yellow ribbons on the knee breeches.

They had stopped at the tailor's on the way to the Beechams' soiree. It had been a desperate bid to get their hands on some lord-type clothes for Henry when they had realized that Meg was not going to recover in time to attend the "sour-ee." It had worked, much to Valoree's disgust. Of course the man had had a proper outfit in just the right size. Well, almost the right size. It had been made for a Lord somebody-or-other and was due to be delivered the next day, but would be delayed now thanks to Henry. He'd offered up a small fortune to be able to purchase it for his own use.

Giving a mutter, Henry tugged at his breeches impatiently. That was the only real problem with the outfit, Valoree supposed. The green waistcoat fit him in the shoulders, but it and the knee breeches were too big at the waist. Apparently the noble who'd commissioned it had something of a stomach, while Henry, who kept trim by pulling ropes and climbing rigging, did not. Now Henry was forced to constantly tug the pants up or else risk losing them. A voice interrupted her musings.

"Lady Ainsley."

Leaning to the side slightly, Valoree peered past Henry's scowling face at the smallish man who was approaching from behind him.

"Beecham," she said. Henry made a face, took one last swipe at her face, then turned to greet the man.

"Ah, Lord Beecham. A pleasure to meet the man who made the arrangements I requested. Good of ye to invite us to this here little swarming," Henry began cheerfully.

"Soiree," Valoree corrected, then forced a bright smile to her face as she nodded at their host. "Lord Beecham, my uncle Henry."

"A pleasure, my lo—Ah . . ." The young man paused, his eyes fixed on the pirate, and a frown began to slip onto his face.

"Is there something wrong?" Valoree asked a touch nervously, only just now worrying over his recognizing Henry as one of the servants that had accompanied her earlier that afternoon. She hadn't thought it a problem, for she had heard that most nobles didn't trouble themselves to notice servants. It figured that Beecham would be one of the few who did.

"I am sorry for staring, my lord," the man said. "It

is just that you look very much like one of the servants I saw with Lady Ainsley this afternoon."

"Ah." Henry nodded solemnly, and Valoree waited for his explanation, knowing he would come up with one. The sailor was a quick thinker. He didn't disappoint her. "That'd be me brother. Half brother, that is. My father's bastard offspring. His mother was one of our maids on the island. When he came of age, we took him on as a servant. Have to look after family, don't ye know." He slapped their host on the back as he said that, nearly sending the slender man to his knees.

Maintaining his feet, Beecham managed a weak smile at the jovial man. Then he glanced to Valoree and asked with real regret, "Your aunt could not make it tonight?"

" 'Fraid not," Henry answered before Valoree could speak, then tried for a conspiratorial look and said, "You know how women are. Fussing over the least little problem. Well, she took to the bo—"

"Bed," Valoree interjected quickly before he could finish. "She was not feeling well and took to her bed."

"I see," Beecham said, and Valoree suspected he did see—if not the whole picture, then that something was wrong with the picture they were trying to present. Sighing inwardly, she sent a quick glance at Henry, relieved when he caught the younger man's arm and whirled him around to propel him toward the middle of the room.

"How about ye introduce us around so we can size up the offerings this evening."

"Offerings?" Beecham asked uncertainly.

"Aye. The *men*. Got to marry this little lady off, don't ye know."

Glaring at the back of his head and following the men into the crowd, Valoree imagined she had one of

79

her blades with her and was sticking it into her quartermaster's arse.

"Have you seen Lady Ainsley?"

Daniel glanced up from the drink he had been contemplating, his eyebrows rising slightly at Beecham's distressed face. "Last I saw her, she was with you and that older gentleman."

"Her uncle." Beecham sighed, turning to peruse the roomful of people unhappily, unaware of the way Daniel stiffened.

"Her uncle?" he asked carefully. "On which side?"

Beecham turned back, his eyes blinking rapidly. "Which side? You mean which side of the family is he from?" The man frowned slightly. "I do not know. She merely introduced him as Uncle Henry. I imagine he is from the mother's side, however, since I do not believe that Lord Ainsley had a brother." He paused to consider that briefly, then shrugged with disinterest.

"He does not visit London much, obviously," Daniel said. Beecham shook his head.

"He has a plantation on one of the islands in the Caribbean. This is his first trip to London in years."

"Which island?"

Beecham frowned at the question. "I . . . I am not sure. I do not think they mentioned which one," he admitted slowly, then waved the question away. "I must find her and make sure she is all right."

"Did something happen?" Daniel asked before he could slip away, and the other man groaned.

"Aye. There was an *incident*."

Daniel's eyebrows rose at his pained inflection. "An incident?"

"Yes." Beecham hesitated, then said, "I had introduced them to several people when *Mother* waved us over—"

Daniel had to smother a grin at the way the man

said the word *mother*, though he couldn't blame him. Were Lady Beecham Daniel's own mother . . . Well, he was just grateful she wasn't. She was a rather unpleasant woman.

"So I was forced to introduce Lady Ainsley and her uncle to her friends; then Mother sent me off to fetch her a sweetmeat. Apparently, while I was gone . . . Well . . ." He whined piteously. "Lady Ainsley's face fell off."

Daniel blinked, bemused. "Her face fell off?"

Beecham nodded, seemingly broken. Then he suddenly straightened, an idea striking him. "Mayhap I should check—"

"Beecham," Daniel interrupted, drawing the other man's distracted attention.

"Hmmm?"

"How do you . . . I mean, how is it possible that her *face* fell off?"

"Oh! Well, it was her . . . er . . . the white stuff that all the women wear." He shook his head with a frown. "It was drying up on her skin and cracking." His frown deepened. "I thought to give warning, but feared to embarrass her, so I did not say anything. She knows now." He shook his head again. "It was horrible, really. I must find out where she got that makeup and warn everyone to stay away—"

"Beecham," Daniel interrupted patiently.

"Oh, sorry. Well, it was drying up as the night progressed. It turned a sort of grayish color as it dried and began to crack. Little bits of it were flaking off for most of the night as I took her and her uncle around. Honestly, we left a trail of the stuff from one end of the ballroom to the other. I believe she must have been aware of it and did not know what to do, for she grew quieter and quieter as the evening progressed. And, of course, she could surely feel it. It seemed to be pulling her face tight."

Seeing that Daniel was growing impatient again, Beecham hurried his story along. "Anyway, apparently Mother asked her a question she could not just nod at as she had been doing most of the night. She spoke, her face cracked, and a great chunk of it fell right off her chin. It bounced off her"—he gestured vaguely toward his chest—"and it plopped into Mother's wine. Of course, Mother's wine splashed out all over her new yellow gown. It will probably stain, and she is quite distressed," he ended somewhat lamely.

Daniel bit his lip hard to keep back the laugh that wanted to escape as he visualized the *"incident."* Taking a moment to clear his throat, he asked, "I take it the lady then disappeared?"

"Fled with her uncle on her heels," Beecham agreed unhappily. "I do not know where they may have gone."

"I would think they went straight home," Daniel proposed, but Beecham quickly shook his head.

"I went out front and checked. Their carriage is still here." When Daniel raised his eyebrows, Beecham shrugged. "Her servants are rather easy to spot. Pink livery." He frowned. "I've never seen men look quite so disreputable in pink livery as hers do. And they are all so big." Shaking his head, he bowed slightly toward Daniel. "I really must find her. I feel somehow responsible. I never should have left her with Mother. Excuse me."

Daniel considered that last phrase as the fellow hurried off. It was more telling than the rest of the tale. Beecham suspected his mother was somehow at fault for the whole affair.

Knowing Lady Beecham, she probably was. She would have seen the problem the girl was having, but rather than taking her aside and helping her repair her problem, as any good hostess would, she had probably sent her son off deliberately so that he could not field questions and the girl would have to speak and suffer the humiliation of a cracking face. Lady Beecham was a rather cold, nasty piece of work. Her friends were not much better, and the crowd of them together . . . Well, they would have eaten Lady Ainsley alive, he thought. But would they? He reconsidered. The woman he had seen eavesdropping at Whister's had not appeared the sort easily chewed up and spat out by anyone, even society's nastiest matrons. No. Just witness the fact that she had not already jumped in her carriage and fled.

He glanced around the room. Where *had* she gotten to then? he wondered. His gaze alighted on Lady Beecham and her crowd of cronies. They were all having a good laugh, he saw. His eyes narrowed as one of the women gestured toward the doors to the balcony, tittering as she did. Daniel stiffened.

Surely that was not where Lady Ainsley had run off to? If so, wouldn't Lady Beecham have told her son, rather than have him run about searching for her? Nay. Of course not. Not if she didn't want the fellow to have anything to do with her.

Positive he was right and drawn by his curiosity, Daniel strode toward the balcony doors.

"Oh, Captain, girl, I'm so sorry," Henry apologized as he found Valoree on the balcony. "This here was a terrible idea. We never should have made ye come out when ye were without the proper stuff." Awkwardly patting her shaking shoulders, he sighed miserably. "Please don't be crying, though. Yer breakin' me heart."

Valoree wheeled around at that. "I ain't crying, ye silly old goat," she snapped, her English slipping somewhat in her hurry to correct him. She had not cried since Jeremy's death. Pirate captains did *not* cry.

"Oh . . . Well, yer shoulders was shaking so hard I—"

"I was laughing," she explained. At his amazed expression, she shook her head. "It was damned funny when my face fell off. Did you see Lady Beecham's face when it plopped in her wine? I thought I'd split a gut right there." She curled her lip. "She was hoping for something of the like to happen, I think, the nasty old bitty. But I don't think she was quite prepared for it to ruin her precious gown like that."

"Nay, I don't think she was," Henry sighed. "And she *is* a nasty old biddy."

"Aye, she is," Valoree agreed, her amusement evaporating as she recalled the woman's false smile and cold eyes. Had Lady Beecham found aught amiss with Henry's account of life on their Caribbean plantation? He had been telling tales taller than the *Valor*'s masts tonight, but then he had always been that way on the ship, too, entertaining the men with some truly imaginative yarns when they relaxed in the evenings. Unfortunately, not ever having moved in such elevated circles as these people moved in, he'd had to make everything up from scratch. And even Valoree, who had not lived the life of a noble since her eleventh year, had seen great, gaping errors in his lies.

Not that he had told many of them at first, but once young Beecham had departed and they had been left alone with his mother and her crowd, Henry had started talking almost feverishly in an effort to draw attention away from Valoree and her cracking face. The more he had babbled away about their huge plantation—the sugarcane, the servants, and the fine "shorties" they held there—well, the more malicious Lady Beecham's smile had gotten, and the more she had eyed Valoree like a hawk eyeing a field mouse. Then she had started interrupting Henry to ask Valoree questions. Henry had tried to answer them, but finally the woman had said, "I asked your niece, my lord. Surely she can answer for herself."

It was then that, with nothing else for it, Valoree had opened her mouth to speak and sent a great avalanche of the white muck sailing off her face. The largest chunk had bounced off her chest into the woman's goblet of red wine, which had then splashed bloodred on her yellow gown.

Taking one look at the woman's horrified face, Valoree had whirled away to flee. But as she'd just told Henry, it was only so that she would not be seen when she burst out laughing.

"I suppose tonight probably ruined everything," Henry said. "We'll never get another invite to one of these here sworings, and we'll never get you married now. I should have listened to Meg instead of forcing ye to come tonight."

Valoree's ears perked up; she was hopeful that this might signal the end of this stupidity and that she might return to her old life, where she felt safer despite the inherent danger of being a pirate. Was Henry admitting defeat so soon? And not because of any fault of hers but because of the men's own miscalculations? Oh, this was too perfect. Better than she had hoped for.

Keeping her relief hidden, she nodded in agreement. "Aye. I doubt we garnered any friends here tonight. We are ruined, I believe is the term." She gave a feigned sigh of disappointment, then headed for the door. "Well, we'd best clear out of here and head home to tell the men."

"You don't really want to walk back through *there*, do ye?" Henry asked with amazement, falling into step beside her. He eyed her face with a wince mingled with doubt.

"That bad, is it?" Valoree asked, pausing.

"I could just nip around and see if there's any way to escape without going through the house."

Valoree briefly considered his suggestion, then nodded.

Henry was off at once, hurrying away, out and through the gardens to disappear into the trees. Valoree waited a moment, then caught herself picking off the chunks of dried glop that still clung to her face. Grimacing, she forced her hands away and walked to the edge of the balcony impatiently. It was then that she spotted the fountain. As she eyed it from where she stood, a plan formed in her head. She hurried down the steps and into the garden.

When he first stepped outside, Daniel thought he had been mistaken; the balcony was dark and empty, and there was no sign of Lady Ainsley. It was quiet and cool, though, a nice change from the inside of the Beecham ballroom. Deciding to enjoy the tranquility for a moment, he moved to the railing and set his drink down. His relaxation was broken a moment later as he glanced quickly up at the sounds of splashing water.

Squinting, he peered out over the shadowed gardens, his gaze stopping upon a dark shape directly in front of what appeared to be a rather large fountain. The shape seemed to be the source of all the racket. After a hesitation, he moved to the steps and down into the garden, making his way silently until he stood directly behind the noisy shadow.

It took his eyes a moment to sort out what he was seeing, and when he did, it was only because the dark shape suddenly shifted and rose up slightly, a head and shoulders appearing above the mass of dark blue skirts that had appeared black in the darkness. The sound of spluttering water continued.

Why would any woman submerge her head in Beecham's garden fountain? Unless she had a desperate need to clean some defective foundation from her face.

"Lady Ainsley?" he asked in disbelief.

The shape whirled on its knees and turned to face him. It was indeed the lady. She peered up at him in dismay, then lurched to her feet, pushing wet hair back off her face and glancing about rather wildly—looking for an escape route, most likely. Shifting forward a bit, Daniel blocked any opportunity for escape, his eyes taking in everything about her.

For a moment they were both silent; then Daniel cleared his throat. "I heard of your incident and thought to come out and check on you."

Her eyes widened. "My incident?"

"The trouble you had with . . ." He gestured vaguely toward her now clean-scrubbed face and thought she winced slightly, but he couldn't be sure in the darkness.

"Oh, aye. Well . . . I seem to have . . . been sold some inadequate foundation," she said at last.

"Ahhhh," Daniel murmured, though he wasn't sure what he meant even as he did so. "How distressing for you."

"Aye," she agreed. "Most distressing."

They both fell silent again; then Daniel, judging that she wouldn't run off on him, stepped back to give her some room. "I see you managed to remove it."

"Hmmm." She grimaced slightly. "I doubt Lady Beecham will appreciate my befouling her fountain."

"Better that than her wine." Daniel laughed, then realized what he had said. Quickly he tried to back-pedal. "I mean—"

"Oh, don't worry about it," the girl muttered, pushing past him and moving a few steps farther into the garden. Her gaze shifted out over the shadows as if in search of somebody; then she glanced back at him with a frown. "Was there something you wanted?"

"Wanted?" His eyes widened. "Nay, I just . . ." He paused, having no good explanation for his presence in the gardens. He shrugged, then searched for something to say. "I trust your appointment with Whister—"

"Went about as well as yours," she finished dryly, then glanced around. "Else I surely wouldn't be *here*."

"I take it you are not enjoying yourself?"

She turned her face toward him in the darkness. "Is that a joke, my lord?"

A bark of laughter slipped from Daniel's lips at her dry question. The girl certainly didn't pull any punches. He liked that. Clearing his throat, he tried a different topic. "Ainsley is in northern England, is it not?"

"Aye," she agreed, turning to peer out over the bushes again.

"I understand your parents died when you were quite young?"

"Aye."

"And your brother, Jeremy?"

Her head turned sharply, and Daniel could almost feel her eyes boring into him in the darkness. He continued.

"Whister mentioned that he died some . . . five years ago, was it?" He waited for her reaction. In truth, Whister hadn't said anything about this girl's brother; Daniel had known the fellow personally. In fact, Daniel had been looking for the man for some time now.

Though the man had been reputedly killed, someone was riding the ocean waves and continuing to loot the Spanish in his place. And whoever that man—Back-from-the-Dead Red, he was called—might be, he owed the king of England his percentage of five years' worth of piracy. If Jeremy Ainsley had thought to escape his contract with the Crown by faking his death, he was mistaken. If it was someone else in his stead, the king wanted him brought in.

Because he was the only one other than the king who had ever met Captain Red, Daniel had been commissioned by the king to bring Jeremy Ainsley to task for his crimes.

Of course, that had all ended a year ago when Daniel's father had died, leaving him Thurborne and all of its problems. It had been rather humiliating to him to have to admit failure after four years of endeavoring, but Daniel had had little choice but to give up his hunt for Jeremy Ainsley or his impostor. He'd had to return to take up his responsibilities. But perhaps here was a chance to rectify that. A little charm, a few compliments, and no doubt Lady Ainsley could be encouraged to give up the information Daniel needed to at least discover if her brother still lived.

"Damn!"

His thoughts interrupted by the curse, Daniel glanced down at the light oval of Lady Ainsley's face, then followed her gaze toward the balcony. Lord Beecham was coming out of the ballroom.

He glanced back to Valoree Ainsley, hoping to continue their discussion, but when he did, she was gone. He peeked around. The girl had ducked behind a nearby tree. It was a poor hiding place, and her skirts were sticking out on either side of the trunk.

Amusement filling him, Daniel took pity on the girl. She obviously did not want to speak to Beecham. With a sigh, he started back toward the steps to waylay the man.

"Psst . . . Pssst! Hey!" A voice came out of the darkness.

Her head jerking around, Valoree squinted at the bushes and trees that Henry had disappeared into several moments earlier. "Henry? Is that you?" she said in a hiss, then glanced nervously around the tree she was hiding behind. Thurborne had reached Beecham and the two men were now talking.

"Well, who the hell else would it be hidin' in the bushes hissin' at ye?"

Her quartermaster sounded cranky. She supposed she couldn't blame him. It had been an awful evening. Casting a nervous glance toward the men on the balcony, Valoree took a deep breath, then skittered across the small open space. She dove into the bushes, crashing into Henry's barrel-like chest. "Oh, there you are."

"Aye, here I am," Henry answered dryly, steadying her.

"Did you find another way out?"

"Aye." Turning, he began to push his way through the bushes. Then he stopped. "Well, it's not an ideal exit," he warned over his shoulder. "But a stone wall surrounds the town house gardens, and one side of it faces onto a street. I thought I could boost ye over the wall, then go fetch the carriage and bring it around to pick ye up."

"That'll do," Valoree answered. Anything to escape. The two set off.

"Here we are," Henry announced a moment later, pausing under a tree and tipping his head back to consider the wall. "What do you think?"

Valoree nodded as she looked at it. It was only a couple of inches taller than she. Were she not in such a clumsy, heavy dress, she would have managed it on her own. "All right. Give me a boost."

Henry locked his fingers and stooped to hold them at knee level. Rucking her skirts up, Valoree placed her booted foot in his hands, then reached out. Grasping the top of the stone wall, she launched herself upward as she pulled with her arms. Henry straightened and boosted her at the same time, and that lifted her high enough that she landed on the wall on her stomach. Quickly she swung one leg up to the side, catching at the wall with her foot and scrambling into a sitting position. Once perched there, she squinted down at him.

"I'll go back through the party, fetch the carriage, and bring it around," he told her.

"Why not just come this way? You can walk around to fetch it rather than go back through the party."

Henry shook his head. "I'm too old to be scrambling over walls," he told her, turning away. "I won't be a moment."

Valoree watched him disappear into the bushes again, then turned to glance at what lay on the other side of the wall. It was more an alley than a street—dark, narrow, and not well traveled. Unfortunately, though there was no one to see her, there was also nothing to see. She began to swing her legs on either side of the wall in boredom. Glancing back the way Henry had disappeared, she tried to calculate how far he might have gotten. He had probably reached the balcony.

She had just decided that when, glancing idly down at the ground just inside the wall, she stiffened. Something metal was glinting in the moonlight. Tugging her skirts out of the way, Valoree felt along the top of her boot for the knife that always rested there, then cursed. It was gone, of course. Must have been bumped out of her boot top as she had struggled to mount the wall.

Straightening, she peered down at it again. Short, sharp, and with a jeweled hilt, it had been passed down through the family for generations. It was almost all she had left of the family that had once been hers. That and Ainsley Castle. But Ainsley wasn't yet hers, and wouldn't be if she couldn't find a husband and get with child.

She couldn't leave the dagger behind. Cursing under her breath, she swung her right leg back over the wall and launched herself off of it. She landed harder than she expected and stumbled to the side, rolling in the

91

dirt and underbrush, then stopped herself and crawled to her hands and knees. Reaching out for the knife, she picked it up, then sat back on her haunches to inspect it. She needed to be sure all the jewels were still present.

The knife seemed fine. Deciding not to risk its falling out of her boot again, she stood and reached up to lay it on top of the wall. Then, grasping the top of the wall with one hand, Valoree tugged her skirts up with the other. Revealing one booted foot, she dug it into the wall, then attempted to pull herself up with both arms. Of course, the moment she let go of her skirts, her second foot tangled in them. With a jerk both her feet slid out from under her, sending her smacking into the wall.

This had been a lot easier with Henry's help.

Daniel had maneuvered Beecham around so that his back was to the garden. He didn't want the other man to spot Valoree sticking out from her tree. Unfortunately, once he had completed the maneuver, as he peered into the gardens himself he found he could no longer see her either. His gaze slid over the shadowed area as he nodded absently at Beecham's conversation, but he could discern nothing.

Where the devil had she gone? he wondered; then he stilled, his eyes narrowing as he spotted movement in the darkness at the periphery of the garden. Someone was sneaking toward the balcony, sticking carefully to the shadows. But it wasn't Lady Ainsley, he was sure. There were no bell-shaped skirts hampering the figure.

Quickly, Daniel turned his head slightly away so that whoever it was would not know they had been spotted. Instead, he watched from the corner of his eye. The figure drew nearer, then hesitated. Suddenly, straightening abruptly, it started forward at a fast clip that sent it sailing by into the ballroom almost too fast for Daniel to recognize the man.

"Who was that?" Beecham asked, turning suddenly. He must have caught a glimpse, however, for with some shock he said, "That was Lady Ainsley's uncle." Excusing himself, Beecham went off after the man at once.

Daniel watched him go, then turned to peer back down at the gardens. Moving to the steps, he walked down them, then paused to glance around before setting off to where he had first noticed the man, at the edge of the gardens. Finding almost at once a rough sort of side path that had been trounced into the trees and bushes on the edge of the garden, he did not hesitate, but began to follow it. After several steps, he heard a muffled curse from ahead and picked up his pace.

The path ended quite suddenly, and Thurborne stepped out of the bushes to find himself confronting the back end of a skirt—Lady Ainsley's—as the woman hung from the wall and scrambled to climb it.

"Damn it!"

Daniel blinked as the woman before him swore again, then briefly settled on the ground. She launched herself upward once more almost immediately, pulling with her arms and scrabbling at the wall with her feet.

"Might I be of some service?" he asked with amusement, chuckling when she released the wall abruptly, stumbled a step back, then tripped over her own skirt and plopped onto her behind in the dirt. The curse she snapped then was nothing any lady he knew would have ever uttered—and certainly not with such believable vehemence.

Moving around in front of her, he reached out, offering assistance. Lady Ainsley hesitated briefly, then slapped her wrist into his hand, her own fingers closing around his wrist like a vise. Before Daniel could recover from his surprise at both the masculine action and the strength in her fingers, she was pulling, and he had to brace himself to prevent being tugged over on top of her. Gathering himself quickly, he pulled even as she did, bringing her to her feet before him.

"Attempting to avoid leaving via the ballroom, I take it," he asked, watching with interest as she busied herself in brushing off her hands on her once pristine skirts.

Sighing, the girl gave up trying to remove the dirt on her hands, then used them to push the damp mane of hair off her face. She propped them on her hips as she considered him. "It seemed an easier alternative."

"Aye," Daniel agreed. "If one can scale this vast wall."

Her eyes flashed. "Do not make fun of me. I could climb this damn thing if I just had my breeches on and not these horrid skirts."

"Ah, but then you might be mistaken for a man," he teased. When she merely glared at him, he turned to consider the wall, then turned back. "Why did your uncle not help you up the wall ere leaving to"—he arched an eyebrow questioningly—"fetch the carriage?"

"He did," she snapped. At his doubtful expression, she rolled her eyes. "Well, do you think he expected me to manage it on my own with all these bothersome skirts?"

"Then why, pray tell, are you down here instead of up there?" He nodded toward the top of the wall and watched with some interest as she ground her teeth together.

"I was up there when he left."

"Then how did you get down here?"

"How do you think?" she asked scornfully. "I jumped down."

"Why?"

She rolled her eyes. "What is this? An inquisition?"

When he merely arched his eyebrows at her and leaned back against the wall, she sighed impatiently and returned to her task. Grasping the top of the wall she leaped and strained to pull herself upward. He watched in fascination for several moments, waiting for her to beg his assistance as most women would, before he realized quite suddenly that she would not do it.

"All you need do is ask," he said at last. She turned, a small struggle on her face. Asking obviously wasn't easy for her, he realized with some wonder. *Amazing.* In his experience, females were always asking for help. They were thought weaker and used that to their advantage. *Pray, my lord, the basket is soooo heavy, if you could but carry it. Oh, my Lord, prithee, I couldn't possibly walk from here to there on my own, if you would but loan me your strong arm to lean on.*

But not this one. She would most likely continue to struggle until doomsday ere asking, Daniel realized. He felt himself soften. Straightening, he caught her arm and drew her away from the wall, then stepped in front of her. Placing his back to the wall, he dropped to his haunches, and held out his interlocked hands. "Up we go."

She considered his proffered hands suspiciously for a moment, then sighed. Positioning herself in front of him, Lady Ainsley reached over him to grasp the wall, then glanced down to find his hands with her eyes.

"On three," he murmured, considering the booted foot she placed in his hands. What odd dress, he thought. "One, two, three."

He pushed, but not too eagerly. She pulled with a grunt, and she landed on her belly on the wall, her lower legs pressed against his face. Grinning, Thurborne slid out from between her and the wall, then straightened and moved behind her, considering her voluminous skirts as she swung her right leg to the side and tried to heft it up onto the wall as well.

"Some more help perhaps?" he teased, watching her skirts swing back and forth as she struggled.

Her grunt of rage was most entertaining. Stepping forward, he slid his hands under her skirts and caught her by her boots. "Up or to the side?"

"Up," she snapped, and he slid his fingers lightly up until he touched something other than leather, laughing at her abruptly cut-off yelp.

"To the side, to the side," she roared, not sounding at all ladylike. Thurborne continued to chuckle as he grasped one leg, lifting and swinging it to the side. A moment later she had broken free from his hold and sat straddling the wall. Immediately, she pulled her other leg up beneath her as if not trusting him not to touch her again. Then she felt along the wall for something. When she didn't find it, she released another curse and turned to glare down at him. Even in the darkness he could see that she was furious.

"If I had my blade with me I'd—"

He never got to hear the end of that threat, for at that moment the jangle of a carriage and the clip-clop of horses reached them both. Glancing over her shoulder, Lady Ainsley muttered something under her breath. Then suddenly, she dropped off the wall, disappearing on the other side.

"What took you so bloody long?" he heard her snap on the other side of the wall.

"Long?" a man cried. "Why, I nearly ran through that there house, then hustled Skully straight on over here. I only left you but a moment ago."

Her response to that was cut off and muffled by the slam of a carriage door; then Daniel heard the conveyance jangle away down the street.

He stayed where he was long after the carriage had rolled away, his mind replaying the incident and certain things that had been said. *I could climb this damn thing if I just had my breeches on and not these horrid skirts.*

*Ah, but then you might be mistaken for a man.*

Nay, he thought uncertainly. It could not be . . . But she had been wearing boots and something else beneath her skirts. And she had said *my breeches*. Still, what did all this mean?

"Daniel!"

Recognizing his mother's voice, Daniel peered back toward the bushes he had walked through to reach the wall. He started quickly back through them, stepping out into the garden to see his mother standing on the balcony, glaring impatiently out into the darkness.

"Oh, there you are, Daniel." She sighed as she spotted him. "Lord Beecham said he saw you out here. Whatever were you doing in those bushes? The party is inside."

"Which is perhaps why *I* am *outside*," Daniel muttered, jogging up the last few steps to join her.

"Oh, really," she muttered with exasperation, turning her cheek up for his dutiful kiss. Once that was out of the way, she stepped back to eye him. "Did you see Master Whister today?"

"You know I did," he answered.

"And?"

"And what? Do not try to pretend you did not know the codicil to Gran's will. She told you everything. No doubt you have known about it for some time."

The woman had the grace not to deny it. Instead, she asked, "I am arranging several small soirees in the next little while. One for tomorrow night even. Is there anyone in particular you would like me to invite?"

He knew what that meant; *Daniel, now that you know you have to marry to inherit your dear grandmama's money, I am arranging a party to parade available females by you. Is there anyone you prefer?*

"Nay."

His mother blinked. "Well, then, I shall just do my best."

Translation, he thought dryly: *Every available female in England shall be invited.*

"Do not bother; I will be unable to attend," he began. Suddenly he paused. "On second thought, I do have someone I wish invited."

His mother's expression, which had begun to turn down with displeasure, abruptly lightened. "Yes, dear?"

"Lady Ainsley."

Her face fell with displeasure again. "Not that woman! Oh, Daniel, you cannot be interested in her! She is the talk of the ball. My God, her face fell off in Lady Beecham's wine. And her uncle is an absolute horror. Completely barbaric, from what I have heard. He—"

"She had an unfortunate experience with some bad makeup, Mother. It was not her fault, and she was humiliated by it." He somehow doubted that the lady in question had really felt much more than a touch of embarrassment—amazing, considering that the situation would have crushed most young women attending a soiree—but his mother need not know that. "As to her uncle, she can hardly be held accountable for his behavior. If you wish me to attend your party, you will invite Lady Ainsley. Otherwise I shall be quite unavailable. For the foreseeable future, I shall attend only balls that she is attending."

His lady mother's mouth dropped open, her eyes wide as she gazed on him. Then she fairly beamed at him. "Oh, Daniel! Of course, I shall invite the dear girl then."

# Chapter Five

"You were a success!"

Valoree paused halfway down the stairs to peer at One-Eye warily. He closed the front door, waved a small piece of paper at her, then snatched up a small stack of four or five more and hurried toward her.

"See! Invites, all of them. Soirees, balls, the lot," he announced with glee, waving the invitations under her nose. "See, there weren't nothing to worry about. I knew ye'd do just fine."

"Do just fine at what?" Henry asked, catching the tail end of One-Eye's comment as he came down the stairs behind Valoree.

"At being a lady," One-Eye explained, grinning widely as he flashed the invitations at the older man. "Invites. Five of them. She must have done us proud last night. She's been invited to more balls and such."

"Pity invitations," Valoree muttered, pushing the papers he held out of her face with disgust and continuing past him down the stairs.

Quick to speak up, Henry followed her with One-Eye on his heels. "Oh, now, I don't think them nobles we met last night would send invites to their sworings out of pity."

"Soirees," Valoree corrected automatically as she crossed the hall. "But aye. Mayhap you are right. Mayhap they invited me for the entertainment value!"

"Entertainment?" One-Eye asked, moving to

Henry's side as they followed her into the small morning room.

Valoree had refused to discuss the evening's debacle once they had returned home last night. She had simply stridden upstairs and straight to her room, rolling her eyes as she'd heard Henry telling the others that all had gone "well enough." So much for the man's leading her to believe that they would give the sorry task up.

Now she ignored One-Eye's questions to glare at Meg. The older woman was already seated at the table, and she looked pretty bright and chipper for someone who had drunk herself into unconsciousness the night before. Her aunt merely smiled blandly back.

Petey entered then with a rack of fresh loaves of bread, still steaming, and Valoree's attention turned to her rumbling stomach. Nodding to the dark-haired, solemn man, she moved toward him as he set the bread on the table.

"Oh, come now. It weren't that bad," Henry soothed. "Ye did real fine for yer first night out."

"Real fine?" Forgetting food briefly, Valoree spun on him in fury. "*Real fine?* A great chunk of my face fell off into the hostess's glass! You call that *fine?*"

"What?" Meg gasped with horror.

"Her makeup," Henry explained quickly, then glared at Petey. "It dried, cracked, and fell off her face. She left a trail of face flakes from one end of Beecham's ballroom to the other."

"What are you looking at *me* for?" Petey asked, eyes narrowing. "I had nothing to do with it."

"Nothing to do with it?" Henry sputtered. "You made the muck up!"

"I didn't make nothing up!" Petey snapped back, drawing himself up proudly. "What do you take me for? I don't know how to make that muck noblewomen put on their face. I cook."

Henry scowled. "I sent One-Eye down to have you make something up for her to wear on her face."

"And I set aside the cake I was making and went down to the docks to see if I could find someplace to buy some proper makeup," the man snapped impatiently. "I wasted two hours searching for some, and when I come back, what do I find? You're gone, my cake batter is gone, my raspberries are gone—"

"Ahha!" Valoree interrupted, turning to glare at both Henry and One-Eye. "I told you it tasted sweet when you got some on my lips."

"Aye, that you did," Henry muttered. He turned to glare at One-Eye. The man raised his hands helplessly.

"How was I to know it was cake batter? You said to go down and see what Petey had whipped up to put on the captain's face. I went down. Petey wasn't around, and there it was. White gooey stuff. It looked like it could have been makeup to me."

"Let me get this straight," Meg interrupted quietly from her place at the table. "You took Lady Valoree to a soiree with cake batter on her face?"

"And raspberries smooshed into my cheeks and on my lips," Valoree added with disgust.

"Raspberries?" Meg stared at Henry with dismay. He shifted uncomfortably.

"Well, it worked. Her face was white—"

"Until it fell off," Valoree snapped.

Ignoring her, Henry continued. "And her lips and cheeks was red like all the rest of them ladies at the swarming."

"All the rest of the ladies at the *soiree* didn't have people picking raspberry seeds off their cheeks all night long," Valoree snapped.

"Oh, dear." Meg sank back into her seat, her face dropping weakly into one open hand.

Valoree was gratified by this display of horror until she noticed the way the other woman's shoulders were

101

shaking. She was laughing! "It was not funny!" she said in a snarl.

"Nay, of course not," Meg said at once, though the words came out with a few chortles. "It is not funny at all," she agreed again, trying for solemnity and failing desperately as a chuckle began to rumble from her belly upward. "Oh d-dear." She gasped apologetically, fighting valiantly to keep the laughter in, but the moment she looked at Valoree, it exploded out of her mouth on a hiccup of sound that quickly grew into a full-blown laugh. "Oh m-my! C-cake batter for makeup."

"And raspberry cheeks," One-Eye added with a grin that died the moment Valoree turned her sour gaze on him. "Well," he said unhappily, "it seemed like a good idea at the time."

Grunting, Valoree glanced toward the steaming bread on the table. Her stomach rumbled. Before she could move toward the food, however, Meg suddenly sobered and looked questioningly at Pete. "Were you able to find the makeup in question?"

The Greek scowled. "Nay. I told you it was a wasted trip."

"I see. Well, that shall be our first order of business this morning, then," she decided solemnly, rising to her feet.

"What?" Valoree asked suspiciously, tearing her gaze from the food.

"Going out to purchase some proper makeup. We cannot have another night like your last." She headed for the door, but paused beside Henry. "Did it really fall into Lady Beecham's glass?"

Grimacing, Henry nodded. Meg shook her head, amusement twinkling in her eyes briefly before she sobered again and ordered, "You'd best fetch some of that gold, Henry. We shall need it." She sailed through the door then, adding, "Come along, Valoree. The bread will still be there when we return."

"Not bloody likely with Bull and One-Eye around," Valoree muttered, snatching up the biggest loaf, and a good-sized hunk of cheese, before following the woman. As she passed a frowning Henry, she said sweetly, "Ye'd best be fetching some of that there gold, Henry. Or have ye changed yer mind and decided we can return to the sea, after all?"

The last part was more a hope than anything else. Valoree would have dearly loved to give up this humiliating venture and return to their lives on the sea, but she knew even as she voiced the words that none of the men was likely to give up yet. She figured she had a great deal more humiliation left to suffer before they would call it quits. And why not? They weren't the ones having to suffer.

"Which do you like best, Valoree?"

Sighing, Valoree peered at the small pots of red color and frowned. She did not have much patience at the best of times, and this little expedition seemed to be evaporating what tiny bit she did have rather quickly. They were supposed to have come in search of makeup. And they were ... now. *Finally.* But they had left the town house several hours ago.

First, "Aunt Meg" had insisted on a stop at the tailor's to see about those dresses Henry had gone to order. Despite her irritation, Valoree had to admit that at least that had proved to be an intelligent move. The little land-rat had horrible taste, and the dresses he had decided on for her had all been atrocious. They were frilly, fluffy, busy little dresses that had made Valoree curse a blue streak when she saw the designs. He apparently didn't realize she was not a frilly, fluffy sort of woman. The tailor was an idiot. She had told him so as she had ripped up the designs he had made, then spent a grim hour hanging over his shoulder and directed him in sketching more acceptable gowns, slapping him in the head or bellowing in his ear every time he had tried to sneak in a ruffle or frill.

They had all—Meg, Valoree, and the tailor—been relieved when that was over. But then Valoree had climbed out of the carriage at the next stop to find they were at a perfumery. Entering the smelly place had given her an immediate headache, one that had stayed with her throughout the hour of sniffing and sampling Meg forced on her. The woman favored flowery odors, forever shoving them under Valoree's beleaguered nose until she'd finally ordered Henry to buy one of them for Meg to get her to leave off.

The woman had fairly beamed at the gift, though Henry had been less than pleased. Still, they had both left her alone to choose her own fragrance then. She had made her choice relatively quickly, picking one that reminded her of tropical breezes and the smell of the ship's hold after they took a galleon rich in spices. Meg had looked doubtful at her choice, but Henry had proclaimed it nectar and paid for it a little more happily than he had Meg's.

Now here they were, finally at the makeup shop. But this part of the expedition was going no faster than the rest of the trip. They had spent half an hour just choosing a foundation, the white base that was spread over a woman's face, neck, and bosom to hide skin problems or scars from the pox. And while Valoree did not have either of those problems, due to her years of sea and sun she had a slight tan—despite the captain's hat she always wore. And tans simply were not the thing at court. Ladies were to have lily white skin and rouged cheeks and lips.

A foundation made of white lead and vinegar had been what the shopkeeper obviously favored, but Valoree had refused to even consider it, no matter how many times he insisted it was the best. She had heard that the concoction made the skin shrivel and turn gray. When he had finally given up on trying to sell her that, he turned to a long description of the other offerings he had; pastes made up of alum and tin ash, others featuring sulfur. She had chosen one with an egg white–and-talc base and stood firm on it despite his efforts to steer her back to the lead and vinegar.

Now they had moved on to the fucus, as he kept calling it—a most unattractive name for the variety of red face paints that were used on both the cheeks and lips. Once again he was insisting on describing their contents. There were madder-, cochineal-, and ocher-based compounds among them, but vermilion, made up of mercuric sulfide, was the one he kept drawing their attention to.

Valoree groaned. There were still kohl and concoctions to brighten the eyes to get through yet. Also, Valoree seemed to recall Meg muttering something about a wig. She envisioned hours of this nonsense ahead, and, frankly, she had already had more than enough. It was nearly the nooning hour and she was dying of thirst. She hadn't had anything to drink since the night before, and the fact that she had eaten the whole loaf of bread as well as the chunk of cheese in the carriage, polishing off a good portion of each on the way from the town house, then finishing them between shops, didn't help.

"Well? Do any of them appeal to you?" Meg asked.

Sighing, Valoree focused on the paint pots again, then shook her head. "I do not care."

"Of course you do, dear. You—"

"Nay. I don't," Valoree assured the woman grimly. "I am hungry and—"

"How can you be hungry?" Henry asked peevishly. "You ate that whole loaf of bread yerself."

Valoree's mouth began to twitch at the resentment in the old man's voice. She had been aware of his hungry-eyed glances at her loaf and cheese, but had ignored them, still irritated that he'd reneged on his claim last night that they would give up this fool's errand of trying to find a husband.

Forcing her amusement aside, Valoree shrugged. "Well, I am. And I am also thirsty. I have not had a drop to drink since last night. So the two of you can make the choices," she announced, turning toward the door. "I am in search of . . . refreshment." She said the word dryly as she walked out of the shop, knowing Henry would gather her true meaning. She wanted a damn drink. A real drink. Rum, or whiskey, or—

"Ah, Lady Ainsley. What a surprise."

Valoree gasped and stepped to the side to avoid colliding with Lord Thurborne as the man suddenly appeared before her, but she did not slow her step. She was too damned thirsty to be bothered with the irritating nobleman. Rather than leaving her to her own devices, the pest fell quickly into step beside her.

"I see I caught you without your blade again," he said lightly, reminding her of her last comment the night before. She had been frustrated to find the knife missing when she had finally gained the wall, but it had only been knocked off to land on the other side. She had snatched it up on her way to the carriage.

"Aye. More's the pity," she muttered now.

"Then I suppose I am safe," he teased. Then, before she could comment, he asked, "Where is it we are headed exactly?"

"*I* am headed for a tav—" Catching herself, she cleared her throat and tried for a less irritated and more ladylike answer. "I am searching for an establishment in which I might partake of refreshment."

"Alone?"

Valoree rolled her eyes at the question. She had been doing things alone since she was eleven. Disguised as a boy, mind you, but alone nonetheless. Ladies, of course, would not take refreshment unescorted—especially in this less than ideal part of town. *Damn!* The rickety little shop that Meg had directed them to was in an area that had once been quite upmarket and expensive, but that was years earlier. Now the buildings were crumbling and the shops were gradually moving out, a less pleasant element moving in.

"I am not alone," she told him grimly. "My aunt and uncle are in the shop I just left, and my men . . . servants . . . manservants . . . are right there." She glanced toward their carriage as she gestured to it, then paused, for while Skully still sat upon the driver's seat, One-Eye was no longer on the footman's stand.

A movement out of the corner of her eye drew her attention to the man standing a step or two behind Lord Thurborne. It was One-Eye, and he had a solemn expression on his face as he attempted to look the part of a footman. Impossible, of course, despite the pink livery he wore. The pink merely seemed to emphasize his long, shaggy black hair, his eye patch, and the fact that he was armed to the teeth. Two flintlock pistols stuck out of his pants, his cutlass hung sharp and wicked at his side, and a leather strap he had fashioned years ago had been slung over his head and hung from one shoulder blade to his waist on the opposite side. It was packed full of blades, all in varying sizes and shapes. He looked like what he was: a pirate who was deadly with knives. But that didn't alarm Valoree nearly as much as the fact that he had come down off of his perch on the carriage to follow her. As if she needed protecting like any other lady!

Fear rippled through her at the damage that was being done to her image as a strong and capable captain. None of the men would have considered her in need of protecting prior to this nonsense. None of them but Henry had even known she was a woman before they'd arrived in London! Until then they had all still supposed her to be Jeremy's younger brother, about to claim his estates and the title of lord.

"My lady?"

Valoree glanced at Thurborne briefly, her breath coming out on a small sigh. "I am sorry, my lord. Wait here a moment, please," she ordered. Then stepping past him, she caught One-Eye by the arm and jerked him around to lead him back to the carriage.

"What do you think ye're doing? I don't need protecting, One-Eye, I may be wearin' a dress, but that don't mean I'm suddenly helpless. I—"

"I know that."

His sharp words silenced her as she paused by the carriage, and she faced him questioningly.

"Well," he explained, "I seen a lot of ladies out and about since we got here, and none of 'em seems to go anywhere without an older lady or a servant following her about like a pup. So when ye came out o' the shop without Meg or Henry, I thought I'd best follow ye . . . For appearance' sake."

"I see." She sighed, relief and gratitude overwhelming her briefly so that she had to turn her head away in alarm to hide the moisture that suddenly dampened her eyes. What the devil was going on here? she wondered with dismay. She hadn't cried since Jeremy's death, yet here she was getting all watery just because One-Eye *didn't* see her as helpless. *Brilliant!* If this was a side effect of wearing a damn dress, she'd never put one on again once she finished this business.

Taking a deep, calming breath, Valoree blinked her eyes rapidly until most of the moisture was dispersed, assuring herself that there was nothing to get upset about here. One-Eye was following her around for appearance' sake, not because he suddenly saw her as a weak woman. Her title as captain was still safe. She hesitated to examine why that should relieve her so, except that her ship and crew were all she really had in the world right now, and maybe all she ever would have, unless she found a husband and had a child to claim her home again.

Clearing her throat, she turned back to One-Eye. "Well, now I have Lord Thurborne to escort me. You should remain here. But take off those damn weapons."

"Take 'em off?" he cried.

"Aye. This is London, not the high seas. You just make yourself look like a silly pink pirate with them. Take 'em off and stick them under the driver's seat or something."

"All of 'em?"

Valoree was about to say "aye, all of them," when she caught the panic in his eyes. The expression made her think for the first time that she might not be the only one feeling like a fish out of water, suffering the insecurity of new roles and such. No doubt going from a swaggering swashbuckler to a pink-clad footman was a difficult transition to make. Sighing, she shook her head.

"One pistol and two of the smaller blades you can keep, but stick 'em in the top of your breeches and close your coat over them." She gestured to the pink livery jacket he had left undone, and pushed back the sides to reveal the white top and weapons beneath. "Just put the others somewhere out of sight, but close at hand."

"Aye, Captain," he said, apparently relieved.

"Good . . . And tie your hair back," she instructed.

One-Eye's hand went to his long black locks in alarm. Valoree sighed. "Only when you are out and about as a footman. Of course, you may wear it as you like the rest of the time."

Sighing, he nodded reluctantly, and Valoree grimaced sympathetically, then glanced toward the man now stepping down from the carriage to join them. Her eyebrows rose. His name was No-Nose, which came from the fact that he had no nose, of course. Well, not really much of a nose anyway. It had been shot off long ago while he was a merchant seaman. The ship he had ridden with had been under attack by Spanish pirates at the time. Once he had healed, he had returned to his ship, but its captain had told him he wasn't needed anymore. He'd been replaced; no one wanted to look on his ugly mug.

He was one of the men Valoree and Henry had hired on to replace the crew members who had died with her brother. Neither of them had cared that he was horribly disfigured. All they had cared about was that he knew his business and did it well. Yet she wished he hadn't been the one driving today. She hadn't really paid attention to who was driving, simply assuming it was Skully. Now she wished he were Skully. She didn't care about the man's nose so much, but she did care that he had long hair. It was a limp, greasy brown, and he too was armed to the teeth—his rotten, half-missing teeth. His presence brought a scowl to her face. "What the hell are you doing here? I thought you were still on the ship."

No-Nose shook his head and propped his hands on his hips. He leaned to the side slightly and spat on the road. "Nope. Came back with the others last night to help at the town house. Volunteered. Didn't know I'd be 'spected to wear this here fancy-pants outfit, though."

"Hmmm." Ignoring his sneer of disgust at the pink livery her men were all being forced to wear, Valoree raised an eyebrow. "And where is Skully? Why isn't he driving today?"

No-Nose shrugged. "Went back to the ship for something. Henry sent him."

"Hmmm," she said again, then sighed. "Well, what I just told One-Eye goes for you, too. Get rid of all

110

your weapons but one pistol and two short blades. Stick 'em in the top of your pants and close your coat. Wear it proper. And find something to tie your hair back with. You both look like a couple of pirates."

No-Nose straightened slightly at that. "Well, and so we should. That's what we are."

"Not right now, you're not," she said as if they were idiots. "You're playing the parts of servants at the moment." They both stiffened, their chests puffing out slightly in offense, but Valoree smiled at them sweetly. "You all voted on this," she reminded them, then her smile disappeared. "And if I have to run around in these damn dresses acting all ladylike, you two can play your parts, too. I expect my orders to be carried out. If they aren't . . ." She let the sentence fade away, a mean look on her face. There was no need to finish the threat. All her crew knew what would happen if they should disobey an order . . . Something bad.

Chin lifting, Valoree whirled away, actually enjoying the way her skirts flew out around her, imagining that it must look impressive as she strode grimly back to where Lord Thurborne patiently waited.

"Come on, I need a drink," she said with a grunt, catching his arm and dragging him along the road a ways before trying to pull him into a tavern. She got him to the door before he balked.

"Just a moment."

Turning at his hesitation, she eyed him impatiently. "What?"

"Well . . ." He glanced up at the sign over the door unhappily. "This is a rather rough establishment for a lady. I do not think—"

"Can you not protect me?" she asked with feigned surprise. He stiffened.

"Aye, of course I can, but—"

"Good." Whirling away, she hurried inside, leaving him to follow or not as he wished.

The noise from the tavern washed over her like thunder as she opened the door, but was a very brief thunder. Her entrance seemed to be noted by everyone rather quickly, and an ominous silence abruptly fell. Ignoring their mute stares, Valoree wove her way calmly through the sea of sailors, ne'er-do-wells, and doxies, to the bar. Pausing there, she waited patiently as the barkeep hesitated, then made his way to her.

He eyed her uncertainly. "Is there something I can help ye with, m'lady?" he asked doubtfully.

"You can poor me a whiskey," she answered calmly, sighing when the bartender's eyebrows rose. He glanced over her head at someone behind her. Undoubtedly that someone was Thurborne. Forcing what she hoped was a sweet smile to her lips, she turned and flashed it at the man, then murmured, "Whiskey settles my stomach, and I am feeling a touch nauseous just now."

Both the nobleman and the bartender continued to stare at her rather blankly, and Valoree's frayed patience was stretched a little further. Eyes narrowing, she turned back to the barkeep.

"I said, it settles my stomach. Ye wouldn't want me to be pukin' on yer lovely bar now, would ye?"

That got a better response. A look of horror overtaking his face, the man snatched a mug from under the counter, slammed it on top, and produced a bottle from seemingly nowhere. He poured out some golden liquid into it.

"Thank you," she said with amusement, lifting the glass to her lips as Daniel gave his own order—ale, of course. Probably for the best, she decided. They didn't serve stuff like she was drinking in the places he likely went. This whiskey was the kind Petey could soak his pots in and never have to scour to get them clean. One could even drink the used whiskey afterward, and it

112

wouldn't taste any different. Yes, sir, this was the good stuff.

Swallowing the rest of the liquid down, she slammed her mug onto the counter, a message to the keeper that she was ready for more. The minute he had refilled it, she moved to the nearest table with an open spot and settled herself on the end of the bench. She needed to drink and try to relax. Daniel followed and settled across from her almost at once, glancing around warily as the other patrons slowly began to speak again—about her, no doubt. They didn't like what they thought was a lady invading their territory. Didn't like it at all. That became rather obvious in a hurry.

"Mayhap we should find another place to—"

"Nay, it's fine here. Just ignore them," she advised, but the approach of one of the sailors made ignoring impossible. He was a big gawky Scot. The man was as big as Bull, with hair as red as Valoree's and a wicked grin that almost distracted her from the fact that he was missing one ear and had a scar in its place that ran down to his chin.

"Hello, lovey," was his opening line, and Valoree arched an eyebrow at him.

"Is there something I can help you with?" she asked, suddenly aware of the way Daniel was tensing across from her.

"Actually, lovey, I was about to ask ye the very same thing." He grinned suggestively. "Mayhap a little male companionship."

"She already has an escort," Lord Thurborne said sharply, bristling all over.

"Does she now?" The big Scot glanced at him with amusement. "Well, it wasn't escorting I was thinking of offering."

Much to Valoree's surprise, Daniel was on his feet before the man could finish turning back to face her. Grabbing him by the shoulder, Daniel wheeled the big lug back around, and coldly glared at him. "I said she has an es—"

That was as far as he got, of course. This wasn't the type of place where men "discussed" their differences. The Scot was on him at once, slamming a fist into his jaw midword, sending him stumbling backward. Valoree sighed, thinking she would have to give up her relaxing drink and intervene on Daniel's behalf. It seemed she would find no peace today . . . anywhere.

But before she could move, he had regained himself and come back at the man, fists flying. Valoree was impressed. The Scot wasn't much taller than Thurborne, but he carried twice his bulk, and had arms as big around as her thighs and fists like pots. But Daniel was the better fighter, apparently—and a dirty one, too, she realized with a grin a moment later as he suddenly kicked the other man.

The Scot howled a note in soprano, his hands suddenly glued to his groin. He tumbled sideways to moan and writhe on the ground.

Straightening his cuffs, Daniel eyed the Scot for a moment, then turned a hard-eyed look on Valoree. "If you have finished your *refreshment*, mayhap we could get out of this *establishment*."

"Well, now," she said with amusement. "As it happens, I am not quite finished. Besides, it appears you've made some friends."

"Friends?" He gave her an angry look.

"Aye. And it appears they'd like ye to stay and play."

Understanding dawning in his eyes, Daniel whirled just in time to see the fist that came flying at him. He tried to avoid it, and while he didn't succeed entirely, he did manage to avoid the worst of the blows. It seemed the Scot had friends—three of them—and they were moving in on him. Sighing, Daniel spread his feet slightly and prepared to do battle.

Gulping down the last of her whiskey, Valoree stood and moved around the fighters to reach the bar again. Setting the mug down for the barkeep to refill, she kept her gaze fixed on Daniel and his new friends as the real fighting began. She wasn't really worried about him, despite the odds. If he could handle the Scot, he could handle those three . . . four . . . five . . . Now, six was getting a bit unfair, she decided irritably.

Grabbing her refilled mug in one hand, she snatched the now empty whiskey bottle from the barkeep with her other, and started back to the table. She paused along the way to smash the bottle over the head of the nearest of the six men. He fell like a stone, crumpling to the wooden floor behind her as she continued on to the table.

Sipping her drink, she watched the remainder of the fight with interest. Daniel was fast on his feet. He was also, she saw with delight, using every dirty trick in the book. There were no fancy fisticuffs here. He was pulling hair, gouging eyes, kneeing, punching, and kicking groins. She couldn't have been prouder had he been one of her own men.

A tap on her shoulder made her glance around to find herself staring at Richard and Scratchy. "What the devil are the two of *you* doing here?" she snapped irritably, then glared at her second mate. "Richard, I left you in charge of the ship. What—"

"Skully came back to relieve me. He said Henry had sent him to give me some time off, too."

"Oh." Sighing, Valoree glanced back at the fight, trying to shrug off the guilt that was suddenly plaguing her for not thinking herself of giving the man time off. "Well, behave yourselves."

The two men muttered acquiescence to that, then were silent for a moment, watching the fight with her.

"He's pretty good," Richard commented after a moment as Daniel tossed one of the men over his shoulder and onto a nearby table. "Is he 'him'?"

"Him who?" Valoree asked distractedly.

"The one what ye're gonna marry," Richard clarified, bringing her head snapping around.

She glared at him briefly, then snapped, "Nay."

"Why not?"

"Why not?" she repeated in amazement. Because he was definitely not the sort to allow her to be in charge; she could tell just by looking at him. But instead she said, "Well, for one thing, he hasn't asked."

"Hmmm." Richard pursed his lips and eyed Thurborne consideringly. "Good fighter."

"Not bad," Scratchy agreed, plucking out a silver of wood that was half sticking out of the rough wooden table and using it to pick his teeth as he considered the continuing fight. "Knows how to handle hisself."

"Hmmm." They were all silent for a moment; then Richard muttered, "Don't suppose we should help 'im out a bit? Just in case it turns out he's thinking of asking?"

"He doesn't need help," Valoree snapped. "He's doing fine. Besides, you know I don't like you men fighting when you're on shore." She winced as one of the men landed a rather brutal blow that seemed to stun Thurborne for a moment, allowing several more blows before he could stop them. The Scot chose that moment to recover from his own injury. Climbing back to his feet, he released a furious roar and charged Daniel. The two men crashed onto a far table, grappling together. Now that the Scot was back in the battle, several more men suddenly found their courage and decided to join the fight as well. Once the odds reached nine to one, Richard couldn't keep silent any longer.

"He may not *need* help. All the same—"

"Oh, go ahead." Valoree sighed, hiding her relief as Scratchy and Richard rushed forward, launching themselves into the fray. Thurborne had done all right for himself, but he was growing tired and could use the help.

"What do you think you are doing?"

Valoree glanced around with a start at that sharp tone, relaxing somewhat when she saw Meg and Henry standing behind her. "Oh, it's you. Done, are you?"

"We finished several moments ago," Meg told her grimly. "And have been searching for you ever since."

"Well, all you had to do was ask One-Eye. He must have seen me come in here."

"One-Eye did *not* see you come in here," Meg informed her grimly. "He claims you ordered him and that poor gentleman with no nose to remove their weapons and tie up their hair, then disappeared. He said that by the time they had finished these tasks and glanced around, you were gone."

"Oh. Well." Valoree gave an unconcerned shrug at the news. "You found me in the end, and that's all that matters, I suppose."

"All that matters?" Meg repeated with dismay. "What matters is that you are presently sitting in a . . . a . . . What are you *doing* in here?"

Valoree blinked in surprise at the razor-sharp edge to the woman's voice. She shifted uncomfortably. "I'm just watching a fight," she answered quietly, reaching for her mug to take a small drink. Her hand was about to close around the cup when Meg slapped it. Snatching the cup, the woman raised it to her nose and sniffed the contents.

"Whiskey?" She exclaimed in horror.

"Aye. Do ye want some?" Valoree glanced toward the bar to wave the barkeep over, only to cry out in shock as pain shot through her head. Meg had grabbed her ear and twisted it. Even now, she was using it to force Valoree to her feet. Following the pull to avoid further pain, Valoree found herself dragged back out onto the street before she was released. Eyes spitting fire, she whirled on the old ex-prostitute, then reached automatically for her cutlass, only to find it missing. With little else to use against her enemy at the moment but words, Valoree sucked in her breath, ready to bawl her out, only to find her mouth snapping shut in surprise as Henry grabbed her arm and whirled her around in the direction of the carriage.

"If you were my daughter instead of my captain, I'd take you over my knee and whup ye," he snapped.

"Me?" Valoree cried in amazement. "But she—"

"She did exactly as an aunt would be expected to do to a brainless whelp who doesn't have the sense to tend to her own reputation."

"I—"

"You were in a *tavern*. A run-down hive full of thieves and doxies. There wasn't a single respectable lady there, including yourself, it would seem."

"Just because I am a woman, it doesn't mean—"

"Woman?" he snapped, turning on her. "This has nothing to do with being a woman. This has to do with being a noble. You are a member of nobility, girl. Or have you gone so far that you've forgotten that? 'Cause your brother never did. He was a gentleman right up to the day he died."

Valoree stiffened, her face paling to a deathly white as he continued.

"Jeremy never would have set foot in a place like that. Not unlessen it was for business. And then he would have left the minute business was done, and found a more respectable place to relax. But *you! You've* got something to prove, don't ye? And what is it exactly, I wonder? That you can crawl in the mud with the rest of the scum?"

Valoree winced at his words, then lifted her chin. "Richard and Scratchy were in there. They are not scum."

"Nay, they're not. But they ain't nobility either and never can be. You are. And that life is just waiting for ye. Why are ye so afraid of it?"

Panic suffused her briefly; then she whirled on her heel and strode toward the carriage. "I ain't afraid of nothing," she said with a snarl.

"I know ye're not afraid of death or pain," Henry called as she stomped back to the vehicle. "But it sure seems to me yer afraid of living!"

# Chapter Six

Her face was hot. Not just hot, but burning. It also itched something fierce. The discomfort had started shortly after Meg had finished putting that glop they had bought today on her face. Valoree had been doing her best to ignore the fiery itch for what seemed like hours, but really she was beginning to think it would drive her mad—if all the fawning women around her did not manage to first.

The Thurborne ball was certainly a different beast than the Beecham party had been. Their hostess, Lady Thurborne herself, had greeted them upon their arrival, been most gracious, then taken it upon herself to introduce them around. There were no snickers behind fans or gloved hands, nor malicious messages being sent from cold eyes. Everybody had been most pleasant.

Valoree would have liked to have believed that it was because Meg was doing all the talking and that the older woman, much to her amazement, carried herself, looked, and sounded exactly as a lady should.

Truly, her performance was impressive. She carried each conversation with apparent ease and grace, leaving Valoree and Henry to smile and nod politely. But that explanation just didn't wash. These people were up to something, Valoree decided grimly. There was no other explanation for the way the women had suddenly crowded around her, cooing and pleading that she attend this ball or that dinner. They were fawning over her as if she were royalty, and it was making Valoree nervous.

Her gaze slid to Henry, and she saw the same suspicion she felt reflected in his eyes. He, too, had noticed the difference. No doubt he had also noticed that, while they were presently the center of an ever growing circle of people vying for her attention, there was not a single man among them. . . . Well, except for Thurborne himself, but Valoree didn't really count him. She had already ticked him off her list of possible husbands, so his presence was easily discounted.

Nodding politely in response to yet another young girl's plea that she attend some function or other, Valoree turned her face away from the growing crowd. Annoyed, she dabbed at the small bead of sweat that was trickling down the side of her face. Despite the crowds and the heat in the room of so many bodies together, Valoree wasn't really hot enough to be sweating. At least not from the neck down, but that stupid wig that Meg had insisted she wear was irritating her scalp something fierce. Since she'd arrived, sweat had begun gathering at her hairline and trailing down her face. Valoree kept discreetly dabbing at it, trying to minimize the damage to her makeup, but really, all she could think was that this was all terribly uncomfortable and a blasted waste of time.

Why, she wondered, was she allowing herself to suffer through this when every single man but Thurborne was keeping himself at a safe distance? Watching the frufarau curiously, but not approaching? Valoree could almost have believed she was wearing her shirt and breeches, and that the women all thought her a man, by the way they were gathering around her. Except that she had never been this uncomfortable in her regular clothes.

"Would you care to dance?"

Valoree gave a start and glanced over to see Daniel Thurborne. The man had a small bruise on his left cheek, but otherwise looked none the worse for wear. "Nay. I do not dance," she answered irritably, then gasped in surprise as he suddenly took her arm and turned her away toward the dancing couples.

"Come now, you shall have to come up with a better excuse than that," he chided gently as he led her unwillingly forward. "Everyone knows how to dance."

"Aye, well, I do not," Valoree insisted, giving a useless tug on her arm.

"Then I shall be pleased to teach you," he murmured sweetly, pausing to draw her around to face him and settling the hand he held onto his shoulder, even as he snatched up her other in his own and set out to dance.

Her hands moved with him; her arms did too, but Valoree's feet stayed planted firmly where they had settled, her legs bracing automatically against his pull as if she were astride the *Valor*'s deck during rough seas. Startled, Daniel halted abruptly and peered down at her feet, then up at her face.

"You really do not know how, do you?" he asked quietly. Encouraged by something in his eyes, Valoree sighed and shook her head. His gaze drifted briefly; then he straightened his shoulders and nodded. "Then I shall teach you. Now, you just—"

"I really do not think that would be a good idea," Valoree interrupted, turning away to head right back toward where Henry and Meg still stood surrounded by women. She came to a dismayed pause, however, upon seeing that every single person in the group they had just left seemed to be watching her. There was nothing like a little pressure to make things easier.

"Well, *I* think it would be a very good idea," Thurborne argued, taking advantage of her pause to draw her back around to face him. "After all, it will be very difficult to find yourself a husband if you do not have the proper skills," he argued. As he did, he replaced her hand at his shoulder and took the other up in his own again.

"What makes you think I am looking for a husband?" Valoree asked sharply.

"Is that not every woman's aim?" he asked with amusement. Then, seeing that she was not amused, and neither was she about to let the question go, he sighed and admitted, "All right, Whister told me the first time you and I met at his office."

"Whister," she muttered disgustedly. "If he is not careful, he will find himself without his tongue."

Daniel bit his lip in amusement at her disgruntled words, then nodded, indicating that she should peer down. "Watch my feet; you are going to follow me."

"Follow you where?" Valoree asked suspiciously.

"In the dance. You will follow my steps. It is easy. The same steps are repeated over and over. Watch." He stepped back, waiting patiently for her to follow, then stepped to the side. She followed and he stepped to the side again. "You should not be too upset with Whister," he said after he had led her slowly through the routine twice. "He only told me because I am in much the same situation."

Her eyes met his. "What situation?"

"I must marry to gain my inheritance as well," he admitted with distaste. Valoree shook her head in patent disbelief.

"You already possess your title and estate. You inherited Thurborne estate and a dukedom from your father some years ago," she announced. His eyebrows rose, and Valoree could have kicked herself. It was Meg who had passed on that little tidbit of news, and Valoree should never have let on that she knew it.

"Aye," he admitted now. "Howbeit, I have not yet inherited the wealth necessary to keep it running."

Valoree blinked. "You inherited the land and title, but no wealth? How is that possible?" How similar was this man's plight to her own, she found herself thinking.

Daniel hesitated, then sighed. "Ah, well, it is not something any one of those women or their mamas who have been hanging about all night could not tell you. My father inherited land and title on his father's death, but had to marry for wealth."

"Your mother?"

"Aye. Her family had a great deal of wealth but no estate or title. It was a perfect match. Mother had a very generous dowry when they married that helped to keep things afloat, but by the time my father died, it had been exhausted. What I was left with was a nice title, a lot of land, and a mountain of debt."

"Hmmm. And this wealth that you have not yet inherited?"

"My grandmother, my mother's mother, died this last spring."

"I am sorry," she murmured, her gaze sliding to the dancers moving around them.

"So am I," Daniel murmured. "She was a grand lady. A wonderful sense of humor." He grimaced slightly as he said that last bit, then smiled wryly and said, "She helped out with some of the worst of the debts while she was alive."

Something in his tone made her glance back, and she could see his irritation at making that admission. Valoree knew instinctively that he had never asked for the old woman's help, and that accepting it had probably been the hardest thing in the world for him. She could understand that. She hated to ask for help, too, and would nearly kill herself trying to do things on her own rather than give in, speak up, and admit she could use assistance. "She sounds . . . nice," Valoree finished lamely, wishing wistfully that she'd had someone similar in her own life after Jeremy had died.

"Nice?" Daniel gave a short laugh. "She was an old harridan. Forever lecturing me that I was not getting any younger, and that I should really marry and start the next line. I tried to explain that, what with trying to repair the damage done at Thurborne, I really did not have time to look for a wife. She always said, 'You will not have time until you make time.' " He grimaced. "I found out that day in Whister's office that she had arranged it so that I would make time."

"Marry and produce an heir, or no inheritance," Valoree said with a smile. She doubted he had taken such a stipulation any better than she herself had. No wonder he had been shouting and stomping about in the office.

"Aye." He smiled wryly. "And when I asked Whister where she had got such a ridiculous idea, he said that she may have heard it from him. That he had another client, a female, whose father had left a similar codicil in his will. And, in fact, that this female client was no doubt, at that very moment, waiting to see him. That she had an appointment with him, whereas I had just stormed to his doorstep the moment I arrived in town."

Valoree grimaced at the reminder of her own objective: to find a husband. Not to inherit wealth, as Daniel had to do—she had a great deal of that. Nay, she had to find a husband so that she might be able to claim land—land that was rightfully hers by birth. They were two opposites of the same coin. "So you are here in search of a wife."

"Much to my everlasting horror, it appears I shall have to take one, aye," he agreed. "And my mother, of course, God bless her soul, has put out the news that I am seeking one."

"Well, that explains the women." Valoree chuckled. His expression changed to slight confusion.

"What women?"

"What women?" Valoree rolled her eyes. "The women all fawning upon me with pretended interest in being my friend. No doubt it is just camouflage. Since you've been near me, so are they. It's an excuse for them to flock around you in hopes of being the 'chosen one.'"

Daniel gave her a strange look, and suddenly Valoree became very self-conscious. "So why are you wasting your time dancing with me?"

Daniel's expression changed to a smile. "So you have noticed?"

"Noticed what?"

"That we are dancing. *You are* dancing. And quite well, I might add."

His words made her realize that she was indeed doing just that, and had been for the length of their discussion. He'd distracted her with talk. She immediately stumbled, her feet suddenly forgetting where they were supposed to be going. Daniel drew her nearer to counterbalance her sudden awkwardness. "How is my dancing with you a waste of time?"

"Well, should you not be threshing out the chaff from the wheat among the eligible young women who are interested in marrying you?" she asked, forgetting her feet to glance up at him again.

"Ah." He nodded in understanding. "I suppose I should. And which are you? Chaff or wheat?"

"Me?" She was surprised by the question, but not so much that she could not answer. "I am sugarcane, hard to cut."

"But sweet," he teased. Her expression turned grim.

"Nay. Not sweet. Never make the mistake of thinking that," she said solemnly. Then, while he was pondering that, she added thoughtfully, "So all your mother had to do was announce that you were looking for a bride, and the eligible women flocked to you like pirates to a keg of rum?"

Daniel gave her another odd look, then nodded. "Pretty much, aye."

"How interesting," she murmured, then glanced up at him sharply. "But you still haven't answered my question. Why waste time with me, when you should be sorting the offerings?"

Daniel was silent for a moment, for in reality he had no idea why he was doing what he was doing with her. He didn't know why he had told his mother he would not attend her ball, or any other function for that matter, unless Valoree and her uncle were invited, or why he had asked her to dance. Oh, certainly, he was curious as to what had happened to Jeremy on the king's behalf, and to get to the bottom of the rumors about Back-from-the-Dead Red, but as curious as he was, he had not even touched these topics tonight. He had been too intent on making her comfortable, teaching her to dance, seeing her smile. He liked it when she smiled. He liked holding her in his arms.

She suddenly stopped dancing and stared at him suspiciously, forcing him out of his thoughts. He raised his eyebrows questioningly.

"You were not thinking that you and I should—that we would . . ." Pausing, she shook her head and gave a half laugh. "Nay, of course not. You would hardly be so silly."

Insulted, Daniel frowned at her as she turned to walk off the dance floor, dabbing at her cheek with her sleeve as she did. Catching her other hand, he pulled

her irritably back into his arms. "I was not thinking
what? That we should marry?" He moved her into the
dance again.

"Forget I even said that." She laughed with a shake
of her head, as if the idea were quite ridiculous, he
noted with mounting annoyance. "I am a touch suspicious on occasion. Of course you were not thinking
that we could marry."

"And—just to satisfy my curiosity, mind you—why
is it that we could not marry?"

Lady Ainsley's eyebrows rose slightly, as if she was
surprised that he need even ask. "Why . . . because . . .
Well . . ." And then she burst out laughing.

Daniel felt his indignation grow. Not that he had
been thinking that they might marry—had he?—but,
well, now that he thought about it, it was not a *bad*
idea. He had to marry to gain the wealth his grandmother had left behind. She had to marry to gain her
land and title. They were both in the same boat, so to
speak. It could be a business arrangement. People did
that all the time. She, however, didn't seem to see the
sense in it. She who needed a husband or, as far as he
knew, would be left with nothing, laughed at the idea
of marrying him—even though most of the ton were
throwing their daughters and granddaughters at him in
hopes of just such a match. "Because *what?*"

Valoree's laughter died slowly away as she realized he
hadn't joined her in it. In fact, he looked quite put out.
"Because we would not suit," she said seriously. "You
are far too . . ." He raised an eyebrow at her hesitation,
and she sighed. "You *are* serious, aren't you?"

His silence was her only answer.

Valoree actually considered the matter, her gaze taking in his deep brown eyes and handsome features; he
had a strong nose, a square, stubborn jaw, a sensual
lower and narrower upper lip. Fitted together it all was

an attractive package. Very attractive. Her fingers slid from his shoulder to his upper arm and she measured and squeezed, testing the muscle there before sliding quickly across his chest, poking to make sure that that magnificent expanse was all his and not padding. Nay, it was all his. She pulled away, and her gaze dropped down over his flat stomach to the fine tight breeches he wore, without those silly frilly ribbons, she noted with relief, and she peered at his strong, well-shaped thighs with interest.

Daniel was as stiff as a marble statue under her inspection, his feet moving automatically in the dance as the rest of him awaited her pronouncement. When she finally turned her gaze back to his face, he eyed her warily and waited.

"My lord, you are a fine specimen of a man. Well built, obviously strong, and no doubt you could supply the babe I need to inherit my family estate. However"—Valoree ignored his grimace—"our characters are simply too similar to make such an option a success."

"What?" He stared at her with amazement, and she rolled her eyes.

"I am far more independent, strong-minded, and strong-willed than the average lady. I am not in the least bit interested in a husband. I would not even ever marry could I get away with it. But I have been forced to do so by my father's will. The man I choose to husband me will not rule me. In fact, I shall probably rule him. You would not like such a thing."

"You are damn right, I would not like it," he snapped. "What on earth makes you think that any man is going to allow you to rule the household? It simply is not done. No man worth his salt—"

"I do not wish to marry a man worth his salt. I wish to marry a man who will allow me to lead my life as I have done since I was nineteen."

128

"You would never respect a man like that," Daniel argued with a frown.

"I do not need to respect him, just to marry him."

"And have a babe with him," Daniel pointed out. She grimaced this time.

"Aye, well, that is a part of the bargain I could do without thinking about for a bit, if you do not mind," she said unhappily, then glanced around. "Oh, look. Meg and Henry have managed to escape your would-be brides. Take me back to them, please."

It came out as more an order than a request, and she could tell Daniel was about to balk at it when he noticed the trickle of sweat sliding down her face. That took him aback. "Aye. Mayhap we should stop. You appear to be overwarm."

His words made her dab at the sweat self-consciously. He released her hand and took her arm to lead her to where Meg and Henry were conversing.

"You did pretty well out there, Ca—girl," Henry corrected himself, casting a quick glance in Daniel's direction.

"Aye. But you should have stopped sooner," Meg said with a frown. "You are overwarm and . . ." She paused midsentence as she reached out with her hanky to dab at Valoree's cheek, just as Valoree turned to give a meaningful glance to Daniel.

"I *did* try to stop. Several times," she announced peevishly. "But Lord Thurborne was not willing to let me." She waited a moment then, for some comment or apology from the man, but he remained silent, his gaze locked on her face. Frowning, she glanced back toward Meg and Henry questioningly, only to see them both just as frozen and fixated on her. Shifting uncomfortably under their combined stares and mounting horror, Valoree glanced from one person to the other. "What is it?"

"Your face," Henry said in dismay.

Frowning, she reached up to feel her cheek where Meg had meant to dab and felt that her movement had turned the dab into a brush that had removed a portion of her makeup. The bare skin underneath felt oddly lumpy.

"Do not touch it," Meg said quickly, pulling her hand away and peering at the spot. "Is your face itchy?"

"Itchy?" Valoree muttered with disgust. "It has been burning and itching all night. It has been nearly driving me mad."

"What?" Meg peered at her with concern. "Well, why did you not say something?" the woman asked in exasperation. Valoree glanced toward Henry, whose expression showed complete understanding mingled with regret. She hadn't said anything because a captain should not complain of minor discomfort. A captain should bear it as long as necessary, then tend to it when the opportunity arose.

"Never mind why she said naught about it," Henry said resignedly. "What do we do about it?"

"Do?" Meg peered at him blankly, then shook her head. "She is obviously reacting to the makeup. We must leave and get it off her as quickly as possible."

Henry's shoulders slumped at that, and Valoree could read the disappointment in him. They had gone to all this trouble. Again. And it had been a flop. Again. She had only danced, or talked even, with one man. Nonetheless, he nodded solemnly. "We leave then."

"Nay. Not just yet," Valoree said suddenly. She turned to Daniel, her mind racing with a plan that was forming even as she spoke. "Who is the biggest gossip of the ton?"

Daniel peered at her in surprise and confusion, then said slowly, "That would be Lady Denholme. Why?"

"Is she here tonight?" Valoree asked hurriedly.

Daniel hesitated before nodding. "I believe she is."

"Where is she?"

He peered at Valoree silently for a moment, then glanced around the hall, scouring the people present until he spotted the woman in question. "She is over there, beside the large woman in white and green."

Valoree followed his pointing finger, then glanced to her aunt. "Meg?"

"Aye?" The older woman moved to her side at once, frowning in concern at her niece's blistered red skin.

"Go and strike up a conversation with this Lady Denholme. Tell her about the codicil in my father's will. Tell her how you must marry me off quickly to claim it. Then tell her it shouldn't be a problem, however, since I am exceedingly wealthy. Make sure you mention that I am desperate and not likely to be picky." She paused suddenly to glance toward Daniel. "Are there any other rather gossipy women here tonight?"

Daniel gave her a look of mixed admiration and annoyance, then straightened to glance around the room again. "Ah, well, Lady Smathers over there, and . . . er . . . Lady Wenback by the tall, skinny gentleman."

Nodding, Valoree turned to Meg again. "After you are finished with her, move on to the other two and tell them the same things. Then come join us. We shall be on the balcony."

Nodding, Meg hurried off to do as she asked. As she did, Valoree began to fan her face with one hand, her gaze moving around the room.

"Damn me." Henry's hissed words drew her gaze around questioningly, and he muttered, "A passel of trouble headed our way." He nodded toward a herd of hopeful mamas dragging their chicks their way.

"Damn." Valoree muttered as she spotted the group. This was the last group she wanted to see. Her gaze

131

shot around to land on Daniel. "They are after you. Go away and they will leave me alone."

"I have a better idea," he answered. Taking her arm, he hurried her through the crowd toward the balcony doors, Henry hot on their heels.

"See, this is what I mean about our not suiting," Valoree snapped irritably as he rushed her out onto the balcony. "You could not just go away as I asked; you had to take charge and drag me along with you."

Daniel said nothing, simply led her down into the garden. Finally he said, "Well, your aunt did say that you should get that stuff off directly, or else ruin your complexion."

"So? And so I shall. As soon as Meg is finished with what I asked her to do, we shall return home and get this goop off my face."

"Why wait?" Daniel grinned and drew her to a halt, gesturing toward a fountain he had brought her too. "It worked well enough last night."

Valoree stared. This fountain was smaller than the mammoth one the Beechams had owned, but much more attractive for all that. Its musical trickle was like some tempting siren's call, promising relief for her face. She could wash off and soothe her face in the cool water. Ease the itching and burning. Enjoy a moment of giving her face a good scratch, all under the guise of cleaning it.

A moan slipping from her lips, she dropped to her knees beside the fountain and thrust her face into its cool, soothing water, her fingers scouring her skin with a vengeance that made up for the whole night of suffering. Lifting her face out of the water a moment later, she sighed in relief. She heard Henry sigh as well.

"I don't suppose ye've got an alley siding on yer garden here, do ye?" she heard him ask as she impatiently tugged off the wig Meg had insisted upon her wearing. Tossing it to the ground, she rubbed at her scalp vigorously as Daniel answered.

"Aye. Along the side there. Shall I help her over the stone wall while you fetch the carriage?" She ducked her whole head into the water, then, thrashing it exuberantly about rather like a dog shaking itself off. She pulled her head back out just in time to hear Henry answer.

"Aye. But give it a couple of minutes. I shall go back inside and wait for Meg, then leave with her, get into the carriage, and have it come around."

"Make sure she talks to all three women, Henry," Valoree called after him as he headed back toward the balcony; then she collapsed back to sit on her heels. She gave a sigh of pure bliss.

"Better?" Daniel asked.

"Aye," Valoree said. Though the itching and heat were still there, her face felt not nearly as bad as it had with all that makeup irritating it. When Daniel offered her his hand to help her up, she hesitated, her gaze moving back toward the fountain. Then she decided that she'd had enough and placed her wrist in his hand, her own fingers closing around his wrist so that they worked together to get her back on her feet. "Where does the alley side your garden?"

"This way." Daniel gestured, then took her arm to walk with her, following the moonlit path to the trees. There, he slid his fingers down to grasp hers so that he could lead the way on the uneven ground, tugging her behind him. At the wall, he paused and turned to face her. "This is becoming a habit."

"What is?" she asked. "My leaving soirees over walls, or my little incidents at balls?"

"Both of those two," he admitted. "But I was thinking more along the line of our meeting in dark, secluded spots."

"Oh, that." Tugging her hand free of his, she stepped

up to the wall, checking its height relative to her own. Of course it was a good foot higher than her head, she thought in annoyance. Who exactly were these nobles trying to keep out of their darn gardens anyway? she wondered. "Well, never fear, it shall not happen again. I am never wearing that foolish muck on my face again."

"Good. You are far too lovely to bother with such nonsense."

Valoree gave a doubtful snort. *Lovely? What nonsense.* She'd had an entire crew of pirates convinced she was a man for the past thirteen years. That hardly spoke of loveliness. "Aye, well, if my plan works, I should have this business done in no time. Then we shall head for Ainsley and I shall not need worry what the fashion is, or what people think."

"Ah, your plan," Daniel murmured softly, suddenly standing directly behind her. He was uncomfortably close, she thought, feeling his heat through his clothes and her own. He wasn't touching her anywhere, yet she was incredibly aware of his presence. She actually shuddered when his breath brushed her ear as he whispered, "Do you really think that simply spreading the word among the gossipmongers will work? You'll just announce that you are looking for a husband, and they shall come?"

"Why not? It worked for you," she said, then frowned at the husky quality of her voice. She had meant to sound slightly derisive. Instead the words had come out slightly breathy, as if she had just swum a long distance.

"Aye, but what sort of man will it bring running, do you think?" He breathed so close to her ear that his lips actually brushed it. She shivered uncontrollably, ripples of something she had never experienced before shimmering through her body. Her mind unable to actually grasp what he had said, she leaned back into him, her breasts rising and falling quickly now.

"I—Ohhh." She gasped in surprise as his lips closed on the rim of her ear. His hands clasped her waist gently, fanning out where they rested as he did some dark and mysterious things to her earlobes that had her turning into pudding in his hands. Moaning mindlessly, she let her head drop limply back against his chest. She wasn't quite sure what he was doing, and almost suspected it was some witch's trick, her reaction was so violent; but she didn't seem to be able to find the presence of mind to care. It felt so damned good, she hardly noticed as his hands inched their way up over her ribs, to climb the mounds of her breasts.

A second moan slipped from her. She arched into his touch, her breasts pushing against the cloth that bound them, her hands coming up to cover his, cupping them closer against her flesh as she turned her head, her lips unconsciously seeking his. When his mouth covered hers and his tongue slid out to trace her lips, she opened instinctively to him, and a series of seizures seemed to ripple through her. Her ears were actually ringing as if in reaction to the shot of a pistol nearby, and she jolted in his arms, a hungry groan slipping from her mouth into his. She turned in his arms, mindlessly seeking a closer embrace.

Caught by her shoulders, Valoree let Daniel press her back against the wall, his knee sliding between her legs and pushing forward and upward. He tugged at the décolletage of her gown, and she felt the cool air on her nipples like a caress before his hands covered them. His lips left hers to travel down her throat in search of the booty he had just uncovered. Gasping and moaning, Valoree pressed her bare shoulders back into the rough stone, arching her breasts out as he plucked at them with his fingers and licked at the bare flesh he had revealed.

It was like some sort of madness. Daniel wasn't

what she wanted or needed, and yet she wanted and needed him with a violence that would have terrified her had she seen it coming. Clenching her fingers in his hair, she dragged his mouth away from her breast, pulling it impatiently back to her own with little care for the slight pain she might be causing. Daniel responded in kind, catching her still-damp hair in his fingers and tugging her head back as far as it would go. Then he gave her the kiss she wanted, devouring her mouth with a passion that stole all her breath and left her panting and gasping and shuddering. He tugged her skirt impatiently upward and found her thigh, and she felt herself further inflamed by that touch. Then he was suddenly gone. Valoree was left blinking in amazement, her chest heaving with her gasps as she saw Daniel had backed away to several feet in front of her, hands clenched at his sides as he struggled for a return of control.

Valoree gaped at him in amazement for a moment; then the clip-clop of horses' hooves and the jangle of a carriage came to her from over the wall, and she realized why he had stopped. Henry and Meg must have finished and were coming in the carriage to fetch her. Good Lord, had so much time passed?

Shaking her head in an effort to try to clear it, she turned to face the wall. Leaning her forehead against it briefly, she was brought back to herself somewhat by the cool, rough stone pressing against her skin. Then she straightened, took a determined breath, and leaped upward, grasping at the top of the wall with her hands.

Daniel was behind her at once, his hands grasping her waist, then suddenly sliding upward again to her breasts. Valoree gave a startled cry, her fingers releasing their hold on the wall so that she dropped to the ground in front of him again. For a moment, her body seemed to sing with a sort of joy as it felt his nearness and touch again, and really, at that point, he probably could have thrown her on the ground and taken her right there, carriage on the other side of the wall or no. But then that joy dissipated as she glanced down to see that he was fumbling to put her décolletage back in place, to cover the breasts he had bared.

Before she could move his hands out of the way and take over the task herself, it was done and his hands had moved back to her waist once more. But rather than lift her up then, he turned her in his arms and tortured them both with another searing kiss that left them gasping and breathless.

"Till we meet again," he murmured near her ear; then he turned her and lifted her upward until she could grasp the wall and help to pull herself to rest across the top of it on her stomach. Her gaze found the carriage a little down the lane.

"There she is. Up a little farther," she heard Henry call just as she felt a cool breeze drift over her naked legs and behind—a naked legs and behind that would have been clad in breeches had Meg not dragged them from her hands and given them to the men to hide. Jerking around in surprise, she saw Daniel's head disappear beneath her skirt, then felt his lips graze the inside of one thigh, then the other. A moment later, he ducked back out from her skirts and smiled at her wickedly.

"Till we meet again," he repeated silkily, clasping her bottom through her skirts. Then he levered her upward once more, and Valoree was distracted with the challenge of gaining the wall or finding herself tumbling off the other side of it. Once she was astride the stone, she glanced back down, but Daniel had disappeared, and she could hear the sound of his footsteps receding through the trees.

"Well, are you comin' down, or shall I come up there and fetch ye?" A hand on her ankle drew Valoree's head around. One-Eye gazed up at her in amusement. His hat was pushed back on his head, his coat undone and pushed to either side of his waist, and he held a glaring lantern that stung her eyes with its light. She missed the sudden change of expression on his face as he caught a glimpse of her, but she didn't miss his concerned comment.

"Lord love us. You did react nasty to that stuff, didn't ye?" She could see him shake his head through her squinting eyes as he released a low whistle. "Your face is all red and flushed . . . and even your lips are swollen. Damn, ye're a mess."

"Thank you," Valoree said sarcastically, slinging her other leg over the wall, but careful of her skirts in the process. Then, holding the hem down with one hand, she dropped off the wall, landing on her feet in front of him.

"Let's get the hell out of here."

# Chapter Seven

"Lord Thurborne is a very handsome man."

Valoree quit shifting impatiently under Meg's ministrations and opened her eyes to peer at the woman presently slathering green muck over her face. It smelled like some sort of garden mixture. Mushed cucumbers or something. Whatever it was, Meg had assured her it would help with the burning and itching, which was the only reason that Valoree had agreed to her slathering yet another concoction on her face. And actually, despite making her smell like a salad, the mixture *was* having a soothing effect on her skin. Exactly the opposite effect that Meg's words were having on her mind.

Valoree needed no help to see Thurborne's attractiveness. She had noticed that upon first meeting the man, but she wasn't generally impressed with the prettiness of a man's face. Unfortunately, she was seeing more and more about Daniel that was impressing her. He was a no-nonsense sort, who did not enslave himself to the present trend toward frilly, fluffy fashions; his waistcoats had almost a military cut to them, and there were no ridiculous ribbons on his knee breeches. She liked that. She thought the rest of the men looked like silly poodles.

He was also strong, obviously a man who used his body for more than posing or primping. She would not be at all surprised to learn that he had been chipping in physically to correct things at his family estate, which he claimed was in such disrepair. He had the shoulders of a workingman, not a dissolute landowner. He had a good sense of humor, and had made her laugh several times last night. Then, too, what other lord was likely to direct a woman to his fountain to have her wash off, then help her climb over his own wall to avoid having to pass back through his guests? He was a sharp thinker, too, and commanding—traits she possessed herself and could appreciate. And damned if he wasn't the finest kisser.

Of course, she reminded herself solemnly, mayhap every man kissed like that. But good Lord, her lips were still numb and tingling, not to mention the inner backs of her thighs where he had pressed those final kisses good-bye.

Aye, she'd like to see more of the man. She fancied she'd even pay a king's ransom to bed him, but marriage? Now that was another thing entirely, and she knew darned well that was the reason Meg was bringing him up. It was what all of her crew wanted—for her to marry and get them their promised homes. So, of course, knowing the man was in the same position as herself, they would look to him as a prime candidate. Unfortunately, Valoree couldn't agree with them. She would not be ruled. And Thurborne was the ruling sort. Just look how he had not gone away and left her alone tonight! How he had not accepted her refusal to dance. Nay, he liked things his own way. Like her. And a ship just could not have two captains.

"Tell me something," Valoree murmured now as Meg opened her mouth to comment again. Closing her mouth, the older woman raised her eyebrows questioningly, and Valoree asked, "Who are you?"

The woman stiffened, her eyes turning wary, and Valoree smiled. "I noticed tonight while you were talking to Lady Thurborne that you know quite a bit about Port Royale. You've been there."

"Nay, I've just listened well," Meg answered quickly. "Sailors will talk while in their cups."

"You *have* been there," Valoree insisted. "You know more about it than I. And you are of noble lineage, for all that you looked like a down-and-out prostitute when Bull found you. No prostitute could walk quite as stiffly or talk quite as precisely as you do. Now I'll ask you again, who are you?"

Meg glared at her silently for a moment, then shrugged indifferently. She turned away to clean up the mess she had made on the small table with her garden medley. "It does not matter. I was hired for a job and am performing it to the best of my ability. That is all you need know."

"I fear I disagree with you." Valoree stood to block her path as the woman tried to carry the bowl of remaining salve toward the door. She stared down at the suddenly nervous woman and said grimly, "If you are a lady and of the nobility, you may be recognized. Then our little tale of your being my aunt could be ruined. I cannot risk that. Who are you?"

Meg hesitated, then turned around to drop her load back on the table. Wiping her hands on the apron she had donned over her gown, she sighed. "You are right, of course. I was born a lady. But you need not fear my being recognized. I left London twenty-seven years ago, married, and lived in the Caribbean. On a plantation even, so that would fit right in with the story we have passed around."

"And your family?"

Her mouth tightened. "My husband died last fall. We had no children, as he could not father them. I have no family."

Valoree heard the pain in Meg's voice at her admission and felt pity for a moment, but she tamped it down. Too many people were affected by this. She could not afford for pity to get in the way of her protecting the men who counted on her. "No parents? No brothers or sisters left here in London?" Her expression made Valoree's gaze narrow. "Which is it? A brother?"

"Sister." She sighed miserably, her head lowering further. "But you need not fear her acknowledging me in any way. She . . . I . . . There was a rift."

Valoree waited a moment, then sighed and moved back to her seat. Settling there, she gestured to the other chair as Meg glanced at her nervously. "You had best tell me all."

Meg sat with resignation, then shrugged unhappily. "There is little to tell. I was young and thought I was in love. I did something foolish and found myself unmarried and with child."

Valoree arched an eyebrow at that. "Why did your family not force a marriage?"

Meg shrugged. "My father probably would have, but I did not tell them. I did not wish the baby's father to be forced to marry me. He did not believe it was his,

141

anyway. He said if I had given myself so easily to him, how was he to know I was not so free with others?" She related her story as dispassionately as if telling the time of day, a sure sign to Valoree that it had been incredibly painful for her at the time.

"I fled to an empty cottage on the edge of an estate my parents owned," Meg continued. "It was in the north. There I had the babe. It . . . it was born dead." Her voice trembled, her hands twisting viciously at her apron. Taking a deep breath, she straightened and finished. "Because I'd fled, my reputation would be in tatters among the ton. It would be quite the scandal. I had to get away, so I caught a ship for the Caribbean, met my husband on it, and was married at sea the day before we landed in Port Royale. I lived there ever since and had absolutely no contact with my family in that time."

Valoree peered at her silently, positive the woman was lying, or at least leaving something out, but unsure how to force it from her. Or if she even had a right to. If it did not affect her, or her men, she really had no need to know. But . . . "Your parents?"

"Dead." The word was said without emotion. "They were both dead within ten years of my leaving."

Valoree nodded slowly. "So this scandal is the reason you believe your sister, Lady Beecham, will not acknowledge you?"

"It is the reason I *know* she will not," Meg snapped, then suddenly froze. Her eyes snapped up to Valoree's, wide with shock. "How did you—"

"She looks just like you," Valoree explained. "She is thinner, meaner, and grayer mayhap, but I saw right away that she has the same features. I just needed something to make me realize it." She paused. "I take it that is why you dragged the bottle to bed and made damn sure you would not have to attend her soiree?"

Turning pink, Meg nodded.

"Did you really drink it all? Or did you just swish a sip around in your mouth and splash some on yourself to make yourself look worse?"

The woman's eyes widened slightly. "How did you guess that?"

Valoree smiled. "Ladies do not drink rum, Meg. You made that clear at Whister's. I thought it odd that you had drunk it."

"Oh, well, there was nothing else available. I had to nag Henry the next day to get him to bring in some brandy and such—just in case I needed another escape in the future."

"Hmmm." Valoree considered the situation, then glanced at her again. "And all the times on the ship when you appeared to be drinking or drunk?"

Meg bowed her head miserably. "The same. I splashed some rum on myself and pretended to be useless. I just wanted to be alone to think."

Valoree accepted that silently. "Have you seen your sister since returning?"

"I have seen her from a distance, but I have not spoken with her," Meg said carefully. "I had intended to avoid any functions it was likely she would attend, and—"

Valoree waved her to silence. "We shall deal with this problem if and when it arises. How did you end up as you were when Bull found you?"

Meg gave a dispirited sigh. "I was robbed. I had hired a hack at the docks to take me to a nice inn. He had loaded everything on top and was taking me to one when I spotted . . . a shop I wished to look in. I had him stop, went in to take a look around, and when I came out, he had just driven off with all my things." She shook her head with disgust at the memory. "I never should have left the carriage. I should have just waited until I arrived at the inn—"

"Most likely you never would have arrived," Valoree interrupted quietly. "It was probably lucky for you that you got out. You have to be careful about things like that. There are men just waiting to prey on women traveling alone. I heard a story of a similar incident the day we arrived in London. A well-bred woman arrived on a ship, hired a hack to take her and her servant to a relative's, and they never made it. The authorities found both women the next morning— dead. All their belongings had been taken, even the clothes off their back."

Meg paled, her eyes going round with horror. To put her at ease, Valoree quickly asked, "So you were left without your things. How did your dress get ruined and—"

"Oh," Meg interrupted irritably. "I . . . Well, I just started to walk. I did not know what to do. I was flustered by the fix I found myself in and did not pay enough attention to where I was headed. By the time I did, it was to find that I had made my way back toward the docks." She grimaced and nodded at Valoree's shake of the head. "Aye, I know it was foolish of me. The area was horribly run-down. The smell alone . . ." She paused and shuddered, then sighed "Well, I realized my folly at once, and turned to head back the way I had come, but had barely done so when I was accosted.

"Right there, in broad daylight, two young ruffians grabbed me and started to drag me into an alley. I screamed, and they koshed me over the head. When I awoke, everything was gone: my jewelry, my cape, my reticule with the last of my money. They had left me lying in a pile of filth. I stank and my gown was ripped and filthy. I was woozy and weak. I could not see any injuries, but I could feel a large bump on the back of my head. I knew I needed help, and as frightened as I was to leave the relative safety of the abandoned alley where I had been left, my head ached horribly and I feared if I allowed myself to lose consciousness, I would die there. I tried to get to my feet, but the world seemed to spin around me, so I had to half crawl, half drag myself out into the street. It was night by then and the streets were much less busy. Those people still walking about simply ignored my pleas for help. I'm sure they thought I was just what I looked like: a fallen woman. Then a couple of young nodcocks, as you would call them, came along. They were drunk and stumbling, and they assumed I was drunk as well. When I raised a hand toward them to plead for help, they thought it was a drink I wanted. They had some fine sport emptying their bottle over me and laughing at my pathetic state before moving on.

"The next person to come along was Bull," she finished quietly. "By that time I was rather resigned to dying, but he stopped and seemed to look me over, then nodded to himself.

" 'How would you like a hand out of the gutter, old girl?' he asked. When I nodded dumbly, he picked me up and started walking, carrying me in his arms as he told me what he was about. 'We need ye fer a job, a respectable-type job—chaperoning our captain. If you do it all right and proper, there's food, clothes, a place to stay, and a cottage of yer own at the end of it. Think you could play a lady?' "

She laughed with real amusement now and shook her head. "I am not even sure if I meant to help you at that point. I simply wished to get away from the docks at the time. I was still rather groggy, my head aching, while you and the dressmaker's wife bathed, dressed, and measured me. But in the morning, when I awoke on the ship, I thought it through. I had no money. No home. And from what I could tell, no family. A cottage of my own on an estate far away from court, with the beauty and peace of the country, seemed a fine place for me to sit and reflect in my old age."

"Aye, I suppose it is," Valoree said, moved. She sighed. Here was another burden for her conscience, another soul whose future it seemed now depended on her.

"If I have answered all your questions," Meg said, standing suddenly, "I think I shall just—"

"Go ahead." Valoree sat back in her chair with a frown as Meg left the room. She had to get married. She had to regain Ainsley and get Henry his roses, Pete his own big kitchen, and Meg a home in which to settle. They all depended on her. Her mind raced, but she kept coming back to the gossips being her best hope. She simply could not bear another party—or any engagement that might result in another debacle regarding her makeup. She had no graces to attract a husband. If a straight-out call sent through the gossips did not work . . . well, she might just have to consider Thurborne.

"Good morning, Valoree. Your face is looking a bit better."

Valoree grunted in response to Meg's comment as she entered the morning room. She knew by the expressions on her men's faces, and by what she had seen for herself upon awakening, that the woman was lying through her ladylike teeth. No doubt she was just trying to make Valoree feel better, but Valoree didn't much care how she looked; she had no balls to attend today. She was just relieved that the irritation had gone away.

"Well, eat up quick there, Captain, girl, and we shall head out nice and early to the shops," Henry suggested with bluff good cheer.

Turning a suspicious glare on the man, Valoree dropped into the seat at the head of the table. Pete

146

immediately carried in a large tray of baked goods that made her stomach growl. "And just what would you be thinking we might need to go to the shops for?"

Her quartermaster hesitated, his gaze shooting to Bull and One-Eye, who sat on either side of her. When the two men nodded in encouragement, he cleared his throat and continued, "Well, ye can't be wearing that slop ye wore last night again, so we'll have to go find you some other muck to—"

"The hell we will," Valoree said in a growl, rising to her feet. "There will be nothing more on my face. Two such incidents were enough."

"Now Captain, girl," Henry tried. "I know—"

"Ho!" No-Nose hurried into the room, excitement lighting his eyes. "There's three fellers at the door, all of 'em lookin' to see the captain. They gave me these."

"Let me see those, Robert," Meg murmured, holding out her hand for the cards he held. Squirming under her use of his real name, No-Nose handed the cards over and waited along with everyone else as she perused them.

"Lord Chaddesley, Lord Alcock, and Lord Heckford," she murmured thoughtfully, tappping the cards against one hand.

"What is it about?" Henry asked, frowning as he moved to stand behind her and peer down over her shoulder.

"I do not know. Lady Thurborne was talking about these three last night. They are all friends who gad about together. They are also second sons—they will not inherit and are in need of wives who are wealthy."

Relief flowing through her, Valoree chuckled. When everyone turned to her, she shrugged. "I would say they are here to offer themselves up for marriage," she proposed. "Meg's little chat with the gossips last night must have worked."

Meg looked taken aback. "Oh, my, of course." She turned to No-Nose. "You shall have to tell them that Lady Valoree is not available today, and to try back tomorrow. We—"

*"What?"* every man in the room, plus Valoree herself, cried out.

Meg sighed unhappily, but her response remained firm. "Just look at her face! She cannot catch a husband looking so. Besides"—her mouth tightened—"it is always best to play hard to get."

Valoree made a face and shook her head. "Nonsense. They do not care what I look like. This is business. No-Nose, show them to the salon and tell them I shall be along directly."

"Valoree," Meg protested, but Valoree ignored her, her eyes narrowing on the hesitating No-Nose.

"You heard my order."

Acquiescing, the man turned and hurried out of the room. Valoree turned to peer at Meg, whose upset was obvious. "This is business, Meg. I am not looking for a happy-ever-after ending. You yourself should know how rare those are. I have seventy-five men and one woman under me, all in need of a home and safe harbor. I cannot afford dreams of a perfect husband or happy marriage. I must be satisfied with Ainsley, one brat, and a husband who bothers me as little as possible." Turning her back on the table, she left the room.

"Son?"

Daniel paused, the tune he had been whistling dying abruptly as he looked about. His gaze fell on his mother, hanging halfway out of a carriage on the road beside him, waving madly in case he should miss her. Smiling, he changed direction and moved to the carriage, taking her hand to press a kiss to it. "Good morning, Mother."

"You seem very happy this morning."

"I am."

When he didn't add any further information, her smile faded. "Would you care for a ride?"

"Nay. Thank you. I felt like walking and sent my driver on ahead." He gestured up the road where the Thurborne carriage waited.

"Oh. Well, where are you going? And what is that parcel? A gift?"

Daniel laughed outright at her blunt questions and shook his head. "You never change, do you, Mother?"

"Nay, of course not. Why should I?" she asked with real surprise. He smiled wryly.

"As it happens, I am headed to see Lady Ainsley."

"Lady Ainsley?" Her eyebrows rose, her eyes filling with speculation. "And your package?"

"Oh." He glanced down at it, suddenly embarrassed, and shrugged. "She had a reaction to her makeup last night. I stopped in at the apothecary to see what they had to offer as aid. They gave me this."

His mother barely glanced at the bundle, her next question already tumbling from her lips. "The lady lives around here? I had not realized that the Ainsley's had a town house in this area."

"Actually, I believe they are renting it for the season from Lord Beecham. It is just . . ." He turned to gesture vaguely up the street, only to pause and frown as he saw a carriage stop before the town house in question. A gentleman stepped down—John Lambert, he recognized as the man conversed briefly with a servant in pink livery who rushed forward—then turned to give instructions to his driver before following the servant to the door of the house. The Lambert carriage had barely pulled away when another had pulled up in its place, disgorging Harry Gravenner. The servant hurried back at once, gesticulating a bit excitedly, then turned to briefly glare at Daniel's carriage.

"Hmmmm," his lady mother supplied thoughtfully

as she, too, watched Gravenner say something to his driver, then hurry up to the house. "It looks as if Lady Ainsley is having many visitors this morning."

"Aye," Daniel said shortly, scowling as the Gravenner carriage drove away only to be replaced by another. "I have to . . ." he began distractedly, but didn't finish the sentence. He turned away from his mother's carriage and hurried toward his destination, his whole mood ruined.

Daniel had woken up in a fine state this morning. He had not bothered returning to the party the night before, but had gone to his club for a drink and some peace. Of course, all he had done was think about Valoree: her spirit; her wit; her funny little smile where one side curved up and the other sort of bent downward as if she not only smiled rarely, but was afraid to indulge often lest she find her reason for doing so suddenly gone; the way she suddenly slipped into less than stellar speech when she was annoyed; her determination, her passion. . . .

He had tasted her on his lips for hours after she had disappeared over the wall, and still could when he closed his eyes and concentrated. He could feel her arms wrapped around him, her fingers in his hair, her body molded to his, could hear her gasps and sighs and groans and moans as he had licked her eager flesh.

Dear God, just the memory aroused him, and he had tortured himself with it for hours as he had pondered things—like the fact that he had to marry and produce an heir to gain his grandmother's inheritance. That she had to marry and get with child to gain her family estate. That he could help give her that baby. Over and over again. In bed. Out of bed. Against a garden wall. On a staircase. On his desktop. In one of the chairs before the fire in his room.

He was thinking with his nether regions and not his head, he knew, but damn, it made his nether regions happy. And really, when it came right down to it, why not contemplate such things? He enjoyed this woman, albeit in an odd sort of way. He found her awkwardness in the ton endearing, her intelligence enchanting, and her independence refreshing. Of course, he would have to curb some of that independence, but the pleasure he anticipated in other areas seemed to make that a small consideration.

He just had to convince her of the smallness of that. Which, he had thought last night, should not be that difficult a chore. After all, she did have to marry to regain her home, and he was a handsome fellow—intelligent, soon to be wealthy, with land of his own, a title, and all those other things that a smart and ambitious young woman sought in a husband. Just look at all the girls and their eager mothers who chased him from ball to ball. They thought he was prime marriage material. And, he had assured himself, it would be little enough trouble to convince her of that, too. His certainty was what had had him whistling cheerfully as he had made his way here.

But that had been when he had thought there would be little if any competition for the woman. Now, as he hurried along the street, watching yet another gentleman leap from his carriage and stride up to the door to rap gaily, he couldn't help thinking that perhaps it would not go as smoothly as he had hoped. And why the hell hadn't he ridden here in his carriage? He would have been here long ago had he not decided to walk off some of his excitement along the way.

"Shall I move, my lord?" Daniel's driver asked as he drew abreast of his carriage. "A servant keeps insisting that I shouldn't park here, but I told him that you said I should, so here I'd be waiting."

"Stay put," Daniel ordered, turning to glare at the fellow now rushing toward him from the town house.

"Ye cain't be parkin' yer hack here. Have yer driver

move it. We don't need the road blocked out front here," the harried-looking fellow announced, and Daniel raised a supercilious eyebrow at the fellow. The man's pink livery was ugly but easy to digest, but hiding his surprise as he took in the man's damaged face took some doing. The butler had no nose! He was also missing several teeth, had long hair, and wore a pistol sticking out of his breeches. Catching Daniel's glance at the weapon, the fellow scowled and fastened his waistcoat. "I said—"

"I heard what you said," Daniel interrupted coldly. "I simply cannot believe your temerity in attempting to order me about."

The man rolled his eyes, not looking the least impressed. "Now see here, them's me orders. I'm to be making sure that you fellers ain't cluttering up the road with yer carriages. If all of ye was to be parking yer hacks out here, no one would be able to get by and the ca—er—Lady Valoree, she was saying she didn't want no trouble with the neighbors, so we're to see the carriages move along once their passengers is out of 'em."

"By all means, do so with the other 'guests.' However, my carriage shall wait right here for me," Daniel announced firmly, bringing a scowl to the servant's face. The man looked about to argue the point, but another carriage pulled up just then, distracting him.

"Oh, now, ye can't be parkin' yer hack here!" he shouted, moving on to the new carriage in a fury. Daniel glanced back curiously to see Beecham stepping out. Blinking in surprise at the surly servant, the nobleman directed something quickly to his driver, and the hack pulled away, leaving him to hurry up the walk.

"Thurborne," he said in greeting, glancing over his shoulder toward the fellow with no nose. "I really must talk to Lady Ainsley about her servants. They are quite—"

"Unusual?" Daniel suggested. "Impertinent? Loud? Disreputable-looking?"

"All of those," Beecham agreed as they paused on the steps to the town house and Daniel rapped on the door with his cane.

If the first servant had seemed somewhat disreputable, the servant who opened the door was downright scary. He filled the door like death, as wide as and even taller than, it was, having to stoop to stand in its frame, completely blocking any passage. His skin was a deep, rich mahogany, his head bald, and his teeth shone as he smiled a white smile that was anything but friendly. "Yer cards."

Daniel blinked at the deep growl and handed his card over, silently eyeing the man's thick arms as he took both it and the card Beecham supplied. Barely glancing at them, the fellow stepped back for the two nobles to enter, then tossed their cards on a tray, where a small mountain of others resided. He gestured toward a door on their left, behind which the sound of voices could be heard. It seemed opening the door and announcing them was not part of his duties.

Amused, Daniel started for the door, only to pause and glance back when Beecham asked curiously, "What did you want our cards for if you had no intention of presenting them to your mistress or announcing us?"

In the process of closing the door, the giant paused to eye young Beecham narrowly. "So's I'll know where to deliver ye if ye cause trouble and I have to knock ye out."

Even Daniel blinked at that announcement, his mouth drawing into an astounded smile. "And how will you know which card belongs to whom?" he asked smugly. "You have quite a collection there, my man."

The fellow's expression didn't change at all; he

merely said, "I'll know." And really, Daniel suddenly suspected the man would. Shaking his head, he turned back to the door and opened it. Having done so, he froze in shock. The room was overflowing with men. There were at least thirty of them in the small salon—and every single one of them was trying to be heard over the others.

"My God," Beecham breathed, moving to his side to survey the room. Daniel glanced at him grimly.

"Aye. It would seem her plan worked," he murmured, not at all pleased by this turn of events.

"What plan?" Beecham asked faintly, his glazed eyes shifting from one suitor to another. Knowing the man's penchant for keeping accounts, Daniel surmised he was counting them.

"Her plan to spread the word that she is wealthy and desperate for a husband," Daniel explained patiently. "She was hoping that it would bring the suitors scurrying. It appears that her plan worked. Every gold-digger in London has shown up." He made a disgusted face, then noticed Beecham's alarmed expression. "Is that not why you are here?"

"Nay!" Beecham cried at once. "At least—Well, the money isn't really important. I mean, money is always nice, but Lady Ainsley is . . . She's . . ." His voice trailed away helplessly, his expression slightly moony.

"Aye. She is," Daniel agreed darkly. Stepping into the room, he made his way through the crowd of male bodies toward where they seemed most dense. That was where he would find Valoree, no doubt. At the center of the hive.

"Your hair is like fire."

"Your beauty is incomparable."

"Your lips are like little rosebuds."

"You are as sweet as honey."

"Oh, your voice is music itself."

Valoree sighed inwardly and tapped her hand impatiently against her side as compliment after compliment was bestowed by the men crowding around her. It was all a bunch of bunk, of course. Her face was red and blistered, her eyes bloodshot, and her hair was lying flat and unfancy upon her back because she had refused to wear her damn wig. She had left it in Thurborne's garden, anyway. In short, she looked like hell. And she knew she looked like hell. Nor was she terribly impressed with all the flowery phrases with which suitors were showering her.

It seemed her plan had worked too well. The salon was filling up by the moment with hopeful would-be husbands. It was nice to have a choice, but really, how was she to choose one from this mob?

A firm grasp on her arm made her glance around to see Daniel.

"Good morning," he mouthed with a wink, then turned and started away, dragging her firmly behind him. Her crowd of gentleman callers immediately began to follow, their silly compliments undiminished as they trailed her to the door of the salon. Stepping into the hall, Daniel pulled her out, then slammed the door in their faces.

"Good day," he murmured, smiling pleasantly as he turned to face her, leaning his weight determinedly against the door and holding the knob firmly. He dug a bedraggled and knotted wig from his pocket with his other hand. "You left this behind last night."

Valoree couldn't help it; she burst out laughing as she took the wig, then shook her head and sighed. "Good day to you, too. Thank you for getting me out of there."

"Yes. It seems your plan worked."

"Too well," she admitted sardonically as the door rattled with the combined force of those who sought to open it.

"Well," he continued cheerfully, "I could rid you of

this problem should you but reconsider marrying me."

Valoree smiled slightly at his words, but shook her head. "I never reconsider a decision. That would make me wishy-washy. Once a decision has been reached, good or bad, it stands."

"That sounds incredibly foolish."

Valoree shrugged, vaguely annoyed but unswayed. She had spent most of her life on a ship, and the last five years as its captain. She wasn't going to allow one man's opinion to change her way of doing things.

"What if there was some bit of information that you did not know before you made your decision?" he suggested. "Surely, should you learn something new, and of import, you would reconsider—"

"That's not reconsidering; that is a new consideration entirely," she told him calmly.

"But that's the same thing!"

"What is two plus two, my lord?"

He blinked at the non sequitur. "Four, but—"

"And what is two plus two take away one?"

"That would be three, but—"

"Exactly. You see. Two separate mathematical problems. With two different answers, despite both having a similar portion."

He stared at her blankly for a moment; then admiration slowly began to shift over his face. "Why, you clever little witch. I believe you could twist some intellectuals into knots with your thoughts. Are you always so logical?"

Valoree blinked at the question. No one had ever called her logical before. A knock at the front door saved her from having to come up with an answer. Turning, she watched as Bull moved toward the door, positive it would be more damn suitors like those they had trapped in the salon.

"Oh, my!" a female voice cried out in surprise, but

Bull blocked Valoree's view of who it was. "Oh, hello, um . . . I am here to see Lady—"

"Mother!"

Valoree blinked at Daniel's irritated voice, then left him alone to guard the salon door—which no longer shook, the suitors apparently resigned to wait in peace. She moved curiously to Bull's side to see that it was indeed Lady Thurborne.

"Oh, Lady Ainsley," Daniel's mother exclaimed with relief as Valoree moved into view. "For a moment, I feared I had the wrong town house. Daniel just waved down the street. He did not point out exactly which one it was and—Oh, hello, Daniel," she said, easing cautiously past Bull and into the entry.

Her son did not look impressed, Valoree noted with amusement, taking in his expression. "What are you doing here, Mother?" he asked.

"Oh, well, I thought mayhap I could help."

"Help?" Valoree asked with amazement. Surely his mother had not come to plead his case as to why she should marry her son?

"Yes, dear." Lady Thurbone whirled toward her, smiling brightly. "Daniel mentioned that he had stopped at the apothecary's to collect some salve for your poor face because you had reacted to—Oh, my!" she interrupted herself in horror. Bull had swung the door wider for a nervous young maid to scamper inside and sunlight spilled over Valoree, illuminating her ravaged face.

"Oh, you poor, dear thing, you!" she cried, hurrying forward to catch Valoree's face gently in her hands, turning it this way and that to examine the blistered skin. "Oh, Daniel. You did not tell me it was so bad! That nonsense you got from the apothecary will be useless."

Then she turned to scowl at her son. "Did you know about this last night?" she asked sharply, and read the answer in his expression. "Well, you should have told me about this. She needs Grandmama's remedy for certain." Sighing, she turned back to stare at Valoree one more time, then released Valoree's face and shook her head. "It is a good thing I stopped by to see what was about. Now, where is your kitchen?"

"Kitchen?" Valoree repeated blankly. Her mind was still taken with the fact that Daniel had stopped at an apothecary's to pick up some salve for her "poor face." For some reason, that fact made her feel all warm and squishy inside. It was a feeling she wasn't sure she liked, but was far better than the irritation all the false compliments her suitors had been raining on her had caused.

"Yes, dear. Bessy will need to mix up Grandmama's remedy." She frowned now. "I wish I had known about this sooner. I would have brought the ingredients, but hopefully your cook will have them on hand. Where is the kitchen?"

"Uh . . . well . . ." Valoree glanced uncertainly down the hall. Petey hated anyone in his kitchen. At sea or on land, it was the one thing on which he tended to stand firm. No one was to mess about in his galley. Not even her.

"This way, is it?" Lady Thurborne asked, moving determinedly in the direction Valoree had involuntarily glanced. "Come along, Bessy," she said to her maid. "There is no time to waste."

"Damn," Valoree said under her breath as the woman sailed down the hall and through the kitchen door.

"You might like to call your aunt in on this one," Daniel suggested with a repressed smile, and Valoree glanced to where he still stood with his back to the salon door.

"My aunt?"

"Aye," he said with something that seemed oddly like sympathy. "And your uncle, too. My mother will march right over you if you do not have plenty of support."

Valoree blinked in amazement at the claim, then shook her head. She was the captain of a pirate ship! The day she could not handle one little old lady . . . Her thoughts died as a clatter in the kitchen was followed by some vigorous cursing. Frowning, she started up the hall, but paused halfway there when Lady Thurborne stuck her head out. The woman gave a brilliant smile.

"I found your cook," she sang out cheerfully, not even wincing at a second round of oaths behind her. "He is the temperamental sort, I see. So is mine. All artists are. Not to worry though; we shall get along famously."

Her head disappeared back into the kitchen, there was a great racket, and then there was complete silence. Valoree hesitated, unsure at that point whether she really wished to know what was going on. Daniel spoke from behind her. "Your aunt was not in there, was she?"

Valoree glanced over to see him nod toward the door he guarded, but shook her head. "Nay, she went up to her room."

"Ah. Good, she will be well rested and in fighting form. Perhaps you should send someone up to get her."

Valoree paused, then sighed and nodded to Bull. The giant left his post by the door and started up the stairs at once. "Find Henry, too," she called after him, then walked toward the salon door Daniel was guarding. "I suppose I had best tend to my suitors while I am at it."

"Is that what you call them?" Daniel asked a bit peevishly, straightening away from the door. "I would have thought greedy gold-diggers to be a better description."

"Oh, sod off, Thurborne," she muttered. With that, she reached for the doorknob and tugged the door open.

159

# Chapter Eight

"Marry me and you can simply tell them all to just go away."

Valoree grimaced at the words Daniel whispered in her ear and sighed. She supposed he had been encouraged by her pause at opening the door. It wasn't that she didn't know what to do. It was that she couldn't believe how many men had responded to the gossip. There were at least thirty of them, and of all ages, shapes, and sizes. If she had realized how easy getting them to her door would be, she never would have bothered with all the nonsense of dresses and makeup and socials. She simply would have sent Henry and Meg to have a chat with the appropriate parties, then sat back to await the arrival of every single male in London who wished to marry money. But now they were here, and she had to weed through them and decide which was the weakest, and in the most desperate straits. She would marry him.

Ignoring Daniel, she straightened her shoulders and addressed the waiting mob of men. "Every single one of you is here today because you heard the rumors yesterday about my being wealthy and needing to marry to claim my childhood home, Ainsley Castle."

She had barely finished making that statement when the men rumbled to life with denials. Oh, no they weren't there because she needed to marry! They were there to bask in her beauty. To wallow in her wit. To enjoy her intellect.

Valoree rolled her eyes. "You can stop your nonsense now," she interrupted. "You can all see that I suffered a reaction to the foundation and fucus I wore to yesterday's ball. There *is* no beauty to bask in. And I am not feeling particularly witty today either. So if you aren't here with an interest in marrying me for my wealth, then you can leave now."

There was an uncomfortable silence as the men peered anywhere but at her. Valoree supposed the sudden shifting and nervous silence were because the lords of the ton were not used to such open honesty in regards to motive. She supposed they all would have been more comfortable to play a game where she pretended they all were ensnared by her feminine wiles, and they pretended she found them the most interesting creatures alive. Well, pirates did not go in much for lies! Their motives were wealth and they made no bones about it. That was the society she'd learned to respect. She had neither the patience nor the intent to lie her way through several weeks of courting, smothered by smarmy compliments that weren't sincere.

Despite their discomfort, she noted, not a single man left the room. Valoree nodded her head solemnly, then said, "To inherit, my husband has to be a member of the nobility. If you are not such, you may as well leave now."

There was a murmur of voices and a general shifting of bodies as first one man, then two others, made their way out of the crowd and moved past where she and Daniel stood by the door.

Well, she thought, three down and twenty-seven to go. "I must also have birthed a child, or be carrying one by my twenty-fifth birthday—which is a little less than nine months away," she continued. There was dead silence in answer. Valoree frowned slightly. She had hoped at least another one or two men might be eliminated by that. They couldn't all be thrilled to bed her. Just as she would have opened her mouth to speak again, Daniel startled her by interrupting.

"Lady Ainsley's uncle will, of course, have you all thoroughly investigated to discover whether you are truly members of the nobility . . . Also, that you have not suffered any injury or illness that might raise some doubt as to your ability to perform the necessary task of providing an heir," he announced pleasantly. A sudden ripple of alarm wound through the group. Valoree watched in amazement as more than half her remaining suitors made a quick exodus.

"All of them could not be unable to produce heirs," she murmured to Daniel in disbelief. He shook his head slightly.

"Nay. Doubtless some of them were not really nobility, but had hoped to be able to convince you they were long enough to trick you into marriage. Then, too, some of them may have skeletons in their closets that they do not wish uncovered by your uncle's 'investigations.' "

Valoree nodded. That made sense. Not that she had a problem with skeletons in one's closet. She had seventy-five of her own, every one of them alive and breathing and eager to see her bound in marriage. Resigned, she eyed the twelve men left to choose from. Then, sensing a presence behind her, she glanced over her shoulder to see Henry standing there, his eyebrows raised as the dozen men left.

"Bull said you were wantin' me," he explained, then gestured to the room at large. "What happened to the rest of 'em?"

"We weeded out the ones who weren't nobles, or able to father an heir," Valoree answered, perusing the suitors that were left. As she turned back, she thought she saw an odd glint in her quartermaster's eye, but he was peering at Daniel.

"What are ye going to do with the rest of 'em?" Thurborne asked.

Valoree was silent for a moment, then turned to glance at him, a slight grimace on her face. "I suppose I shall have to spend some time with each to see which one would suit best."

"Or you could save yourself the trouble and marry me," Daniel put in. Valoree saw Henry regard the man again, and she quickly moved to squash that notion.

"I already know you would not suit. She turned to Henry. "Take them all to the dining room. Schedule visits with each of them so that I can see what they are about, Henry. If we work this right, we could be out of this stinking town by week's end."

Nodding, her right-hand man faced the men. "All right. We're moving into the dining room now. I'll get ye names and schedule each of ye with an appointment to return, then ye can leave. Follow me."

Valoree and Daniel stood aside as the crowd vacated her salon, each man pausing to give her smarmy smile, and kiss her hand with varying degrees of a passion. Each assured her they could not wait for their visitation. Shaking her head as she watched the last man troop out the door, Valoree released a breath with what she told herself was satisfaction. There was not a single real man among the bunch. This endeavor to find an easily subdued mate should be quickly successful. The feat she had thought impossible was suddenly beginning to look simple.

"Alone at last," Daniel murmured, pressing a kiss to her neck that made her jump in surprise and wheel on him.

"That'll be enough o' that, it will," she snapped, quashing the shivers the brief caress had sent through her. There was a time for business and a time for fun after all—and she was still on business time.

"Your language is slipping," he said with a wicked smile, insinuating his arms around her waist and pulling her stiff body against his own. "I notice it tends to turn into something resembling the speech of a dockside doxy when you get excited." His hands slid down her back to clasp her bottom and urge her tighter against him so that their lower bodies were molded together. "Oddly enough, I find that excites me. Can you tell how much?"

"You—"

"Daniel!"

Releasing Valoree at once, Thurborne leaped guiltily away at his mother's scandalized roar from the doorway, then caught himself. Scowling at her, he quickly affected a slightly wry smile. "Done playing in the kitchen, Mother?"

Before she could respond, Meg appeared behind her. "Why, Lady Thurborne! What a pleasant surprise. Zachariah said we had company, but did not mention who it was."

Valoree was puzzling over the name Zachariah when she caught a glimpse of Bull moving across the hall, his face contorted with mingled embarrassment and displeasure. *Zachariah?* She hadn't even known that that was his real name. *God's teeth!* It was no wonder he preferred to be called Bull.

"Do come in and sit down." Meg urged Daniel's mother and her maid into the room and toward the chairs and settee. "Valoree, dear, will you ask one of the men to have Peter bring us some refreshments? Tea, and perhaps some biscuits or scones," she added pointedly.

Just in case I thought rum and a side of beef would do, Valoree supposed with vague amusement, turning to walk out into the hall. When she did, she noticed Bull was missing from his spot by the door. She supposed he was down in the dining salon with Henry, sizing up her suitors. No doubt all the men were. It affected them, after all. No doubt the bloody bastards thought they could vote on which one she married, too. Well, let them. She didn't care what they did at this point. In fact, she didn't really much care which she married. Although, had her life been a normal one, and her needs not so specific, she had to admit that Thurborne would have been an interesting option. He reminded her very much of her dearly departed brother, at least in his determination and strength. Aye, she liked Thurborne.

But she had been in charge of her crew for too long to give up her power to another and play the submissive, dutiful wife. Not that she even could have if she had wanted to. She had no skills in that area—didn't know the first thing about it, and didn't want to. Being a lady and wife seemed incredibly boring next to her years of adventure on the high seas.

"Ah, Lady Ainsley."

Drawn from her thoughts, Valoree looked blankly at the fellow she had nearly walked into, recognizing him as one of her suitors. He was a hard one to forget. The man's name was Alcock, which was fitting since he dressed like a peacock. He was also short with a scrawny little neck and shoulders, and a rather wide rump. A most unfortunate physique, she decided as he drew her hand into his and lifted it to press tiny butterfly kisses across her knuckles.

With his lips still pressed to her hand, he peered up at her in what she considered a rheumy manner. "Truly you are as lovely as a fresh summer day. How it pains me to say *adieu*."

"Aye. Me, too," Valoree lied, snatching her hand back. Then, using it to catch his elbow, she propelled him firmly toward the door. "Now watch your step on the way out," she sang out with feigned good cheer. Pulling the door open, she gave him a shove that sent him stumbling out into the street, and she closed the door behind him with a snap.

"Lovely as a fresh summer day indeed," she muttered with a scowl, fully aware she looked anything but lovely. Unless one liked rashes . . .

"Henry!" she yelled, starting up the hall, then paused when the door to the dining salon opened. Henry's head popped out. "Cross Alcock off the list. He's too damn prissy for my liking. And have Petey fetch some refreshments; we have company."

Henry's gaze shot around the entry questioningly and Valoree sighed. "Lady Thurborne has joined her son in the salon."

Nodding, Henry turned back to the room, addressing someone. A moment later One-Eye slid out and moved into the kitchen to pass her message on to Petey.

Leaving them to it, Valoree returned to the salon in time to hear Meg saying in a pained voice, "I fear her uncle was not very strict with her over the years. He had no idea what to do with the poor girl, and it has been up to me to try to instill a lifetime's lessons in manners in a very short period. She is coming along nicely, of course, but still occasionally forgets some little thing. Such as that ladies never raise their voices," she added, turning to eye her "niece" with some annoyance.

"She is doing fine."

Valoree's answering glare at Meg faded abruptly, replaced with amazement as Lady Thurborne championed her. "She is a lovely girl, and with perfectly lovely manners. I must confess that I myself sometimes forget and call out to, or for, my servants more loudly than is thought proper."

Meg smiled doubtfully at that, but Valoree chose to ignore her. Lady Thurborne continued, "Daniel mentioned to me that Lady Valoree had suffered a reaction to her makeup last evening, so I thought I would come over and see if there was not something I could do."

"Oh, that was very kind of you," Meg answered, *tsk-tsk*ing as she peered at Valoree's ravaged face. "I fear we have just not had much luck with cosmetics on the girl. Last night was the second foundation we have tried since arriving, and the second time we have had problems. I fear she just is not suited to such concoctions."

"Well, it certainly does not seem to have affected her popularity any," Lady Thurborne said brightly.

"Yes, well," Daniel piped up, "it appears Lady Valoree is in much the same boat as myself. She must marry to gain her inheritance. *Someone* let that slip, and it has made the gossip mill. Every second son and down-on-his-luck lord in London showed up here today."

"Oh!" Lady Thurborne's eyes widened slightly; then she confided, "Well, I *had* heard something about that. About the will, I mean. Actually, I am surprised that you are not married already, dear. Surely there were some marriageable men on that island you grew up on? Which island was it?"

Meg sidestepped the question for her. "As to meeting marriageable men, I fear Henry, Valoree's uncle, was not very interested in society. It was not until we married that Henry understood the importance of society and a coming-out and marriage. Hence the reason Valoree is coming out at such an advanced age."

Valoree's head whipped around at the "advanced age" comment, a scowl darkening her expression. She wasn't *that* old.

"How old are you, dear?" Lady Thurborne asked with curiosity. Valoree hesitated, then answered reluctantly.

"Four and twenty."

"Oh, dear!"

Valoree grimaced at the woman's shock and dismay. She'd reacted as if she had said sixty.

"Aye." Meg's expression was disconsolate, but Valoree swore she saw a spark of humor in her eyes. "Such a problem. And then there is the codicil to her father's will, which adds even more urgency to the issue of marriage."

"I heard about that, too," Lady Thurborne confided. "I was told that to inherit, she has to be married and have a babe—or at least be with child—by her next birthday. When is that, dear?"

"A mere nine months away," Meg answered.

"Oh, dear!" Lady Thurborne exclaimed, again. "Well, then you must get to work on it at once." Her eyes moved to her son speculatively before announcing, "Daniel is in a similar situation himself."

"Is he?" Meg asked with interest, and Valoree turned to glare at the man in question, silently willing him to do, or say, something to stop anyone from suggesting what obviously came next.

Daniel peered back innocently for a moment, then intercepted his mother as she opened her mouth to speak. "I suggested to Lady Valoree that we team up to solve both our problems," he claimed, making Valoree gasp in horror. "But alas, she refused me."

"What?" Both women gasped as one, gaping from Daniel to Valoree. Even Lady Thurborne's maid looked shocked that Valoree had refused the man. Lady Thurborne shook her head.

"Well, Daniel. 'Tis no wonder she refused. No girl wishes to be proposed to so cavalierly. They like romance, sweet words, and charming gifts. No doubt those gentlemen Bess and I saw parading down the hall as we came out of the kitchen will offer those things if you will not. There must have been a dozen men—were there not, Bessy?" She glanced toward her maid, her eyes suddenly widening as they landed on the bowl the girl stood patiently holding. "Oh! The salve!"

She was on her feet at once and hurrying over to dip a finger in the bowl's contents. "I think it is still all right," she said at last. "But, really, we should have applied it at once."

"Aye, before it putrefied." Daniel chuckled, suddenly at Valoree's side. Glancing up at him, Valoree found herself staring with fascination at his eyes. They sparkled with life, and actually seemed to twinkle in his handsome face.

"Well, shall we do it over here?"

Forcing her gaze away from the woman's son, Valoree saw that Lady Thurborne had moved to a chair by the fire and was now waiting for her expectantly.

"Come, Valoree. Sit here and we shall have you looking and feeling better in no time."

Valoree's gaze slid from the bowl to the seat the woman was encouragingly patting. She really did not want any more stuff on her face.

"Mother's concoctions are really quite miraculous," Daniel announced, his eyes alight with laughter. "She is infamous among the ton for them."

"I have helped quite a few people over the years with one ailment or another." Lady Thurborne smiled modestly. "Come, dear. Sit here."

"I do not think—" Valoree began, only to be interrupted by Meg.

"Oh! A brilliant idea, and so kind of you to think of it." The woman was suddenly at Valoree's other side, giving her a poke.

"Hey, that hurt!" Valoree exclaimed, glaring at her. She turned that glare toward Daniel as a laugh slipped from him.

"I am sorry, dear. Why do you not sit over there as Lady Thurborne suggested?" Meg urged, adding under her breath so only Valoree could hear, "Or shall I fetch Henry and the men to vote on it?"

Furious but unwilling to be further humiliated, Valoree moved reluctantly to the chair and took a seat. The moment she did so, the three women closed in on her, blocking any possibility of escape as Lady Thurborne's maid dipped her fingers in the bowl of goo.

Craning her neck slightly, Valoree examined the contents. It was gray with reddish chunks in it. She opened her mouth to ask what it was, then snapped her lips closed and leaned back as far as she could in an effort to avoid the maid's hand—it had come out of the guck with a nasty glob of salve on the fingertips and moved toward her face. Unfortunately, seated and surrounded as she was, there was no escaping. It was cold and slimy as the maid began to smooth it around.

Valoree immediately wrinkled her nose at its smell. "What is it?"

"An old family recipe," Lady Thurborne told her, watching the application closely. "It is passed on only to family members."

"What a shame," Valoree lied. Not that Lady Thurborne seemed to notice. Daniel did, though, and she was gratified by a snort of amusement from him. She found herself thinking that she liked it when he laughed. Especially when she'd made him do so. He had a nice laugh, full and deep and robust. His eyes sparkled, and his teeth flashed. And he *had* all his teeth—with not a brown, gray, or black one among them. Pretty impressive, she thought. He was a handsome man. She had seen prettier men, perhaps, but there was just something about him that appealed to her.

"You could have it if the two of you married."

Valoree blinked at Lady Thurborne's sly words, her mouth dropping slightly. Then Meg added, "Oh, would that not be nice," in a vaguely amused tone. Valoree glared at the older woman, quite positive Meg knew that she had no interest at all in making Daniel her husband. He was too . . . Well, he just wasn't right for what she had in mind!

"You should not grimace, dear. You will get wrinkles," Meg lectured sweetly. Valoree glared at her silently as her face was quickly covered in chunky slime.

"Oh, *my*, Mother. What wondrous stuff this is. I believe I see an improvement already," Daniel said as he peered over the woman's shoulder at Valoree's face. Her eyes immediately snapped to him, spitting fire, but he merely winked in response. His mother turned and slapped him playfully on the arm.

"Oh, do behave, Daniel. You should not even be here. Why do you not go visit with the men?"

"Because this is far more interesting, and even educational."

"You know," Lady Thurborne murmured, drawing Valoree's gaze back to her expression as she peered thoughtfully at Meg, "you look terribly familiar, my lady. Is it possible we have met in the past? Perhaps ere your journey to the Caribbean?"

"Me?" Meg stammered. "Oh, nay. *Nay.* I have been in the Caribbean since I was quite young. Quite young." She glanced around a bit desperately; then her gaze settled on the door. In a voice strident with sudden anxiety, she added, "I had best go and see to those refreshments. Our cook appears to be taking his time with them."

"Oh, nay!" Valoree shot out of her chair, her first opportunity to escape presenting itself. "I shall tend to that. You should stay and visit. Who knows, mayhap you and Lady Thurborne knew each other as children."

Meg looked quite upset in the glimpse Valoree had of her face as she slid out of the room—distraught even, almost in a panic. It was enough to make Valoree feel a touch guilty. Almost. Not being used to the sensation, she shrugged her shoulders uncomfortably as she strode down the hall. It did not help. The guilt remained solidly across her shoulders like a cloak. This nobility business was really starting to irritate her. Nothing was fun anymore, not even a little good-natured spite!

Cursing under her breath, she pushed through the doors into the kitchen. She had barely registered the empty room and the open back door when something slammed into the back of her head. Lights exploded behind her eyes, nausea rolled up from her stomach, and then those lights faded to darkness.

The hue and cry coming from somewhere near the back of the town house was the first indication Daniel had that anything was wrong. Aware that the women were following, he moved swiftly out of the salon toward the shouts and cries of alarm down the hall. There, a good half-dozen of Valoree's suitors were clogging the entrance to the kitchens.

"What is it? Let me through," he ordered, making a path where there had been none even before the men began to shift out of the way. Reaching the front of the pack, he found himself staring down at an even tighter circle that consisted of Valoree's uncle and the men who passed for her servants. They were bent over an unconscious Valoree. Kneeling beside the girl, her uncle reached for her shoulder and turned her onto her back. A horrified gasp immediately went around the men.

"My God! Look at what they done to her face," the servant with the eye patch cried as Valoree's uncle sat back in dismay.

"That is salve," Daniel explained, pushing through the servants to kneel beside her. "Did she faint?"

"The captain don't—" An elbow in his side silenced the one-eyed fellow's scornful comment.

"My niece is not prone to fainting fits," Meg said quickly, drawing Daniel's attention from the servant.

"Aye, and not only that, she just don't do it," the fellow missing his nose muttered.

"And she didn't this time, unless she hit her head on the way down." Henry announced that as he pulled the hand that he had cradled her head with away, revealing a stain of blood.

"On something like this, maybe?" the cook said sarcastically, bending to pick up a bloody rolling pin.

"Seems more likely it would fall on her than her falling on it," One-Eye said grimly, turning to coldly eye the suitors. "And I'm wondering which of you helped it fall."

" 'Tweren't none of them," Henry snapped as Daniel pulled a hankie out to press to Valoree's head. "Couldn't have been. They were in the dining salon with you, me, and Bull. Petey—you found her, didn't you? Where were you?"

"Out haggling with the fishmonger." He gestured to a spilled basket on the floor by the door. He had obviously dropped it in his rush to get to his mistress's side; his purchases were spilled out onto the floor.

Henry nodded, then glanced at Daniel and the women questioningly.

"We were in the salon. Lord and Lady Thurborne, her maid, and myself," Meg said quietly.

"Ye didn't hear or see anything?"

"I was the first one out the door, and did not see or hear anything except your cook shouting, and you men rushing into the kitchen," Daniel said impatiently, lifting Valoree into his arms. He stood. "I am taking her into the salon to be attended to. I suggest you have the servants search the house. It is doubtful you will find anything, but it cannot hurt to be sure."

"Aye-aye," Valoree's uncle agreed, rising as well. "Bull, see the men into the dining salon, I'll be along directly. One-Eye, Skully, No-Nose, you start searching the house. Whoever it was is probably long gone by now, but look anyway. Petey, clean this mess up."

Daniel heard the orders being issued as he carried Valoree out of the kitchens and back down the hall toward the salon. Meg, his mother, and her maid immediately followed.

# *Chapter Nine*

"Captain?"

Valoree murmured groggily, wincing as her head protested her return to consciousness. Blinking her eyes open, she moaned, then quickly pressed them closed again.

"Ye'd best call the others."

"Aye."

There was a rustle as someone left her side, then a door opened. A high, piercing whistle rent the air, and she recognized Skully's voice shouting. "Hoy! She's awake!"

Groaning, Valoree raised her hands miserably to press them to either side of her head. She felt as though someone were doing a dance on it. If she'd had the strength, she would have risen from her bed and ripped the man's tongue from his mouth.

"Captain?" One-Eye's voice sliced through her head, and she let her hands drop away in despair.

"Aye. I'm awake," she said in disgust, just to shut the two men up. Then, forcing her eyes open, she struggled to sit up as she saw that she was lying in bed. Reaching out, One-Eye quickly propped pillows behind her and grasped her under the arms to assist her in leaning against them. Had she been in a better mood, Valoree might have thanked him. As it was, she didn't bother. Instead, she grunted as Henry and Meg rushed into the room with the other crewmen at their heels.

"How're ye feeling?" Henry asked anxiously as he reached her bedside.

"Like hell," Valoree snapped, then scowled around at the faces surrounding her. "What happened?"

"Ye don't remember?" he asked. Valoree sighed.

"Would I ask if I did? The last thing I remember is that Meg wanted to go check on the tea. I said, nay, I'd do it. I walked into the kitchen and then . . . what happened?"

"Someone knocked you out," Meg said quietly.

"Koshed ye over the head with Petey's rolling pin," Henry added.

One-Eye leaned forward. "Did ye see anything?"

Valoree frowned, then shook her head. "Not much. I opened the door and had a brief glimpse of the open back door. I thought the room was empty, stepped in, and . . ." She shrugged.

"Open?" Petey scowled. "I closed the door behind me when I went out to meet the fishmonger at the gate. It was still closed when I came in to find you on the floor."

Valoree's eyebrows rose, then wrinkled in pain. "No one passed you at the gate?" The Greek shook his head. "Who was the first person through the kitchen door?"

"That'd be me, I think," One-Eye answered. "We were in the dining salon, heard Petey's shout, and came running."

"Did you see anyone in the hall as you came out of the dining room?" Valoree asked. The man shook his head. Sighing, she peered around at the rest of her men and Meg. "Did *any* of you see *anyone* who didn't belong in the house?"

175

"Nay," her aunt murmured. "Lord Thurborne, his mother, and her maid were all in the salon with me when we heard the shouting. By the time we got into the hall, it was crowded with your suitors."

The men nodded in agreement. No one had seen anything.

"I had the men search the house afterward, but they didn't find anything."

Valoree nodded at Henry's announcement. "Is everyone still here?"

"Nay. I finished with scheduling appointments nigh on an hour ago, and Lord and Lady Thurborne left about the same time. Right after the first time you woke up."

"The first time?" She peered at them blankly. "I have been awake before?"

"Aye, but you were pretty groggy."

Valoree felt shocked by that news. "So what was decided?"

"About what?" Henry asked blankly. Valoree made a face.

"Unless I miss my guess, Thurborne wouldn't have left unless he had decided what had happened and ensured to his satisfaction that it wouldn't happen again. What did he decided?"

"Oh." Henry shifted. "We all agreed it must have been some petty thief hoping to grab a trinket or two, but that you surprised him in the kitchen and got koshed for your trouble."

Valoree accepted that with a grunt. It made sense. There was no reason for anyone to be whacking her over the head otherwise. At least, not here. Now, if this were Spain, or maybe even France or Holland, and people knew who she was . . . Well, that was another story. But here in England? She did not even know anyone here, other than her own men and the few people she had met so far.

"Thurborne suggested we post someone to watch the back door as well as the front for a while, to keep an eye out, just to make sure," One-Eye added. Valoree nodded again. Sensible and cautious. She figured he'd think that way.

Groaning, she lay back on the pillows and made a face. "Well, you can all stop looking at me like I am at death's door," she said in disgust. "I am fine."

Her men straightened, muttering an agreement to that, but not looking as though they really believed it. Valoree blamed it on the dresses she had been forced to wear. They never would have looked at her like this after a koshing before they'd heard she was really a girl. When she was Captain Valerian, they would have gone about their work and left Henry to tend to her wounds. Now they all thought her so fragile they had to see for themselves that she was all right, and even then they looked reluctant to look away or leave her. Hell, she might drop dead while they weren't looking!

"Oh, go on, get out of here," she said in a snarl. "My head is pounding something fierce."

"Aye, come on, let her rest," Henry ordered, straightening and urging the rest of the men away from the bed. "She'll be fine. She's suffered worse than this before."

"Go ahead. You too, Meg. I am fine," Valoree added when the woman hesitated.

Nodding, the older lady moved away, exiting through the door Henry held open for her. Valoree wasn't terribly surprised when he then closed the door and returned to her bedside. Being the only one who had known her true sex, he had always been the one to tend her when she was ill or injured—and he had also always tended to fuss over her like a mother hen.

"Do ye need anything?" he asked, settling himself on the edge of the bed.

"Nay. Thanks," she added a bit gruffly, then waited,

knowing him well enough to suspect he had something to say. She didn't have long to wait.

"Daniel seems a fine boy," he murmured, and Valoree glowered at him. Lord Thurborne was a man, not a boy. Still, Henry called anyone under his own nearly sixty years *boy* or *girl*.

"Aye," she agreed at last.

"He is smart, strong, and handsome. Virile, too."

"Aye," Valoree agreed, trying not to smile at that last comment. What would Henry know about that?

"You noticed, then?" he asked hopefully. Valoree made a face.

"I would have had to be blind not to notice."

Henry nodded sagely. Then he blurted, "I think he'd be willing to marry—"

"Forget it!"

Henry blinked at the hard tone of her voice as she cut him off. "Why? You like him, don't ye? I can tell ye like him. And—"

"Henry, I need a husband I can control, and Daniel does not strike me as very controllable."

The old man scowled at that reasoning. "A wife ain't supposed to control—"

"A normal wife, mayhap, but I am not a normal woman! There is nothing normal about me," she said.

He hesitated at that, then peered down at his hand as he began plucking at the linen sheets. "I know you haven't had the usual childhood, girl, but now is your chance for a normal life. Wouldn't you like to set down your burden and lean on—"

"I leaned on Jeremy once," she interrupted quietly. "I have learned my lesson."

"Jeremy didn't mean to let you down. He didn't mean to die. He—"

"Jeremy never ever let me down," she said harshly, then glanced away. After a moment, she added, "But when he died . . . I was lost. If not for you, Skully,

One-Eye, and Petey—Well, who knows what would have become of me? The men could have voted in another captain and I could have found myself suddenly alone and destitute. I probably would have ended up dead, or a prostitute. I will not ever be weak like that again. I want to run my own life. No surprises, no—"

"Passion?" Henry suggested sadly. "I understand what ye're saying, girl. But do you?"

She felt surprise at that, then asked warily, "What do you mean?"

"What I hear ye saying is that ye're afraid." She started to protest, but he waved her to silence. "Ye're afraid to be hurt again. To love and lose. To care and suffer. To do those things, ye gotta give up control. I've said it before: ye've no fear of dying, but ye're terrified to live." Seeing her closed expression, he sighed and got to his feet. "Ye must be tired. I'll leave ye to rest. Yer first visit with one of them suitors is midmorning tomorrow."

". . . and she had a mole cut to look like a carriage and horses that she insisted on wearing right above her lip. It was the most disgusting thing, and yet she thought herself so clever for it."

Valoree forced a smile as Lord Gravenner tittered at his own ancodote. He was the second of her scheduled visits of the day. Unfortunately, he was just as boring as Lord Shether, her first. Shether had talked of nothing but himself: how clever he was, how fashionable, how everyone adored him. Gravenner talked about everyone else: how stupid they were, how ugly, how terribly unfashionable and dull. *Really!* She didn't know which was worse. She did know, however, that both men were idiots and off her list of prospective husbands. Lack of personality aside, she didn't think that either man could be quiet long enough to accom-

plish the task of getting her with child. If she were
even capable of allowing them near her.

Both men had decided on a "nice walk in the park"
as their courtship activity, and Valoree had briefly
wondered if they were separated twins. Still, she'd
found the proposal fine for the first appointment, so
she, Shether, Meg, and Henry had set out on a walk
with good cheer. Half an hour into their promenade
around the park, they had run into Daniel, who had
"just happened" to be out for a stroll himself.

Honestly, Valoree had been relieved to see the man.
By that point, she had too long listened to a nonstop
diatribe from Shether about his favorite topic—
Shether. At first she had thought that the man was
simply trying to let her know as much about himself
as he could to help her make her decision, but by the
time they had run into Daniel, she had begun to think
that the man was simply a bore. Lord Thurborne's
amused and rather snide little comments when he
joined them had only proved her right.

"Shether is well known as an expert on himself,"
had been one of Daniel's quips. It had made her eyes
widen, her hand covering her mouth to hold back a
laugh, and that laugh had nearly escaped when Shether
had agreed enthusiastically.

"Aye," he'd said. "He was an expert on himself.
Why he could tell her . . ." And off he had gone, not
even seeming to realize that the comment had been a
poke at his egotistical personality. By the time they
had said good-bye to Daniel to return to the town
house, Valoree's mouth was sore from biting it in for-
bearance, and the muscles in her cheeks ached from
the effort not to laugh. She had instructed Henry to
cross the man off the list the moment he had bidden
them *adieu* and ridden off. Alas, they had entered the
town house to find Gravenner waiting in the salon,
eager to announce that he, too, had decided on a pleas-

ant little walk. Sighing, Valoree, Meg, and Henry had trotted out again, following the exact same path they had just trodden, this time running into Daniel right away. Stunned to find them there again, or so he proclaimed, he had fallen into their group and murmured, "Lord Gravenner is the one to ask should you wish to know anything at all about the ton. He is quite in the know. A *very* sharp fellow."

Valoree had raised an eyebrow at the twinkle in his eyes as he'd said that, then turned her attention to Gravenner. He, too, had agreed with Lord Thurborne's assessment. "Oh, my, yes. I know everyone and everything. For instance . . ." And off he had gone, into an attack on seemingly every member of society. "Lady Braccon is a cow, she . . ."; "Lord Snowtan is a dullard, he . . ."; and so on and so forth. Valoree, aside from beginning to suffer aching feet, was heartily sick of the man with his cruel quips and snide remarks. If it weren't for Daniel's gentle little jibes at the man—jibes Gravenner, just like Shether, did not seem to grasp—she would have told Gravenner to shove off and have headed home long ago. Instead, she was seeing the humor in the situation, sharing silent laughter with Daniel, and actually enjoying herself in an odd way.

"Well, here we are."

Meg's voice, heavy with relief, made Valoree glance around in surprise to see that they had returned to the town house.

"Aye. I can hardly believe it. The hour passed like mere moments in your company." Lord Gravenner turned to take Valoree's hand. "It has been a true pleasure, my lady. I can hardly wait to enjoy your company again."

Bending, he pressed a kiss to her hand, then nodded to the group at large and turned to get into his waiting carriage. Valoree turned away as it pulled off, her gaze moving to Henry.

"Cross him off the list?" the older man asked solemnly.

"Aye. Who is next?"

"Ye've a free hour between now and the next one," Henry informed her, pulling a piece of paper out of his pocket and contemplating it briefly before scratching out an entry, presumably Gravenner. "I thought I'd best put rest periods in once in a while—in case one of the appointments ran over time."

"Hmmm." Valoree nodded, impressed with his forethought, then started for the door. "Well, I do not know about the rest of you, but I could use a drink."

"I intend to put my feet up," Meg muttered, following her into the town house. "I certainly hope the rest of the suitors have something a little more entertaining in mind than walking about jabbering about themselves . . . or sniping about everyone else."

"So do I," Valoree muttered dryly, stripping her gloves off her hands as she crossed the entry to the salon.

"What you need is to give your feet a good soak, Meg," Henry commented, following Daniel in and closing the front door.

"Oh, that does sound lovely." The older woman sighed, then shook her head. "Mayhap later. We should—"

"There's no better time than now, *wife*," Henry argued firmly.

Pausing by the sideboard, Valoree glanced over in time to see the man catch Meg by the arm, drag her around a startled Daniel, then pull her out of the salon.

"Henry, what are you doing?" Meg gasped, struggling to free her arm. "I cannot soak them now. Valoree cannot be left alone with a gentleman caller. It is not proper."

"It ain't improper if no one knows about it. 'Sides, she can take—"

The door closed behind the older couple with a firm snap.

Valoree and Daniel were both silent for a moment, staring at the closed door; then their gazes met.

"Well," he began with a smile, "I would guess that means that I have your *uncle*'s approval."

"Aye," Valoree admitted, then frowned and glanced back to the sideboard. She busied herself preparing a drink, then asked politely, "Did you want refreshment, my lord?"

"Please." The sound of his voice right behind her made her start slightly in surprise. Forcing herself to ignore him, she finished pouring two drinks, drawing it out as long as she could before picking up both and turning reluctantly to face him.

"Here you are." She held one glass out.

"Thank you." His voice was deeper than usual, softer as he closed his hand over hers on the glass. "Now perhaps you could tell me something?"

Valoree glanced up to meet his gaze, amazed to find herself suddenly nervous. "I . . . What would that be?"

"What it is I have to do to convince you to reconsider."

She didn't play dumb. She knew he was referring to her considering him as a potential husband, and her lips tightened slightly in self-defense. He was a tempting package. Especially when he stood this close, his body and lips a hairbreadth away, his hand gently warming hers around the cool drink. She took a deep breath to try to clear the effect he had on her senses, but it just made things worse as she inhaled the scent of him.

"I told you, I do not reconsider," she began almost desperately, but he interrupted, finishing for her.

"Unless there is a part of the equation that was left out. And there is, you know."

Valoree paused in surprise, her head cocking to the side. "What?"

Taking both glasses, he reached his arms around her to set them both on the sideboard. Then he caught her shoulders and drew her toward him, whispering, "This." And then his lips covered hers, warm, soft, and seductive.

As before, Valoree was lost at once. Opening her mouth beneath his even before he issued the invitation, she sought the heat and excitement she had experienced in his mother's garden. She had been yearning for a repeat performance since that night, and was honest enough to admit it, at least to herself, as she wrapped her arms around his neck, arching so that her breasts pressed tightly against him through their clothes.

Muttering a sound of surprised delight into her mouth, Daniel thrust his tongue inside, his hands slipping down her sides to grasp her waist. He inched forward, pressing her back until a sword blade couldn't have fit between her and the sideboard, or her and himself. When his mouth left hers to trail down her neck, she tipped her head slightly to the side, releasing a murmur of pleasure. Then she shuddered and brought her head back around to press a kiss to, suck, then nip at his neck in return, enjoying the slight roughness of his skin against her lips and tongue.

"Vixen." Daniel chuckled breathlessly, raising his head to kiss her lips again as he grasped her by the waist and lifted her to sit on the sideboard. But then his kisses became more teasing than satisfying. He alternated between brushing his lips lightly over hers, then nipping at her.

A growl of frustration slipping from her throat, Valoree caught her hands in his hair to hold his head still. Covering his mouth with hers in mute command, she thrust her tongue into his mouth and dared him to a duel. It was a dare he met with enthusiasm as his hands moved to busy themselves with the fastenings of her gown. He wasn't fast enough for Valoree's liking. Releasing her hold on his hair, she slid her hands between them, undoing the laces herself and tugging her gown shamelessly open, arching and gasping into his mouth as he tugged her chemise down and closed his hands over her aching breasts.

"Beautiful," he murmured, tearing his mouth away and lowering his head to suckle at one hardened nipple.

Moaning, Valoree shifted, closing her legs around his hips and drawing him nearer as she wrapped her arms around the top of his bowed head. She pressed one cheek to his soft hair.

"More," she said softly by his ear. Daniel chuckled against her breast at the urgency in her voice, then straightened and pressed a quick kiss to her eager lips.

"More, hmmm?" he murmured against the side of her mouth. His hands dropped to grasp her ankles, then slid slowly upward over her calves, pushing her skirts before them.

Shuddering, Valoree nodded and sought his mouth with hers, but he evaded her, pulling back slightly to watch her face as his hands crested her knees and eased up the insides of her thighs.

"How *much* more?" he asked huskily.

Suddenly unable to catch her breath, Valoree met his gaze, her mouth parting and her tongue darting out to wet dry lips she then bit as his hands met in the middle. Eyelids dropping slightly, she stiffened under his touch, her posture suddenly perfect.

"All of it," she managed to get out in a raspy voice, then glanced down to see a slow, satisfied smile creep over his face.

"You will not be sorry," he assured her gently, moving in to give her a brief, passionate kiss as he continued his caresses. Pressing a trail of kisses across her cheek to her ear, he added, "I shall make all the arrangements. You need not worry about a thing."

"Arrangements?" That was really the only word that made it through Valoree's passion-soaked mind as the tension inside her mounted.

"For the wedding." He laughed, nipping at her ear.

"Oh, that." Shaking her head, she insinuated her hands between their bodies and began to tug at the buttons on his shirt. "I did not mean *that*. I meant I wanted more of what you are doing," she said with a snort. Her head snapped up in surprise, her eyes searching his face as he suddenly removed his hands from under her skirt and stepped back. He crossed his arms and glared at her. He was angry, she realized with surprise. "What?"

"Do I understand you to say that you have not changed your mind about marrying me?"

"Nay, of course not," she said, surprised that he would think so. Taking in his grim expression, she realized he was quite upset. Sighing, she slid off the sideboard and moved forward, placing her hands gently on his crossed arms. "Do not take it so. I like you and am attracted to you, but nothing has changed. We simply would not suit."

Uncrossing his arms to avoid her touch, he propped his hands on his hips and said in disbelief, "You mean you are letting me touch you and make love to you like this when you have not decided to marry me?"

"Well, sure. And why not?"

"Why not?" He gasped in horror. "Mayhap things are different in the *Caribbean*; but here in England, *ladies* do not behave so with just anyone. They save themselves for their husbands."

"Really?" Valoree asked. She heard his doubting emphasis on the word *Caribbean*, but ignored it as she had the way he seemed to emphasize *uncle* when he spoke of Henry. She was gathering that he didn't believe their cover story, yet for some reason she was more interested in this new bit of information at the moment. It seemed more relevant, since her body was throbbing and aching with desire for him. Too, she found what he said hard to believe. Men didn't seem to wait to have sex until they were married. The members of her crew certainly didn't. Every single one of them had been with almost every willing woman there was in the warmer ports, and no doubt those on leave were having a good go at those here in London at this very moment.

In fact, Valoree was the only one on board the *Valor* who hadn't been with a member of the opposite sex. She had not even been kissed until Daniel. But, living a lie as she had, it was only because the opportunity to do so had never come up. Valoree had no interest in women, and she could hardly have brought men on board to satisfy any baser needs she might have had. Besides, she really hadn't had any until now. An oddity, that, she thought. None of the men, not One-Eye with his charming smile and ways, or even Bull, who was pure muscle and handsome as hell, had made her feel the way she felt with Thurborne. She supposed it had something to do with growing up with them; she thought of those men as family. But whatever the case, now she no longer needed to hide the fact that she was a woman, and she was attracted to the man before her—why not have him?

"Yes, really," Daniel said in exasperation and Valoree was drawn back to their conversation.

"Hmmm." She peered at him doubtfully. "So you're a virgin, too?"

"Too?" Daniel seemed to sag with relief, apparently pleased by the unintentional admission. Then what she had asked sank in, and he frowned. "Nay, I . . . Only women must refrain until after they are married."

"Aha!" she crowed a bit derisively. "Ladies are the only ones who must restrain themselves! Not men! Now, is that not interesting?" she asked. "Who exactly would it be who made up that rule, do ye think? Men, mayhap?"

"Aye, but—"

"Now, why do you suppose that is?"

"So they would know that any heirs born of the union are theirs," he answered.

"Oh, of *course*," she said with a sneer. "That *must* be it. It would not be another way to control women. Nay, of course not."

"Well." He smiled slightly. "No doubt they enjoy the fact that it also makes women behave a certain way. But the fact is, a man—even myself—does not wish to leave his family estate and name to someone else's by-blow."

Valoree's eyebrows rose slightly; then she nodded her head. "I suppose I can understand how that might be an issue in the normal course of things," she admitted, then shrugged. "But nothing about my situation is normal. I am the one with the land and title. I also must produce an heir. And as it is a business deal, whomever I marry will have no rights in the matter of what I do with my body. So . . ."

Stepping closer, she pushed his undone shirt off his shoulders, licking a path from his right nipple up to his neck as she did. Then she pressed her breasts against his chest, kissed him just below the ear, and murmured, "Help me make a baby."

Daniel was tempted. Oh, dear Lord, was he tempted. He had never been quite so much so in his life, in fact. His body was screaming at him to just do it. Just grab her, drag her down to the carpet, push her skirts up to her belly, crawl between her sweet legs, and thrust himself into her until he cried out and spilled his seed.

Unfortunately, he wasn't so far gone that his brain didn't still work, and it was pointing out the reasons why he shouldn't. For instance, it certainly would not help him out of his predicament of needing to marry. And if he did have to marry someone, Valoree was his choice. But that aside, if he did go ahead and take what she was offering, and she married one of those other oafs on her list of suitors, he would be imagining that man enjoying her body, and knowing what it felt like to do so. That would be sheer torture. Then again, she might be willing to continue to allow him access to her body after she married one of those other oafs— but he would still know that when she went home at night, another man was enjoying crawling between her sweet thighs. On top of that, what if his seed took? If he did take her as he wanted to, and she did produce a child as she must to inherit, he would always wonder if the child was his, and would have to live with the fact that some other bastard was raising him.

"Thurborne!"

Glancing down with a start as she squeezed his hard manhood through his pants, Daniel stared at her with fascination. She wanted him. That desire was written all over her face. Her cheeks were flushed, her eyes held a mixture of desire and impatience, and her naked nipples stood proud and erect. Aye, she wanted him. Badly. *Hmmm.* Mayhap this was a weapon he could use in his war for her hand in marriage.

Sniffing, he crossed his arms and lifted his chin so that he could glare down his nose at her self-righteously. "Nay."

She blinked once, then drew her head back in amazement. "Nay?"

"Yes. Nay. I am not helping you have a child that will bear someone else's name," he announced primly. But then he added, "However, if you would care to reconsider and agree to marry me . . . well, then, of course I would be obliged to—"

"All right."

Daniel paused and stared at her in amazement. He hadn't expected it to be this easy. "All right?"

"Aye. All right," she repeated, then reached up to tug her gown off her shoulders. It dropped to the floor, leaving her standing in a pool of silk in just a pair of tight black breeches.

Very nice tight black breeches, he decided, taking a step back toward her before catching himself and stopping. This was too easy. He gazed at her face suspiciously for a moment, then asked, "You are agreeing to marry me?"

Her mouth twitched with irritation at his making her clarify, and he watched a struggle take place on her face; then she snapped, "I am agreeing to reconsider."

"Not good enough." Whirling away, he continued his walk to the sideboard, poured himself a nice stiff drink, and downed it in one gulp.

"Thurborne!" she snapped again, stomping a foot in impotent rage.

Daniel turned to glance at her, then wheeled abruptly back to the sideboard. Damn, she was a sexy little bundle when she was furious! "Call me Daniel," he called over his shoulder. "We know each other well enough for that, I should think."

Instead she called him a string of words that he had never heard put together before. Actually, he decided, tossing back another drink, he had never heard a lady say even one of the words she had just uttered, let alone all of them together in such a creative manner.

She was still muttering some inventive, though not very pleasant, things that she would like to do to him a moment later when the rustle of clothing made him glance back to see that she was donning her gown. Even that action was sexy, he thought glumly, turning back for another gulp of brandy before reaching up to straighten his own clothes. He had barely finished doing so when there was a tap at the salon door and it was pulled open by Henry. The man peered hopefully inside.

His expression drooped immediately upon seeing the two of them standing so far apart; then his gaze narrowed on Valoree.

Daniel glanced toward her to see that while her hair was a touch disheveled, her dress was back in place. She also looked as sour as a lemon, however, and was glaring daggers in his direction. Ignoring her, Daniel smiled pleasantly at Henry. "Come to join us?"

"Nay." he glowered at them. "The next suitor's here."

"Hmmph." Valoree started for the door even as Henry pulled it open and stepped aside. Daniel couldn't at first see the man in question. He did, however, see Valoree's response to him. She stumbled to a halt, her eyes widening slightly, then flashed a brilliant smile and moved forward again, holding out her hand. A figure immediately stepped through the door to take the proffered appendage, lifting it for a kiss.

Daniel stewed. Henry had let him know shortly after the incident that had left Valoree lying unconscious on the floor in the kitchen that his hope was for Daniel and Valoree to come to an understanding. It had happened after Valoree had been carried to her room and while the women were undressing and tending to her. The two men had waited in the salon, and Henry had confessed as much, then informed him of her first suitors and their intended activities. He had also said that there would be an hour between the first two and the third fellow that Daniel could take advantage of, but he had not mentioned who the next fellow was. Now Daniel nearly groaned aloud as he recognized the

191

golden-haired man with the winning smile. *Hawghton. Of all the bloody luck!*

"My lord." Valoree moved a step closer to the man as he released her and straightened, and Daniel felt his hands clench at his sides.

"Lady Ainsley," Hawghton purred in his perfect voice, flashing her his perfect smile. "I must say that your beauty is a pleasant surprise. I fear the rash you were sporting yesterday did not show you off to advantage."

Daniel grimaced at that. She *was* looking lovely today. Her face was free of makeup, and completely recovered thanks to his mother's miracle salve. Probably one of the only times that one of her damn salves had actually worked, too, he thought bitterly. That figured.

"Thank you, my lord. It is *so* kind of you to say so," she purred, then tossed a glare in Daniel's direction, as if to underline the fact that he had not.

"Oh, Thurborne," Hawghton greeted, as if just noticing his presence. "I did not see you at first, old man." Then a concerned expression crossed his face. "I am sorry, did I get the time wrong? Mayhap my appointment was not until later."

"Oh, do not mind *old* Thurborne." Valoree's voice was heavy with disgust. "He's a friend of Uncle Henry's."

Daniel glanced at her sharply and she smiled at him in a cold-eyed way that told him she had guessed from the start how he had "just happened" to be in the park. Well, he supposed he should have known she would figure it out.

"I see," Hawghton murmured, his gaze moving between the two of them. Then he seemed to come to some decision and turned on his most charming smile. "Well, then. I thought mayhap we could attend the theater this afternoon. They are performing Sir George

Etherege's "She Would If She Could." It is supposed to be quite amusing."

Nodding, Valoree started toward the door. "I shall just go fetch my aunt and uncle and we can be off." Then she paused to examine Daniel pointedly. "Shall I see you out, my lord? You *were* just leaving, were you not?"

Nodding, Daniel set the drink he had been holding down, then moved silently toward her. She didn't wait for him, but stepped out into the hall, leaving him to follow. By the time he had reached the hall, she was at the front door and pulling it open.

Pulling the door to the salon closed with a snap, Daniel crossed to Valoree determinedly, caught her about the waist, and drew her against his chest. She tried to bring her arms up, but he had pinned them nicely to her side. Then she opened her mouth, probably to bestow upon him a few more of her colorful endearments, but he covered her mouth with his own, taking full advantage of the moment.

Valoree didn't crumble right away—she did have some backbone to her—but when he pushed the door closed with his foot, caught her hands, and held them behind her back with one of his so that the other could roam freely over her breasts, she at least stilled and stopped struggling. It took several minutes of thorough kissing and fondling before she actually began to kiss him back, but only a moment or so more after that before she was as liquid fire in his arms and moaning into his mouth. That was when he stopped.

Taken by surprise, she sagged against the wall and watched blankly as he straightened his cravat and cuffs.

"I just thought I would leave you something to remember me by," he said with a wink, then opened the door and slipped out quickly. A growl of rage slid from her throat and she grabbed a vase from the table beside her. Daniel pulled the door closed and chuckled as he heard the smash of glass behind it.

The battle lines, it seemed, had been drawn.

# *Chapter Ten*

"I cannot believe you did that!" Meg snapped, climbing into the carriage and seating herself across from Valoree so that she could glare at her through the darkness. "What on earth is the matter with you? Are you deliberately trying to ruin any possibility of finding a husband and claiming your inheritance? Because if you are, you are doing a fine job of it!"

"There is nothing the matter with me," Valoree snapped impatiently. "Scrantom was feeling me up with his stinky old foot under the table!"

"What?" Meg blinked in amazement, seeming at a loss for a moment; then she sighed impatiently. "Well, that may be, but an old man playing a little footsie—"

"Footsie?" Valoree snorted her disgust. "He had his foot under my skirt, halfway up my thighs, and was still moving upward until I put a stop to it."

Meg bit her lip. "Oh."

"Aye, oh," Valoree said in a snarl, turning her head to glare out the window of the stationary carriage. It was stationary because they were waiting for Henry and *him* to come out.

*Him* was how Valoree thought of Daniel Thurborne now. Just *him*. The man was a canker on her butt. A wart on her nose. A pus-ridden carbuncle on her arse.

In short, he was making her life absolute hell. He was everywhere she went. There wasn't a moment's peace from *him*. Every walk, every dinner, every *anything* one of her suitors chose to do during their appointed times with her . . . *he* was there. Which might not have been so bad had he simply been present. More often than not his wit and charm turned what would have been hellacious hours spent in the company of boring, whining, or just plain weak men into bearable chores.

Unfortunately he did more than that. He teased, and chatted, and made her laugh, waiting the whole time like a vulture. And the moment the opportunity presented itself, he pounced, taking her in his arms and making her dizzy with passion, working her into a frenzy of want, then stopping and walking away, leaving her a bundled ball of knotted nerves. And it was hell.

He didn't even have to kiss or touch her anymore. The moment she saw him, Valoree's body began to hum with want. Should he brush against her innocently in passing, a jolt of desire shot through her like lightning. And forget fighting it. At first she had tried to avoid any situation he might take advantage of, but now she sought them out. Now she looked for them. He had worked his frustrating magic on her behind trees, in hallways, under stairways, and even, once, in a closet. But all each episode did was make her more miserable. And she was reaching the breaking point. Even losing control of her life didn't seem like such a horrible price to pay to gain release from this terrible frustration. And that scared the devil out of her. Back-from-the-Dead Red, scourge of the Caribbean, the pirate feared by the Spanish, French, and Dutch alike, was laid low by the need for a man between her legs.

Not just any man. *Him*. Only *he* would do. Oh, she had tried kissing her various suitors, and even a bit more on the less repulsive ones. But it was like trying to substitute wine for rum. Wine was sweet but not very strong; rum was spicy and had a kick. Valoree wanted the damn kick! But she didn't want to have to marry the kicker. *What a pain.*

A titter from Meg drew her head around, and Valoree peered at the older woman in question. "What is so damn funny?"

"Oh, dear. I was just thinking of Lord Scrantom's face when you slammed your knife into the table beside his hand. I think he relieved himself on the spot." She covered her mouth to keep a laugh in, then shook her head. "Then when you pulled it out—"

She began to laugh helplessly, and Valoree smiled slightly as she recalled the moment. It *had* been rather funny, now that she thought of it. She had tugged the knife out of the table in the sudden silence, nonchalantly turning it over, to hold it half an inch in front of Scrantom's quivering nose so that he could see the decimated insect on its end. "A fly," she had said, as if that explained everything, "Pesky little things. They like to crawl up under a lady's skirts and tickle her legs." Then she had shot her gaze to him coldly and added meaningfully, "I hate things that crawl up my skirts and tickle my legs."

The man had gone into a dead swoon. Valoree had wiped the fly off on his sleeve and stood to leave the room, saying, "Cross him off the list, Henry. He wouldn't survive long enough to get me with child." Then she had come out here to wait in the carriage for them to join her, which Meg had done almost right away. Daniel and Henry, the only other guests at Scrantom's dinner, hadn't yet come out.

"Where is Henry?" she asked impatiently.

Meg leaned forward to peer through the window at the town house. "I am not sure. I thought Henry was right behind me, but—Oh, here they come."

Valoree leaned forward to see the men chatting as

they walked toward the carriage. They parted at the end of the walk, Thurborne moving toward his carriage, and Henry hurrying over to where Meg and Valoree waited.

"Come on," he said cheerfully, pulling the door open. "I invited Thurborne back for something to eat, since Scrantom's shenanigans cheated us out of half our dinner. He's offered us a lift in his carriage."

Valoree blinked in surprise that Henry had known what the man was about, then frowned as what he said sank in. "What's wrong with *our* carriage?"

"Nothing, if ye don't mind riding in a sea of silk," Henry muttered in disgust. "It's too damn small for the three of us, let alone all four."

"Well, he can just follow in his carriage," she argued, but not with very much force behind it. A moment later, as Henry pursed his lips and looked down his nose at her, she heaved a sigh and started out of the carriage. Satisfied by her agreement, Henry turned to tell No-Nose the change of plans.

She supposed she wasn't really fooling anyone by such a weak protest, at least not Henry. He knew her too well to be fooled by it, but she felt better that she had at least made the effort. Valoree attempted not to look too eager as she walked from one carriage to the other. She even muttered something unpleasant under her breath when Daniel winked at her as he helped her inside. A heartbeat later, they were all seated, and Valoree was cursing herself for her weakness as the carriage they now rode in moved out to follow the rented hack home.

The Thurborne carriage *was* larger than the one the men had rented for their stay in London, but Daniel didn't seem to be aware of that. He was sitting squeezed up against her, his hip and outer thigh pressed against hers, and his arm rubbing hers with the movement of the coach as he chatted with Henry. It was all what she had hoped for, of course, but it was sheer hell anyway. Amazing, the things that you could learn about yourself when put into new situations. For instance, until she had come to London and met Thurborne, Valoree hadn't had a clue that she had such masochistic tendencies.

She was berating herself for a fool when there was a sudden shout of warning, the shriek of horses, and a loud crash. The carriage lurched violently, throwing Valoree against Daniel, but a glance out the window showed a wagon tipping on its side even as it was pulled past by two panicked horses.

"Are you all right?" Daniel asked, helping her to sit up again once the carriage had stopped.

"Aye," Valoree assured him, then peered out the window as Daniel turned to check on Henry and Meg. Her gaze moved toward the road at the back of Thurborne's carriage, the direction the wagon had gone. She saw the vehicle had stopped some distance back, lying on its side in the road. The driver was whipping the horses, trying to get them to move anyway, to drag the wagon away. When they wouldn't budge, he gave up, and ran off down the road. Muttering under her breath, Valoree then turned to glance to the expanse of road at the front of Thurborne's carriage. What she saw there made her blood run cold and had her scrabbling to get outside.

"What is it?" Daniel asked, noticing her panic, but Valoree didn't stop to tell him. Stumbling from the carriage, she ran toward the wreckage of the hack her men had rented.

"One-Eye!" she yelled, hurrying toward the first man she saw. Flung to the side of the lane, he sat up slowly, shaking his head as she dropped to her knees beside him. "Are you all right? What happened?"

"Don't know," he answered dazedly, shaking his head again. "I guess we crashed. There was a bang;

then I got thrown from the back of the hack."

"Is anything broken?" she asked worriedly as Daniel reached them.

"Don't think so." He moved one limb, then another with caution. "Nay, I'm fine. What about the others?"

"You stay here and rest a minute; I'll go see." She patted his back, then stood and moved toward the front of the spilled carriage, aware that Daniel was following her. She heard him curse as he looked over what remained of the rented hack, but didn't look herself. She had seen the wreckage when she had peered out the window of his coach. The hack had tipped, smashing into the stone wall along the front of a town house. The top had been torn off, its sides had caved in, and the bottom was twisted. She doubted anyone would have survived had they been inside.

She found Bull and No-Nose off to the side at the front of the carriage. Bull seemed fine as he knelt by the other man, but No-Nose was not. His leg was broken, the bone poking clean through the skin.

"Sorry, Captain," No-Nose apologized. "That wagon came out of nowhere. Headed straight for us. I tried to move out of the way, but . . ." He shook his head.

"Shut up, No-Nose," Valoree muttered, kneeling by his injured leg and beginning to rip at the hem of her petticoat. "Help me here, Bull. We have to straighten this out. Are you hurt anywhere else?"

"Nay, I—Aaaahhhh," he screamed, then began to curse a blue streak as Valoree and Bull set to work on him.

Valoree pressed her lips together and did what had to be done, or at least as much as she knew. Scratchy would have to have a look at it when they got him back to the ship. He was the doc. But she knew No-Nose would be lucky to keep the leg.

"Damn," Henry swore upon spotting No-Nose's injury as he and One-Eye reached them. "How the hell did this happen?"

"A wagon came around the corner, pointed straight at us," Bull rumbled. "No-Nose tried to get us out of the way, but the other fella was comin' on too fast. We couldn't avoid getting hit, and we both jumped off just before it hit."

Henry blew out a breath, then asked, "He gonna be all right?"

"He'll live," Valoree answered shortly, unwilling to make promises about keeping his leg. Her gaze moved to Bull. "I can finish up here. You and One-Eye go tip that wagon back on its wheels and see if it will move. If it still works, bring it back here. You'll need it to take No-Nose back to the ship."

"I'll give 'em a hand," Henry said, chasing after them as the two men hurried away.

Daniel shifted, drawing her gaze to him. She had quite forgotten he was there.

"No-Nose?" he said softly, raising one eyebrow. "Ship?"

Lips tightening, Valoree turned back to trying to stanch the flow of blood from No-Nose's leg.

"Here." Meg was suddenly beside her, ripping a length of material from her own petticoats and offering it to Valoree, even as she attempted to reassure the man. "You will be all right, Robert."

Even in pain as he was, the man managed to grimace at the use of his proper name.

When she had done the best she could for him, Valoree glanced around. Daniel had moved off to help the men. They had the wagon back on its wheels, but instead of bringing it back, had paused to chat with a stranger. The four men she knew were standing in a semicircle, apparently listening to the other, who was gesticulating wildly.

Clicking her tongue impatiently, she stood and

roared, "Quit yer lollygagging, ye shiftless bastards! I've a wounded man here!"

Jaw dropping to his chest, Daniel wheeled around to peer at her in amazement. One-Eye and Bull, however, rushed to the wagon and leaped onto the driver's bench, immediately turning it to ride back toward her. Henry stayed, though, apparently trying to soothe the stranger. The man was getting more excited by the moment.

"Sorry, Captain," One-Eye apologized, holding the horses steady as Bull leaped down to lift No-Nose into the back of the wagon. "That fella back there is the owner of the wagon."

"Oh, he is, is he?" she said in a snarl, turning to start toward where Henry was still talking with the man.

She was given pause when One-Eye called out, "Aye, but he weren't driving it. Some fella stole it from him on the next block. He chased after him on foot and came on the accident after it happened."

Valoree hesitated, her gaze moving to where One-Eye was struggling to control the horses. The man was a sailor. He didn't know the first thing about driving. As far as she knew, Skully and No-Nose were the only members of her crew who had any skill with the beasts. Sighing, she turned back toward the three men still talking down the street. "Henry! Bring that man over here!"

Henry glanced toward her, hesitated, then started to lead the man back. He was about Henry's height and nearly as muscular, his face covered with soot. He had been delivering coal to the town houses when his wagon had been stolen, she guessed. The bottom and sides of his conveyance were stained black from the dust of the coal.

"This is your wagon?" Valoree asked as soon as he was close enough to hear without her having to shout.

"Aye. The dirty blighter stole it. I—"

"One of my men is injured," Valoree interrupted shortly as he stopped before her. "I need to get him to the docks. Can you take him?"

The man hesitated, displeasure shifting over his features. "Why can't ye just take him in *your* damn carriage? He not good enough to dirty the seats?"

Valoree stiffened, her eyes narrowing to cold slits that were usually a warning to her men that they were treading a dangerous path. "His leg is broken. He needs to be kept flat. The carriage is too small for that. He must be returned to the docks in your wagon. What I am asking you, is whether you wish to do the driving and be recompensed for it, or whether you wish to stand here and watch it be taken. Now, which is it?"

The man's gaze slid from her to Bull, to Henry and Daniel, then lastly to One-Eye seated on the driver's bench. "Ah, hell," he muttered, starting for the bench.

Turning to Bull, Valoree murmured, "Both you and One-Eye go with him. See he's paid when he gets you there."

Nodding, Bull turned and hefted himself into the back of the wagon. The driver climbed up to join One-Eye, who had shifted to make room for him. The vehicle was off almost at once. Valoree waited until it had turned the corner before turning to move back to Thurborne's carriage.

The four of them were silent on the way back to the town house. Valoree was fretting over No-Nose. She almost asked Daniel to take them to the docks several times, but then changed her mind. It would just mean more questions. She already had enough on her plate what with having to explain about the ship to him, and she knew she would have to. The nobleman kept looking at her. Of course, he was always looking at her, but he was looking at her differently now. Now, he kept casting curious glances her way.

Sighing, she leaned her head against the wall of the carriage, relieved when they stopped at their destination a moment later. They trooped silently inside and went directly to the salon. Valoree moved to stand by the fireplace as Henry quickly fixed everyone a drink. He handed these out, then glanced at Daniel questioningly. "Are ye still hungry?"

Thurborne smiled wryly, but shook his head, as did Valoree when he glanced her way. Henry's gaze then moved to Meg, who sighed and set her glass on the table, then stood. "Actually, Henry, I think I am more tired than hungry. It has been a most eventful night. If you will all excuse me, I am going to retire." She left the room to their murmurs of good-night; then Henry downed his drink and headed for the door as well.

"I'm going to talk to the men. Goodnight, Thurborne." The door pulled quietly closed behind him before Valoree or Daniel could say farewell.

Now the questions would begin, Valoree thought. She lifted her glass to drink from it, but Daniel didn't ask questions. Instead he was suddenly behind her, his hands on her shoulders, his thumbs rubbing the bare flesh of her collarbones. He pressed a kiss to the back of her neck. Swallowing the rum in her mouth, Valoree stood perfectly still, amazed to see that the hand holding her glass was beginning to tremble.

The shaking became much more violent when his hands slid down her arms, then beneath to reach around and cup her breasts. Twisting her head, Valoree sought his lips with hers, sighing into his mouth when he accepted the invitation. He kissed her passionately, one hand dropping down over her stomach, then lower, until it rested between her legs. There, he pressed gently. She groaned, barely aware of the splash of cold liquid on her skin as the glass she held tipped dangerously. Then he withdrew his hands, and his lips, and gave her a quick peck on the nose.

Eyes blinking open, she stared in amazement at his retreating back, then whirled toward the fireplace, throwing her glass in the fire with a vulgar curse. Leaning her forehead wearily against the mantel, she heard the front door of the town house open and close quietly. She was still standing there several moments later when the door to the salon opened again.

"Captain?"

Sighing, Valoree straightened, took a deep breath, then turned to peer at Henry. "Aye, what is it?"

He stared at her uncertainly for a minute, concern flashing across his face. "Are ye all right?"

"I am fine. Why shouldn't I be?" she snapped. "Is that all?"

"Nay, I wanted to talk to you about the carriage accident."

Sighing, Valoree moved to one of the chairs and sank into it wearily, then gestured for him to sit in the other. "Have you heard from the ship? Is No-Nose going to be all right?"

"Aye. One-Eye and Bull returned with Skully just a minute ago. Scratchy is looking after No-Nose. Says it was a clean break and he might even keep his leg."

Valoree relaxed slightly at that news. "Good."

"Skully's going to arrange for another hack first thing in the morning. We paid for the other."

"Also good." They were both silent for a moment; then Valoree frowned.

"What is it?" Henry asked, waiting.

Valoree met his gaze, her thoughts shifting for a moment. "I want you to have a couple of the men go out tomorrow and talk to that wagon owner again."

"Why? What is it ye want to know? Do you not think it was an accident, pure and simple? The fellow stole the wagon and in his excitement to get away, went too fast and lost control."

"Maybe," Valoree murmured, then shrugged. "Just

have them find out everything the owner can tell them about the fellow he saw steal it."

Henry nodded slowly; then they both fell silent for a moment. At last he asked, "Have ye made up your mind yet?"

She peered at him in surprise. "About what?

"About which one to marry," he answered. "Scrantom was the last of 'em on your list. Ye've visited with all of them now."

Valoree looked away toward the fireplace. "Nay. But I've narrowed the list."

"Aye, ye've done that, all right. Ye've only got Hawghton and Beecham left on it."

"Aye," Valoree agreed.

When she didn't say anything else, Henry said, "Should I send a letter around to those two, inviting them by for ye to have another gander?"

Sighing, Valoree let her head fall back on the chair and closed her eyes. "Aye, aye. Go ahead."

"I'll write 'em up before I go to bed so one of the men can run them around first thing in the morning. Good night."

She didn't hear him get up, but she did hear the door open and close. Sighing, she turned her head toward the fireplace and stared into it for a moment, picturing Hawghton and Beecham in her mind.

Hawghton was a handsome man, mayhap even more handsome than Daniel. He was also a charmer like Daniel. But, unlike Thurborne, who Henry told her had spent most of his time out tending to his estates since inheriting, Hawghton neglected his affairs and lived in London, where he could enjoy the high life. Gambling appeared to be his downfall. He, unlike most of the others, was not a second son. He was a firstborn son who had inherited a great deal of wealth with his title when his father had died three years earlier. He had also gambled most of it away in the short time since.

Or thrown it away on some mistress or another. Henry had seen to looking into each man. Hawghton liked gambling, women, and drinking. Between the three vices, he couldn't seem to hold on to a coin. Still, that didn't bother her much. Once the child was born and he was no longer necessary, she could set him up in town on a nice allowance that he could gamble away as he pleased.

What bothered her was that during their appointment, when they had gone to the theater—the only appointment she had managed without Daniel being there—she had glimpsed a flash of fury in the man. It was as they were leaving Drury Lane. Someone had jostled him and he had turned in a rage, his face suddenly beet red and looking as if he meant to strike the unfortunate passerby with his cane. Valoree had shifted then, drawing his gaze, and Hawghton had forced himself to relax and immediately release one of his charming laughs. All as if the incident had never happened. But the moment had stuck in her mind. The man had a temper, and a second appointment was only to assure herself of that. She would not marry a man who might raise his cane to her. She'd have to kill the bastard then, and she had enough troubles without that.

That left Beecham. He was a perfectly nice man, unlike Daniel, who was an evil, irritating bastard. He was smart, unlike Daniel, who didn't know enough to take a woman when she offered herself. He was also good with money. In fact, from what Henry could find out, he had absolutely no need for her money, so she was not quite sure of his motives for offering to marry her. That was bothersome. He had taken her to a coffeehouse for his appointment, and Valoree had enjoyed herself. Daniel had shown up, of course, but he had not done anything at all to emphasize any faults Beecham might have. She supposed he didn't really have any. He didn't rattle on about himself endlessly, or talk snidely about others. In fact, he was a very quiet man. He didn't sniffle or whine as Haversham had . . . or had that been Griswold? He did not waste his money on gambling like Hawghton, and he certainly had not tried to slip his foot under her skirts like Scrantom. He was just a nice man who would make a fine husband.

But there would never be any passion there. She was positive of that. Beecham had not tried to kiss or touch her in any way during his appointment, but she knew despite that, his kisses would be just as mild and unassuming as he was. Unlike Daniel's kisses, which curled her toes and singed her insides.

Sighing, she leaned her head back on the chair, closing her eyes again, her mind drifting. She heard the men moving about, talking quietly as they made their way to bed, but she was suddenly too tired to bother getting up to go to bed herself. She knew she was falling asleep right there in the chair, but couldn't seem to rouse herself enough care.

She wasn't sure what it was that woke her. Perhaps it was a sound that disturbed her dreamless rest, or perhaps it was her neck, which was stiff and sore from nodding off in the chair. Whatever it was, she woke abruptly, her eyes darting around the dark room. The fire had gone out while she slept, but the smoky scent of it was still in the air.

Grimacing at the pain in her neck, she rubbed at it irritably and forced herself to get up. Bed was where she belonged. She stumbled toward the line of light beneath the salon door, thinking she would have to cuss out the men in the morning for such foolishness. They were obviously getting lazy on land if they were not even bothering to put the candles out before retiring. The last thing they needed was a fire.

The wave of warm, thick smoke that rolled over her as she opened the door was enough to wash such thoughts from her mind. The light had not been from candles at all, but from across the hall. The library door was open, and showed the fire licking its way up the drapes covering the window inside.

Bellowing at the top of her lungs for her men, Valoree hurried into the room, taking in the situation at a glance. The drapes were ablaze, and the fire was spreading from there. Running forward, she snatched at the curtains, ignoring the pain that shot through her fingers as she did, and ripping the drapes from the window. She let go as soon as they fell, then grabbed up her skirts and proceeded to try stomping on the flames. Someone grabbed her from behind and moved her out of the way.

"Get out of here! Your skirts'll catch fire. Go wake the others!" Henry shouted, pushing her toward the door.

Valoree hesitated, then left him to it and charged up the stairs, roaring at the top of her lungs as she went. One-Eye met her as she reached the upper landing.

"What's going on?" he asked, still half-asleep but waking up quickly.

"Fire," Valoree snapped, pausing to push Meg's door open without knocking. "Get up!" she yelled, hurrying in to shake the old woman awake. "Move it, Meg. We've got a fire below."

"What?" the woman muttered, sitting up groggily, then immediately began coughing. The smoke had followed Valoree upstairs and was now rolling across the ceiling in large, billowing waves.

"Come on!" Valoree tugged the woman out of bed, grabbed a wrap off the chair, tossed it around her shoulders, and bundled her quickly out of the room. She was just in time to see Bull and Skully head down the stairs. Hurrying the older woman along, Valoree ran her down the stairs and pulled the front door open.

She was about to shove Meg through when Henry shouted, "It's out!"

Pausing, she whirled to stare through the smoke-filled entry toward the men coming out of the library. "What?" she asked in amazement.

"It hadn't got far," he explained, waving his hand in front of his face and moving to join her where she and Meg now stood in the open door. "I managed to get the drapes put out, and your shout woke Petey. He came out of his room off the kitchen, grabbed a pail of water on the way, and threw that over the rest." He shrugged. "That was the end of that."

Sighing, Valoree sagged against the door frame, breathing in the fresh air that was rushing into the entry even as the smoke drifted slowly out. "What happened? What started it?"

Henry shook his head, pausing to cough, then spat out through the door before saying, "There was nothing that could have started it accidentally. I put the candle out after I finished writing them invites to Beecham and Hawghton."

"You're sure?" Valoree asked sharply, then took in the affronted look that immediately covered his face. Of course he was sure. Despite her thoughts on seeing the light under the salon door, she knew none of the men would make a mistake like that. Thirteen years had trained them well. You had to be extra careful about things like that on board ship. You couldn't run out a door, or climb out a window to escape a fire on a boat. Your only options were burning to death or jumping ship, then either drowning or being shark bait.

"Aye, I'm sure," he said testily. "Besides, it looked like the fire started with the drapes at the window behind the desk chair, and there ain't even a table there, let alone a candle that might have sparked it."

"It's a curse, that's what started it," Skully muttered. "Someone's put a curse of bad luck on us for sure,

209

'cause that's all we've had since we came to London."

"There's no curse," Valoree said impatiently as the men began to shift. There could never be a more superstitious lot of men than pirates. And the last thing she needed right now was for the men to start harping on bad luck, curses, and such. "As far as bad luck goes, aye, we've had some, but we've had good luck, too. We haven't lost a single man in five years of pirating. What other crew can claim that?" she snapped, then sighed and went on. "As for these 'accidents?' calling them a curse is foolishness."

"Aye, she's right," Henry agreed. "We can't just claim it's bad luck; there have been too many instances for that."

"And too many for them to be coincidence, even." she continued. "But they still could be. The first incidence we thought a robbery attempt, and it may have been. If so, we were lucky. They got away with naught and we suffered little but a knock on my head."

"What about the carriage accident?" One-Eye asked. "No-Nose broke his leg."

"Aye, and if you ask me that was luck, too. Had Henry, Meg, and I been in the carriage instead of riding behind in Lord Thurborne's hack, we would be dead now. No doubting it. I say one broken leg is better than three dead any day." She allowed that to sink in, then continued. "As for the fire, we were lucky again. It was caught early, it's out, and no one was hurt."

She sighed again, a frown twisting her mouth. There *had* been too much bad luck. Even she could see that, but she didn't want the men to get jumpy. "We *have* been lucky. But I want to make sure there is nothing to worry about. Tomorrow I want a couple of you men to go talk to the owner of the wagon again, and find out what you can. Then ask around near where the accident occurred, see if anyone saw where the fellow who was driving ran to."

"You think it wasn't an accident?" Henry said. Valoree paused.

"I don't know. I'd just feel better finding out what we can." She glanced over the men, then sighed. "I will see Lord Beecham and Hawghton again tomorrow and decide which of them to marry; then we can get out of here. Then it will be over. Now it's late. Why don't you men head off to bed?"

Meg was the first to turn away to leave, but the men did follow. Valoree stood staring around the library once they were gone, frowning at the fact that, somehow, a curtain with nothing nearby to hold a candle had been aflame. If she were the superstitious sort, she might believe it was a curse, or some such thing as Skully had suggested. But Valoree wasn't superstitious. She was slightly cynical. And to her the answer seemed quite clear that someone had set it.

But who?

Sighing, she left the library as well, but she didn't seek out her bed. Instead she crossed the hall to the salon, only to find Henry there, seated on the settee, dealing cards out on the low table before it.

"Hazard or hearts?" he asked as she moved to the sideboard to pour them both a drink.

"Hearts," Valoree murmured, carrying glasses over to join him. He knew her too well. She should have realized he would know she would not simply retire and risk another fire, or any such accident, befalling them while they slept. He had figured she would sit up all night to stand guard against any further "accidents" while everyone slept, and meant to keep her company.

Picking up the hand he had dealt himself, Henry

announced, "Skully and Bull are going to spot us in a couple of hours; then One-Eye and Petey will take over for them."

Valoree just grunted and picked up her cards.

# Chapter Eleven

Valoree closed the door behind Hawghton with a snap and turned to eye Henry. "When does Beecham get here?"

"He should be along shortly. I scheduled them one after the other. Hawghton left a little early."

"Aye, well, you can cross him off the list. Beecham it is," she announced, walking back into the salon.

A few minutes later, Valoree was sitting staring into the fire when Henry entered. Forcing herself to sit up and doing her best not to look as depressed as she felt, she raised an eyebrow in question. "Aye? What is it, Henry?"

"Well." The man hesitated, then straightened his shoulders and decided to get to the point without any shilly-shallying. "The men and I were talking, and we've decided ye shouldn't marry Beecham." Seeing her eyes narrow, fiercely, he quickly went on. "He's too weak for ye, Captain. Ye'd walk right over him; then ye'd loathe him for lettin' ye. Ye need someone stronger, like Thurborne there."

"I—" she began harshly, but he interrupted before she could blast him.

"So One-Eye's gone back to the boat to let the men know what's about, and have them take a vote on who we want ye to marry. I'm thinking they'll all vote for

Thurborne, too, once One-Eye tells 'em they should. We surely wouldn't have done this had we not known ye really like the man anyway. We've all caught ye shilly-shallying with him at one point or other during the last two weeks. We know ye like the fella."

Valoree flushed at his announcement, her face heating up like toast over the fire as she realized that she and Thurborne had been spotted in their passionate clinches.

"I—" she began furiously, but paused abruptly, her mind ticking over what he was saying. They were going to vote she should marry Thurborne. She'd get a lifetime with the man. It meant a lifetime battle for her independence, and a lifetime struggle not to be secondary to him, but also a lifetime of passion, of finally gaining satisfaction from the man, of his finally scratching the unbearable damn itch he had worked so hard at building within her. And it was not even as if she was giving in. They were basically forcing her to do it.

Or were they? If she gave in on this, mayhap they weren't forcing her at all, and weeks from now . . . well, perhaps months . . . Okay, it would probably be years. Years from now, when her itch was scratched and she came out of her desire-fogged state, she would awake to find she had given up her independence for something that would not last. She had to consider that. But she wasn't given the chance as Bull opened the door and rumbled, "Beecham."

Valoree frowned at the news that the man was there, then glanced at Henry. "If you have finished arranging my life?"

Nodding, Henry turned and moved toward the door. Bull stepped out of the way for Beecham to enter. Her "uncle" paused to greet him on the way out, then murmured something about instructing Petey to prepare a tea tray. With that he left them alone. Unlike he did whenever Daniel was present, this time Henry left the door open.

"Thurborne's not here?" Beecham asked in surprise. He came to join her by the fire.

Valoree made a face at the question. Apparently it had not gone without notice that Daniel always seemed to be hanging about. She hoped that he wasn't also aware of their "shilly-shallying," as Henry had put it. Beecham was too nice a man for her to wish his feelings or his pride hurt.

She blinked as that thought ran through her mind and stuck. Beecham was too nice a man for her to deliberately hurt. *Damn* . . . She was going soft! She would have blamed it on being in London, but she knew that wasn't the only reason behind it. It was Meg's influence, her disapproving looks, her gentle remonstrances.

It was also the dresses she was forced to go about in here in London. Meg had forced the men to return all her breeches and boots to the boat after she'd discovered her niece in them. That had left her with little choice but to go about with the air running up under her skirts, and those silly, useless slippers as her only foot covering. It was hard not to feel feminine in that gear. And it was also Daniel, with his kisses and caresses, making her feel like a woman for the first time in her life. But being a woman did not feel so bad when his arms were around her, and the heat was burning her up from the inside out.

Aye, she was going soft, she admitted with regret.

". . . that is why I have always admired Thurborne. I know *I* would never have had the courage to deal with and hunt down privateers and pirates."

"What?" Valoree cried in amazement as Beecham's words registered. Obviously she had missed a great deal of something that the man had been saying, and some very important things, too. Seeing his startled expression, she forced herself to speak more calmly. "I mean, I fear you spoke so fast I did not gather all that." It was true. If he had spoken slower, she might have tuned back in at an earlier point. "Hunt down pirates and privateers?"

"Aye. That is what he was doing in the Caribbean all those years. At first he was just the king's man, assessing the cargo of various privateers in the area and taking the king's forty percent. But then when that Captain Red died—Are you quite all right? You appear pale. Are you not feeling well?"

"Nay, I am fine." Valoree forced a smile to her lips. "I am just suffering an aching head. Please go on."

"Anyway, there was a famous privateer called Captain Red. Living in the Caribbean, you probably heard of him. It was rumored that he was actually a lord, trying to remake the fortune he had lost, but only the king and Thurborne would know for sure. At any rate, the poor fellow was captured by the Spanish, but it was just after he had turned in his cargo for assessing. They say that the Spanish were so furious at being cheated out of the treasure they had expected, they tortured him and his entire crew to death."

Not his whole crew, Valoree thought grimly. Only those who had been aboard at the time. A skeleton crew, just enough men to get Jeremy where he was to meet the assessor. She and the others had been in port, collecting the supplies they would need for the next trip out. And the Spanish had gotten the gold.

"But then rumors began to circulate," Beecham went on, "that Captain Red and his crew had come back from the dead to seek vengeance and wreak havoc on the Spanish for what had been done to them. Ship after ship after ship claimed that the dead captain and his crew appeared out of nowhere, out of the very mist, materializing suddenly on the deck of their ships. There was never any ship, just the crew."

Valoree's mouth twitched at that with nervous humor. Their attack on that first ship had worked so well, they had used it repeatedly: leaving the new *Valor* anchored in a safe cove, rowing out in a small piragua or two, then drilling holes in the small boats and climbing aboard their targeted ship to take it over. With each craft they had taken, the story of Back-from-the-Dead-Red had grown until the very sight of them on deck was enough to send the crew of whatever ship they boarded either to their knees to plead for their lives or scurrying to drop their own skiffs into the water to get away. That had left them with, not only whatever treasure each carried, but the ship itself to sell. That was how they had made the money they had needed to replace so quickly.

Of course, they had taken an occasional ship in the usual manner, chasing them down in the *Valor*, boarding, fighting, and winning, but always at dusk or dark when they could continue the charade of Back-from-the-Dead Red. Sailors were a damned superstitious lot, and that charade had given them the edge more times than not.

"The king was irate about this, of course," Beecham related. "Privateering is one thing, but pirating quite another."

"Yes," Valoree assented. *Good Lord, yes.* If the king didn't get his share, the whole letter of marque was null and void—even if the pirates in question attacked only the king's enemies, and never bothered their own countrymen or ships of countries that were allies. Unfortunately, when Jeremy had died, the name of the assessor and next meeting place arranged with the man had been lost as well. Thus, Valoree and the men had been unable to keep everything as aboveboard as they would have liked. Still, they had saved the king's portion, always counting it out painstakingly to be sure that his share was there. They had stored it in a warehouse here in London when they arrived, and waited for the king to contact them. She'd assumed he would as soon as he knew that Lady Ainsley was in London. He had known Captain Red was her brother, of course. But he had not yet called on them, and frankly, Valoree had been so wrapped up in this husband business, the matter had quite slipped her mind.

"So, since Thurborne was one of the few people besides himself who had met this Captain Red, the king sent him out to seek the truth of the matter— whether there really was a ghost pirate running amok out there, or if Captain Red had survived after all and was taking advantage of the tales of his death to keep the entire portion of the treasures he took."

Valoree blinked in surprise. She had never considered anyone might think that, but, she supposed it made sense. Unfortunately, she had more important things to consider. For instance, what this all meant to her and the men. If Thurborne had been the assessor, then he knew that Jeremy was Captain Red. And if he knew that, he knew she was his sister. So why had he not come to her and requested information? Why not ask her the truth of the matter? Had he been hanging about all this time in the hope of learning some further information for the king?

Quite suddenly she remembered the night before and what had happened after the carriage accident. She had unthinkingly mentioned the ship. Daniel had heard her and echoed the word. Valoree had fully expected him to question her on the matter once they returned to the town house, but he had not. He had merely kissed and caressed her, then left. But he had not returned this morning as was his usual habit. Where was he? Out looking for her ship? And now that she was thinking along those lines, she recalled all the times he had emphasized certain words like *uncle* or *your island* or *the Caribbean* with some hidden meaning. She had

217

paid little attention, and had wasted little concern over such matters at the time, but she was now beginning to attach a terrible significance to them.

Mayhap they should not have waited for the king to send someone around. Mayhap he would not. Mayhap he would merely have them all arrested and hanged.

Cursing, she leaped to her feet and started for the door.

"Is there something amiss, my lady?"

Valoree paused, then glanced back blankly at Beecham. She had quite forgotten all about his presence. Recovering herself, she managed a smile. "Nay, my lord. It just suddenly occurred to me to wonder where that tea is that my uncle said he would have sent. I will not be a moment," she assured him, then slid out into the hall to find herself facing Henry, Pete, One-Eye, Bull, Skully, and Meg. They all stood there, huddled in conversation, but fell silent and turned to face her as she closed the door.

"What?" she began, scowling. Henry held up his hand to silence her.

"One-Eye and Skully just got back from the ship, and the crew has voted. Ye marry Thurborne."

"You men are incredible," she said with disgust. "You cannot vote on a thing like that. I shall marry whom I please."

"Nay, according to the contracts—"

"According to the contracts, any decision that affects you men and your life aboard ship is up to the vote," she said shortly. "So, aye, mayhap you could force me to marry, but once I marry and reclaim Ainsley, your lives aboard ship end. Then you become land rats. And that means all your contracts are null and void. So I will marry whom I please, and I am marrying Beecham. In fact, I am going to go tell him so right now."

Turning on her heel, she threw the door open and marched right back in, closing the door behind her with a slam. She was so angry, she was halfway across the room before she realized that she had not told them about Thurborne, and that they would still have to take care of that situation right away. Sighing, she whirled reluctantly back, then changed her mind. She could tell them all about that later. First she would arrange things with Beecham.

Smiling, she returned to her chair and had just seated herself when the door opened and Meg rushed in. "Oh. Hello, Lord Beecham," she said brightly, ignoring Valoree's glare as she moved to join them. "How are you today?"

"My lady." Beecham stood at once, bending to kiss the older woman's hand when it was offered. Valoree sat frozen, throwing glares at the woman that were studiously ignored.

She had no doubt that this was supposed to prevent her from announcing Beecham as her choice for a husband. Meg had made herself scare every other time that John Beecham had been present. Valoree was not sure if it had been because she feared being recognized as his scandalous aunt, or if the sight of him just brought back the pain of the rift with her sister. Still, whatever it was, Meg had always chosen to absent herself when he was about, leaving Henry to tend to the matter of chaperoning—a job he had done miserably, allowing her countless moments of fraternizing with a man who was most likely trying to get them all hanged.

"How handsome you look this afternoon, my lord," Meg was saying, seating herself beside Beecham on the settee and beaming at him widely. "You must tell me who your tailor is so that Henry can pay him a visit. The clothesmaker we have been using is barely adequate."

"Oh, well, I would be pleased to share his name," the man assured her quietly. "He is quite the best one in town, in my opinion, Top-quality work at a fair price."

"Oh, marvelous. It is so hard to find that nowadays, is it not? So many overcharge and—"

"Aunt Meg," Valoree interrupted in a warning tone, and Meg turned to her innocently.

"Yes, dear?"

"I was about to speak of something important with Lord Beecham."

"Were you, dear?" she murmured, then brightened as the door to the salon opened and Petey entered, carrying a tray. Henry was hard on his heels. "Oh, look. Here is the tea!"

Sighing, Valoree sat back in her seat impatiently and crossed her arms. They could delay all they liked, but she *would* marry Beecham. She watched with grim displeasure as the two men walked to her side. Pausing there, Petey held the tray silently as Henry lifted a cup of tea and offered it to her.

Giving him a you-are-pushing-your-luck-mightily stare, she reached impatiently for the cup. But her pesky crew did not move on then; they stood waiting. Valoree arched her eyebrows irritably. "What?"

"Ye have to try it," Henry announced, adding when Valoree began to frown, "Petey's afraid he may have made it too strong."

Rolling her eyes, Valoree lifted the cup to her mouth and took a curious sip, nearly spitting it out in surprise. There was heated spiced rum in the cup.

"Something wrong?" Henry asked innocently, giving her a wink when she glanced up at him. Valoree shook her head, her shoulders relaxing.

" 'Tis perfect," she said quietly, knowing that this was Henry's way of saying he was sorry. From the time that she had boarded the *Valor* at the age of eleven, any time she was feeling sick or just plain unhappy, Henry had always brought her some heated, spiced rum. Of course, Jeremy had not known that. At least, she didn't think he had known. But just the taste of the warm drink on her tongue made her soften toward him affectionately. As unlikely as it seemed, this crusty old pirate had been the equivalent of nanny, friend, and tutor to Valoree from the moment she had become Valerian. And he still was her friend, confidant, and even tutor in some ways. Especially when she was reacting in anger rather than using her head; then he always settled her down and helped her to see what she was doing.

"Drink up. Tea's good for what ails ye, and there's plenty of it," Henry said cheerfully as he moved around her chair toward the settee, Petey following.

Smiling slightly, Valoree took another drink, enjoying the spiced flavor and the warm, fuzzy feeling it gave her as it went down.

"Thank you, Henry," Meg murmured, accepting her own cup as Henry took it from the tray and carefully handed it to her. Lifting it to her lips, she took a sip and smiled as she swallowed it. "Oh, my. It is good, is it not?" she asked, smiling at Valoree, who grinned back, nodding as she took another swallow.

Valoree knew darned well that Meg's cup would not have rum in it. Despite the way she had tried to fool them all at first that she was a drunk, she didn't drink much at all. Her cup would hold tea and nothing else. Of that she was sure, and the thought of the trick that she and Henry were putting over on them struck her suddenly as quite funny, making her chuckle aloud.

Henry and Petey paused on the way to Beecham to turn to glance at her with amusement. Meg lifted one querying eyebrow. "Something funny, dear?"

Valoree shook her head. "Jusss thinking," she murmured, frowning when she heard the slur of her own voice.

"Oh, well, drink up," Meg murmured. Valoree nodded, dutifully swallowing another gulp, then leaning back in her seat with a sigh as she watched Henry continue toward Beecham. She was suddenly quite tired. She supposed it was the lack of sleep last night, when she and Henry had sat up playing cards and guarding against another "accident." She hadn't really lost much sleep, though, just a couple of hours; then One-Eye and Bull had taken over for them. Or had it been Petey and Skully? Mayhap it had been Skully and One-Eye, or Petey and Bully—*Oops, Bull*. She chuckled again, and Henry paused in the process of lifting Beecham's teacup off the tray.

"All done? Shall I fetch you more?" he asked pleasantly.

"Oh, aye." Swallowing the last of her drink, she held the cup out, laughing again as it teetered and swayed before her.

An exclamation drew her gaze to Beecham to see the teacup Henry had been holding tumbling out of his hand and down toward the nobleman. It seemed to Valoree to fall in slow motion. She saw it turn upside down as it went, the liquid spilling down to hit the man on the shoulder, splashing down the front of his waistcoat even as the cup finally caught up, bouncing off his shoulder and smashing to the ground in a thousand pieces.

Falling back into her seat, Valoree began to laugh uproariously as she let the cup she held drop to the floor. It was all too funny—especially their expressions. Beecham was jumping up with alarm, his eyes wide as those of a fish. Meg was looking horribly apologetic and leaping and jumping around like a frog as she wrung her hands. Henry was doing his best to mop up the mess up with Petey's help as they urged Beecham toward the salon door. Oh, it was hysterical!

\* \* \*

"Really, this is awful, I am so sorry. Please forgive us," Meg murmured worried and repeatedly even as Henry closed the door behind the departing man, then leaned weakly against the wall beside it. She sighed miserably. "I wish there had been another way."

"Well, there wasn't, so it's no good fretting over it," Henry assured her quietly, then reached out to pat her shoulder awkwardly as Petey hurried back into the salon to check on Valoree. "Does he know ye're his mother?"

Meg froze at that, her eyes going wide. "I—He is not—"

"He's yer son," Henry said firmly and dryly. "And there's no doubting it. Your sister may look quite a bit like you, but she hasn't got those lovely blue-as-the-sky eyes with the gold flecks. I doubt anyone does."

"*You* could tell Lady Beecham was my sister, too?" she asked in alarm. "Dear Lord, what if everyone—"

"Everyone hasn't figured it out," Henry reassured her quickly. "Valoree has a good eye. She recognized ye were sisters, then talked to ye about it. Afterward she told me. I don't think even she has figured out that Beecham's yer son, though. The only eyes she's been looking into lately is Thurborne's."

"Aye." Meg sighed. "I do not understand why she is so set against marrying him. He is perfect for her. My John . . ." she paused, flushing slightly, then continued, "Well, John is a nice young man, but he is no match for her."

"Not yet," Henry agreed quietly. "But he'll become stronger. He is still quite young. He needs a little seasoning, is all—seasoning he never would have got had he married Valoree. She'd have stepped on him and kept him there under her foot until his spirit died."

"She's asleep."

They both turned to glance at Petey as he came out into the hall to make that announcement.

"Good. The potion worked," Henry murmured wearily.

"Aye," Petey agreed quietly. "But she ain't gonna like it much when she wakes up and figures out what we did."

"It's for her own good," Henry said defensively. "We're trying to save her from making a mistake she'd regret the rest of her life." Turning, he peered down the hallway toward the kitchens. "One-Eye! Skully! Bull!"

The three men came out of the kitchens on the double, a question in their eyes. But only One-Eye asked what they were all wondering. "Is it done? Did it work?"

"Aye. Bull, go fetch her out to the carriage. Skully, help Meg bundle up some of those fine dresses for us to take with us."

"What do you want us to do?" One-Eye asked, moving up beside Petey as the other two men and Meg moved off to do what he had asked of them.

"We need to move the chests out and make sure everything is locked up tight. Who knows how long it will take ere we convince those two they are meant for each other?" Henry paused, clicking his tongue in irritation. "And I'd best send a message to Beecham, tell him we're off to the country for a bit. This town house is paid up for another five months and he might wonder if we just disappear."

"What about Thurborne?" Pete asked as Bull carried an unconscious Valoree out of the salon.

"We'll collect him after we get the captain back to the ship," Henry announced, reaching to open the door for Bull, only to freeze when a knock sounded on the other side. Bull immediately changed direction, turning away from the door and continuing across the entry and on into the library with Valoree. Henry grabbed

Petey's arm and pulled him out of sight on the other side of the door, then gestured for One-Eye to open it.

Daniel rapped his cane on the door, then set it on the ground and turned to peer idly up the road as he waited for it to be answered. He was running a bit late. He had hoped to have all his questions answered and to have gotten here by noon, but the answers he had received to his questions had not been satisfactory. He had wasted the whole morning and a good portion of the afternoon finding out nothing. So much for his hopes of being able to sort out the mess that seemed to be swirling around Valoree. And it seemed to him to be a rather huge one.

First, there was the matter of Back-from-the-Dead Red. The king had finally heard that Lady Ainsley was in London in search of a husband. He was demanding answers now regarding her brother's demise, or lack thereof. Daniel had rather hoped the man wouldn't find out for a bit longer. At least until Daniel had gotten her to trust him and give up her stubborn resistance to marrying him. He knew if he didn't get her to agree before she found out about his past, she probably wouldn't trust him enough afterward.

Daniel grimaced at himself and the spot he was in. He had never before been interested enough in any woman to do more than offer her a quick roll in the linens—or possibly two. Yet here was a woman who wanted that roll and nothing else, and he was the one who wanted more. Hell, he wanted it all. She was unlike any woman he had ever met. She was strong, intelligent, decisive. He respected her. He also wanted her with an ache that was beyond anything he had before experienced. The last two weeks had been hell. He had thought that was so damn clever when he had decided that he would use her desire for him to crumble her defenses and convince her to marry him. If he had realized the agony of torture he would be causing himself . . . Well, hell, he still would have gone ahead with the plan. He was even beginning to think it might be working. Or perhaps he was just fooling himself, he thought wryly, and sighed.

This woman was a magnet for trouble, though. First there was the king and his desire to solve this Back-from-the-Dead Red business; then there were the rash of accidents around her. They had decided at the time that she was knocked out that she had probably walked in on and surprised someone out to rob her. And he probably would have been satisfied with that if it were not for the carriage accident. That had bothered him a great deal. And the description her men had given of how it had occurred was positively worrisome. From what was said, it had almost sounded as though the crash was deliberate. Daniel had been doubtful enough of its being an accident, and he had decided to look into it.

But Valoree's "servants" had beaten him to it, already talking to everyone he had thought to ask—from the various household help of each place on the street where the accident had taken place, to the owner of the wagon itself. They had all mentioned that a fellow with a patch over his eye, and a mate of his who was as big as a mountain and dark as death, had been by to ask the same questions. Daniel had at once recognized the descriptions as fitting two of Valoree's rather disreputable manservants. He had also learned from the owner of the wagon that the fellow with the patch on his eye had mentioned a fire at the town house late last night.

It had all only left Daniel more convinced than ever that there was something going on, but he hadn't a clue exactly what or why—just that Valoree was as much a magnet to trouble as she was a magnet to him. And that he had best resolve all this soon, before someone got killed—or he died from unsatisfied desire. He just had to convince her to marry him; then he could lay his cards on the table, tell her all, and together they could work out everything. So today he was determined to get her to agree to marry him—even if he had to blackmail her with his knowledge that she was Back-from-the-Dead-Red to do it.

The opening of the door drew Daniel from his thoughts, and he turned to find the servant Valoree called One-Eye peering out at him. The man's one good eye widened incredulously at the sight of him; then he slammed the door in his face. Astonished, Daniel could hear excited chatter from the other side of the door. Unfortunately, the wood muffled it enough that he couldn't tell what was being said.

Shaking his head in disbelief, he rapped firmly on the door again. It opened almost at once this time, and Daniel arched one eyebrow with incredulity. "Lord Thurborne to see—"

"I'm not daft; I know who ye are," the man muttered in disgust. "I'll see if she's in."

The door slammed in his face again.

Shaking his head in bewilderment, Daniel sighed and prepared to wait. It seemed they were playing a new game. Hard to get, perhaps? Or let-the-randy-bastard-wait-on-the-doorstep-until-I'm-ready-to-grant-him-an-audience?

The door opened again, all the way this time, and One-Eye gestured for him to enter, then peered out at the street as he did. "Is that yer carriage?"

Daniel glanced out and nodded. "Aye."

"Hmmm." He didn't look pleased at the news. Frowning, he pushed the door closed, then motioned toward the door to the salon. "Well, go on in. She'll be along directly."

Shaking his head, Daniel turned and walked into the salon. He considered making himself a drink, then decided to wait until Valoree arrived. He had barely come to rest in a chair, when her Uncle Henry entered, followed by a man he recognized as the cook.

"Good day, Lord Thurborne. How are you?" Henry asked cheerfully. He didn't wait for an answer, but announced, "Valoree will be along in a moment, but she asked me to see to yer comfort and offer you a refreshment, so Pete mixed up a couple of special warmed spiced rums for us."

"Warmed spiced rum?" Daniel asked curiously, accepting the cup Henry lifted off the tray and handed to him.

"Aye. They're real tasty and warm the stomach, helping a body to relax." He took a cup off the tray himself, nodded at the other man, who immediately turned to leave, then seated himself across from Daniel. He smiled at him over his own cup as he lifted it for a sip. "Try it. Ye've never had anything like it."

# *Chapter Twelve*

Valoree felt like hell. Her mouth was as dry as Jasper's smile, and her head felt like it was splitting in half. She was pretty sure of that. Grasping it in both hands, she held on to it tightly, just to make sure her brains didn't fall out. Then she slowly, carefully opened her eyes—only to blink them closed again rather quickly. She'd died and gone to hell for her sins. That was the only explanation for the burning blur of light that attacked her eyes upon opening them.

Groaning, she tried to lie still for a moment, then realized that it wasn't *her* moving; it was the bed. *Dear*

*Lord!* Someone or something was moving the bed about while she lay on it. Forcing her eyes open, again, she raised herself up on her elbows and squinted about in the hope of discovering who it was, only to find there was no one there. It didn't take her poor woolly mind more than a minute or two after that before she realized that the bed she lay in wasn't the huge four-poster from the town house, but the wee hard cot of a ship. Her ship. She was on the *Valor*, and that was what was moving.

How the devil had she gotten here? she wondered, dropping weakly back onto her bunk. The last thing she remembered was . . . *Hmmm. What was the last— Oh, aye! Beecham!* She had been about to arrange things with Beecham. That was it. But then Meg had come in, and then Henry and Petey had brought the tea. Only it hadn't been tea. At least hers hadn't been. Henry had fixed her some of his special hot spiced rum and—

Her eyes blinking open again abruptly, she rose up in the bed like the resurrected dead, roaring at the top of her lungs. *"Henry!"*

"So you decided to kidnap the two of us and *force* us to wed?" Daniel asked in disbelief.

Henry shifted. He stood a few feet from the bed, where Daniel now sat rubbing his sore head. "Aye. Well, she's too damned stubborn to marry ye elsewise, and you two belong together. Ye're perfect for each other. Just being around ye has softened her up some already. And ye need a woman who will be a challenge, else ye'd lose interest right quick."

Daniel raised his head to stare at him. "You know so much about me in such a short time?"

Henry shrugged. "Ye learn to take the measure of folk right quick in our line of work."

"Speaking of which, what exactly *is* your line of

work?" Daniel asked silkily. Henry pursed his lips, considering the matter briefly, then shook his head.

"I think I'll just let you and the captain sort that one out."

Daniel grunted, then pressed his hands to either side of his head. "What the hell was in that damn drink you gave me?"

"Head's bothering ye, huh?" Henry asked solicitously.

Daniel impaled him with his eyes, then suddenly frowned as a thought occurred to him. "How did you get me out of the town house without my driver causing an uproar?"

"In a chest."

"A chest?" Daniel cried.

"Aye." Henry grimaced at his upset. "We put ye in Valoree's dress chest and carted ye out."

"And Valoree?" he asked dryly.

"We wrapped her in a tapestry."

"Great, I . . ." Daniel began, then paused as a sudden bellow, not unlike the sound a wounded bear might make, reached them from the next cabin. "Correct me if I am wrong," he murmured with sudden amusement, "but I do believe that was *your* name she was singing out in her *soft* voice."

Henry's mouth tightened, his eyes narrowing on Daniel at the comment; then he sighed and turned toward the door.

"Just a moment." Daniel stood, grabbing at the nearest item at hand to steady himself. It turned out to be a chair. He waited until the other man had turned back questioningly, then said, "Whatever you gave me has left me with a weak stomach. If I do not get out on deck and breathe some fresh air soon, you will be sending someone in here to scrape the contents of my stomach off the floor."

"Go ahead," Henry told him. "Ye're not a prisoner.

Ye're a guest." Then he left, closing the door behind him.

Daniel stared at the door in amazement for a moment, then shook his head. "A guest. Of course. I do not know why I thought otherwise." Shrugging, he started cautiously across the floor.


Henry wasn't quick enough. Valoree was off the bed and on her third shout for the man by the time her cabin door opened and he stuck his head warily inside. Spying her standing, grasping the edge of her desk for balance as she tried to shake off the last of the effects of the drug he had given her, the man forced an innocent smile. "Aye, Captain?"

"Don't you 'Aye, Captain' me, you—" she began, taking a threatening step toward him; then she paused to grasp the desk again as the room swayed dangerously about her. "What have you done?" she snapped. Then, before he could answer: "Never mind that. I can see what you've done. Well, it won't work. How far out of port are we?"

Henry didn't question how she knew they had left the London docks. She had lived on a boat long enough to tell the difference between the relative calm of a harbor and the roll of the sea. "About a day out," he admitted. Her mouth tightened.

"Well, you get your arse up there and tell them to turn the ship around. We're going back!"

"Ah, now, captain-girl," he started in a wheedling tone. It died as her gaze narrowed on him.

"Stow it, Henry. I'm so mad at you I could—" She almost seemed to choke on her anger, then waved him away in disgust. "Get out! I'll give the orders myself. But know this, Henry: you men haven't stopped anything. I *will* return and I *will* marry Beecham. All you've managed to do is delay it."

Henry hesitated, then twisted and backed out of the

cabin, closing the door quietly behind him.

Muttering under her breath several things she would like to do to the man, Valoree made her way cautiously to the chest by the bed and knelt beside it. Throwing it open, she rifled through it briefly until she found her knee breeches, white shirt, boots, belt, and short waistcoat, then began to undress where she sat, transforming from Lady Ainsley into Captain Valerian in a matter of moments. Then she crawled back to her feet and stumbled for the door, pausing only to grab up her cutlass, knife, and pistol on the way. She needed some fresh air, or she'd surely puke up whatever it was Henry had put in her drink—if there was anything left in her stomach to heave out, which was doubtful.

She felt better the moment she stepped out onto the deck. The roiling in her stomach died an abrupt death as she turned her face up to the sun and drew fresh sea air into her lungs. She had missed this like a starving man misses food. Fresh clean breezes, not the foul-smelling, polluted air in London. And the constant overwhelming racket that was the city: the rattle of wagons, the clip-clop of horses, the shouts of vendors selling their wares. None of that assaulted her ears. Here there was only the clang of the rigging, the sound of the waves hitting the hull, the whisper of the breeze, and the flap of the sails. Dear Lord, how she had missed this. Maybe she wouldn't punish the men too harshly for this action, after all. Maybe she could forgive them this. She already felt rejuvenated after only a few moments. And it was only a two-day delay of her plans.

Aye, she decided, a peaceful smile curving her lips as she peered around at the crew, who all watched her with wary attention. She would . . . hang them all by their damn toes from the rigging!

"What the hell is *he* doing here!" she roared, her gaze having found and frozen on Daniel.

In the silence that followed her cry, Daniel merely smiled at her crookedly. "Back-from-the-Dead Red, I presume?"

Valoree's eyes widened on the man calmly crossing the deck toward her, dressed in only a shirt and breeches, his hair a bit mussed, and a charming smile on his face. He was as handsome and appealing as she had ever seen him. Her heart turned over in her chest.

"Bull," she said calmly.

"Aye." The tall man was at her side at once.

"Take Lord Thurborne up to the crow's nest and hang him."

Daniel gaped at her in the brief silence that followed, hardly noticing how pale she had suddenly gone, or that her hands were clenched into tight fists, knowing only that she had just sentenced him to death.

"Ye can't be hanging him!" Henry cried in dismay.

"Aye!" One-Eye backed the quartermaster up. "We brought him here to marry ye!"

She silenced the men with a gesture, then turned, her expression as smooth and emotionless as stone. "I am still the captain of this ship, unless you men want to vote me out of the position right now. And, as captain, it is my job to see to your safety—even if you idiots are too damn stupid to tend to it yourself!"

"Now just a danged minute! We—"

"You brought one of the king's spies aboard ship. Specifically, the very one the king assigned the task of finding and bringing in Back-from-the-Dead Red and his crew."

There was a sudden silence at that, uncertainty beginning to show on every face.

"And, that is about as far from intelligent as I want to see you men get."

"Spy?" Henry said after a moment. "Are ye sure?"

"Aye. Beecham told me last night. Or the other day. Whatever damn day it was that you perpetrated this ridiculous folly. He was the king's assessor in the Caribbean. He was the only one besides the king who knew what Jeremy looked like, and his true identity. He was sent to track us down. Now"—she turned to Bull—"do as I say. And do it quick. And make sure his neck breaks when you throw him over; I don't want him to suffer. None of this is his fault."

Nodding unhappily, the man grabbed for Daniel.

"Now just a damn minute," Daniel snapped, dodging. "I was the king's assessor, that is true, but I am not to bring you in, just question you."

He stopped talking and concentrated on struggling with Bull as the larger man tried to grab him. In the end, others had to step forward to help. It took eight men to entirely subdue him. They ended up having to tie his hands behind his back and his feet together so that Bull could sling him over his shoulder and cart him toward the main mast. One-Eye and Jackson followed.

"Never mind none. She won't be hanging ye," One-Eye whispered as they neared the mast. "She's just letting off some steam. The captain has a bit of a temper."

Bull shrugged his shoulder, getting a better grip on Daniel before rumbling, "One-Eye's right enough on that. She'll let us get ye up there and all; then old Henry will talk her some sense. Then she'll change her mind. Happens all the time."

"She often decides to have people killed?" Daniel asked incredulously as he bobbed on Bull's shoulder, then lifted his head to try to avoid knocking it repeatedly against the man's wide back.

"Nay," One-Eye admitted reluctantly. "As far as I can recall, she's never ordered it afore." When Daniel cursed at that, he added calmly, "But then that just proves what I'm saying. She's not ordered anyone killed ere now, so she's not likely to start with you. She likes you."

"You could have fooled me," Daniel said, letting his head drop down again wearily. The muscles in his neck were beginning to ache from holding his head at such an awkward angle.

"I don't know, One-Eye," the other fellow trailing argued. "She looked pretty riled to me. 'Sides, ye're wrong, she has so ordered someone killed. Twice now."

"She did not," One-Eye denied.

"Aye, she did. Lemmy and Jake. They was hung, then tossed overboard for shark bait."

One-Eye's mouth tightened grimly. "Those were the rules, Jackson. We all know the rules. We were told 'em ere we ever signed up. Yer to leave 'prudent women' alone if they're unwilling, else yer done in. We all know that."

"Aye," Jackson agreed with disgust, then turned to Daniel's bouncing head to explain, "It's a woman thing. She's a woman, so she hands out harsh punishment against a man who messes with women."

"It's *not* a woman thing," One-Eye snapped impatiently. "That rule was made by her brother when he ran the ship. He got it from the rules of Captain John Philips. It's not a woman thing at all. 'Tain't decent to be forcing somethin' on a lady that she don't want, and if ye're having to be told that, ye'll most like be hanging from the crow's nest someday, too. Ain't you got a sister or nothing?"

"No."

"What of a mother? I know ye gots one of them. Everyone has one of them. How would ye like to go to visit her one day and find some snake trying to force hisself on her?"

Jackson shrugged. "I'd be asking what she was doing letting him in the house in the first place."

"Aye, he'll be hanging from the crow's nest some-day," Bull rumbled grimly.

"And just like she did for Lemmy and Jake, she'll simply say, 'You know what must be done,' then leave and wait in her cabin," One-Eye predicted. He peered down at Daniel and explained. "She's got no stomach for killing. It's why I'm sure she ain't really meaning to hang ye. She ain't gone to her cabin. She's still standing on the deck, letting Henry yammer at her. She's just sharpening her spleen some. Ye'll see."

Daniel fervently hoped so as the man called Bull lugged him up the rope ladder toward the crow's nest above. Tied and trussed as he was, fighting was no longer an option. His life was fully in the hands, and at the whim, of the woman standing on the deck below watching them. Daniel's life had never been in any but his own hands before. Not another human's, anyway. It was a new experience—one he didn't like very much. Not very much at all.

"Here we are," One-Eye announced as Bull set Daniel down. The man said it as cheerfully as if they had just arrived at the theater.

"Well," Jackson said as the three men now glanced down at the deck, "she's not yelling at us to stop yet."

"Nope," Bull agreed unhappily.

"She's still watching, though."

"Yep," the other two men said.

"Looks pretty angry still, too. She don't look quite ready to spare him."

"Nope."

"I'm thinking she's still wanting to hang him."

"Seems so," One-Eye said, his voice heavy with dis-appointment.

They were all silent.

"Did you bring the rope?"

One-Eye frowned at that question from Bull and shook his head. "Seemed a waste of time. Expected her to call a halt the moment we got up here."

"Hmmm."

"I'd best go down and fetch some, huh?" Jackson suggested.

"Aye. Mayhap the delay'll give her a chance to remember she's not bloodthirsty."

Nodding, the man started down the rope, and One-Eye and Bull turned their attention back to their captain.

"I don't know," Bull rumbled with a shake of his head. "She's looking pretty mean."

"Always did have a temper," One-Eye muttered.

"Aye."

"And she sure is riled this morning. His calling her Back-from-the-Dead Red probably didn't help."

"Yep." They turned to glare at Daniel briefly for being foolish enough to do so; then Bull nudged One-Eye and nearly sent him tumbling out of the crow's nest. "And you thought they would be perfect for each other."

"You agreed," the fellow said mildly, steadying himself.

"Aye, I did. Guess we were wrong," he said sadly. "Here comes Jackson back with the rope."

"What's Henry doing down there?" One-Eye asked as Jackson mounted the last of the ladder and handed up the rope.

"Babbling his head off, tryin' to convince her to spare him," Jackson announced. Bull began to attach the rope to the rail.

"What's she saying to his babble?"

"That his knowledge could put us all at risk, something we should have thought of ere bringing him here. That her job is to lead us and keep us safe, and it is a job she has to see to."

"Hmm. That's true enough," One-Eye agreed with a sad sigh. "I see Richard and Petey are on deck now."

"Hmm. They're trying to assure her that Danny here won't talk none if they just are allowed to chat with him."

"She buying that?"

"Not for a bowl of beans."

They all sighed, then Bull finished tying the rope and sighed. "Shame."

"Real shame."

"Pity."

"She'll regret it later," One-Eye assured Daniel quietly as he slid the noose over his neck.

"Most likely she don't even like it now," Bull commented, scooping him up and carrying him to the edge. "She can't stomach killing."

Daniel could feel the large man's arms tense as he prepared to heave him off the rail. Silently he began to pray.

"You cannot, you simply cannot, do this!" Henry cried with dismay, watching Bull fit the noose around Thurborne's neck. "He is a lord, a—"

"He is a threat to each and every one of you now that he knows who you are. If we return him to London, he will head right to the king to turn us all in."

"Not if you marry him. If you marry him, he'd become master of this ship. The welfare of all these men would be his. Look, this isn't his fault. At least give him the chance. Marry him, bed him a couple times. Get with child; then, if he doesn't come around and look like he'll keep the secret, we can make ye a widow. But you'll have fulfilled the requirements of your father's will. Then we can still claim the land." Henry watched her jaw tighten, her expression telling him that she was at least considering the idea. He had to restrain himself from telling her to think a bit quicker as he glanced warily up at the crow's nest. Bull was lifting Thurborne into the air in preparation to toss him over. If she thought too long, it would be too late, but he already knew pestering her wouldn't work. She did what she wanted, in her own time, too. She always had.

"Halt," she called suddenly to the men above. Henry tried not to sag with relief as she began to pace before him. It was obvious she hadn't made up her mind, but he wouldn't pester her. It wouldn't help if he did. All he could do was wait until she had thought it out.

When she suddenly stopped to whirl and face him, Henry felt himself stiffening to attention anxiously. "Very well, Henry. I'll marry the bastard to save your hide and his. But if he doesn't show signs of coming around right quick, you will be making me a widow. You *personally*."

He nodded solemnly, hiding his relief as she continued. "And I won't be either forgetting or forgiving this action, you sneaky old tar."

"What did she say?" Bull asked, glancing down at the deck where the captain appeared to be chewing Henry out.

"Sounded like 'Halt' to me," One-Eye muttered, peering hopefully down.

"Nay, it was 'Toss.' " Jackson joined them at the railing.

"Toss?"

"Aye, as in 'Toss 'im.' Toss him over."

"She wouldn't say 'Toss,' " One-Eye snapped impatiently. "She'd say, 'Get on with it,' or 'Throw him over,' or maybe even 'Toss him over,' but she wouldn't just say 'Toss.' "

"Well, I think she said 'Toss,' " Jackson said a bit peevishly.

"I'm pretty sure it was 'Halt,' " One-Eye argued. Bull agreed. "Sounded like 'Halt' to me."

"Me, too," Daniel supplied.

"See, that's three to one."

"Well, he *would* say that, wouldn't he?" Jackson asked with disgust.

"Hoy!"

They stopped arguing at that second shout, and Bull leaned a little farther over the side, dangling Daniel a little farther over too, as he peered at the man who had called—Henry.

"Fetch him down!"

Relaxing, Bull stepped back from the rail and set Daniel on his feet.

"There, ye see?" One-Eye commented with obvious relief, stepping forward to remove the noose from his neck. "I told ye she wouldn't see ye dead. 'Tweren't yer fault ye're here."

Daniel merely stared at him numbly. He was rather numb all over, actually. He couldn't seem to feel a thing: not his legs, not his arms, not even anger. He was just numb.

Other than removing the noose from around his neck, they did not bother to untie him further. Bull simply slung him over his shoulder, then swung out onto the rope ladder, carting him down just as he had carted him up. Despite the awkward position, Daniel was rather grateful. He did not know that he could have managed the climb down—what with not being able to feel his legs and all.

Valoree watched grimly until the men were halfway back down the ladder, then glared at Henry and turned to stalk back into her cabin. The men had certainly gotten her into a fix this time. She had truly thought she would have to see the man dead. She hadn't wanted to, and had felt a shredding sensation in her chest as the man was led up the ladder to the crow's nest. That shredding had intensified a hundred-fold as she had seen them place the noose around his neck, but she had truly seen no alternative. Her brother had left these men in her care. The knowledge Daniel now held, thanks to their foolish interference, had made him a terrible threat to them all. It was her job to see he never betrayed them. Just as it was his job to betray them.

But if she married him, something she had been resisting doing from the start, the men became his responsibility by English law. He would hardly turn himself in. Not that she was pleased to be giving up control this way, but faced with that or seeing an innocent man, king's spy or no, dead, well . . .

Sighing, she dropped into her chair wearily. Mayhap she had been dreaming anyway to imagine that she could marry and retain her independence, even if she had married someone like Beecham. Legally he would have been lord over her and all she owned anyway, and the men might very well have accepted that.

Pirates they might be, but they were oddly traditional for all that. Hence the reason she had pretended to be a male for the past thirteen years. In truth, she might be grateful for the change as well. While there was a certain amount of satisfaction ordering these men about, some of the responsibility weighed heavily. Her decision today, for instance. There was no pleasure in ordering the death of a man. None whatsoever. She had done it twice before, but those times the men had been scurvy dogs deserving of their fate. Too, she had left the men to the chore and retreated to her cabin. It was not that she lacked the courage to watch it, but simply that she had no desire to. She did not care to watch garbage being tossed over the side of the ship each day either.

As for Daniel, he had been a different proposition entirely. His death, were she forced to see to it, was not of his own making, or even remotely his fault. The blame lay solely on the shoulders of her men. That put her in a quandary. She would have to punish them for that. They had gone on their own initiative and done something they had known she would not wish, and their actions had resulted in what could still mean the death of a blameless man. That was why she had not been able to leave the deck during his execution. He did not deserve to die, and she felt she had to acknowledge that by witnessing it.

But mayhap now he would not have to die. Not if he would still marry her. The tap at the door when it came did not surprise her. Nor was she surprised when Henry entered. She had expected as much, desired him to follow her, even. That was why she had glared at him hard before coming to her cabin. He had, as usual, understood.

Now he closed the door of her cabin and faced her solemnly, waiting for her to speak.

"He may still have to swing," she announced abruptly.

Henry grimaced. "It's all my fault."

"Aye, it is," she agreed heavily.

The quarter master sighed. "How many lashes?"

Valoree glanced away with a frown. Henry already knew that he would be receiving punishment, or mayhap he was assuring her with his words that he understood she had to inflict it to maintain control of the ship. Also even that he deserved it.

"It depends on whether he has to die or not," she decided at last.

Henry nodded solemnly.

She shifted impatiently and muttered, "I know little about marital law. Do you or any of the men?"

"If ye marry him, all that is yours is his," he assured her eagerly.

Her mouth tightened. "I fail to see what makes you so damn happy about all of this," she said in a snarl. "If I marry him everything is his. If I do not, everything goes to someone else. Either way I lose every-thing—including control over my own destiny."

Henry blinked at that and frowned slightly. "Aye. Well, it is the way of the world, girl . . . er . . . Cap-tain." Expelling a breath, he took a step closer. "If ye want my opinion, yer future will be brighter in the hands of Daniel than with Beecham, and that's a fact. I—"

"I *don't* want your opinion," Valoree snapped, her mouth twitching. Then she shook her head impatiently. "You do not understand at all. There is no threat that someday *you* shall be forced to give up all your au-thority and respect to stand behind a woman!"

He blinked in surprise at that. "But I've already done that. When I agreed to work fer you."

She frowned at him impatiently. "You are being de-liberately obtuse, Henry. You know what I mean. You can leave my employ if you wish."

Sighing, he moved closer again. "You are like a fish swimming against the stream. Do you tell me that you truly do not grow weary from all the responsibility? That you do not sometimes wish to lay down your heavy load and allow someone else to carry it? You have shown spirit and courage by your leading of the men so far, but I know it wearies ye."

"I'll not deny that. But to share it with someone would be preferable to being ruled by another."

"I'm suspecting Thurborne will bear the worst of the burden, but allow ye the freedom to be yourself."

"You suspect," she repeated tiredly. "But what if he does not?"

"Do you truly think ye would be happier with Bee-cham?"

"Aye, he—"

"Is a boy wanting seasoning. By my calculations, he'll grow to be very like Daniel in time, if given the chance. You would not give him the chance. It might work out anyway, but most likely would not. Besides, to be honest, I don't think ye'd enjoy bedding him like you will Daniel. Lord Thurborne sees ye for what you are; there are no illusions. He's smart and strong. Ye respect him for that, and don't bother denying it. And ye want him."

When she stiffened at that, he shrugged. "It's plain talk I'm giving ye but there is no time for other. Ye want him. And he wants you. You respect him and I would imagine after today he must return the sentiment," he added. "It's more to start on than a lot of people have."

"But will he wish to marry me after I almost had him hanged?"

Henry grimaced. "Aye, well, that may be a problem. He's probably none too pleased with any of us right now."

"If he will not marry me, I will have to see him dead."

"Aye," Henry answered, "Mayhap we could give him some time for his temper to cool."

"How much time?" she asked dryly. "We do have a time limit."

"Aye, eight months to make a babe," Henry murmured, thinking for a moment. "Let's give him a week or so. We'll sail south a ways and give him some time to relax and get over today, then put it to him real diplomatic-like."

"How diplomatic can you put 'Marry me or swing'?" she asked dryly. Henry smiled and shrugged.

"Just give him a week."

Sighing, Valoree leaned back in her chair and nodded. "A week. Maybe a couple days more. But then we will have to deal with him and return to collect Beecham."

"Aye-aye." Henry turned to open the door. "I'll just

go have a chat with him and get the lay of the land."

"You do that," Valoree said.

Stepping onto the deck, Henry glanced about, his eyes widening as he saw Daniel seated on a barrel with Bull, One-Eye, Jackson, and Skully gathered about him. He was untied. He was also gulping down rum as if there were no tomorrow.

"Henry." One-Eye smiled at him as he approached and passed over a mug. "We were feeling like a touch of rum after that. Came mighty close, didn't it?"

"Too close," Daniel muttered into his mug before tipping it to his mouth again.

The men all nodded solemnly.

"Think the captain would mind?"

Henry shook his head.

"How many lashes are we to have?" Bull asked at last.

"It depends."

"Lashes?" Daniel frowned from one to the other as he lowered the mug from his lips. "What do you mean?"

"Well, we went against the captain in bringing ye here," One-Eye explained. "It almost cost your life."

"It still might," Henry muttered into his drink.

Daniel glanced at him sharply. "What?"

"Nothing."

"How many lashes?" Bull repeated.

"It depends."

"On what?"

"On her mood. Pour me another mug."

# Chapter Thirteen

One-Eye and No-Nose joined Henry at the rail, one on either side, taking in his grim expression silently for a moment before One-Eye said with a grunt, "What's got you looking all prune-faced?"

"I've been thinking about the captain and Thurborne."

"Aye, well, that's enough to make a grown man cry," One-Eye groused. The last two weeks had been hell on board ship. Thurborne had stormed around looking like thunder—refusing even to look at the captain, let alone speak to her—and the captain in turn was getting crankier and crankier with the crew. Meg, the first morning after the near-hanging, had tried to smooth things over between the couple. She was chewed out by both Valoree and Thurborne for it, and had since taken to staying in her room to avoid the unpleasant atmosphere. The men weren't so lucky. They had work to do to keep the ship sailing southward, and they could only try to stay out of the way. Worst of all, it was looking like the stupid man would hang after all if something wasn't done.

"They're both too damn stubborn for their own good," Henry complained.

"Aye," No-Nose agreed. "But I say it's mostly *his* fault." When Henry and One-Eye peered at him questioningly, he shrugged. "He's letting his pride stand in the way. The captain's a fine woman."

"Aye, she is. But she's not exactly the kind of woman he is used to," One-Eye pointed out.

"Well, if she were, she wouldn't be the captain, now, would she? Besides, like other women or not, she's got her fine points—which anyone could see if they bothered to look. For instance, she's smart."

One-Eye nodded. "Never met a smarter woman."

"She knows more curses than I know words," Skully pointed out, drawing the three men's attention to the fact that he, Bull, and Petey had joined them.

"Aye, and she never loses at poker," One-Eye said as he, No-Nose, and Henry turned to face them. He added, "Much to my dismay."

"She holds her drink well," Henry pointed out, and No-Nose nodded in agreement. "Drinks like a fish and still manages to sail a straight course."

"Never gets the *mal de mer*," Petey murmured; then they all began throwing in various merits.

"Born to the water."

"Not a touch squeamish."

"Never ever like to faint."

"Cut off Jeb's leg without a grimace when he got the gangrene."

"Not afraid of hard work."

"Pulls rigs and ropes with the rest of us."

"Climbs the rigging like a monkey."

"A fine figure."

"Fills her pants well." They all nodded solemnly as they watched her crossing the deck in her tight black breeches.

"But is that what a lord wants?" Petey asked quietly after a moment of silence. The other men looked at him as if he were mad.

Then Skully muttered, "He's right. Just look at them noble ladies. Ye never see one but she's all trussed up in one of those gowns they near to spill out of. They wear those silly wigs and they faint if they drop their hankies—"

"Nay, I'm thinking they drop their hankies cause

they're fainting, not the other way around," One-Eye corrected.

"The point is that if that is what the average noble likes, our lady is . . ." He twisted uncomfortably, unwilling to state even in his own mind that she was inadequate in any way. He didn't have to finish his sentence, however; the other men had caught his point. One-Eye got angry at the slur to their captain. He turned on Skully furiously, but Henry stopped him with a touch.

"Nay. He has a point."

"A point!" One-Eye glared at him.

"Aye. It's what I was pondering over when you and No-Nose came to join me," he admitted, then grimaced as the man glared at him. "Just think on it, One-Eye. Why would the women all rush about hampered by such heavy skirts and acting so frail should the men not like it?"

One-Eye frowned. "Well, what sort of fool would want a weak-willed, stupid, helpless creature for wife?"

"A nobleman," Petey answered grimly. One-Eye frowned.

"Truly? Ye truly think Thurborne's being so stubborn 'cause . . ." He paused suddenly and shook his head. "He was panting after her like a randy bull in London."

The other men began to nod in agreement.

"She was wearing a dress in London," Henry pointed out quietly. They all went still. "And she was also acting ladylike, at least as ladylike as she can."

Realization and alarm mingling on their expressions, the men were silent for a moment. Then One-Eye snapped, "Well, what the devil are we to do about it?"

"Well, I've been thinking on that, and I have an idea," Henry announced eagerly, eliciting a groan from the rest of the men.

"We still don't know how much hide your last idea is going to cost us, Henry."

"Aye, but I didn't know all the facts then. She didn't tell me about what Beecham had told her. This one is a *good* idea."

"Oh, let him talk," One-Eye said. "We'll at least hear him, then decide."

"What?" Valoree turned to peer at Henry and One-Eye in amazement. They had approached her above deck a moment before and said they needed to speak with her. Nodding, she had led them down to the captain's cabin. She had expected it would be about Daniel. She had given the man two weeks to calm down from his anger over almost being hanged, but he hadn't softened one whit as far as she could tell. It was looking as though she was about to have to make a hard decision, but she had kept putting it off and putting it off. The men, it had seemed to her when they had said they wished to speak, had decided they had all waited long enough. But then they had begun to speak, and she had been so shocked by what they said that she wasn't sure she could have possibly heard them right.

Henry cleared his throat, then repeated himself. "I said the men have all voted and decided ye should wear a dress from now on."

Valoree stared at him blankly. "They want me to wear a dress? On board a ship?"

One-Eye and Henry both nodded.

"You expect me, your captain, to order you all about wearing a dress?"

"We voted on it."

"You voted." She stared at him blankly; then her temper flew. "Now see here, Henry!"

"We also voted that if ye won't wear a dress, ye're to step down as captain," Henry finished, wincing even as he said the words.

Valoree dropped into her seat, her face expressionless, but her eyes full of pain. Henry sighed. "We're doing this for yer own good, Captain, girl. Thurborne's not losing any of his temper, and we're thinking if ye just wear a dress like ye did in London, maybe he'd remember he cared for ye. Then . . ." He sighed.

Valoree turned her face away. "Is that all?"

Henry and One-Eye exchanged a glance; then Henry straightened his shoulders and announced, "We voted ye let Meg teach ye some ladylike things."

Her jaw tightened. "What sort of ladylike things?"

"Walking and talking and how to laugh in that high, tinkly way that ladies do."

"I see." She was chilled through.

"We also voted, and ye can't cuss or drink no more."

Her head snapped around at that. "Are you done?"

The two men glanced at each other, then nodded.

"Good," she said grimly. "Now get out."

They hesitated, but then moved to the door. One-Eye paused there and nudged the older man. Henry glanced back to add, "We need to know yer answer right quick, so we know if we're having to vote in a new captain or not."

"I will give you my answer as soon as I have decided if you are all worth it," she responded coldly. "Now get out."

This time the two men left, and Valoree sank back in her seat. Much to her amazement, a moment later she felt a wetness on her cheeks and reached up to touch it in disbelief. She hadn't cried in so long. To cry now because they wanted her to wear skirts was just plain silly. But, of course, that wasn't what she was crying about. She was crying at the fact that it had finally happened. They were threatening to take away her position, something she had clung to like death since losing Jeremy. It was the only thing she had left in her life. What would she do if she were not captain?

A bitter laugh suddenly slipped from her lips, and she got impatiently to her feet to pace the small cabin, rubbing her upper arms with her hands as she did. They had basically voted to take that position away from her when they had all determined that it was time to retire, claim Ainsley Castle, and settle down.

Another knock at the door made her stiffen and slowly turn. "Enter."

Her expression was cold as she watched the door open, and did not soften when Meg entered. "What do you want?"

Meg peered at her silently, then sighed. "I thought mayhap you would like to talk."

Valoree's mouth twisted slightly. "You heard, did you?"

"Of course. I had a vote, too."

"Of course." Valoree sighed and turned quickly away. She paced to a map stuck to the cabin wall, a map of the Caribbean, and stared at it blankly.

"They really are trying to help," Meg explained quietly. "They care about you a great deal." When Valoree remained silent and unmoving, the woman added, "And so do I."

Valoree shifted impatiently. "You hardly know me."

"I know you are intelligent, brave, and noble."

Valoree snorted at that. "I'm a pirate. *Noble* is not in my vocabulary."

"You are a privateer," Meg said firmly. "You carry a letter of marque from the king himself and have dutifully saved his portion over the years. It is stored in a warehouse until you can arrange to see the king and have it delivered. Which you intended to do as soon as you had sorted the matter of your inheritance."

Valoree was silent for a minute, then muttered, "Henry has a big mouth."

"Why do you not simply tell Thurborne that?" Meg

asked quietly. "It would resolve your problem with the king. Mayhap even resolve your problem with him."

Sighing, Valoree returned to her desk chair and sank into it, gesturing for Meg to take the seat across from her. "The letter of marque was made out to Jeremy. I am not sure that it would protect us without him."

"Oh, surely—"

"And I do not have it," Valoree finished quietly.

Meg's eyes went wide. "What—"

"It went down with the original *Valor* when the Spanish sank it."

The woman frowned at this news, then said, "Aye, but surely the king will recall? He must; he sent Thurborne to look for you."

"Aye. Even before I knew that, I had hoped that he would recall assigning Jeremy a letter of marque, allow that it protected myself and the crew, and would simply take his portion and be happy. But that was before the men kidnapped Thurborne—his man, and a noble. I fear that might make him a little less pleased to grant us his favor."

"Oh, dear, I see," Meg whispered, frowning. "This all rests on Thurborne, then."

"Who is quite angry at me for ordering him hanged."

"Aye, well." She made a face, then straightened her shoulders. "Then I think you should do as the men have decided: don your loveliest dress and try to charm the stockings off of him."

"Do I have a choice?" Valoree asked. Meg's expression softened again.

"Oh, Valoree. You fight so hard not to be the things you are."

Valoree stiffened at the soft words. "What I am is the captain of a pirate ship," she said quietly.

"Nay. That is just a role you took when forced. What

you are is a lady, born of nobility and soon to return to your home."

"I am a pirate captain," Valoree insisted. "And have been for five years."

"Are you a man then, too?" Meg queried, arching an eyebrow.

"Nay, of course not."

"Nay," Meg agreed with a nod. "You have lived as and pretended to be a man for thirteen years, but that does not make you one. You were born a female member of nobility, and will die one. Playing at pirates is just something you did, not who you are. It is high time you realize that and stop playing. Pirate captains retire, die, or are voted out. Being noble lasts a lifetime. This ship may sink, but Ainsley will not, and so long as you marry and provide an heir, it will always be there for you." She paused, breathing heavily in her excitement, then sighed. "I suggest you stop deliberately doing everything in your power to look and sound and act like a seadog, and start using the ladylike words, manners, and abilities I know you have."

At Valoree's startled expression, she nodded solemnly. "Oh, aye. I figured out quite quickly that you were stomping about and muttering your curses, using slang and poor manners just to try to put off your suitors. I recognized you just as you recognized me for a true lady. What I did not understand at first was why. Now I think I do."

"Oh?" Valoree said warily. Meg nodded.

"You were hoping to avoid marriage. Having a family and children is risky. You might love your babies. You might even come to love Thurborne, which is why you refused to even consider him. Loving someone means risking heartache should you lose them, and you have had quite enough of that in your young life, have you not?"

Valoree made a face and shook her head. "Nonsense. As you said that day outside Whister's office, my crew are my family. I care for *them*. I am not afraid to love."

"I was wrong," Meg said simply. "Because if you loved them, you would have married Thurborne the moment he offered, and not chanced having to return to pirating, where they are all at risk of being injured or dying." Standing, she moved to the door, then paused to glance back and say, "*They* care for you. So much so that they *will* take away your captaincy if they think it will make you do what they ultimately believe will make you happy. And they believe Thurborne will do that. So do I." Then she stepped out and pulled the door closed behind her.

Valoree released a breath and sank back into her seat, a frown tugging at her lips. Meg was right, at least about her manners. She did know how to speak properly, how to walk properly, and how to dine and behave in company. She may have been forced into the role of cabin boy while they had worked to remake their lost fortune, but Jeremy had seen to it that she knew how to behave. There were no great dining halls on the *Valor* for all of them to eat together, so the men ate in shifts. But Jeremy and she had had their meals in his cabin, where he had made sure she retained her proper eating habits, and had insisted they hold polite conversations. He had also insisted on her using proper English all the time, even around the crew—something the other men had teased and harassed her for at first.

Aye, she had been behaving badly mostly on purpose, but she had told herself it was for the benefit of both herself and the men. They would have grown bored in no time living the quiet life in the country, she'd assured herself. Then they would pine for their lives of privateering, but it would be too late. In truth, Valoree had resented the men's voting to retire. She had been actually relieved when Whister had said she had to be married and produce an heir. Then she had thought that they would give up this foolishness and return to the sea. But they had voted she should marry. So aye, mayhap she had planned to behave badly in the hopes of frightening off suitors, but she hadn't really had to. Not much, anyway. Fate had stepped in, tossing those calamities with the face whitener and fucus at her, and things had seemed to be going her way without her aid until Thurborne had stepped in to put a fly in her pie. She couldn't turn him down without risking the men's getting irate and refusing to follow her. It wasn't as if he were an old troll or something. So her plans had changed again, and she had decided she must find a replacement were she to refuse him. Beecham had seemed the one least likely to cause her problems.

But the rest of what Meg said, that bit about being afraid to love lest she get hurt, and her not really caring for the men or she would wish them out of the risky business of pirating—well, surely that was not true? She was no coward. Besides, she did care for the crew.

Valoree grimaced as she realized she could not even think the word *love* in regard to her own feelings. And she silently acknowledged that she had been selfish. The men wished to retire. She should wish to see them safely out of the business. And she did, but . . . where would that leave her?

Her gaze moved to the signet ring on her hand. Jeremy had pressed it into her palm as he had died, and she had worn it ever since. It had been too large, of course, but string wrapped around the base of her finger had made it stay on. It had always meant a great deal to her, even more than the land it represented. It was all she really had left of her family—that ring and the men who had survived when Jeremy had died. That was what she had always thought. She'd refused to include Ainsley, the home that had witnessed the death of both parents—it caused her too much pain. And that was when Valoree realized that Meg was right.

She had closed off her heart when Jeremy had died, afraid to love and lose. She had refused to marry Daniel, not because he was too strong or would not let her lead, but because she liked, admired, respected, and maybe even loved him a little already. And because she knew that she could love him wholeheartedly if given the chance. But that would mean risking the pain of loss if anything happened to him, and that possibility frightened her more than losing her own life in battle ever had.

She had been behaving like an idiot and a coward, and it was high time she cut that out. Standing, she moved to the chest that held the gowns she had ordered in London and began to sort through them. She would wear gowns. She would not swear. She would not drink. She would be the best lady she knew how to be, and she would charm the stockings off of Daniel. This time, when he asked, she would marry him in a trice. Then they could start making that baby she needed to reclaim Ainsley.

Thurborne was not in the mood to be charmed. Valoree came to that conclusion after wasting two straight weeks on the effort. She didn't charm anything off him, let alone his stockings. She couldn't, since he would not even talk to her. Valoree worked hard at the effort, trying everything she could think of. She tried sweet smiles. She tried polite conversations. She tried teasing him for being so grumpy. In desperation, she even lowered her neckline until it was beyond decent, but all she got from him on each attempt was a cool-eyed look and a grunt. He wasn't charmed at all. And Valoree, who had been incredibly patient, in her own opinion, had finally had enough. It was time to take action. With that intent, she had called Henry to her cabin. Now she faced him across her desk and said the only thing she could think of to save the situation: "Get him drunk."

"What?" Henry gaped at her.

"You heard me. Get him drunk."

Henry hesitated. "But—"

"Henry, we do not have time for any more playing about. There are barely seven months for me to get with child. I must get moving on the matter, and to preserve Thurborne, he must marry me. So get him drunk. We shall hold the ceremony and I shall consummate the marriage."

"You'll be needing a little help from him with that task, Captain, girl," Henry mentioned a little tentatively. "And who will marry the two of you?"

"You will have to go ashore and bring back a minister."

"Go ashore where?" the quartermaster asked. "We have not reached land yet."

"We will reach Port Royale by nightfall," Valoree told him calmly.

"We made good time," he murmured with surprise, but knew her sense of these things. She shrugged.

"Aye. One or two storms and only a couple days of lee wind. A good strong wind the rest of the time more than made up for it." She sighed. "Get him started on the drink, Henry. I want him well sotted when we reach Port Royale and you fetch the minister back."

Less than twenty-four hours later, Valoree watched the men row back toward the ship with a frown. They had been preparing a "love nest," as they insisted on calling it, on a nice secluded stretch of shore for her and Daniel. Calling it a battle arena probably would have been closer to the truth, she thought derisively as she watched the small boat reach the *Valor* and the two men begin to clamber up the rope ladder. She suspected Daniel was not going to be pleased this morning when he learned that they were married. Why should he be? Nothing else she had planned had gone her way.

Oh, aye, Henry had done as she had requested and gotten Daniel thoroughly drunk the day before. He had challenged him to a drinking game, then cheated his pirate head off. By the time they had reached Port Royale, Daniel hadn't even been able to stand on his own, let alone see straight, and forget about any ability he might have had to think.

The men had had to prop him up for the ceremony, which had made the minister, at first, refuse to perform it. It had taken a lot of talking, gold, and even threats to get the holy man Henry had found and fetched to cooperate. Especially as Daniel had obviously hardly known where he was. Still, he had kept raving on about how she was "my Valoree" and her passion was "soooo hot." Apparently the drink had made him forget all about his irritation over her trying to hang him, and this helped reassure the priest.

Unfortunately the moment the ceremony was over, and the minister had walked away, Daniel had collapsed to the deck in an unconscious, sodden heap. One-Eye and Skully had immediately carried him down to her cabin and laid him out on her small cot. There, Valoree had attempted to consummate their marriage, only to learn—firsthand—what Henry had meant by her needing Daniel's cooperation to accomplish it. The man had lain flat on his back, snoring away as she had undressed him, then continued to lie there. *All* of him had just lain there.

Consummation had been impossible. She had spent the night dozing in her chair, then got up this morning to give orders. She supposed this latest plan had come to her in a dream, for she didn't recall thinking it out. But whatever the case, she had ordered the men to set sail around the island until they reached a secluded

cove she recalled, then instructed Henry to sit with
Daniel and wait for him to wake up. She had told the
man that the moment he did, he was to pour some of
that sleeping potion—the one they had used to get her
and Daniel aboard this ship—down his throat. But not
too much. She wanted him out only long enough to
set her plan in motion.

Leaving him to it, she had gone off to converse with
Petey about what she wanted him to prepare for this
plan, then had had One-Eye, Bull, and No-Nose help
her take several things ashore. The last trip to the cove
had been to take the food she had had Petey prepare,
and the unconscious Daniel. After arranging him as she
had ordered, the men had piled back into the dinghy
and shoved off, hurrying back to the ship. They were
not to return until dusk the next night—unless it rained
or there was a problem.

Now she just had to wait for Daniel to wake up.
Which shouldn't really be long. Henry had assured her
he hadn't given him much of the potion, and he had
already shown signs of stirring when Bull had carried
him ashore.

A voluble curse from the trees behind her a moment
later proved her thought correct. It was time to begin.
Resigned to the battle ahead, Valoree turned and
started up the sand to the trees.

# Chapter Fourteen

Daniel took another look at his bound hands and cursed again. What the hell had happened? The last thing he remembered was waking up with a terrible hangover from the drinking game he had obviously lost, and Henry nursing some foul-tasting liquid down his throat. Then he'd woke-up here?

Where was here, exactly? he wondered a bit hazily. His first thought was that he had been staked out in the sand and left to drown. But he wasn't on sand really, and there was no sign of water. Though he *was* staked out. Two good-sized posts had been driven into the sand on either side of, and up a little from, his head, just off the carpet of silky soft cloth he lay on. His hands had been bound to them. Similar posts at the other end held his feet spread-eagled.

"Would you like a drink?"

Daniel glanced down sharply to the woman now standing between his bound feet as she eyed him warily. He glared at her for a moment, then asked between clenched teeth, "What exactly are you up to now? Hanging me was not good enough, so you have decided to stake me out in the sun and let me die a long, slow death from thirst?"

He realized how stupid that sounded the moment the words finished leaving his mouth, considering that she had just asked him if he wished a drink, but he could do little to take them back now.

"I believe you have to be left out in the sun for that," Valoree asserted calmly. She moved to pick up a bottle that had been laid out on a barrel a short distance away. There was also bread, cheese, and what smelled like some sort of roasted chicken there as well, he noted with interest. He watched her pour a glass of wine half-full, pick up a spoon, and move toward him. "As you can see, I made sure they put you in the shade."

Daniel glanced around briefly to see that he was staked out under a group of nice shady trees. He turned toward her again as she knelt on the silky material beside him. "Oh," he said. "So how do you plan to kill me?"

Pausing, she met his gaze briefly and frowned. "I did not have you brought here to be killed," she snapped, and he gave her a morose smile.

"Well, do forgive me for slighting you by thinking so. It was not that long ago that you were ordering me hanged from the crow's nest."

Valoree released a sigh, then shrugged. "I was not happy about it. But you *are* the king's spy, and I *did* vow to protect my men as captain. I had little choice but to see to that to the best of my abilities."

Daniel felt himself soften somewhat, then frowned. It was as simple as that to her. She had a responsibility as captain to see to the safety of her crew. He supposed he could understand that. He had been in similar situations and had to make comparable decisions. He had even understood that when Henry had explained it to him, when Meg had explained it to him, and One-Eye, Skully, No-Nose . . . Hell, the whole crew had had a go at him about it over the past month, each of them ending their little chat with: "We'll just keep this little talk betwixt us two, hmmm? No need for the captain to know 'bout it. She'd think I was fussing in her business."

Aye, Daniel understood her decision, and he wasn't really angry about it either, though he couldn't have said the same right afterward. Once his temper had cooled a bit, he had realized that he was half to blame for the fiasco himself. If he had been honest from the outset and simply cleared up the mess over her brother and Back-from-the-Dead Red from the beginning, none of it might have happened. But he'd be damned if that meant he was going to let her get away with marrying him to save his life. Not that he didn't want to marry her, but who the hell needed that? He did not need her throwing it in his face every time they had a disagreement over the next fifty or sixty years: *I only married you to save your life. I should have let you swing!*

*Nay.* If they married it would be because she had finally admitted her desire to do so, not under the excuse of saving his hide. The thing of it was, he was pretty damn sure she did want to marry him. Or at least that she wanted to sleep with him. But he wanted to hear her say it. If she would just say it, he would become the most agreeable, most cooperative of men.

A sigh of impatience from her drew his head around as she asked, "Do you want some of this or not?"

Daniel eyed the liquid suspiciously. He was thirsty, but . . . "Is it poison?" he asked, his gaze narrowing at the spoonful of wine she had poured out of the glass and was moving toward his lips.

Rolling her eyes, she lifted the spoon to her mouth and swallowed its golden contents.

"There. See? No poison. Now do you want some?"

Face expressionless, he nodded, and she quickly poured out another spoonful and tipped it into his mouth when he opened it. Then she fed him another spoonful, and another. It was a perfectly ridiculous way to drink, and most unsatisfactory. He felt like a child, and his thirst required a full glass or two poured down his throat to quench it, not these little trickles of the stuff.

"If I am not here to be killed, why am I tied down?"

he asked after several spoonfuls, when his frustration got the better of him.

Valoree hesitated, then admitted, "Because Henry was worried about how you would take the news I have to impart. He was unwilling to leave us here without a guard unless you were tied down."

His eyes narrowed at once at that. "What news? And why could you not impart it on the ship?"

"Oh, I could have," she assured him quickly, then added, "but I wanted privacy for the other part."

"The other part?"

"Aye."

"What other part?"

"The part that comes after the news," she said evasively.

Daniel shifted impatiently, tugging at his bonds in frustration. "Well, what bloody news?"

She hesitated uncertainly, then asked, "Would you not like some more wine first?" When his only response was to glare at her angrily, she shifted unhappily and asked, "Do you not remember anything about last night?"

Daniel blinked at the question. He was rather fuzzy on that subject. It was all a sort of pink haze. Pink and fuzzy. "What happened?"

"We got married."

He immediately began to struggle as if she had stuck her blade in his arse, his hands and feet pulling furiously at the ropes that bound him, curses rolling off his tongue in fury. He snarled as Valoree eased warily away from him to watch from a safe distance. After a few moments of fruitless struggle, Daniel stopped and glared at her. Panting, he raged, "The hell we were!"

Valoree moved silently to a sack beside the barrel, withdrew a piece of paper, and returned to hold it before his face. It was a marital contract, and his signature was right there on it beside hers, albeit a little sloppy.

"Henry fetched a minister from Port Royale, and Jasper took care of obtaining the special license. You said 'I do' and signed. We are married."

Daniel stared at the paper for the longest time, then glanced toward her smugly. "I will have it annulled."

Sighing, she looked away from him briefly, then back hopefully. "Would you like more wine?"

"Oh, no." He shook his head firmly. "I'll not touch another drop of anything but water until I've had this marriage annulled."

Sighing, she walked back to replace the piece of paper in its sack, muttering, "I guess you leave me no choice, then."

"What? You are giving up?" he asked with disbelief and not a little disappointment. Had he been wrong? Did he mean so little to her? Where was his lady pirate? Where was her fight?

Finished putting the license away, she straightened and turned to calmly move back toward him. "Nay. I am not giving up. I am simply moving on to accomplishing the task myself."

"What task?" he asked suspiciously. Her gaze dropped at once to the area south of his waist and north of his knees.

"A little raping and pillaging."

Daniel's jaw dropped in amazement; then an incredulous grin stole across his face. "And how do you plan to accomplish that without my cooperation?"

Her gaze still on his nether regions, she arched an eyebrow, her relief showing as she commented, "It appears I may have some cooperation with that task. Just enough to see the deed done, no doubt."

Daniel didn't have to glance down to understand her meaning. The very thought of the raping and pillaging she had mentioned had made his one-eyed soldier decide to stand at attention—and it certainly was doing that. It was standing so straight and eager, she could probably fly her Jolly Roger from the damn thing. Since there was no sense in arguing the point, he decided to simply lie there and see how things developed. Until she picked up a knife from the barrel and moved toward him.

"What are you planning to do with that?" he asked warily.

"Well," she mused calmly, "it seems to me I cannot undress you all tied up as you are."

His eyebrows rose as she moved down by his feet, then knelt between them. "So you are going to let me go?"

"Not quite," she said cheerfully, then slid the knife between his leg and knee breeches and began to slice upward. She was most efficient; were he a fish, he would consider himself filleted, he thought grimly as his knee breeches dropped away from one leg. Straightening, she performed the action again on his other leg just as quickly. Then she shifted further upward to sit between his spread thighs, making two more slices, each one neatly cutting the cloth from where her last slicing motion had left off, up to and through the waist of his breeches. Leaving the cloth lying over him, she then tossed the knife aside and straightened to stand consideringly between his feet.

Daniel swallowed and waited. He supposed he had expected her to lift her skirts and drop to mount him in just as quick and efficient a manner as she had sliced his clothes away. She didn't. Instead, she reached out suddenly and began to undo her bodice, watching his face as she did. Once done, she pulled the garment off first one shoulder, then the other and let it drop between his legs. Her overskirt followed, then the kirtle, and then her partlet. Daniel licked his lips as her corset and petticoats slipped away next. She was left in a chemise so thin that through it, he could see the triangular shadow between her legs and the round darkness that were the areolae of her breasts.

Her gaze slid back to his manhood now, a slow smile spreading on her lips. Daniel didn't have to look down to see what caused that smile. He had been unable to do anything but grit his teeth and bear it as he had grown stiffer with each removed item, his erection growing and lifting the loose cloth of his breeches away from his flesh.

Winking at him, she bent slowly and grasped the hem of her chemise, drawing it slowly upward. It was only then that Daniel realized she had forsworn hose and garters, and was barefoot. Probably a smart thing to do to negotiate the sand here, he thought distractedly as she slowly straightened, uncovering her calves, her knees, her thighs.

Daniel swallowed audibly as she revealed the nest of curls at the apex of her thighs. It was as bright as red as the hair on her head. His gaze paused there briefly, losing several of her movements, but he caught up as she lifted the gown past her breasts, and his eyes widened. They were swollen and full, with nipples that at the moment were tightly erect and a cinnamon-brown.

Daniel had to bite his lip to keep from groaning aloud at that. Her little striptease had excited her as much as it had him, it seemed. She was definitely no shrinking violet. Tossing the chemise to join the small pile of clothes to the side of where he lay, Valoree stepped over his thigh to kneel beside his chest. She bent over him then, her hair falling forward like a curtain to hide her face from view as she began to undo the fastenings of his shirt.

"Untie me." Daniel's voice was harsh from the strain of watching, silent and unmoving, but she ignored him, undoing the last of the buttons. She pushed the cloth of his white shirt open with a sigh, her hands running over his chest as she did, her hair tickling across his belly, which tightened at once in response. She slid one hand down over his stomach to sweep the remains of his breeches out of the way, her hand brushing across his hot flesh as she did, making him close his eyes in exquisite pleasure. *Damn!* She had barely touched him and his body was already threatening to explode. It was the anticipation. He knew bloody well that she would not untie him. That she would mount him with that damned sexy smile of hers, and ride him until he—

His eyes popped open as she trailed kisses down his chest and across his stomach. "What are you doing?" He gasped in horrified wonder as she pressed the little kisses to his hip, then shifted between his legs.

"Sometimes," she murmured against the flesh of his thigh, "when the men go ashore, if they are feeling generous, they have been known to send back a prostitute or two for the men left behind," she told him, her hand closing around his manhood and squeezing curiously. "They are not supposed to and risk a whipping for doing so, but a half a dozen times or so over the years, I have come across the men engaged in various acts with these women. Twice the women were on their knees—"

"Oh, God!" Daniel gasped as she rose up slightly, her breath brushing against the excruciatingly sensitive tip of his manhood as she spoke.

Pausing, she grinned at him slightly and announced, "You are getting bigger still. I did not think you could."

"Ohhh, God!" Daniel groaned as her mouth closed over his tip and she suckled at him like a babe at its mother's breast. It was rather obvious that she didn't have a clue what she was doing. She was experimenting with him like a child with a toy. She sucked, then she licked, then she nipped, and it didn't matter that she had no idea what she was doing, for the very fact that she was doing it—and the view he had of her eyes and face as he looked down his body at her—was driving him insane.

"Untie me," he rasped desperately, then added, "I think I am coming lose anyway. Just—" Daniel fell into relieved silence as that got a reaction out of her. Shifting, she reached up to check the hand nearest her, and Daniel licked his lips as one breast jiggled gently just a bare few unreachable inches to the side of his face. Then she leaned over him to check the other wrist, and that breast was suddenly an inch above his face. Lifting his head, he licked hungrily at the flesh on the underside of her breast; then he nipped at its peak before closing his mouth over the nipple and drawing it into his mouth.

Valoree had gone still at the first touch, but had not removed herself. Now she groaned as he laved her hungrily, her body trembling as she stretched over him.

"Untie me," he murmured against her skin. "Come. Untie me."

Groaning, she straightened away from him, shaking her head. "Nay. You are just trying to seduce me into setting you free."

"Nay, I . . ." Daniel paused as she stood, then stepped over him so that she had one foot on either side of his hips. For a moment, he had a view like no other; then she lowered herself carefully, frowning as his splayed legs forced hers out at an awkward angle as she tried to position herself above him.

"You cannot do it with my legs like that. Untie me and I will—" Her sudden grasping of his shaft with one hand to try to position him made him stop and bite his lip again as arrows of sensation shot through him. "You cannot," he managed again in a strangled voice, groaning in relief when she suddenly released him and stood.

Retrieving her knife, she moved silently to his feet and freed first one, then the other. Daniel pulled his legs closed as she tossed the knife aside again, then returned to her earlier position, kneeling astride him. Grasping him in her hand, she shifted slightly, peering down as she lowered herself, shifting him as she sought her entrance using his flesh as the probe. Daniel groaned at the combination of her firm hold on the base and the warm, wet flesh closing around and brushing over the tip of him as she played find-the-entrance. Just when she had found it, he muttered her name. She paused to peer up at him questioningly.

"Aye, my lord?"

Daniel nearly laughed at the polite title, then shook his head. "My hands."

"I will not untie you, my lord," she asserted, but he shook his head.

"No. My hands. They feel odd."

Her gaze slid up to his hands and she gasped in alarm. She released the hold she had on his manhood and leaned over him to quickly loosen first one bond then the other. It was not enough that he could escape his captivity, but enough to let some blood back into his hands. Daniel, who had deliberately pulled tight on his bindings to cause such a necessity, immediately licked at any flesh in his path like a starving dog licking the juice from his lord's plate. His tongue roved over her breasts, between them, and at the undersides. Anything that jiggled into his path received a like treatment as she worked. A moan of disappointment slid from his lips as she eased away from him, only to be silenced by her mouth as she kissed him, licking his lips as he had hers so many times, then slipping inside with her tongue to explore him aggressively before receding to allow him to explore in return.

He kissed her desperately, groaning again when she ended the kiss, then sighing as her lips brushed over his chin, his chest, then found and fastened curiously on one nipple. She licked and nipped experimentally as she slid her hand back down to find and squeeze his staff as if testing it for usability. Then she slid down again, settling herself over him, and began to probe herself with the tip once more, wiggling as his flesh rubbed over hers. Apparently enjoying the sensation, she did it again, and Daniel moaned at the exquisite torture. She paused then, peering at him curiously. "Does that hurt?"

"Oh, God, no." He groaned. "It feels good."

"Really?" Valoree leaned forward slightly, bracing her free hand on his chest as she again brushed him against herself, rubbing his hardness across her soft, damp warmth. She admitted a bit breathlessly, "I like it too."

Tugging at his bindings, Daniel closed his eyes as she continued to manipulate him, pressing him harder against herself with each caress, and moving farther forward and farther back each time until he felt his tip nudge against her opening. She paused then, suddenly, and he opened his eyes to see that she was quite flushed, her lips partly open, her eyes sleepy with desire. He knew he was in much the same state, and opened his mouth to again beg her to untie him, but just as he would have, she eased herself slowly backward, wriggling and shifting as she went, easing him into her narrow passage. When the tip met the membrane that proved her innocence, she paused, her gaze meeting his, and Daniel immediately gave up his restraint. He raised his knees slightly behind her and thrust upward, plunging through with one quick push.

They were both still then, and Daniel frowned at her expression.

"Are you all right?" he asked in concern. She nodded, but not very convincingly, so he asked curiously, "Did it hurt much?"

She made another face and sighed. "Just enough to dampen the pleasure."

"Untie me and I will—"

"Nay." She shook her head abruptly. "Next time, mayhap. I will see this well and truly consummated before I release you."

"Once the maiden's veil is broken it is consummated."

Valoree shook her head. "I will have your seed. Just in case you try to claim I was not a virgin and nothing happened."

Daniel opened his mouth to argue again, but then snapped it shut as she braced a hand behind her on his knee and began to rise off of him. It allowed him to slide partway out of her before she lowered herself onto him fully again. She watched his face as she moved, her expression curious, and Daniel felt self-conscious at first, until what she was doing made him close his eyes. She was driving him crazy. It was slow torture. She raised and lowered herself with a languid deliberation that was teaching him the meaning of frustration. All he wanted to do was rip the damn posts out of the ground, clasp her buttocks, and take control of the speed. He wanted it faster, harder, more, and she was driving him insane with this leisurely ride.

"Untie me!" he yelled in frustration, and she stopped, tilting her head slightly and frowning.

"Am I doing it wrong?"

Seeing the worry on her face, Daniel shook his head. "Nay. I . . . I would touch you. Untie me and let me touch you."

"Where?" she asked with interest.

"Your breasts." He tugged at his bindings. "I would close my hands over your breasts and . . ." He paused when she glanced down and cupped her own breasts, peering at them. Still holding them, she peered at him curiously.

"Why do men like breasts so much? Surely you get no pleasure from touching them. Yet nearly every time I have come across my men with the prostitutes they sneaked aboard ship, they always seemed to have their hands on their breasts—no matter what else they were doing. And even you always touch and fondle my breasts first thing after kissing me. Why is that?"

"Why?" He stared at her blankly for a moment, then shook his head. "Because they are beautiful, and they are soft, and they feel good. Do you not like it when I touch your breasts?"

"Aye, I like it when you touch them," she murmured honestly.

"Well, so do I." He shook his head wryly. "It is a good thing women carry the breasts, for if men had them, they would be fondling them all the time."

She laughed huskily at that and Daniel smiled; then his humor faded. She was still cupping her breasts, but that was all.

"Close your eyes," he said suddenly, and when she peered at him questioningly, he nodded encouragingly. "Go on, close them." He waited until she had, then continued, "Now touch yourself. Hold your breasts. Caress them like I would and pretend it is me."

She hesitated for a moment, then closed her own hands over her breasts, clasping them briefly before catching the nipples between her thumb and fingers. As she pinched and rolled them tentatively, a sigh slipped from her lips. Daniel watched her and felt himself swell further within her. As if suddenly remembering what she had been doing before the interruption, she began to ride him again, raising and lowering herself in that excruciating leisurely rhythm as she continued to caress herself. Her hands slid away from her breasts to smooth over her belly, then moved back to her breasts, up over her collarbone and shoulders, then returned. Her lips parted slightly again, her cheeks began to flush, and her head fell backward. Daniel gritted his teeth, his hands clenching with building excitement, but his mind screaming at the slow, sedate pace.

Which was perhaps why he was so surprised when his excitement suddenly overtook him. It came on him without warning. He felt his toes curl toward the bottoms of his feet and his body tense; then he jerked at his bindings and cried out, exploding inside her with unexpected force.

Eyes closed, heart still pounding in his chest, he felt her lean forward on him to kiss his cheek; then she briefly rested atop him. He had nearly dozed off moments later when finally she slid off. He felt first one of his hands, then the other, go slack as she released him, then heard her move away through the sand. Opening his eyes curiously, he turned his head to watch her walk naked down to the ocean. She waded for a moment until the water reached her knees, then dove in, and Daniel rubbed his wrists absently as he watched her frolic. She did not swim long before turning to shore again.

He watched her rise out of the waves, too far away to see clearly, but was able to imagine the beads of liquid rolling over her rosy flesh. He closed his eyes as she made her way back toward him. Hearing the rustle of material, he peeked one eye open to see her drying herself with a piece of linen, then closed it again when she tossed the scrap of cloth aside and turned toward him. There was a pause before he sensed her kneeling beside him. It took a concentrated effort for him not to flinch in surprise when her cold, damp hair brushed his arm, but then she cuddled up against him. Burrowing her head into the crook of his arm and chest, she laid one hand gently on his stomach, and relaxed.

\*   \*   \*

Something was pulling at Valoree's wrist. Frowning sleepily, she tugged against it, her irritation replaced with confusion when she couldn't seem to free her hand. Turning her head, she blinked her eyes open and stared blankly at the rope binding her wrist to a post. Then her head snapped around to find Daniel kneeling on her other side. She instinctively started to lift her free hand from the sand where it lay by her hip, but he caught it easily and smiled.

"Good morning," he murmured with a sweet smile. The expression turned wry as he began to bind that wrist to the opposite pole, ignoring her attempt to retrieve her hand. "Well, not morning exactly. Midday, I would guess."

Finishing with her wrist, he straightened and moved down to her feet. Valoree began to scrabble sideways to avoid him, but there was only so far she could go with her wrists tied down. Daniel grabbed her ankle after only a short chase and dragged her back into place to secure her to the post. She cursed herself for having left the ropes in place.

"What are you doing?" Valoree asked furiously, lashing out at him with her free foot.

Catching it easily, Daniel shifted to kneel on it to keep her from kicking him as he finished binding the first foot. Then he turned his attention to tying that one as well.

"There we are," he murmured as he straightened from his task, his eyes widening with a sudden thought. "You must be hungry. Would you like something to eat?"

Valoree let out a breath, her body relaxing wearily. "What do you want? Is this my punishment for trying to hang you?"

Daniel smiled gently. "I am not angry at you for trying to hang me."

"Oh, aye. Why do I find that hard to believe?" She glanced pointedly toward one bound wrist.

"I am not," he assured her quietly. "You did not go through with it, and you were in a tough spot at the time, thinking that I meant to turn you in to the king."

Valoree eyed him warily. "Thinking that you meant to turn me in? Did you not intend to?"

Daniel shook his head. "Nay. I did mean to sort that business out eventually, but I never intended to see you hanged. Why would I ask you to marry me if I planned to do that?"

Valoree made a face. She hadn't thought of that, but did now and suggested, "Well, it would see that you inherited your grandmother's money, without the irritation of a wife to get in your way."

His looked surprised. "Now why did I not think of that?" When her mouth turned down in anger and she began to tug at her bindings, he chuckled softly. "The only problem is, I need an heir as well as a wife. I cannot get an heir from a dead wife."

He stepped over one outstretched leg and knelt beside her on the silky cloth, languidly surveying her, then lightly running his fingers over her flat stomach. Valoree instinctively tightened her abdominal muscles, then raised her head up slightly to peer at him suspiciously. "Why did you tie me down?"

"Because I intend to torture you," he announced cheerfully, spreading out beside her and bending his arm at the elbow so that he could rest his head upon one open hand.

"Why?" she gasped in amazement.

He smiled and ignored her. "Why did you marry me?"

Her expression went solemn, her eyes again wary. "So that I would not have to hang you."

"Hmmm. I thought you might say that," he said pityingly, tracing his fingers lightly over her hip.

Valoree immediately began to wriggle beneath the featherlight touch. "Cut that out!"

Daniel raised his eyebrows. "Do you not like me to touch you?"

"Not like that. It tickles," she snapped.

"Does it?" He shifted his hand lower so that his fingers whispered lightly up the inside of her thigh. "Does that tickle?"

Valoree gritted her teeth. She would not ask him to stop again. It seemed this was part of his torture. Though only he and the good Lord knew what he intended to torture her for.

"Tell me that you *want* me," he whispered by her ear suddenly, and Valoree turned to gape at him in amazement.

She could not believe that he would threaten to torture her, then expect her to say something like that. What the devil was wrong with the man? Well, the answer to that was obvious. He was mad. If she had known a bit sooner, she might have let him swing.

Her thoughts were distracted when he suddenly lifted himself up and leaned close to her breast. She thought at first that he meant to lick or suckle her there as he had done in the past, but instead he paused, his mouth mere inches from the nipple. His breath rippled against it as his eyes turned toward her face. "Shall I lick you? Kiss you? Shall I suckle your breast?"

Her nipple already reacting as if he had done so, tantalized by the fanning of his breath, Valoree pressed her mouth firmly closed and turned her head. Hearing a rustle as Daniel moved away, she released her breath in a sigh. One of relief, of course, she told herself firmly, only to stiffen as he returned. She refused to look at him, staring grimly toward the water and wondering if he would leave her tied up until the men came back, and just how exactly he intended to torture her, and to what purpose. Then a splash of cool wetness on her chest made her gasp and glance around sharply to see him smiling as he tipped a glass of wine onto first one breast, then the other. The golden liquid immediately ran down them, a small puddle forming between and slightly below her breasts.

"What are you doing now?" she asked sharply, and he smiled at her again.

"Torturing you," was his husky reply. Then he bent to lick at the shallow pool of wine before following the trail to the breast nearest him. He cleaned the liquid from her with long, slow strokes of his tongue.

"T-this is your torture?" she asked shakily, watching his tongue slide out to graze the tip of one painfully erect nipple.

"Aye," he breathed against her damp skin, sending shudders through her. "How do you like it so far?"

Valoree sagged back onto the cloth-covered sand with a sigh that turned into a nervous giggle. She sensed rather than saw his eyes seeking hers out, and met his gaze silently as he frowned.

"You did not think I meant *torture* torture, did you?" he asked, the beginnings of a scowl tugging at his mouth. Valoree hesitated.

Had she? Had she really thought he had meant *torture?* she asked herself. She suspected the answer was no. Valoree knew herself well enough to realize that she would have done quite a bit more cussing and struggling, rather than lying there tensely to see what was to come about, if she had truly believed he meant to harm her. Still, she didn't know what he was up to.

"Nay," she whispered at last, and he relaxed.

"Good." He turned his attention to her other breast now, laving it as he had the first. Valoree swallowed, her fingers closing into fists as she silently watched. She was a touch uncomfortable lying there, helpless, as he kissed and licked her. She wanted to touch him, too—wanted to run her hands through his hair, over his chest, down his back. Which, of course, he had claimed he wished to do, too, when he had been tied up.

His hand replaced his mouth at her breast, and his lips moved upward, kissing a trail to her mouth before covering it with his own. He kissed her discomfort away, his hand squeezing and massaging her breast as he did, his finger plucking and rolling her nipple.

Valoree moaned into his kiss, her body arching off the silky material between herself and the sand, her fingernails digging into the flesh of her palms. Then she was gasping for air as he released her mouth, his attentions moving to explore other vistas. His lips grazed her cheeks, her chin, her ear, her neck, until they returned to her breasts. But this time he gave them only cursory attention before his tongue led him down her stomach, pausing to dip into her belly button, before he continued on to her hip, licking the hollow there.

Valoree was writhing—shifting, arching, and moaning mindlessly beneath his attentions. Daniel shifted to kneel between her legs, and she opened eyes she hadn't even realized she had squeezed closed to see him quickly untying her feet. She thought he would enter her then, and she wanted him to. Dear God, that was what she wanted most in the world at that moment, to feel his flesh fill hers. But he didn't. Instead, he grasped one ankle and lifted it in his hands until he could press a kiss to her instep.

Valoree jolted as if he had bitten her, her body responding with amazing sensitivity to the touch. It seemed he could do anything to her, touch her anywhere, and it would be erotic. She pressed herself back into the sand, twisting her head and moaning aloud as his lips moved up the inside of her leg, pausing to nibble behind her knee. He shifted to lie between her legs so that his mouth could meander up her thigh.

She continued to thrash beneath his touch, uttering a continuous, mindless moan until she felt his breath between her legs. Then she went as stiff as wood, her nerve endings screaming, her eyes shooting open to stare blindly at the trees overhead. She cried out and arched upward off the ground, sending the birds winging from the trees above as he pleasured her in a way she had heretofore only ever heard her men talk of a woman doing to them. He did things with his mouth that brought tears to her eyes and sobs bursting from her lips. She raced toward something wondrous. Then he stopped.

The trees slowly came back into focus before her swimming eyes, and Valoree found herself lying panting on a scrap of silk in the sand, her body clamoring in protest. Raising her head slightly, she peered blankly down the length of her body and saw that he was watching her, waiting.

"Tell me you want me."

Valoree felt those words breathed against the trembling flesh of her womanhood all the way up to the roots of her hair. Her entire body was screaming with the desire he would have her speak aloud. Could he not see that?

"Say it," he instructed. "Say, 'I married you because I want you. Not to save you from hanging.' "

Suddenly recognizing the vulnerability in him, Valoree felt some part of her heart crumble with the understanding. "I married you because I wanted to, and *I want you*. I want you inside me. Right now."

A slow smile twisting his lips, he glanced down to the damp flesh he had been devouring and blew on it softly, sending tremors through her body. Then he leaned down for a lick, and another, his teeth grazing her swollen skin and making her close her eyes and sob in need. With that, his touch changed slightly, and she peered back at him to see that he was caressing her with his fingers, continuing to urge her passion back to the blaze it had been. He shifted to his knees and moved further up between her legs. There, ceasing his manipulations, he slipped his hands beneath her bottom. Lifting her slightly, he nudged her legs farther apart to make room for him between them, then guided himself slowly into her.

A moan erupting from deep in her throat, Valoree tugged mindlessly on her bindings, yearning to hold him. She wanted to wrap her arms around him and draw him close, a need that only increased as he withdrew himself from her with agonizing slowness, watching her expression the whole time.

"More." She groaned in agony, and Daniel smiled a slow, sexy smile.

"More?"

She nodded desperately, bucking upward in an effort to urge him on, but he caught her thighs, restraining her, then grasped her ankles and bent her knees to maintain complete control. He slowly slid himself back into her.

"Greedy," he chided with a grin when she struggled with him, trying to force him to her will, but his control was slipping, and he apparently decided to give her what they both wanted. Releasing her ankles, he dropped forward, his hands landing on either side of her body, his mouth dropping to nip at one breast as he drove himself completely inside.

Gasping encouragement, Valoree wrapped her legs around his hips and met his thrusts eagerly. Some few moments later, he took them both to where that wondrous something waited and showed her just what it was again and again until he joined her in it.

# *Chapter Fifteen*

"What are you doing?"

Working at the laces of her gown, Valoree turned back to smile down at Daniel warmly. He was nude and still sleepy-eyed, his hair disheveled as he leaned up on one arm to peer at her. Good Lord, the man was sexy. "I am getting dressed, my lord."

"Nay," he protested on a yawn, leaning forward to grab at her skirt. "Come back to bed."

"Bed?" Valoree laughed, dancing away to avoid being caught.

Smiling wryly, he glanced down at the now crinkled and sand-dusted cloth she had laid out for Bull to place him on the day before.

It had been well used and it showed. The man was insatiable. He had not let her sleep more than a few minutes since his first awakening after their arrival. Not that she was complaining. She had enjoyed herself immensely.

Shrugging away the question of a bed, Daniel peered back at her, the hungry look she was beginning to recognize taking the place of his sleepy expression. His voice, when he spoke, was husky and seductive. "Come back here. I am not done with you yet."

Valoree felt a flutter in her lower belly at his words, and would have loved to shed the gown she had just donned and slip back into his arms, but she shook her head regretfully instead. "Nay. The men w—" Her gaze sliding toward the beach, she stopped as she saw the *Valor* sailing slowly around the point and into view. Right on time, of course. She had said dusk, and here they were.

"Very well. And here I thought that you wished to get with child."

Valoree glanced around at that to see that he was now rooting through the remains of the supplies she had had brought over. "What do you mean?"

Shrugging, he smiled at her innocently. "Just what I said. We will never produce an heir this way. Especially when we only have—what is it now?—little better than seven months to produce one?"

"Well, surely we can manage the task in that time." She raised an eyebrow at his pursed lips. "What?"

"I was just thinking that it took my parents three years ere they begat me, and according to my mother they were quite dutiful in their nightly attempts. How many years were there between you and Jeremy?"

Valoree's eyes narrowed. "Eight, almost nine—but there were two stillborn babes between us."

"Hmmmmm." Giving up his search, he straightened and caught his hands behind his back, then began to pace naked before her, his head tilted upward, eyes to the sky as he began to figure aloud. "Now, let us see. Three years on my side, and . . . Well, let us just say three between each child with your parents, too. Now, there are three hundred sixty-five days in a year. In three years that would be one thousand and ninety-five attempts they made to create a child before one was produced. Of course, that is only if your parents were as dutiful as mine in attempting it every night. Do you think they were?" Pausing before her, he ignored her gaping expression and raised his eyebrows in polite inquiry.

"Are you saying you think it will take a thousand and ninety-five couplings for us to produce the heir we need to inherit?" she asked with amazement.

"It would seem so." He smiled innocently, then

tilted his head to calculate again. "And we have just over seven months. But, of course, you should be a couple months along else no one will know. Therefore, let us say we have five months to accomplish the deed. That means we have . . . Well, roughly we have to make the attempt at least nine times a day to inherit." He lowered his gaze to her again. "How many times have we attempted it today?"

"Husband?"

"Aye?"

"Shut up and kiss me," Valoree muttered, slipping her hands up to catch his face and draw it down to her own. She hadn't fallen for his line. She wasn't that naive, but he was just so darn cute.

Their passion was quick to reignite. His mouth shifted, and he sucked at hers as his tongue thrust out aggressively. He backed her against the tree that had shaded them these last two days, quickly beginning to undo the laces she had just done up. Finishing with them, he pushed her gown off her shoulders, shifting her chemise out of the way at the same time. Covering her breasts with his hands, he slid one naked thigh between hers and raised it slightly to rub her through her gown. When he bent suddenly, his face dropping toward her breasts, she thought he was going to suckle her, and her nipples puckered even harder, but he straightened again almost at once, his hands brushing up along her legs under her skirt.

Squirming against the tree, Valoree gasped, her eyes opening and landing right on the small dinghy that was being lowered over the side of the *Valor*. She had forgotten all about them.

"Damn," she said under her breath, stiffening at once, her hands going down to catch his as they slid between her legs.

"What is it?" Daniel glanced over his shoulder and hesitated briefly, then turned back and kissed her again, sliding a finger into her moist heat to caress the nub that hid there.

"Nay." Valoree groaned, pulling her lips away and gasping as he began to drive her wild with a combination of kisses along her chin, ear, and neck, and the friction he was causing between her legs. "The men."

"Ignore them. They will go away," Daniel assured her. Catching one of her hands with his free one, he drew it down to press it against his swollen flesh. Valoree released a breathless laugh that ended on a moan as he thrust one finger inside her.

"Daniel," she cried pleadingly, caressing his arousal and pushing at his shoulders at the same time.

"It will take them a minute to get here. We have time." Reaching down to catch one of her legs beneath the knee, he hooked it around his hip, then clasped her bottom and lifted her slightly. Releasing his manhood, she reached up to clasp his shoulders as he drove himself into her, her teeth biting the flesh of his shoulder, her fingernails digging into his back as he began a rhythm that was fast and exciting, pounding into her like waves on a beach until they both shattered with the pressure.

Valoree went slack against him for a moment, then opened her eyes to see that the dinghy was only halfway between the *Valor* and the beach. Grinning impishly, she straightened slightly, waiting until he lifted his head from her shoulder and met her gaze before announcing, "They are only halfway here. We have time to do it again, my lord."

Dropping his head to her shoulder, Daniel released a half groan, half laugh as she whispered silkily into his ear, "By my counting, we have to do so at least four more times today. To reach the number you estimated."

She felt him begin to grow hard within her again, and chuckled breathlessly as she wriggled against him, her muscles tightening around him encouragingly.

"Aye," he murmured suddenly. "Four more times. Let us see if we cannot make it three."

Valoree laughed happily, her heart soaring as she leaned forward to kiss him. She felt at that moment as if she had found heaven, and that mayhap marriage would not be so bad after all.

Marriage was hell.

It was two months since those incredible two days and one night in the isolated cove in the Caribbean. They were only a warm memory now. Married life wasn't anything like that time had been. In fact, marriage was very much as she had feared it would be, with Daniel taking over her life as if she were a child. Oh, it had not started out that way. It had been a gradual turn.

They had returned to the ship with One-Eye and Skully, then sailed back to Port Royale to load up on goods and such, then had ended up staying there two weeks. Valoree had decided the men should have some shore leave ere they set out on another protracted ocean voyage. Meg had spent that time visiting old friends on the island, so Valoree and Daniel had spent the two weeks almost exclusively in each other's arms. Oh, they had left the ship several times, to play on the beach, to go for picnics. But always they had ended up in each other's arms. It had been almost as blissful as the two days in the cove, except that now there were occasional interruptions by Henry or one of the other men. Valoree had begun to notice the difference then.

The first time Henry had come to her with a question, he had hesitated, his gaze going from her to Daniel and back again, as if he wasn't sure who to ask. In the end, he had addressed it to the room at large. Valoree had frowned at that, but answered, giving orders as always. But the trend had continued. So long as

Daniel was present, the men all seemed at a loss as to whom to address. The matter had bothered her so much that when they had finally set sail for London, she had been careful to go on deck to give her orders only when Daniel was sleeping. The rest of the time had been spent naked in her cabin, working hard at making the heir required by her father's and his grandmother's wills. Very hard. Extremely hard.

Between Daniel's determination to learn every inch of her body, and her need to check on her men, their location, and to give out orders while he slept, Valoree had hardly gotten any sleep at all that first week of the journey. Ah, but it had been worth it—until she had come down with a summer cold, probably from her lack of sleep and being worn out.

Daniel had coddled her then, bundling her in blankets and fetching her hot spiced rum. Valoree had slept nearly around the clock for over a week. By the time she had recovered and made her way on deck again, it was to find that he had taken her place. Oh, the men still called her captain, but it was to him they now turned with questions, and when she gave an order it was only to see the men glance toward Daniel before carrying it out.

Valoree's first instinct had been to go into a rage and demand the respect due her as captain. But then she had thought better of it. The men *were* traditional, and she knew they would believe it was a man's place to rule. It was one thing for her to be captain when they had thought her a man—and even mayhap once they had known she was a woman, so long as she was seeking the husband they needed to retire. But now that she was married and had a husband, by law he was her ruler, and therefore theirs. Thus, she had bitten her tongue and returned to the cabin, determined to wait it out. Daniel was an intelligent man. He even had natural leadership qualities. But he had not spent the last thirteen years aboard ship with these men. He would slip up, and she would be there to show him—and the men—that being a lord did not make him a captain.

Valoree had spent the rest of the journey back to England in the cabin, claiming she was still feeling under the weather and desired the rest. In truth, she had been pacing the floor and waiting—something she had never done well.

Sighing, she shifted in her chair and tried to concentrate on the chapbook she had sat down to read. Chapbooks were what she had filled her time with since arriving at the Thurborne estate two weeks ago—tales of banditry, terror on the high seas, and adventure. One-Eye had sneaked them to her. There were romances in the stack, too, but she avoided them. Valoree had had enough romance to last a lifetime, and it wasn't all that it was chalked up to be. She had found that it lost some of its appeal quickly when the rest of one's life was empty. Actually, she was beginning to resent Daniel and the effect he had had on her life. Time had seemed to fly by when her life had had purpose; now it dragged like an anchor along the bottom of life's ocean. It didn't stop her from enjoying his touch and caresses, but somehow they had lost some of their luster.

A sudden great clatter and crashing from below made its way up to the sunroom where Valoree sat, and she sighed. Petey and the Thurbornes' cook, Eleni were going at it again, no doubt. Those two were having a battle over who ran the kitchen. Eleni had been head cook here for several years and was determined to keep it that way. Petey had always been "the captain's" cook and was determined to keep that position. The two had been throwing pots around and having shouting matches since the *Valor* had laid anchor two weeks ago.

Instead of going to London, they had sailed the *Valor* to the Thurborne estate, anchoring off the point that the castle itself stood on and reaching shore by dinghy. That had been Daniel's decision. He claimed he had things to tend here, but she suspected he was keeping her away from society so she wouldn't embarrass him. He had since insisted on hiring instructors to teach her "what she needed to know to get by." She supposed she couldn't blame him. After all, she had been rather a flop during her coming-out. Added to that was the fact that she just wasn't like other women. She supposed he would rather keep her here, out of the way of the ton. Mayhap he was even beginning to regret marrying her.

Daniel had wanted the men all to wait on the *Valor*, but they had had one of their votes and decided that the same men who had accompanied them in London would come to the Thurborne estate with them. So, Henry, Meg, One-Eye, Skully, Bull, and Pete were all hanging about the castle somewhere. Meg usually spent her time helping Henry in Thurborne's gardens, where the old tar spent his time driving Daniel's gardener crazy with questions and opinions. Skully, One-Eye, and Bull divided their time between riding into the village to try to romance the local girls and hanging out around the stables. The three men appeared to have developed a passion for good horseflesh.

It all left Valoree alone, feeling like a fish out of water in this fancy castle with self-effacing servants, and with a husband who was forever busy running his estate. Valoree had spent most of the last two weeks cuddled up with chapbooks in the chair she now sat in. She had not even really looked around much. She had discovered this room and stayed put. It was the room with the least number of breakables in it. There had not been a lot of fancy little delicate things in Valoree's life. At least not since living on the *Valor*.

Fancy breakables had no place on a ship that dipped and rolled on the high seas, and the Beecham town house had been furnished, but with just the essentials such as furnishings and cooking pots. There had been no easily destructible things there. Here at Thurborne, Valoree was almost afraid to walk around, lest she knock over and smash one of the fancy and delicate items her husband seemed to have everywhere.

Sighing, she set the book down on her lap and peered around the small, sunny room unhappily. She could see her future quite clearly if something did not happen soon. The days stretched out before her, an unending parade of hours spent sitting here, staring off into space, miserable, as she waited for mealtime, when her husband would reappear from whatever mysterious chores to which he was tending. Good Lord, how did other women stand it? Her life had been full of tasks up to now. There had always been some chore or other to accomplish aboard ship: sails to mend, ropes to check, maps and charts to read, orders to give. Even as a child her time had been full of lessons and chores. But Valoree had no idea what women did once they were married and beyond the schoolroom. Was there anything to do at all besides stare around?

The only good thing about it was that, if *she* was bored, her men, stuck on the boat with its cramped living quarters and lack of entertainment and women, must be near climbing the rigging by now. She was positive that trouble would break out soon, and then they would see who was the real captain.

"My dear girl!"

Valoree's head snapped around, her eyes widening in amazement as they fell on Lady Thurborne barreling into the room, arms outstretched, a wide, welcoming smile on her face. Guiltily shoving the chapbook she had been reading down under the cushion she sat on, Valoree stood, and felt her body stiffen as she was engulfed in a cloud of rose-scented taffeta.

"Oh, my dear girl! I wanted to tell you how happy I am to welcome you as my daughter-in-law," the woman trilled in her ear gaily, then pulled back to smile. "I was beginning to think that Daniel would never marry. I feared even the requirements of Mother's will would not move him to it. But you managed it, you clever girl! Come sit with me; we must chat."

Valoree allowed herself to be drawn over to the settee, her expression bemused. "When did you arrive? How did you know we were here?"

"I arrived just now, dear." Lady Thurborne dropped onto the settee, dragging Valoree down with her so that they sat half turned and facing each other. "That nice young man with the unfortunate missing nose arrived with Daniel's letter, telling me you had married and were here."

"No-Nose," Valoree murmured to herself. Three months had seen his leg heal quite well, though he still limped.

"And the moment I read that, I had the servants start packing, the carriage drawn around, and I headed here."

"Oh," Valoree murmured, then glanced toward the door with a frown as another round of clattering, crashing, and curses in both Greek and English reached them.

"What on earth is that?" Lady Thurborne asked, rising anxiously.

Valoree sighed and waved her concern away. "It is just Petey and Eleni going at it again"

"Eleni?" Lady Thurborne sat down with a frown. "Daniel's cook?"

"Aye. She and Petey, my cook, are struggling for who is in charge. They have several battles a day."

"I see," Lady Thurborne murmured with a frown,

then tilted her head slightly to the side and peered at her consideringly. "You do not look happy," she announced.

Valoree sat a little straighter. "Oh, I—" she began, but Lady Thurborne waved her to silence.

"What do you do with your time?"

Valoree hesitated slightly, then gazed around the room rather blankly.

"Being a lady is much different from being the captain of privateers, I imagine," she said now, and Valoree nearly fell off the settee in shock. Smiling at her expression, Lady Thurborne explained. "Meg told me everything."

"Meg did?" Valoree asked in amazement. "When?"

"The day the men drugged you both and took you back to your ship to sail out. She did not wish me to worry about Daniel's suddenly going missing."

"Did Henry know?"

"Yes. Apparently he was not pleased with the idea, but she convinced him it would be right—that I might be able to keep Daniel's driver quiet about his going missing from your town house. And she was correct. I did handle the man."

Valoree peered at her with confusion. "Why?"

"Why did I help the plot along in that manner? Well, because, my dear, I wanted to see Daniel married, settled, and starting on my grandbabies. And it did seem to me that he wanted to marry you, only you were reluctant to agree."

"You do not mind that he married a pirate?" she asked with disbelief. Lady Thurborne grinned.

"Actually, I think it is all rather exciting and romantic. Though I think you are being rather hard on yourself, my dear. You are not really a pirate. You are a privateer. Meg explained about your keeping the king's portion to give to him." She tilted her head again and said, "It must be very hard for you, though.

291

I fear I did not think of all this from your point of view. No doubt Daniel took over everything the minute you were married. He has a tendency to do that," she added with irritation. "And doubtless he did not consider that someone who has led the adventure-filled life you have, would need something other than embroidery to fill her time."

"I do not *do* embroidery," Valoree said with disgust.

Lady Thurborne laughed. "Somehow, I do not think Daniel really minds."

"I fear you would be wrong," Valoree muttered.

Lady Thurborne glanced at her sharply, but before she could comment, the sound of a rather ostentatious throat-clearing filled the room, drawing their attention to a short, flamboyantly dressed little man standing in the doorway.

Valoree sighed at the sight of him, then forced a smile for Lady Thurborne when the woman glanced at her questioningly. "My dance instructor," she explained. "Daniel's idea."

"Oh." Lady Thurborne looked nonplussed for a moment, then patted Valoree's hand and stood. "Well, I shall just go see how Bessy is doing getting things put away in my room, then."

Master Henderson smiled beatifically at Lady Thurborne as she passed him, then closed the door behind her and started toward Valoree.

"My lady!" Taking the hand she offered, the man bent low, pressing several sloppy kisses over her knuckles as he murmured, "My dear, dear, sweet lady. What a delight to see you again."

Valoree snatched her hand back and glared at the man suspiciously as he straightened. He was a bit effusive for her taste.

"I understand that Master Carson will not be with us anymore to play the music." He gave a sad little moue, then sighed heavily before murmuring, "Then we shall have to make our own music, shall we not?"

Daniel was coming from the kitchen, where he had been trying to sort out yet another disagreement between Petey and Eleni, when he spied his mother bearing down on him like an avenging Valkyrie. Cursing under his breath, he managed a weak smile. "Mother. When did you arrive? Someone should have informed me you were here."

"I wanted to see Valoree first," she announced. "Then I went to speak with Meg. And now I would have a word with you. At once," she added firmly, and turned on her heel to lead him into his library.

Daniel followed curiously, vaguely amused at the way his sweet, slightly conniving mother was storming ahead of him. But his humor turned to shock the moment he closed the library door and she whirled on him in a fury.

"I have never been so disappointed in you in my life, Daniel!" she cried. "What have you done to that poor girl?"

"Who? Valoree?" He blinked at her in bewilderment. He had never before heard his mother raise her voice above a mildly strident tone in his life. Lady Thurborne was ever sweet and gentle, using trickery to get her way, as most ladies did, rather than straight confrontation. "I married her, Mother. That is all I have done."

"That girl is miserable."

"Nonsense," he said irritably. "Where is she?"

"With her dance instructor," she announced with a disgust that made Daniel frown. "And that is another thing I would talk to you about. Why are you forcing her to take lessons?"

He released a short laugh at that. "I am not forcing her, Mother. She wants to learn to be a proper lady."

293

"A *proper* lady?" She gasped in horror and he scowled.

"You know what I mean."

"Aye," she said slowly and almost sadly. "I do know what you mean. 'Tis no wonder she feels as though you do not think she is good enough for you."

Amazement filled him. "Did she say that?"

"Not in so many words, but I gather that Meg fears she feels that way."

"Well, it is not what I intended. I just do not wish her to be embarrassed or uncomfortable in society. She—"

"She speaks several languages quite fluently," Lady Thurborne interrupted, and he turned to her in amazement.

"What?"

"Aye." She nodded slowly. "And the fact that you do not know that tells me that you have not even talked to Valoree about her 'lessons.' "

"I just assumed—" He scowled, then shook his head. "I will tell Master Thomas he need not continue the language lessons."

"You need not bother," Lady Thurborne said dryly. "Valoree sent the man off the first day."

Closing his eyes, Daniel sighed. "Tell me."

"It would appear that your Master Thomas explained to her on his first day here that she was a woman, and therefore inferior, but that he would attempt to force some intelligence into her poor female mind." Daniel winced at the news, and his mother nodded.

"As you can imagine, Valoree took exception to that and told him, in Latin, that she had learned her languages as a child under her brother's tutor, then had continued them well into her teens under her brother's tutelage. She told him that she spoke Latin, German, and French quite fluently, and that if he ever spoke to her in such a way again, she would cut his tongue out

294

and shove it down his sorry throat. Your Master Thomas apparently turned quite pale at that and left. He has not returned since."

Sighing, Daniel began to rub his forehead agitatedly. "Well, someone should have told me she could speak—"

"Which is the music instructor?" she interrupted, and he paused in his rubbing to eye her warily.

"Master Carson."

She nodded. "Master Carson has not been here since the third day."

"Tell me," Daniel repeated, moving around his desk to sink wearily down into a plush chair.

"From what I gather, he started her on the lute for the first two days, then decided she had absolutely no talent and switched to the harpsichord. Unfortunately, his method of teaching was to rap her knuckles with the handle of his horsewhip when she hit the wrong key. The third time he rapped her so, Valoree smashed the lute over his head and told him that if he ever showed his face here again she would stick his whip handle up his—er—well, you get the idea. He left at once and did not return."

Daniel snapped his lower jaw, which had dropped open upon hearing this news, then arched one eyebrow suspiciously. "What of the dance instructor?"

"I told you, she is with him now. Apparently he has not given her any trouble yet."

"Thank God," Daniel muttered, then scowled. "If she had told me she could speak languages fluently, I never would have hired Master Thomas. And had she told me about Carson rapping her knuckles, I certainly would have handled it, but—"

"She did not need you to handle it," Lady Thurborne said heavily. "She can handle herself. That is the point."

Daniel stared at her blankly for a moment, obviously

not understanding her meaning. At last he began, "Aye. Well, I shall arrange for new tutors on the morrow, but—"

"Daniel!" she cried in exasperation. "You have not heard a single thing I said!"

"Of course I have, she . . . Oh, well, of course, she will not need a language tutor, I had not realized that she was fluent in the languages, but a music and dance instructor would—"

"Why did you marry her?"

He blinked at the question. "I hardly think—"

"You married her because she was strong, independent, and *different* from all the rest of the women of the ton, did you not?"

He smiled warmly, his eyes beginning to sparkle. "Well, yes, I—"

"Then why are you now trying to turn her into another one of those vain, feckless females you despise so much?"

Daniel blinked in amazement at her words. "I am not—"

"Aye. You are. You are trying to turn her into something she is not. And in the process, you are making her feel that she herself is not good enough."

"She wants to learn. She—"

"Have you asked *her* if she wants to learn? Obviously not, or you would have known she is fluent in several languages," she pointed out.

"Well, how was I to know that? She did not protest when I suggested it, and she is not shy with her opinions. Just look how she handled those tutors."

"Oh, Daniel." His mother sighed unhappily. "How did you, my son, end up this dense?"

"What?" He stared at her with anger.

"There is a vast difference between how she will handle you and how she will handle a tutor. Your opinion matters to her. Theirs does not. At least your opinion probably did matter to her. By now, I would think she is beginning to resent you."

"Resent me? Why would she resent me?" he asked.

"Meg says you have taken her men away."

Daniel rolled his eyes at that. "They are not toys, Mother. I cannot 'take them away.' "

"They are her crew."

"How the hell would you know they are her *crew*?" he asked in sudden realization. It was her turn to roll her eyes.

"Meg told me."

Daniel eyed her warily. "And you do not mind?"

"Mind?" She laughed slightly. "She got you before a minister, did she not? Anyone who could manage that is the perfect daughter-in-law for me. Besides, you need a strong woman or you would be miserable. Now give her back her crew."

He shook his head. "I have not—"

"Daniel, Meg says that the men see Valoree as their captain, but that the way they see it, you, as the husband, are above her. Therefore, you are above them and her both, so they listen to you rather than her. Do you not see? You have taken all authority away from her without even trying, and she has no way to fight it."

When he remained silent, a small frown tugging at his lips, she added, "Meg also told me that you had sent a request to the king for an audience."

His eyebrows rose slightly. "Aye."

"And that you have not mentioned it to Valoree."

"I do not wish to upset her," he said dismissively. Lady Thurborne glared at him in exasperation.

"This is what I mean, Daniel. You must not treat her so. She can handle a little upset and more."

"She was ill on the trip back to England. Feverish and weak, and she is with child. I will not have her upset."

Lady Thurborne's eyes widened in amazement. "With child? Valoree is with child? Has she said so?"

"Nay." He frowned. "She may not even realize it. Henry is the one who told me."

"Henry?" she screeched. "Henry told you that Valoree is with child? How on earth would he know and she not?"

Daniel grinned at her outrage. "Henry is the one who tended to getting her what she needed aboard ship all these years as she pretended to be a man. He knew every time she had the flux. He says she has always been as regular as the tide, but she has missed two since the wedding. If the next one does not arrive, then we can be pretty sure she is with child."

Lady Thurborne dropped weakly into the chair in front of his desk. "And he does not think she knows?"

That question made him frown slightly. "He is not sure. No one has ever actually sat her down and discussed the facts of life with her. All she knows she has learned from men's bragging as she grew up, when they thought her a man."

Lady Thurborne made a face at that, then said, "Daniel, you have to straighten things out. If she is with child, she should know. And you really cannot exclude her from everything like this."

Sighing, he rubbed his forehead again, then nodded. "Aye. Of course. I will talk to her. I—"

A crash in the hall outside his library made Daniel pause. The scream that followed had him on his feet and hurrying to the door. Throwing it open, he gaped at the screaming man holding his ankle and rolling about on the marble floor at the base of the stairs.

"It's broken! You broke my ankle! You—"

"That's less than you deserve, ye weaselly bastard!" Valoree roared, starting down the stairs toward him.

"What the hell is going on here?" Daniel shouted, drawing the attention of both his wife and her dance instructor as he strode out of the library, his mother hard on his heels. "Valoree, get down here! What did you do?"

"Oh, my lord." Master Henderson gasped, grabbing at his pant leg. "She broke my ankle, my lord. Look. How can I teach with a broken ankle? She has ruined me."

Shaking himself free, Daniel peered at his wife questioningly while his mother knelt to examine the man's injury. He knew bloody well Valoree wouldn't have thrown the fellow down the stairs without a good reason, and judging by her furious expression, it was a doozy.

"Being the ignorant female that I am, my lord," Valoree quoted her language instructor sarcastically, pausing at the bottom of the steps to glare over Henderson at her husband. "I cannot be sure, but mayhap you can clear the matter up. Is it normal to dance so close that a man's chest rubs against yours?"

"She is lying! I was teaching her proper dancing."

"Or how about his lips slobbering over my neck? Is that proper?" she continued.

"Lies!" he screeched despairingly.

"And is his hand *really* supposed to rest on—and squeeze—my arse?"

"It is not broken," Lady Thurborne murmured, straightening from the instructor with distaste. "Just sprained."

Eyes narrowing, Daniel bent toward the man, only to pause and whirl as the door suddenly crashed open behind him and Jasper stumbled through it. Ignoring Daniel, he paused before Valoree, panting heavily.

"What is it?" Valoree asked sharply as Henry followed, Meg on his heels.

"Trouble," Jasper said in a gasp, out of breath from his run. "The ship."

# *Chapter Sixteen*

Trouble did not begin to describe what they found when Valoree, Daniel, Henry, and Jasper rowed the dinghy back out to the ship and climbed aboard. Jasper had said that Richard had sent him after her because two of the men, Jackson and Chep, were fighting. But during the time it had taken for Jasper to row ashore and fetch them back, the two-man fight had turned into a free-for-all. Even Richard was now busy banging heads.

This, of course, was exactly the sort of thing for which Valoree had been waiting. But before she could act, Daniel had snatched Jasper's flintlock pistol out of the waist of the man's breeches and fired it into the air. The blast it made brought the fighting to an abrupt halt, and the men turned slowly one after another to warily eye her husband.

Valoree had just begun berating herself for being too slow and letting Daniel take control, when he turned toward her and said quite loudly—loudly enough for every man present to hear—"I believe these men and their behavior are your responsibility, wife."

Valoree's eyes widened at that, her jaw dropping slightly in amazement, for the behavior going on today was all his fault. Then he winked, a gentle smile tugging at his mouth as he added, just as loudly, "You *are* their captain."

He stepped to the side then, leaving her to stare at her crew for a brief moment before gathering herself together. "Who started the fight?" she asked at last.

Chep stepped forward almost at once. "Me. I threw the first punch."

"Nay, it was me." Jackson elbowed him aside to take his place.

One man after another then began to step forward, claiming they had instigated the whole affair. Valoree nearly smiled at the loyalty her crew had to each other. They had simply been pent up on the ship too long. They needed to let off some steam, and the fight had given them the chance. None of them wanted Jackson or Chep flogged for giving them that chance.

"Enough!" she shouted, working at keeping her face stern. "It is obvious you do not have enough to keep you occupied. Since you all have so much energy, I'm thinking we should careen the ship." A groan went up all around, but Valoree ignored it and glanced around for her second mate. "Richard."

"Aye?" The man moved to her side at once.

"Make sure everything's strapped down, beach her, heave her over, and careen her. I want every man here working on this."

"Aye, Captain."

Nodding, Valoree glowered at the rest of the men. "We won't be here much longer. No-Nose should return soon with the message from the king and then we'll head for London and you can all have leave. In the meantime, if I hear of another fight out here, I'll flog you all. Understood?"

"Aye-aye, Captain," was murmured back at her. Valoree nodded, then turned and walked silently back to the rope ladder they had used to mount the ship, aware that Henry, Daniel, and Jasper were following.

"What is careening?" Daniel asked quietly later. They had returned to the castle, assured Meg and Lady Thurborne that all was well; then Daniel had asked Valoree to join him in the library. Now he stood on one side of his desk, with her on the other, as he awaited her answer.

"Careening is when you run a boat ashore, heel her over on her side, and scrape the barnacles and seaweed off her bottom. Sometimes scraping does not suffice and they have to be burned off. Once the men have finished with that, they will caulk any of the leaks they can, replace rotten planks when caulking will not do, and seal it."

"It sounds a large undertaking."

"It is. But it is necessary if you want to move fast—and pirates have to move fast."

Daniel shook his head. "You are not a pirate anymore, Valoree. You are Lady Thurborne."

"Aye," she agreed calmly. "But I had to have them do something, else they'd kill each other out there."

He must have noticed the way she was glaring at him, for he frowned. "What? You are looking at me as if what happened out there today were my fault."

"Aye," she agreed.

"Well," he contended, "that fight was certainly not my fault. I wasn't even there."

"Aye. But you are the one who insisted that we sail here to Thurborne, then anchor off your beach." When he gazed at her blankly, she shifted in disgust. "Daniel, those men have been stuck on that boat for more than a month and a half."

He tapped his lips, thinking, then sank back into his seat unhappily. "Aye, of course you are right. I did not think about that." Sighing, he looked up at her. "You, of course, had thought of that, but did not bother to mention it to me. Am I right?"

She gave a brief nod.

"Why did you not say something?"

"You did not ask."

"Valoree." His mouth twisted in irritation. "You could have told me anyway."

"Aye, I could have," she agreed grimly. "Just as you could have asked before taking over my ship."

Daniel leaned back in his seat to eye her silently. After a few moments, he capitulated. Moving forward to rest his arms on the desk, he said, "As soon as this careening business is done, we will sail down to London so that the men may have some leave. As you say, we can wait just as well there as—"

When he suddenly paused, Valoree tilted her head, wondering at his thoughts. "What is it?"

"How did you know that I had sent a request to the king for an audience?"

She snorted. "Your mother told me that you had sent No-Nose to her with a message informing her of our marriage and taking up residence here."

He raised an eyebrow. "So?"

"So you would hardly tell her, and neglect the king," she pointed out. "Really, Daniel, I do not know why you married me when you think me such an idiot."

His eyes widened in surprise. "I do not think you an idiot."

"Oh, aye," she agreed sarcastically. "And that would be why you hired those bloody instructors, and thought to take over my crew?"

"Nay, I . . . ." He paused then, obviously thinking. "I am sorry, Valoree," he said at last. "It would seem I have not been going about this very well. I thought—"

"You thought to turn me into one of those brainless twits that flit about the ballrooms in London," she interrupted furiously, all the pain she had not really realized she had been feeling coming out. "Well, you can stick that plan in your cannon and shoot it, my lord, because I have no interest. And you can try to take over my men if you like, but you will have a battle on your hands. That crew is the only family I have."

"You have me now."

"Oh, aye," Valoree agreed. "If I learn to play the

303

harpsichord and dance. Well, I don't have to do that for them, and I don't *want* to do that for you." Turning on her heel, she started for the door.

Daniel was after her at once, hurrying around his desk and reaching the door in time to prevent her opening it; he placed a hand against it over her shoulder. Pausing, she stood stubbornly facing the door and refusing to look at him. Daniel sighed, then raised his other hand to the door, moving his body closer until he was pressing against the length of her.

"I do not give a damn if you can play the harpsichord," he said quietly, leaning his cheek against the back of her head. "I do not care if you can dance, either, though it would be nice to dance with you."

"Then why—"

"I am a fool; that is why," he murmured by her ear, then lowered his hands to clasp her shoulders before sliding them down around her waist to draw her stiff body back against him. "My mother was right. I detest all those simpering, sad creatures of the ton and always have." His hands slid up to cup her breasts. "Your independence, strong will, and intelligence are what attracted me to you from the moment you asked for a rum at Whister's. But it scared me, too."

Valoree started to arch into his caress, but stilled and tried to turn to face him. Daniel held her in place with his hold on her breasts. She turned her head, trying to look at him, her lips opening to speak then, but he silenced her with a kiss. Ravishing her mouth as he slid a hand down between her legs, he pressed her back against him.

"Daniel, I—" she began as soon as he broke the kiss, but he covered her mouth with one hand and began tugging her skirts up with the other.

"Shut up, Valoree and let me talk for once, hmmm?" he chided gently. She stiffened, but relaxed again and nodded. He released her mouth to use both hands to draw her skirts up between them as he continued. "Your independence and even your crew mean that you do not really need me."

"Nay," she protested at once, trying to turn to face him again, but Daniel stopped her by grasping her legs. He had bent slightly behind her to find the bottom of her skirts, and now clasped her just above the knees, keeping her facing the door. When she stopped trying to turn, he started to straighten, drawing his hands up as he did. But while he could keep her facing the door, he just couldn't keep her quiet. As she wriggled under the glide of his fingers over her skin, she whispered, "I need you. I need a husband and babe to inherit Ainsley, just as you need a wife and babe to inherit your grandmother's bequest."

"I need you for more than that, Valoree," he said against her neck.

"M-more?" she murmured distractedly as he caught her at the hips and drew her lower body away from the door slightly, even as he pressed her upper body against it.

"Aye. I find myself having strong feelings for you." Reaching between them, he began to work at the fastening of his breeches. "I think—Nay"—he sighed, pausing to lean his head against hers—"I know I love you."

"You—" Valoree began in amazement, then gasped and bit her lip as he suddenly slid into her from behind. Her hands clenched into fists against the door on either side of her forehead, and she moaned as he slightly withdrew.

"I love you," he repeated in a voice that almost sounded pained. He pushed into her again. "I love your body. I love your laugh. I love your passion. I love your intelligence." He thrust inside of her and withdrew as he spoke each sentence, then added simply, "I love . . . *you*."

"I—" He stopped moving within her as she started to speak, waiting, and Valoree hesitated, then tried again. "I . . . I—care for you, too," she got out at last, rolling her eyes at her own words even as Daniel suddenly leaned weakly against her. He uttered a shaky laugh.

"Just what every man in love wants to hear." There was amusement in his voice, but pain, too. Valoree tried once again to pull away and face him, but once again he stopped her. "Nay." He pressed a kiss to the back of her neck, then reached up to begin caressing the flesh of her breasts and belly again. "I can wait. You need not lie to me," he murmured, resuming again the rhythm he'd begun. "But we shall make a vow. I will try not to take over, or treat you like an idiot or child, and you will not tell me that you love me until you mean it. Deal?"

Valoree knew a good deal when she heard one and nodded at once, then turned to peer at him in surprise when he suddenly withdrew from her. Grabbing her hand, Daniel pulled her to his desk, cleared one end of it with a sweep of his free arm, then pulled her into his arms for a quick, hard kiss. A moment later he turned her around, bending her over the desk, tugging her skirts up, and thrusting himself into her.

It felt to Valoree almost as if he were staking a claim, gaining control the only way he could, since he had promised to try not to take over. At first she lay still against the desk. But as he bent forward until his chest was against her back, one hand snaked around to slide between her legs, and he began to caress her even as he nipped at her shoulder through her gown. His mouth then moved up to her ear. Within moments he had her panting and thrusting back into him, giving as good as she got until they both found satisfaction.

\*     \*     \*

Valoree caught herself humming under her breath as the carriage rolled along, and she paused abruptly, shaking her head with a laugh. She had been doing that a lot lately—humming a cheery tune as she went about her life. She felt happy. Things were going well.

It had been a little over three weeks since Daniel had confessed he loved her. Now that it was out in the open, his attitude and behavior toward her had changed. She had never really noticed, but until that day, he had only actually shown anything approaching affection for her when trying to get under her skirts. The rest of the time he had worn a slightly cynical smile, as if he found her, and everything else, terribly amusing. It had made him seem slightly distant, aloof. Not that she had recognized it at the time, but now she did. Now she saw the difference. Every time he looked at her now, there was love in his eyes. When he smiled, it was a softer smile, full of emotion. He no longer hid from her.

He also no longer tried to take charge. She had been in obvious control of the men since that day, something the *Valor*'s crew seemed to accept without a problem. She supposed it helped that Daniel had handed her back that power with his loud comments on the ship about their being her responsibility, but whatever the case, she gave them their orders and they listened without question.

Valoree had also found something with which to fill her time. Much to Daniel's everlasting horror, it was bees. Honeybees. Valoree had discovered them during a visit with Daniel to see Lord and Lady Mobley on the neighboring estate. The invitation had arrived a few days before Daniel's confession, but it wasn't until after that day that Daniel decided to accept it. Valoree suspected it was his attempt to prove that he wasn't ashamed of her. She, on the other hand, had agreed to prove that she could act like a lady. They'd had a wonderful time.

Well, all right—not wonderful. Valoree had been bored to tears until Lady Mobley had taken her out to see her bees. She had been smitten with them from the first. She wasn't sure why. Perhaps it was the constant risk of being stung. Or the quiet that had to be kept around them to avoid instigating an attack. Or maybe it was just that she found, as time passed, that she was developing a terrible craving for the sweet nectar they made. Whatever the case, she had promptly decided that bee keeping was how she would fill her time since she was retiring from privateering. Anyway, she had started studying up on the little honey makers right away. Daniel had taken it all in stride, positive she would grow bored with her project. But she hadn't. Not over the two weeks that passed before No-Nose arrived back with the king's response, not during the couple of days that had followed as they had prepared to head to London, and not over the several days since their arrival back in that noisy, crowded, stinky town.

They had arrived midmorning, given the men their orders, left Richard in charge of assigning the men leave, then had sent Meg and Henry back to the town house they had rented from Beecham, to keep up appearances. Her aunt and uncle could hardly just disappear, and certainly would not move in with them at the Thurborne town house—not in any normal course of events. So until Daniel could clear everything up and they could return to Thurborne Castle, those two were to continue to stay at the Beecham rental. Which meant that Skully, One-eyed Joe, Pete, and Bull were all there, too—back in their pink livery and continuing the masquerade.

Daniel and she had continued on to his town house. There he had given her a tour, introduced her to the staff, had luncheon with her, and sat in horror as she announced her intention to make some purchases while they were in town. It wasn't that she wished to spend money that horrified him. It was what she had told him she intended to buy: all the equipment she would need to start a honey-making operation of her own.

She smiled to herself now as she thought of it. From his reaction that day, and the two since, she was beginning to think that Daniel had more than a usual dislike of bees. He really was not reacting well to the idea of her having thousands of them. Not that she had let it stop her. Valoree had been leaving the town house every afternoon since their arrival, and returning just before supper every night with more stacks of things she would need to run an apiary. She could hardly wait to get home and get started on it. Just the thought of all that sweet honey—

The carriage came to a halt, drawing Valoree from her thoughts. Leaning forward, she peered out the window to see that they had arrived back at the town house, and she smiled in anticipation as the footman opened the door for her to get out. She could hardly wait until her husband saw her latest purchases. He would turn green, she knew, and, oddly enough, she looked forward to it. She was finding Daniel's distress quite amusing for some reason.

That was probably a shameful thing to admit; no doubt enjoying torturing one's husband really wasn't a good thing. But for some reason, the more upset he got at the idea of all those bees buzzing around, the more she enjoyed the idea. It was rather like the satisfaction she had experienced as a young girl when she had eaten pickled cucumbers dripping with raspberry preserves, all to make Jeremy—who had always suffered terribly from seasickness—run for the side of the ship. This was probably a flaw in her personality, this enjoyment of torturing those she loved.

Valoree paused halfway up the walk to the house,

her eyes growing wide as she realized what she'd said. Those she loved? *Those she loved?* She loved him. She loved Daniel. Didn't she? She had just thought that. She had. Right? Would she give her life for him? She'd rather not, but probably would. Could she see growing old with him. Happily? Oh, dear Lord, she could! She could see herself torturing and making love to him by turn until he was a randy hundred-year-old with no teeth. She loved Daniel.

The door to the town house opened and Bawden, Thurborne's butler, peered out, reminding her that she had stopped halfway to the house. Flashing a beaming smile at the older gentleman, Valoree rushed forward, nearly flying into the house.

"Good afternoon, my lady. I trust you had a good day?"

"Yes, thank you." Valoree laughed, tugging her gloves off. "Is my lord husband back from his club yet?"

"Aye, my lady," the man said in his dignified voice as he took her gloves. "He asked that I inform you that he has gone above stairs to change; then he shall join you for supper."

"He is already finished with his dress and is ready to join his beautiful wife at their supper," Daniel corrected, coming down the stairs and smiling at Valoree. "You may tell Cook she can start serving now, Bawden."

"Very good, my lord." The servant headed off in his dignified walk as Daniel stepped off the last step. Valoree launched herself at him at once, throwing her arms around his neck and kissing him passionately as he closed his arms about her.

"Mmmmm," Daniel murmured, rocking her gently from side to side as the kiss ended. "I missed you, too."

Valoree chuckled softly, then sobered. "I have something to tell you."

"Oh?" He cocked an eyebrow with interest. "And what would that be?"

"I—"

The front door opened, interrupting her, and they both turned to see the footman come in carrying several packages. Daniel groaned at once.

"More?"

Grinning, Valoree nodded, then took his hand and led him down the hall to the dining salon. Tugging him inside, she whirled to lean against his chest and reached up to caress his face softly. "Now, as I was saying. I—"

They both turned as the door to the kitchen opened and Cook entered carrying a large platter bearing stuffed fish.

"Mmmmm. That looks delicious," Daniel flattered the flushed woman, who smiled her pleasure at the compliment. His gaze slid back to Valoree apologetically and he urged her toward the table, then held her chair out for her. "Sit down, darling. We—"

"My lord?"

"Aye?" Daniel turned from pushing Valoree's chair in for her, looking questioningly at Bawden as the man hesitated in the door.

"A gentleman to see you, my lord," the man explained the intrusion. "I told him you were at dinner, but he said it was important. I put him in the salon. Shall I tell him he will have to wait?"

"Nay. I shall see to it, Bawden." Daniel gave Valoree another apologetic smile, then bent to press a kiss to her forehead. "I won't be a moment," he assured her, then slid from the room.

The clank of the platter being set down drew Valoree's gaze back to the table, and she found herself gazing down at a whole fish, stuffed. Eyes, scales, fins, everything had been left wholly intact. Valoree felt her stomach roll in protest and abruptly stood.

"M'lord, I thought you should know—"

Valoree stiffened as she recognized Henry's voice before it was silenced. Frowning, she hurried out into the hall. The salon door was closed, muffling the conversation coming from inside. Rushing to it, she reached for the doorknob, then hesitated, and pressed her ear to the door instead.

"What? How did it happen?" she heard Daniel ask in amazement.

"The fellow was hiding in Valoree's room," Henry responded. "Skully went in to collect the rest of Valoree's things as ye ordered him to, and surprised the fellow."

"What fellow?" Valoree muttered to herself.

"Is there something I can get you, my lady?"

Straightening abruptly, Valoree turned wide-eyed to face Bawden. "Oh, I—" Thinking of no excuse, she simply shook her head. "Nay, thank you."

The man hesitated, then nodded and turned on his heel. As he took himself off, she turned back to the door to listen again.

"Is he all right?" Daniel was asking with concern.

"He broke an arm in the tumble down the stairs." Henry sounded upset.

"Great," Valoree sighed. "Another broken limb." London was turning out to be far more dangerous to her crew than the seas. She could almost believe that they *were* cursed. Then she realized that Henry had asked to speak to Daniel, and she frowned. He should have asked to speak to *her*. He hadn't. He was bringing the news to Daniel. And Daniel wasn't calling her in on this. So much for the man's not taking over.

"And the other fellow?" Daniel asked inside the salon.

"Dead. Broke his neck on the way down the stairs."

They went down the stairs together, Valoree guessed, frustrated that she had to do any guessing at all. Skully must have surprised him, a struggle ensued, the fellow got away and made a dash down the stairs, and Skully'd gone after him.

"Do you recognize him?"

"Nay," Henry's answer reached her through the door. "Never seen him before, though Bull says he looks like the chap what was driving the carriage that crashed into ours."

Valoree cursed under her breath at the same moment as Daniel.

"Then that was not an accident." Her husband sighed almost too quietly for her to hear.

"It would seem not."

"Then the fire probably was not either." Daniel cursed again. There was a moment of silence; then he asked, "Is there anyone in London who might bear a grudge against Valoree or a member of her family?"

Valoree rolled her eyes at that. Just like a man. The fellow was in her room, so he had to be after her. He didn't even consider that unless he had been in the house before, he wouldn't know whose room was whose. That he would have to search around. Or that maybe he hadn't meant to go into that room at all but had been in the hall, and had ducked into her old room to hide when Skully had come up the stairs.

"Nay. She was just a child when she left England aboard the *Valor*. This here husband-hunting trip was her first trip even to London," Henry said.

"The rumors said that the Spanish killed her brother."

"Aye. Some Spanish bastard did him in." Henry's bitterness was clear.

"How? And why?"

"Didn't she tell ye?"

"She has not talked of it at all."

Silence, then: "It was after he went to meet with you for the assessing. He left, heading back to collect us, but the Spanish had found out that Jeremy'd be meetin' with ye. One of our crew was feeding them information in various ports, I reckon. They lay in wait, thinking he would leave you, collect the rest of his treasure, then head back to join us. But he headed right back for us. He wanted all the men present to collect the treasure.

"The Spanish lay in wait, then stopped and boarded them, none too pleased that the Valor had so little on her. The captain offered them all quick deaths if they gave up the treasure. Jeremy said no, but he changed his mind once they started to torture the crew. He told them then, but the bastard was enjoying himself. He had fun with the men, doing horrible things to them."

Valoree shuddered where she stood, recalling the sight that had awaited them when they had finally found the spot where Jeremy lay. She and the rest of the crew had collected all that they needed for the trip back to England, then relaxed at a tavern, checking infrequently down at the docks for their ship's return. They hadn't at first worried at how long it was taking. But when night fell and Valoree's brother still had not returned, they had begun to fret.

The next morning, while it was still dark, they had hired a piragua and set out to look for the *Valor* and its crew. And they had found them in a cove not unlike the one where Valoree and Daniel had consummated their marriage. They had spotted the mast first. The Spanish had sunk the *Valor* in that harbor, but it was not deep enough to cover the ship. The main mast had stood out of the water, its Jolly Roger waving sadly in the breeze. They had rowed the dugout canoe to shore, silent and grim as they had passed body after body floating through the water. Yes, the Spaniard had done horrible things to those men. Not one body had been unmutilated. But none of the bodies they had passed had been Jeremy's.

Valoree had leaped from the dugout canoe as soon as they had reached water shallow enough in which to walk, nearly losing her pants as they were dragged at by the waves. She had been wearing a set of Jeremy's clothes, as she had just had another growth spurt and had outgrown all her own. Holding Jeremy's breeches up impatiently, she had waded ashore and begun checking the bodies strewn about like so many dropped chess pieces. Checking face after face of men she had known and lived with for eight years, she had desperately searched for her brother.

It had been a nightmare. She had been able to read, quite clearly, the horror in each man's glassy eyes and open mouth. A little piece of her heart had broken away with every friend that she found. And then she had come upon Jeremy.

Valoree had been amazed to find him still alive, and then horrified at his state. They had staked him out in the sand, naked. His body was cut from one end to the other, none of the wounds more than an inch apart. Then they had poured honey over him and left him for the insects and animals. She guessed that the way they had decided to kill him was the reason he still lived when they arrived. It must have taken hours to cut him like that.

She still had nightmares where she held him in her arms. He gasped, "Spanish . . . bastard . . . Ohhhh." Sobbing, she had clutched him close as he cried out, telling him to hush, to rest, to save his strength. But he had known he was dying. He'd gasped out, "Question-mark shaped scar . . . neck. Told them where treasure . . . Lost all. So sorry. Val—"

"Then he pressed the family ring into Valoree's hand and died," Henry's sad words drew her back to the conversation in the room beyond the door, and Valoree closed her eyes, shuddering.

"My God," Daniel's horrified words reached her.

"Aye. She hasn't been the same since. Closed herself up and didn't care 'bout nobody or nothing except finding and killing the bastard who did that."

"She never found him?"

"Nay. We never did."

"How did you convince her to give up the hunt?" Daniel asked.

Henry gave a dry laugh. "Didn't *convince* her. Voted on it." She heard his sigh through the door. "We had regained the money needed to set Ainsley to rights last summer. But she didn't want to stop and we . . ." There was silence, then: "But, finally we had a vote. The men were ready to retire. It seemed to us that we were just giving the bastards more of our time. We were giving up a portion of our lives for them. Still, the captain was obsessed. We talked about it, and the men—well, they still thought her a man at that time, a lad really— but they decided it was for the captain's own good. So we voted, and once we voted, she had no choice."

"No choice," she heard Daniel murmur. "You took the power away from her."

"It was for her own good," Henry insisted grimly. "She had no business being out at sea any longer. She was there out of necessity at first, and that was one thing. But in the end, it was no longer necessity."

They were both silent for a moment; then Daniel said, "So you know of no one who would wish her dead?"

"Nay. But the men are spooked, and Meg . . . Well, she was nigh on hysterical. Took one look at the dead fella and went right white. She's wanting to get out of here. Wants us to tell Valoree that she's with child, have her announce it, claim Ainsley, and head there right now. And the men are right behind her."

Valoree gave a start. She hadn't realized that anyone had guessed her secret, though she supposed she should have known that Henry would figure it out. He had always helped her with the flux when it came on her: getting rags for her to use, serving her hot rum to ease her cramps. Of course he would have noticed she had missed the last two. Well, three now.

She had kept the secret to herself, though. She wasn't even sure why, except that she had wanted to wait first and be sure she didn't lose the child.

"I just can't figure why anyone would wish to harm the captain," Henry said. "Maybe Meg's right and it doesn't matter as long as we get her out of town. She's taking this really hard. She was fussing over Skully something fierce."

There was silence for a minute; then Daniel spoke, his voice drawing nearer the door. "I want to have a look at this fellow. Maybe I know him and—" His voice died as he opened the door to find Valoree on the other side. She had managed to straighten, but not to move away before he opened the door.

"What—" he began, but Valoree interrupted him.

"I was just coming to tell you that your dinner is growing cold," she said quickly, then glanced past him, her eyes widening in feigned surprise. "Henry! Is something the matter? What are you doing here?"

The two men glanced at each other; then her husband said, "He just came around to let us know that they have settled in at the town house."

"Oh?" she asked archly, her gaze fixed on the older man. He squirmed under her hard-eyed look, but remained silent. It was Daniel who spoke next.

"Aye. Valoree, I am afraid I have to go out. I will not be gone long, but I want to check on something," he announced, stepping out into the hall and forcing her back a step. Henry slid past, too, as soon as Daniel had cleared the doorway, sidling nervously toward the front door. Valoree frowned at him, then tried to speak, but Daniel continued right on as he shifted sideways and began to back toward the door as well. "Why do you not go back and finish your meal? You need to keep up your strength. I will explain everything later. Much later."

"But—" The door closed in her face and Valoree slammed her hand against it impatiently. "So much for discussing things and not taking over," she said in a snarl, her mouth twisting with displeasure. She was damned tired of being led around by the nose.

Pulling the door open, she looked out in time to see the carriage pull away. A sudden throat clearing behind her made her pause and glance back at Daniel's butler. "Aye?"

Bawden hesitated, then; "Is my lady going somewhere?"

"Aye."

He hesitated at the hard word, then, apparently deciding he would be in more trouble from Daniel should he not ask, he straightened his shoulders. "Shall I order a carriage?"

"I can walk. It is not far," Valoree said dismissively. With that she walked out, pulling the door closed behind her.

She was halfway up the walk to the gate that fronted Daniel's town house when she heard the door open behind her. "But, my lady, where shall I tell my lord you have gone should he return?"

"You will not have to tell him anything," Valoree tossed back grimly over her shoulder. "I am walking to my uncle's town house, which is where he is."

"Oh." There was uncertainty in his voice; then she thought she heard him sigh unhappily as she stepped through the gate and pulled it closed.

Valoree was so angry, she was nearly halfway to the Beecham town house before she started to feel the early evening chill. The night was damp and foggy. But then, from what she had seen since being in London, it usually was, she thought grimly. Rubbing her arms, she berated herself for not thinking her plan through first and grabbing a cloak of some sort. Ah, well, it wasn't much of a walk from one town house to the other. Two short blocks. Still, her gaze slid alertly around the shadowed street as she went, trying to pierce the drifting mist and watch out for possible problems. Luckily she didn't see anything to be concerned about.

She was a mere two houses from her destination when something made her stop. Freezing, she saw a cloaked figure slide out through the front door. Instinctively, Valoree moved closer to the stone fence beside her, trying to be less noticeable as she watched the figure scurry to the gate. She recognized Meg right away. Her size and the fact that a light-colored gown kept peeking out from under the cloak made her identity an easy guess. When the other woman reached the walk and turned away from Valoree to hurry up the street, she immediately followed, her thoughts churning. The woman was obviously up to something she shouldn't. But what she was doing was anyone's guess.

Already chilled Valoree hoped as she set out after her that Meg wasn't planning to go far. No such luck. The woman walked for what seemed like forever, rushing down this road, then hurrying up another. She should have taken the damn carriage, Valoree thought irritably. It wasn't safe for a woman to be wandering the streets alone. Well, a woman who couldn't protect herself at any rate. Of course, if Meg had taken the carriage, she wouldn't have been sneaking—Skully would have had to go with her, too. Also, Valoree herself couldn't have followed on foot.

It was a relief when the older woman finally paused

in front of a town house. She didn't approach it at first; she simply stood out front, staring up at it, uncertainty in every line of her body. She even turned back the way she had come—toward Valoree, who had to quickly duck behind a tree to avoid being spotted— but she took only two steps before pausing again. Doing so, she straightened resolutely, turned back, hesitated, then started up the walk to the house. Valoree watched from her position behind the tree as the other woman knocked. A moment later, light spilled out over Meg's cloaked figure as a servant opened the door. As he stepped aside for her to enter and the door closed, the night was left dark and silent once more.

Frowning, Valoree peered up at the dwelling, wondering whose it was and what business Meg could possibly have there, then back the way they had come. It suddenly occurred to her that she probably couldn't find her way back. She had been more focused on Meg than on the route the woman had taken. Although she doubted even if she had paid attention to the path that she would be able to recall it. The woman had taken more twists and turns to get here than Valoree could count on both hands.

Sighing, she turned back to the house. She had a bad feeling about all of this. The very fact that Meg had gone about this all so sneakily was enough to make Valoree edgy. First, a fellow was caught in their house, where he broke his neck and Skully his arm in a tumble down the stairs, then Meg slipped out to come here. Valoree seemed to recall Henry saying something about the woman being terribly agitated and wanting them to leave London for the country. Of course, Daniel would not have agreed to that. He was still waiting for his audience with the king.

Drumming her fingers against the tree she stood behind, Valoree considered the house. She could wait here for the other woman to come out and follow her back to Beecham's rental, never being the wiser as to the reason behind this journey, or she could just sneak up to the house and have a look inside. Perhaps she might even figure out who Meg was meeting.

Action was more attractive to Valoree than standing about, so she slid out from behind the tree and walked quickly to the townhouse gate. Slipping through it, she eased it closed, then made her way up the path, doing her best to stick to the shadows as she went.

She didn't notice the man trailing her until it was too late.

# *Chapter Seventeen*

"You want I should get rid of the body?" Bull asked, drawing Daniel's gaze away from the face of the dead man with amazement.

"Get rid of it? No. We have to call in the authorities." Seeing the uncertainty on the men's faces, Daniel grimaced and straightened. "It was an accident. A fall down the stairs. No one is at fault here, and he was an intruder. But the authorities should be notified." He glanced around, his gaze landing on One-Eye.

"I'm on my way," the other man announced, then turned to open the door, only to pause and glance back. "Which authority, exactly, would it be I am going to fetch?"

Daniel glanced toward the man, his mouth opening to answer, then snapped it shut as he saw John Beecham standing at the doorstep, gaping in at the body on the floor.

\*    \*    \*

"Damn." Valoree reached up to massage her aching head. It did seem she had a tendency to wake up sore-headed lately. At least this time she had seen the man who hit her. She had heard the snap of a fallen branch behind her as she approached the town house, turned, and caught a quick glimpse of his face before the handle of his flintlock pistol had struck her in the temple.

"You are awake."

Valoree glanced up with surprise at the woman who hurried to kneel at her side in the dim, dungeonlike room. "Meg."

"Aye." The other woman sighed, then asked at the same time that Valoree did, "What are you doing here?"

Valoree made a face. "I saw you sneak out of the town house and I followed to see where you were going. Someone knocked me out as I was creeping up to the window to peek inside," she admitted, then arched an eyebrow. "And you?"

"I came to see my sister," the woman admitted grimly. Valoree's eyebrows rose.

"Lady Beecham?"

"Aye. I was shown to the salon, went to peer out the window, and someone must have entered behind me. I was hit from behind, too."

"Has this something to do with the man who broke his neck falling down the stairs?" At Valoree's question, the older woman nodded solemnly. "You recognized him?"

"He used to work for my father. I would imagine he was with my sister now."

"So the attacks . . . ?"

"Were all aimed at me, I am afraid," Meg admitted sadly.

"Hmmm." Valoree was silent for a moment, then beetled her brows. "Would you care to fill in the bits you left out when last we spoke about your past?"

Meg hesitated, then blurted, "John is my son."

"John?" Valoree frowned at the name and started to shake her head, then paused, her eyes widening. "John Beecham? Lord Beecham was the lover who got you with child, then did not believe it was his?" When she nodded, Valoree sighed wearily and shifted to get up off the cold, damp floor on which she had been sitting. They were in some sort of storage room. It felt like a wine cellar, but there was no wine, just crates and boxes. A single candle was the only light. Kind of them to leave even that, Valoree supposed as she eased onto a nearby crate. Rubbing the back of her neck in an effort to relieve some of her discomfort, she raised her head to peer at Meg. "Go on."

Sighing, Meg settled herself on a crate near the door, tears beginning to shine in her eyes as she stared unhappily down at her hands. "Meg is short for Margaret. My full name is Margaret Jean Kettleworth."

"Nice to meet you, Lady Kettleworth," Valoree said dryly. "But can we skip to the pertinent parts? I suspect we haven't much time." When Meg nodded, but looked at a loss as to where to start, Valoree prompted her. "How could you be John's mother? Lady Beecham—"

"Stole him," Meg interrupted bitterly. "She stole him and lied to me." Closing her eyes, she lowered her head wearily. "As I told you, I loved John's father." A smile tilted her lips gently in reminiscence. "He was such a handsome man. Tall, debonair—"

"You had an affair." Valoree interrupted, speeding the story along.

"Aye." The word was a sigh. "His mother held a large rout at Beecham Castle before he was married. Lots of people were invited. It was a marvelous affair. Hunting during the days. Dancing at night. The last night there was a masked ball. I did not recognize him at first, but he did me. He said it was my perfume that

323

gave me away." Her smile returned. "He said—"

"Meg," Valoree interrupted impatiently. The other woman nodded.

"Aye, I am sorry. Toward midnight, we slipped out to the bailey for some fresh air, but it was full of people, most of them quite drunk. One of them bumped into me and spilled something on my skirt. It was red wine, and my gown was white. John was furious. I was afraid he would challenge the hapless man to a duel, he was so angry. I dragged him away, pulling him into the stable, begging him to show me his horse in the hopes of calming him down."

"And you made love in the hay," Valoree rushed the story along again. "Then what happened? Did he not ask you to marry him?"

"He did not get the chance," Meg said with a sigh. "Afterward, he led me back to the manor, saying we had to go see my parents, that there was something he wished to ask them. But my sister came across us as we entered. Aghast at the stain on my gown, she rushed me off to help me tend to it. It was beyond repair. I had to change. I told Blanche what had happened, and that I thought the question he meant to ask was for my hand in marriage. She took my gown and suggested she go tell him to come fetch me in twenty minutes, then left me to change. I did, then fell asleep waiting. He never came." Her bewilderment as she said those last words was obvious.

Valoree frowned slightly. "What happened the next day?"

"He gave me the cut direct," she admitted. "I stayed away from the balls and parties after that. It hurt too much to see him. But three months later, I realized I was with child."

"Did you tell *him?*"

She shook her head. "I did not know what to do. I turned to Blanche"—she grimaced at the name—"but she was quite affronted. She said he would have to take responsibility. I resisted at first, but Blanche was brutal about the matter. I had made my bed, and now must face the consequences, she said. He was supposed to be at the Crichtons' ball that night. Blanche determined to go and drop the information in his lap. It would be his problem after that, she claimed. I stayed home, too humiliated and afraid to go. When she returned, it was to tell me that he had laughed at my situation and said it probably wasn't even his. That if I had lifted my skirts for him so quickly and easily, how was he to know I did not do it for others? It could be the stable lad's child for all he knew."

"Men!" Valoree snapped in disgust, and Meg nodded unhappily.

"I did not know what to do. I think I would have hurled myself out the window if my sister had not been there. Instead, she convinced me to go stay in a cottage on the edge of Kettleworth land. I took only my maid and spent most of my time walking in the woods. Three months before the child was born, Blanche arrived. She kept me company through the last few months."

"And your son John was born."

"Yes. It was a terrible ordeal, he was so large. But when I asked to see the child, she kept saying I should wait until after I had rested. The next morning, she told me they had not wanted to tell me while I was so weak, but he had been born dead. Then she told me that rumors of my being with child had reached London, that my reputation was in ruins, and that John, the child's father, had married."

"Not mentioning, of course, that she was the one who had married him," Valoree added dryly. Meg nodded in misery. After a moment of silence, she continued.

"I did not care what happened at that point. I could

not return to London. John was lost to me forever, and our child was buried in an unmarked grave in the local church. Once again, I was ready to simply give up on life. But Blanche convinced me to go to the islands, make a fresh start. She bought me tickets on a ship, packed me up, placed a large sack of gold in my hands, and saw me off."

"So you went to live on the islands," Valoree prompted.

"I met a man on the ship to Port Royale. His name was William Gilchrist. He looked very much like John and he was sweet to me. He fell in love with me. I did not love him back. Still, I allowed him to convince me to marry him. The captain married us on our last morning at sea."

"Did you find no happiness with him?"

"Of a sort," she murmured. "We built a fine plantation during those first years of our marriage—growing sugarcane. We both worked hard and prospered. It was one of the wealthiest plantations on Port Royale. But as years after year passed with no children"—she shook her head—"he started to drink and let things slide. He began to refuse to allow me to help out, or make decisions when he was 'indisposed.' I knew the plantation was failing, but it wasn't until he died that I found out just how bad things were. There was very little left that was not owed. By the time the creditors were paid off, there was enough for a ticket on a ship home and not much else. I decided to return to my family.

"I met a young lady on the ship, a fellow passenger who had not been away from England long, and she filled me in on the latest gossip and happenings. She knew quite a bit about this family and that. Without revealing myself, I was able to learn of my parents' deaths. She also said that she thought the older daughter had married some lord from the north. She claimed it had happened four months after the younger had run off with some stable lad. Quite a family for scandal, she had joked. The older one had barely escaped a scandal herself, rumor had it. Right after the wedding, she had gone to live in the country. Eight months after that she returned with the heir. When I asked her what was scandalous about that, she said the ton had been all atwitter. The child was much too large to be a newborn. It had looked at least six months old."

"And you realized it was your son," Valoree murmured quietly.

But Meg shook her head. "Nay. Not right away. You see, she was so sketchy on details. And she did not know the name of the lord. Besides, you must understand, all those years, I had thought of Blanche as my savior. I would not have believed . . . not until I saw it for myself."

"Which you did?"

"Aye. As I told you before, I hired a hack when I arrived in London to take me to an inn. But I did not stop to look in a shop. We passed by John's parents' town house on the way. I was watching the house, of course, curious to know if he lived there still, or if his parents did. I saw my sister come out of the house and get into a carriage—"

"And then you realized!"

Meg smiled sadly, but shook her head. "You give me too much credit. I thought she had been visiting, perhaps, or some such thing. I told the driver to follow the carriage. She stopped outside of a dressmaker's. I asked the driver to wait and got out to follow her inside. As I entered, a shop girl rushed forward to greet Blanche, addressing her as Lady Beecham. *That* is when I realized. I simply stood there in shock; then the shop girl spotted me and started forward, asking if I was all right. Blanche turned to look at me. She started to look away again, then froze, her eyes coming back to me with equal shock. Then I turned and stumbled out of the store."

"But your carriage was gone."

"Aye. So I started to run. I just wanted to get away."

"And you ended up by the docks, where Bull found you," Valoree finished.

Meg nodded with a sigh. "Aye, and his offer of a warm, dry bed with a sweet small cottage later, where I could ponder my memories of John's father, seemed as good a way to end my days as any."

Valoree gaped at her. "Ponder your memories? You still love him?"

"Aye. Foolish, perhaps, but I always felt there was some explanation for what had happened, something I was not seeing. He had courted me. We had been so happy together. I could not believe all of his feelings were feigned."

"They were not."

Both women glanced sharply toward the door at that announcement. It was open now, and Lady Beecham filled the entrance with her considerable bulk.

"He loved you terribly. Right up until the very day he died," she said sadly. Then, "Meg, I have done you so many wrongs I cannot even count them. And in the end I think I made myself more miserable than you. That night when you came in from the stables you were all aglow. So gloriously happy. I wanted that for myself. And I didn't care how I got it. I didn't even really plan what I did that night. It simply popped into my head, wholly conceived, as if the devil himself had whispered it to me. I stashed your gown in my room and went to find John, but instead of telling him to collect you from our room, I told him to meet you in the stables. Then I flew back to my room, changed into your costume and mask, and slid out of the house.

"I had been by the stables earlier that night to check on my horse. When I was there, I had seen that the stable master was drunk to the point of near oblivion. When I returned, he was not much better. When John arrived, it was to find a woman he thought was you in the stable master's arms.

"I had thought that he would simply turn and walk away. But he didn't. He pulled me away from the man and began to beat him viciously. I was terrified. I thought he would beat him to death. I ran back to the ball and sent a couple of men out to the stables to stop him, then hurried back to my room to change into my own clothes.

"I just stayed out of the way after that to see what would happen next. I was afraid you would talk to him and my plot would unravel, but when he gave you the cut direct the next morning, you seemed to give up on him. I had been feeling guilty about my impulsive actions, but that convinced me that what I had done was right. I told myself that you did not deserve him if you were not willing to put up even a bit of a fight for him."

"How was I to fight?" Meg interrupted sharply at the criticism. "He would not even look at me, let alone speak to me."

"How would you know? You never tried to talk to him!" Blanche snapped back with resentment. "I would have cornered him, forced him to tell me why he was treating me so shabbily after our night together."

Meg sank back onto her crate looking uncertain as Blanche continued. "Instead, you avoided him—not going to any of the same parties, leaving if he showed up at any you attended."

"It hurt to see him. I was so ashamed."

"Well, perhaps if you had used some courage instead of slinking away like a naughty puppy, things would have turned out differently. After the first couple of weeks, he stopped trying to avoid you. He was actually stalking you from ball to ball. I suspect he would have accepted any lie you chose to tell him, simply to keep you near him; he loved you that much. But you ran."

Meg bit her lips, tears rushing from her eyes in rivulets.

"Then you realized you were with child. I was afraid you would go to him out of desperation and tell him. I knew he would marry you then. Even if he believed the child was not his, he would have married you. So I said I would go tell him. But I didn't. I didn't say anything to him. I returned home that night, lied to you, and convinced you to take yourself off to the country to have the child in seclusion. Once you were gone, I told him and everyone else that you had run off to elope with a stable lad. And they believed it. Then I waited for my opportunity. As I had expected, he began to drink heavily. One night he got quite drunk and I was there, insisting on seeing him home. Of course, once there, I wouldn't leave until I was sure he was all right.

"I had thought that he would turn to me for comfort. He would make love to me, and I would have him." She gave a harsh laugh. "But I nearly had to rape him. It was nothing as you described. It was quick, rough, and sloppy, and he kept calling your name. He passed out on top of me. I waited till near dawn to be sure that his servant would see me leave—in a panic, of course—so that he could report it to his master lest he was so drunk he would not recall that he had taken my innocence. Then I waited. I expected him to do the chivalrous thing and propose to me. The next time I saw him, however, he was uncomfortable and as apologetic as could be, but he did not propose. I was furious, but played sweet and waited.

"I had hoped that our one time would get me with child, as it had with you, but once again I was disappointed. So again I lied. I told him I was with child from our night. At last, he did the honorable thing. We were married a week later. On our wedding night, he walked me to my door, kissed me in a fatherly fashion on the forehead, then walked off to his own room, not to bother me again. Foolishly, at the time I was relieved, for I had been agonizing over how I would explain that my body had not changed. The next morning at breakfast I began my great plan to fool the ton. I would remove myself to the country during the remainder of my pregnancy, have the child there, and not return for nine months at least so that no one should suspect that we had married due to my pregnancy. He said that was fine, even saw me off. Then I came to see you.

"He never asked me where I was going or how he could contact me, and I told myself that was grand, because then I would not need lie or fear his finding me with you. I was a fool, deluding myself. The fact was, he didn't care about anything anymore, really. Except making money for the future generations of Beechams."

Sighing, Lady Beecham peered at her sister. "Of course, you realize now that your child did not die. I had him taken to a nearby inn with a servant until I could persuade you to leave on a boat. I remained at the cottage until eight months had passed since my arrival; then returned triumphantly with your child. I was positive that presenting John with an heir would seal our relationship. That he would be grateful and learn to care for me. What I had not expected was his complete indifference.

"He barely even looked at the baby, nor myself, really, when we returned. He did not come to my bed again. Did not even speak to his own son as he grew. And I realized what a huge mistake I had made. My life with him was as cold and barren as a fallow field in winter."

"Poor you."

Meg gave a start at Valoree's words and glanced at her in surprise, as did Lady Beecham. Valoree took in their identical expressions with disgust. "Surely you are not falling for this sad tale and feeling sorry for her?" she said in a snarl. "She ruined your life. She stole the man who loved you, your only child, and your very life! You should have ended up here, happily married and raising a passel of Beechams. Instead you ended up married to a drunk in the islands. And it's all her fault."

"Nay. It is not." Meg said quietly. Valoree gaped at her. "She is right: I did not fight for him, and I should have. Instead I ran away like a coward. And it is not her fault I married Gilchrist. That was entirely my own decision. I made my own decisions, made a mess of my own life."

"But if she had not—"

"Yes, she lied. She told several whopping lies. And I never took the time to rectify or even check on them. I let pride lead me, and fell hard."

"But—"

"I should have gone to John that first day he cut me, demanded to know what that was about. I might have been insulted, or even hurt, but I was hurt already, and at least things would then have been cleared up. But I did not have the confidence in myself, or him, to do it. And not having that confidence, I should never have made love to him."

"Fine," Valoree snapped impatiently. "You made your own decisions and are willing to forgive her for messing the relationship up between the two of you. But she's been trying to kill you since you came to London! Are you going to take the blame for that as well?"

"I have not been trying to kill her."

Both Meg and Valoree looked over doubtfully at that, but it was Valoree who spoke. "Let me guess. You weren't really trying to kill her; you were simply baiting traps. If she fell into one of them, it was her own fault for not being more careful?"

A flicker of impatience crossed Blanche's face at that. "I did not bait traps, either. It was John."

"John?" Meg gasped in dismay. "My own son wishes me dead?"

"I am afraid so."

"Does he not realize that she is his mother?" Valoree demanded.

"I explained everything to him the day I spotted you in the dressmaker's. I feared you would approach him and tell him anyway, so I did it first."

"If he knows she is his mother, why would he want her dead?"

Blanche grimaced. "I fear it is precisely because she *is* his mother that he wishes her dead." When both of the women facing her merely stared at her blankly, Lady Beecham explained, "He fears that if it comes out that he is not my son, but Meg's, he will lose his title and everything that goes with it."

"Because you were married to Beecham and his true mother was not?"

"Exactly."

"Well, surely that is not really that big a deal? No matter the mother, he is still Beecham's only son. No one would contest his inheritance."

"I fear he is not willing to take the chance."

"I can see you did a fine job of raising him," Valoree said sarcastically.

"It is difficult to raise a child properly when the father makes it obvious that he does not give a damn about either of you."

Valoree grimaced, seeing some truth in her words,

but changed the subject. "So you intend to simply stand by and let him kill us?"

"Nay, of course not. I slipped down here to set you free."

"What! Well, why the devil didn't ye say so?" Valoree rolled her eyes. "Never mind, I don't want to hear it. But I shall give you a tip, Lady Beecham." She moved quickly to the door, Meg on her heels. "When in times of peril, 'tis usually best to leave the explanations until all parties are safely away. Or at least to explain on the way to safety. We could have been halfway to Spain by—" She paused abruptly as she reached Lady Beecham, her gaze narrowing on the man who suddenly appeared behind her.

Catching her expression, Blanche Beecham glanced over her shoulder, her eyes widening in alarm. "John," she said nervously. "I thought you had gone to your club."

"I stopped at the old town house on the way to ask Lady Ainsley's aunt and uncle how long they had determined to stay. I had a prospective renter to take their place. I found Thurborne there, examining a man who had apparently broken his neck and died in a fall down the stairs. When I recognized him as that wastrel servant of yours, Addams, I returned home."

"Oh." Her hand fluttered down toward her bag nervously, then suddenly dug inside and came out holding a pistol. "Get out of the way, John."

"Blanche?" Meg said uncertainly. "What?"

"Oh, do shut up, Margaret," Blanche snapped impatiently. "I am sick unto death of your whining and sniveling. If only you had died in Port Royale as I had hoped and prayed all this time, none of this would be happening."

Valoree threw her hands up in disgust. "Let me guess: everything you just said was a lie. You *are* the one after all, and John is innocent."

"Not quite," she said grimly. "I told the truth about what happened in the past."

"Well, bully for you," Valoree answered.

"How could you do that to my father?"

"You shut up too, John. I had her convinced that you were behind the attacks and that it was all her fault. Given a few more moments, I would have had them both convinced to keep quiet about it all and simply to slink back to the islands."

"I do not slink," Valoree protested, and Lady Beecham made a face.

"Nay, but you would have kept your mouth shut for Margaret's sake."

Valoree shrugged, because she probably would have. After all, it hardly benefited her to have Meg's true identity exposed. There would be questions then about where she had been all her life and with whom.

Lady Beecham turned back to John. "You see? If you hadn't interfered, this would all have gone well. But nay. You had to interfere. Like mother, like son," she said with a sneer.

"But why did you want me to believe all those horrible things about John?" Meg asked in confusion, and Blanche turned on her in fury.

"Because you would not die, damn you! Time after time Addams tried to kill you, and time after time you seemed to sail through the attempts. And now he is dead."

"He was quite inept," Valoree told her dryly. "I presume it was he who knocked me out in the kitchens?"

"Aye. He heard my sister say she would go see if the tea was coming and he crept off to the kitchen, but it was you who entered."

"Hmmm." Valoree nodded. "You should have gone down to the docks and hired someone from there to do your dirty work. No one down there would have muffed the job. I do not suppose you would care to share the name of the fellow who knocked Meg and I over the head tonight?"

"Why on earth would I do that?" she asked irritably.

Valoree shrugged. "We might go easier on you when we decide how to deal with you."

"Deal with me?" Lady Beecham peered at her with a sort of amused horror. "Who are you? Do you not see that I have a pistol? Do you *want* to be shot?"

Valoree grimaced at that, wishing she had remembered her blade. She was truly going soft, else she would have worn it. But it was so difficult to carry about now that she no longer wore boots. A movement drew her gaze past John Beecham to see Daniel walking grimly up the hall, Henry, One-Eye, Pete, and Bull at his heels. "Oh, hello, husband," she greeted him cheerfully.

Lady Beecham swiveled her head in horror, and Meg's son promptly took the opportunity to snatch the gun from her hand.

"Very good," Valoree murmured, impressed with the man's fast thinking and agile motion. Perhaps Henry was right: with a little seasoning, Beecham just might measure up to Daniel someday.

"Thank you," Beecham murmured, flushing slightly at the praise, then turned the gun on the woman who had stolen him from his true mother. She started to sidle toward the door. "What do we do with her?"

They were all silent for a moment; then Valoree suggested, "Well, that depends. Who has control of the Beecham money?"

"I do," John admitted, obviously perplexed as to the relevance of that.

"Good. I suggest you hire someone to take her to Port Royale. Set her up in a teeny little cottage there, and give her a small stipend, just adequate to see her fed and able to buy a new dress once a year."

"Nay!" Lady Beecham turned to John in outrage,

obviously horrified by the idea. "Nay. Son, you could not be so cruel."

"Actually, I think I could," John murmured, seeming to like the idea. "After all, it is no more than the life you sentenced my real mother to, is it?"

"Valoree!"

Grimacing at Daniel's irate growl, she raised her eyebrows at John. "I take it you brought these men along?"

He nodded apologetically. "As soon as I said that Addams was my mother's servant, they were determined to come have a talk with her."

"Valoree? What are you doing here?" Daniel asked, slipping past John to move to her side, concern now mingling with her anger. "How did you get here?"

"Visiting?" she suggested, laughing as John dragged Lady Beecham from the room. Meg followed her son. Valoree's crewmen hesitated, then followed as well, leaving Valoree to peek at Daniel's black expression and sigh. "I decided to walk over to the town house after you left, but when I got there, Meg was slipping out. So I followed her here."

"You walked?" He stared at her in horror. "At night? By yourself? Valoree, you should not be taking such risks in your condition."

"I am with child, Daniel. Not ill."

"You know?"

"I know what? That I am with child? Well, of course I know. What sort of idiot do you take me for?"

"Well, when did you plan to tell me?" he asked shortly.

"When did you plan to tell me that Skully had broken his arm fighting off this Addams fellow?" she snapped right back.

They were both silent for a moment, glaring at each other; then Daniel slid one hand wearily over his face. "Valoree, we have to—"

"Another deal for you to break?" she asked.

He gave her a hurt look. "Nay. I will not break it. But in return we have to work together. You have to share with me. Everything. Can you do that?"

She stared at him silently, knowing what he meant. She had kept the news of the baby to herself, and she was trying to keep her crew to herself, too. And by doing so, she had shut him out of those portions of her life. It was as if she thought that by compartmentalizing everything, she could hold on to it all.

"I will try," she said finally.

"That is all I ask," he assured her, pulling her into his arms and holding her close to his heart.

# *Chapter Eighteen*

Valoree stepped out on deck and stretched in delight, her head tipping up to the sun and her eyes closing as she breathed deeply of the fresh sea air.

"Good morning, Captain." Strong, warm arms closed around her from behind, and a chest pressed against her back. Large hands flattened themselves against her well-rounded stomach.

Smiling at that deep voice in her ear, Valoree lowered her head, her hands moving to rest on Daniel's arms as she leaned into him. "Good morning, Captain," she whispered back. She gave a sigh—the deeply satisfied sigh of a woman whose life was as good as it could be. These last months had seen everything straightened out. A visit with a doctor to verify her pregnancy had been enough to see both Daniel's grandmother's money, and Ainsley estate, released to them. That had only left the meeting with the king.

Much to Valoree's pleasure, Daniel had taken her along with him for the royal audience. Too, it had gone much more smoothly than she had hoped. Daniel had explained the matter of Jeremy's death and Valoree's continuation in his stead. She herself had explained the reasons she had not yet delivered the king his portion.

The king had been very understanding. Valoree suspected it was due to the meticulous accounting they had presented to him, and the scrupulous care that they had taken in ensuring his portion was set aside. And the fact that it was easily—and immediately—deliverable surely helped their case as well.

"You, slept well, I hope?" Little butterfly kisses along her throat drew Valoree from her thoughts. She laughed huskily.

"Like a babe rocked to sleep in its mother's arms." Turning in his embrace, she leaned her stomach into him and pulled his head down for a sweet kiss.

"Mmmmm," he murmured; then his gaze slid past her. He smiled wryly.

"What is it?" she asked, glancing around.

"The men," he said, but needn't have bothered. She could see that every single man on deck was watching them with big, silly, self-satisfied grins on their faces. No doubt every single one of them was congratulating himself for his part in her present happiness. And she supposed they had all played a part. For if they had not voted that she marry, then kidnapped the husband of their choice, she wouldn't now be married to the man standing before her. So . . . let them gloat a bit, she decided, then watched as Daniel placed his hands on her belly. He hadn't been pleased at the idea of this trip. He had refused to come until the spring, claiming that there was little the men could do in the way of building their cottages, repairing Ainsley, and planting their crops until then anyway.

Valoree suspected he had also hoped that the baby would show itself early and that any worry would be out of the way. The men had therefore been stuck traveling between the ship and Thurborne Castle, taking their turns at each place, and suffering horrible boredom through the winter. Come the first sign of spring, Valoree had announced determinedly that they had to get the men to Ainsley. Daniel had agreed, though not happily, and they had prepared the boat to journey around England to the other side. It was the long way there, for certain, but the men had wanted it that way. Not three of them knew how to ride a horse, and traveling wagons had made them all flinch at the thought, so here they were, heading for Ainsley and the lives they had always wanted.

Daniel had claimed that the pirates would get tired of the pastoral life in no time. He felt sure they would be clamoring for their old life ere summer. Valoree half suspected he was right, but the only solution they had come up with was to keep the ship. Should such an event happen and they wished to return to sea, the Thurbornes could arrange for legitimate shipping expeditions that the men could perform.

"You realize that our child is going to be the most spoiled brat in all of England," Daniel murmured, rubbing one hand gently over Valoree's belly.

Valoree laughed. "And how do you come to that conclusion, husband?"

"Well, just look at these sea dogs. Every single one of them cannot wait for him to be born, and every single one of them thinks he should be the godfather."

"And every single one of them *shall* be *her* godfather," Valoree said. At his astonished look, she chuckled. "Think on it. That way, should anything happen to leave her without us, she will have the best help a girl could ask for."

Daniel shook his head and pulled her into his embrace. "That will never happen."

"It happened to me," she murmured solemnly into his chest. His arms tightened around her as if to protect her from the memory of her loss.

"Captain!" They broke apart at once at Richard's shout, both of them turning toward where the other man hung over the crow's nest waving down at them. Both of them called out at the same time, "What is it?"

"A ship! Westward ho!"

Both of them moved to the rail, squinting in the direction Richard was pointing. Indeed, there was a ship, and it was sailing toward them at a fast clip. Valoree's hands clenched, a frown curving her lip. She had a strange feeling. . . . Whirling away from the rail, she shielded her eyes and peered up at her second mate. "What color's the flag?"

Richard raised the glass to his eyes and toward the oncoming vessel. Valoree knew when he finally lowered the tube that it wasn't good news. "She's flying a black flag, Captain."

There was a moment of complete silence as the crew absorbed his words. They had never been on the receiving end of a pirate attack before. But for this trip, they were flying England's colors, and the hold was stocked full of furniture, provisions, tools, and seeds. They were carrying everything they had thought they might need to turn Ainsley back into the home it had once been. Riding low in the water from all the weight, they no doubt looked a prime catch.

"What do we do, Captain?" Daniel asked solemnly as the men began to draw nearer. Valoree peered at him in surprise. Despite his claim that they would make their decisions and rule together, and despite his discussing most, if not all, things with her before announcing the decisions they came to, she had truly thought that at the first opportunity, he would take charge and relegate her to a subordinate position. Instead, he appeared to be putting her in charge and stepping down. Seeing her amazement, he gave a half-smile and shook his head.

"There is no time for our usual discussion here. A decision has to be made and made quickly. And you are the more experienced one in this situation, Valoree. When we encounter a crisis where I am, I will take charge, but right now it is you." His words were almost gentle. "What do we do? Try to outrun them?"

Pushing her thoughts away for later consideration, Valoree concentrated on the problem at hand. "We're too heavy with all the goods for Ainsley in the hold. We'd never escape."

There were grunts and nods of agreement from the men, and Daniel seemed to agree. He looked annoyed though. "Then we surrender?"

"The hell we do!" Valoree gave him a stare as though he were mad, an expression the others bestowed on him as well.

"Well, those are our only two options. Outrun them or surrender. What else—"

"We fight," Valoree announced. The men immediately cheered at the announcement. Daniel was a little less pleased.

"Fight? This ship is full of goods, not weapons, and there are women and children aboard," he reminded her grimly, his gaze dropping to her belly. Valoree waved him to silence.

"We will not fight outright," she said patiently. "Though if I were the only woman aboard we might. However, I am not the only woman aboard," she continued quickly when he began to look quite angry again. "But we are not weaponless." Turning away from him, she sought Henry with her eyes, and he quickly moved through the men to her side. "Break open the crates below. Every man gets two flintlocks and a cutlass. And set some men to carting the cannons up here." Henry started off with all haste, the others following.

"Valoree, I love you. And I know you are the more experienced at this," Daniel said unhappily. "But your experience is with attacking, not defending. I really think we should just surrender and hope for the best. Our chances—"

"Are quite good, actually," Valoree interrupted with a grin, her eyes sparkling as she peered around the deck, quickly making plans in her head. "They think we are simply a merchant ship. We are riding low. They'll expect us to have a couple dozen men at most. We have seventy-seven."

"Seventy-six," he corrected, glaring meaningfully at her stomach. "And twelve females."

"Seventy-six men, and *thirteen* women," she laughed, rubbing her stomach meaningfully. She headed toward the helm, eager to talk to Bull.

Daniel caught her arm and swung her around to face him. "This is serious, Valoree. I do not want you or the other women in jeopardy."

Sighing, she touched his cheek gently, her smile turning sad. "We already are, husband, and nothing you can do can stop that."

"But if we surrender—"

"They will kill us. Or worse," she added quietly. "Have you forgotten what pirates did to my brother and his men?"

"You do not know that these men are the same type."

"And you do not know that they are not. I would rather not take the chance. Not with my life, not with your life, and not with little Jermina's life," she added, patting her belly.

"Jermina?" Daniel cried.

Valoree let out a sad little breath. "Nay, hmmm? I did not think so, and truly I do not much care for the name either, but I thought it would be nice to name her after my brother," she murmured wistfully. She sighed again, then gave a small shrug and turned to continue on toward Bull. Daniel was right at her heels.

"All right. You have convinced me it is too risky to surrender. So what is your plan?"

"I am not sure," she admitted. Pausing, she turned to see that he had frozen, gaping at her and horrified. "What?" she asked.

"What?" he repeated in disbelief. "You just told me that you do not have a plan!"

"Nay, I—"

"Aye, you did. I heard it quite plainly," he argued. Valoree rolled her eyes.

"I did not say I did not *have* a plan. I said that I was not sure of it. I am still working it out." Valoree explained patiently.

"Oh." Some of his anxiety eased, though not much. "Well, what are you thinking of, then?"

Shrugging Valoree turned away and continued on toward the helm. "I am thinking that we will appear to surrender and allow some of them to board. Then, when they are least expecting it, we will attack."

"That's it?" he cried, following her to the helm. "That is your whole plan?"

"My lord, the simple plans are usually the most successful," she said exasperatedly, forcing a smile for Bull's sake as she arrived beside him. "Go as quickly as you can. I know we are weighed down right now, but I want you to get every last bit of speed out of the *Valor* that you can manage."

"Aye-aye, Captain."

"Why? I thought we were going to seem to surrender?" Daniel asked worriedly. Valoree had to count to ten to keep from snapping at him.

Once she felt sure she would remain calm, she turned to him with a decidedly forced smile and explained. "If we appear to surrender too easily, without making at least an effort at escape, they will surely become suspicious. Do you not think?"

"Oh, aye," he mumbled. She shook her head sympathetically.

"Husband, you appear to have difficulty with giving up control of this situation. Mayhap you should go below and have a drink."

Daniel smiled wryly. "I am not behaving well, am I? Well . . ." He glanced toward the ship that drew nearer with every passing moment. It certainly sailed under a black flag. "I will try to do better. I trust you. Truly I do. You are an excellent captain. All the men say so."

"Aye. And I am," Valoree agreed proudly. "And as captain, I think you would feel better if you have something to do."

"Aye, mayhap I would," her husband admitted.

Valoree glanced around. "Why do you not go tell Henry that once he has finished handing out the weapons, I want the crates they were packed in for the trip broken and thrown overboard. In fact, mayhap you could oversee that."

"Aha." Daniel nodded. "I can do that." He started to turn away, then paused and swung back. "But why?"

Valoree almost snapped at him that it didn't matter why; she was captain at the moment and that meant he was to follow orders without question. But then she reconsidered and forced herself to explain. "If we were truly trying to escape, we would attempt to lighten our load by throwing goods over."

"Ah, so you hope to fool them by throwing the parts of the crates over."

"Aye. But empty crates would float for a minute or so ere sinking, so you are going to break the crates into single slats, then have men carry them with the flat and largest sides facing the oncoming ship. And drop them into the water as if they are heavy."

"Clever," he said with a sudden grin. "I shall see to it at once."

"Great." Valoree felt some relief as he finally walked away, then chuckled under her breath.

"What's so funny?" Bull asked beside her.

"I was just thinking that as much trouble as he is having giving up control in this crisis, I would be worse were it me."

"Aye," Bull agreed solemnly. At the rather stiff look she threw his way for agreeing so quickly, he shrugged. "Just look how much trouble we had getting ye married to him."

Muttering under her breath, she walked away in search of the women.

"Oh, God. I should have insisted you stay below."

Valoree tore her gaze away from the small dinghy paddling toward them across the short span of water separating the two boats, and frowned at Daniel.

They had pretended to attempt to outrun the pirates now crossing the water eagerly toward them, then appeared to surrender reluctantly when it was obvious that they could not. Pulling the English flag down, they had replaced it with a white shirt, the best they could do for the colorless flag that was the traditional signal of surrender. In response, the other boat had fired one single cannon off the starboard bow as a warning not to try to flee, then laid anchor a safe distance away, just far enough not to have to worry about the two swinging around in a current or stiff breeze and hitting each other. Then the pirates had lowered the small boat, filled it to overflowing with men, and begun to make their way across to mount the *Valor* and claim her as their own. They left some of their crew aboard their own ship, of course, with the cannons trained on the *Valor* as an obvious threat.

Still, they thought the *Valor* a simple merchant ship, carrying goods, perhaps a dozen or so men, and few if any weapons. They were in for a surprise. And at that moment, Valoree was experiencing the same mounting tension and tingling expectation she had always enjoyed when climbing silently up the sides of the craft they had taken themselves. Anticipating the battle ahead, she thrilled at the danger. She felt incredibly alive as she always had. Yet this time, she felt almost an equal amount of terror as well. That was new. Always before she had felt only a burning sort of rage, a desperate desire for revenge, a longing to find herself facing the scarred Spanish bastard who had killed her brother, and a complete lack of concern with death. Now, however, she knew with a certainty that she would never again be Back-from-the-Dead Red—and never could be.

Now the possibility of death was like a cloud inside her head, numbing the part of her brain she needed most and making her hand tremble slightly with the fear of it. She wanted to live. She wanted to spend her life with Daniel, to see her babe born, to watch it grow. And she knew instinctively that her fear was what could get her killed.

"Aye, I should have locked you in the cabin. A woman has no place amid this men's work. And this plan is madness, pure and simple. It will never work. I was a fool to listen to a woman and her hare-brained schemes. Here I was letting you act as captain out of pity and—"

"Pity!" Valoree turned on him in amazement as his words finally sank through her fear and she realized what he had been saying. She couldn't believe the words had spouted from his mouth. After all his proclamations of love and admiration, after finding her *so* intelligent! Now the truth was out. Eyes narrowing to glowing orbs of rage, Valoree put her nose to his and said in a hiss, "You'd best be saving some of that pity for yourself, husband, for after we take care of these bastards. Then I'll be turning my attention to you, and you can count yourself lucky if ye ain't hanged from the crow's nest after all."

Then she turned away to move toward the other women, pausing after only a step to whirl back. "And ye'd best not mess your part up, sirrah, or I'll cut your tongue out and feed it to the fish ere I have ye hanged."

Unfortunately, unlike her men, who were now watching the exchange warily, Daniel didn't look a bit cowed by her threat. He merely grinned and gave her a wink, which served only to infuriate her further. Hand clenching around the cutlass she held hidden in the folds of her skirt, she turned her attention to the other men and said in a snarl, "Look lively; they're boarding. You know what to do."

The men turned to see that she was right. The ropes that had been lowered over the side of the boat were moving slightly and creaking under the weight of the men climbing them. Her crew immediately began to take their positions, and Valoree turned away to stomp over to the other women. Eleni was one of them. She and Petey had more than resolved their differences in the Thurbourne kitchen over who was in charge—they had married just two weeks before setting out for Ainseley. Meg was there, too. Though John had begged her to stay and live with him at Beecham, Meg had feared causing him problems. Instead, she claimed she preferred the idea of a nice little cottage at Ainsley. "Close to Henry and his roses would be nice," she had told Valoree in confidence.

The rest of the women were the wives or the soon-to-be wives of other crew members—except for Helen, the sweet, dark-haired girl who had taken up the role of lady's maid to Valoree. She was the only single young woman on board. Still, the way One-Eye kept trying to charm her made Valoree think that the girl wouldn't be unwed for long. Eleni, Meg, and Helen were the only females who were keeping a brave face on. The others were all shaking in their skirts, a couple even giving in to terrified sobs. The ruckus rubbed Valoree's already raw nerves.

"Quit yer sniveling," she snapped. "Ye'll just be drawing attention to yerselves that way."

That seemed to scare the sobs right out of them, she saw with some satisfaction. Turning herself slightly so that her sword hand was hidden between herself and the group she stood in front of made her advanced stage of pregnancy more obvious, and that was fine, too. It made her appear harmless.

"You men ready back there, One-Eye?" she said in a hiss.

"Aye, Cap'n," came the soft answer.

"Good. On my signal."

"Aye."

"Nice work," Henry muttered, moving to Daniel's side once Valoree was out of earshot. When he simply raised an innocent eyebrow at the remark, the older man said, "She was losing her nerve. You gave it back to her by making her too mad to remember to be afraid."

Daniel shrugged. Right at that moment, he didn't know if he had done the right thing. He had seen the fear, had known it wasn't normal for her and therefore was not something she could easily overcome, and had instinctively done what he'd needed to do. But now he almost thought he should have left her afraid. He would rather she stayed out of the fray with the other women. That was something he knew she wasn't likely to do now that her fear was under control again.

"Never seen her like that before," Henry admitted. "Guess ye're softening her up some. A good thing, I think."

Daniel looked skeptical. "What? Not sorry to see the end to Captain Back-from the-Dead Red?"

Henry considered that seriously for a moment, then sighed. "She sure was something to see. No fear. All rage. Taking on any and all comers, and that anger was her finest weapon. Her lack of fear scared the hell out of any man with the sense to want to live."

At Daniel's expression, he continued. "More often than not that attitude convinced them of the wisdom of surrendering. Not every time, mind ye. She proved her worth with a sword, too—more times than I care to remember. And she showed us that all those years of us men training her weren't for naught. But she was lucky. We all were. That luck couldn't hold out forever. Jeremy's death proved that. Nay." He shook his head. "We're best out of this business. Jeremy would want her out of it."

Daniel was silent for a moment, then said softly. "I am surprised that he allowed her to be trained with the sword."

Now it was Henry's turn to look skeptical. "Considering the life we led, it would have been more surprising had he not."

Daniel murmured in reluctant agreement, then stiffened as the first of the pirates clambered over the side of the ship.

There were twenty in all, and every one of them was armed to the teeth. Compared to them, the twelve men of the *Valor* in evidence besides Daniel and Henry looked almost respectable. And that, he realized suddenly, had most likely been Valoree's intent. These men were the ones still possessing all their limbs and bodily parts. Not a patch, a peg leg, or a missing nose among them. They were also wearing simple breeches and shirts with one weapon each, generally a cutlass. They had no special leather vests or belts bristling with blades or pistols.

Brilliant, he congratulated her silently as the pirate captain came over the side last. That, he thought, was telling. The man was a coward. Daniel had heard very little about Valoree's days of high-seas robbery—by his own choice, for while Valoree was quiet on the subject, the men had been eager to regale him with tales of their daring. But after learning that she always led the attack and was the first over the side of the ship, he had shied off hearing more. Perhaps when he was in his dotage, and already gray, he would be better equipped to handle hearing how she had put herself in danger. But now his poor heart could not bear it.

At that moment, however, he felt a thrill of pride at the fact that, captain or not—and having that choice— still she had always led the attack. This man did not have that courage, and while that lowered him in Daniel's estimation, it also made Daniel extremely wary. There was nothing more dangerous, in his opinion, than a coward. One never knew what lengths they would go to to save their own skin.

These thoughts running through his head, he watched grimly as the pirate captain slowly perused the ship, taking in each man, then the women, before settling on Daniel and Henry. He moved toward them at once, a supercilious smile on his face as he took in Daniel's matching maroon velvet waistcoat and the silly beribboned knee breeches Valoree had insisted he wear. She had said it would make him look more fey and less threatening. Daniel tried not to grimace as the man's gaze then dropped to the pink hose she had also insisted he wear. He had recognized them at once as part of the livery the men had sported while they paraded as her house servants, but had donned them without argument, knowing there was a purpose behind her every order.

Promising himself he would wipe that smirk off the man's face at the first opportunity, he began to wave the hankie she had pressed into his hand, in what he hoped would appear a nervous fashion. Then he pressed it to his upper lip and tried to look as small and "fey" as a six-foot man with broad shoulders could as the fellow paused before him.

"Ye'd be the captain of this here vessel," the fellow decided, addressing Henry with a barely discernible Spanish accent.

"Aye," the quartermaster calmly lied.

The fellow accepted that readily, then nodded in Daniel's general direction without bothering to look at him. "Owner?"

"Aye," Henry said again. "And ye are?"

There was a tense moment of silence; then he smiled. It wasn't a very pleasant smile. "Have your men drop their weapons."

Henry hesitated, then gestured with his hand, and there was a brief symphony of clumps and clangs as the men dropped their pistols and cutlasses.

The pirate captain made a similar gesture, and several of his men began to move around, collecting the dropped arsenal. Once that was done, he turned back to Henry. "What are you carrying?"

"Linen, taffeta, silver, iron, and a bit of gold, but not much," Henry said—exactly what Valoree had told him to report as their cargo. Furniture and food might have just angered the fellow and gotten someone shot before they were ready for fighting. Claiming too much of value might have made him suspicious, however.

The pirate seemed satisfied with the list. He merely nodded, then held out a hand, palm up. "*Your* weapon."

\*    \*    \*

Valoree watched silently as Henry pulled out the flint-lock pistol she'd had him put in the top of his pants. He handed it over slowly, laying it in the man's palm before reaching to remove his cutlass. It was while he was distracted with the second task that the pirate captain struck. She saw him swing the gun at Henry and stiffened, but before she could utter a word, an alarmed cry from Meg pierced her ear. It was too late for Henry to avoid the blow, however, and he went down like a stone beneath it. He fell unconscious to the deck.

Meg immediately tried to rush past her then, no doubt to help Henry, but Valoree grabbed her arm and held her back, stepping in front of her when the pirate captain peered curiously toward them. Their gazes met briefly, and she found her chin rising despite her best efforts to appear frightened. Then he broke the glance and turned to address his now unarmed captives.

"I am Captain Álvarez of the *Bastardo*. This is my ship now. And you will now have your choice: a slow death or a fast one. Those men who cooperate and help us transfer the cargo will die quickly and as painlessly as possible. Those who do not, but ask questions, or are too slow to follow orders"—he glanced down and kicked the unconscious Henry viciously, then smiled pleasantly as he finished—"will be sport for my men. That means keel-hauling, eating your own tongues, things of that nature," he explained in a bored tone, then shrugged. "I would offer some of you the opportunity to join my crew, but I have just taken on several from another ship, and so need no more men."

"Now, Captain?"

Valoree heard One-Eye's hissed words. He sounded furious. Of course. But then, all the men would be outraged. It was one thing to kill a man, quite another to torture him to death. And really, offering to kill him quickly if he sweated to help the people who were about to kill him was just a touch too damned evil. This Álvarez needed to learn a lesson.

"Nay," she whispered back. "Wait."

Álvarez turned toward her again, and she at first thought he had heard her admonishment to One-Eye, but when she took in his expression, she decided he hadn't; he was just now turning his interest to the women.

"You ladies, of course . . ." he said as he walked toward where they were grouped together midship. "You shall not die . . . right away." He smiled at Valoree, who was in front, as if he had just done them the greatest of favors; then his gaze dropped to her stomach. He grimaced. "We shall have to dispose of that."

She saw the rage flash over Daniel's face and knew her own no doubt mirrored it, but merely turned her head away from Álvarez, avoiding his eyes to glance over the position of the various men aboard her ship, then toward the Spanish vessel and the sea between. The small dinghy they had used to bring the first load of cutthroats over was halfway between the ships, heading back for reinforcements.

She caught movement out of the corner of her eye, and turned back in time to see Álvarez catch Helen by the arm and drag her against his chest.

"You are a pretty little thing. You can entertain me personally, sí?" Álvarez told the girl, chuckling as she began to struggle against him.

"I do not think so," Valoree answered pulling her cutlass out and sliding it against his throat. "Not right *now*."

If the pirate captain was startled to suddenly find himself on the business end of a sword, he managed to hide it well; he even smiled as he regarded her.

"A woman with spunk," he commented, apparently amused by the situation. He nodded back toward where

Daniel stood stiff and silent beside the unconscious Henry. "His wife?"

Valoree nodded silently.

"Well, you are too much woman for him. I will show you what a real man is like, yes?"

He released Helen then, and Valoree tensed to see what he would do next when explosions rang out nearly directly behind her. The cannons, of course. It seemed One-Eye had understood her emphasis on the word *now*. She had been so distracted, she hadn't heard or smelled the burning fuses. She saw shock suffuse the pirate captain's face, then understanding as he realized why the women had been standing where they had, and what they had been hiding with their many skirts. There was a second set of booms as the cannonballs found their target.

A horrible rending sound rang out, and everyone turned to see the main mast of the Spanish craft suddenly crash onto its deck. The screams of its sailors were drowned out, however, by the roar of Valoree's own crew. They began pouring out of every door and hole in the *Valor* and leaping from beneath canvases laid over apparent cargo. One fellow even rose straight up out of an empty barrel, its lid flying off as if under the impact of an explosion. The deck suddenly crawled with men, all releasing bloodcurdling screeches.

Valoree turned back to Ávarez, aware as she did that Daniel was approaching the man from behind. But the satisfied smile on her face died, replaced with shock as a movement twisted the kerchief at the pirate's throat, revealing the top of a scar. A buzzing suddenly filling her ears, she reached out to snatch the kerchief away. Her eyes glazed over with a combination of rage and horror as she saw the question mark-shaped scar at the base of the man's throat. She could hear Jeremy's raspy breath in her ear again, could see his bloody body she'd held in her young arms.

"A question-mark-shaped scar . . . throat. Spanish bastard . . . ohhh," he had said in a gasp. She had thought he was calling the man a name, then gasping in pain. But, nay, he had been naming the ship. Dear Lord, all this time—

A second set of explosions shook her out of her shock in time to see Álvarez raise a pistol toward her. Her eyes widened at the sight of it and the man's other hand reaching for her, ignoring the cutlass at his throat, but before she could react, the pirate suddenly stiffened. Valoree never heard the shot; her ears were still ringing from the boom of the *Valor*'s cannons. She just saw the way Álvarez's eyes dilated, pain and surprise flashing across his face; then a thin trickle of blood spilled from the corner of his mouth. He stumbled forward, falling against her. Valoree tried to step away, but her feet tangled up in her skirts in her hurry to avoid him. She stumbled, and would have fallen with the man if the other women hadn't caught her, but they did and held her up as he went down.

Daniel lowered the flintlock he had used to shoot Álvarez. Dropping the spent weapon to the deck, he reached inside his now open waistcoat for the second pistol he had stowed in the top of his breeches and moved quickly forward, prepared to shoot the man again. But one glance at the pirate captain told him there was no need. The man was dead. Daniel's gaze slid to his wife then, and concern filled him at her pallor.

"Valoree?" he asked taking her in his arms and holding her stiff body close, "Are you all right?"

She nodded silently in response, but he could feel her tremble in his arms. He frowned as he held her close, his gaze shifting questioningly to the other women. Blank confusion and small shrugs were his only answer. None of them knew what was wrong.

"His throat!"

Daniel glanced around to see that Henry was up and walking about, assisted by Meg. The older man lowered the hand that had been rubbing the side of his head, then pointed to Alvarez. "The scar."

Daniel glanced down at the villain's throat, confused. Squinting at the scar at the base of the dead pirate's neck, he saw that it looked very much like a question mark. At that, he stiffened, his gaze shooting back to Valoree. "Your brother's murderer?" he asked incredulously.

Nodding silently, Valoree stared at the man, watching unmoving as his blood seeped out, staining the deck.

"Well," Henry said after a moment. "When this bastard's ship was spotted, I figured that we might be having that same bad luck that we ran across in London. But it seems you were right after all, Captain."

When Valoree tore her gaze from the pirate's corpse to give him a questioning look, the quartermaster shrugged slightly. He winced as the movement caused pain from his wounded head, but he explained. " 'Tweren't bad luck at all. We won." His mouth curved into a big grin as he spoke, then he added more solemnly, "And this here about closes the door on the past. Don't it? We vowed for life and vengeance, and Jeremy now's got it. He can rest easy."

"Aye. That he can," Valoree agreed, and Daniel could hear that she was fighting tears. He knew that she would never cry in front of her men, but also that this moment meant very much to her.

"Captain?" One-Eye's voice broke in.

"Aye?" Valoree answered at the same time as Daniel. He squeezed her arm, giving him her strength—if she wanted it.

"What do you want we should do with the pirates?" the first mate asked. Daniel stiffened as he waited for

Valoree's decision. These were the men who had murdered her brother. Would she resist avenging herself upon them?

His wife stared blankly at One-Eye for a moment, then glanced over the deck of the *Valor II,* taking in the fact that every last Spaniard was lying on the deck. Those foolish enough to fight had been killed or injured, and those who had surrendered at once had been ordered to lie on their stomachs on the deck. They were now guarded by several of her grim-faced men. Her gaze slid over toward the *Bastardo.* With satisfaction, she saw that it was sinking fast. "Is the dinghy still afloat?" she asked.

One-Eye raised an eyebrow. "Aye."

"Then throw them over. Those still alive can swim to the dinghy. Those dead"—she shrugged with disinterest—"let the sea have."

Daniel remained silent, only nodding in mute agreement. Then he swept Valoree into his arms.

"You are in charge, One-Eye," Valoree announced as he headed for the cabins with her in his arms. "Clean the ship of this slop, then head us for Ainsley. Henry," she added, catching his upset, "you're to let Meg tend to your head—and no argument about it."

The older man made a face, but nodded.

Relieved it was over, Daniel started down the stairs with his wife in his arms. "Your plan worked," he said with a combination of pride and love as he carried her through the open door of their cabin. Pausing inside, he kicked the door closed with one booted foot, then carried her over to the bed. There, he deposited her gently.

"As did yours," she murmured back, sitting up on the bed and leaning against the wall. He began to disrobe. "What are you doing?"

"Getting out of these damn clothes. I feel like a dandy in them."

Valoree grinned. "You don't *look* like a dandy in them. If anything, my lord, I think pink emphasizes your manliness."

Daniel grunted as he stepped out of the awful knee breeches, leaving only the pink hose and white linen shirt. "Somehow I do not think Álvarez agreed with you."

"Álvarez was not a woman," she murmured, her face stiffening slightly at the name. The man would be a raw topic for quite a while.

"What did you mean, my plan worked? This was all *your* plan."

"The getting me angry part was not part of *my* plan," she answered dryly, reaching out to undo and help remove his hose. Daniel's body took interest in being disrobed.

"Oh, that." He shrugged slightly as he stepped out of the stockings, then straightened, his linen shirt dropping down to cover his body's reaction.

"Aye, *that*," Valoree said, tugging at his shirt, urging him down to her level. When he knelt accommodatingly before her, she captured his face in her hands and pressed a sweet kiss to his lips. "Aye, *that*, my lord husband," she murmured, breaking the kiss before he could deepen it. "Thank you for recognizing my weakness and helping me to overcome it."

"Fear is not weakness, Valoree," he responded. "Only a fool does not feel fear."

"Then thank you for being my strength today, for helping me to do what had to be done." she said softly. Her fingers slipped from his face to fall to his shoulders, and Daniel clasped her face in his much larger hands.

"Today and always, Valoree. Whether dead or alive. I love you."

Her eyes filled with tears at his gentle proclamation, and she tried to turn her face away.

"Nay, do not try to hide from me," he murmured, holding her face firmly in his hands and catching the first tear that slid from one eye with the tip of his thumb. "Please. Never hide your feelings from me. Not your fear, not your pain, and not your love."

She went still at the last word, and he sighed and lowered his own head. "You give me your passion, Valoree, and it is beautiful. Your anger, your laughter. Your lovemaking is freer and more impassioned than that of any woman I have known, but I want more. I love you."

Valoree felt guilt swamp her at those words. She had known for some time that she loved Daniel, but the opportunity to say so had never really come.

Ah, who was she kidding? The truth was that she had been afraid to say those words. Some part of her had feared that if she admitted her feelings she might lose this man as she had lost her mother, her father and her brother. Until today, she had never feared dying or being injured; she had feared living. She had feared caring and losing those she cared for. It was time to stop being a coward, time to give Daniel what he so freely gave her. Love.

She opened her mouth to do just that, then paused to bite her lip in pain. Her stomach had suddenly cramped. It was not the first spasm she had suffered through today, but it did seem a lot more violent than those that had been tightening her stomach since the *Bastardo* had been spotted. Of course, that distraction might have made those earlier contractions seem less severe. . . . She forgot the pain briefly as Daniel raised his head and caught the expression on her face. She knew at once he was misinterpreting her reaction. He probably thought she was unsettled by the thought of voicing her love for him.

When he started to pull away, she caught at his shirt, determined to tell him what he needed to hear. His expression turned hopeful as she opened her mouth, but all Valoree managed to get out was a garbled, "I-ugh-oh," as she was struck by another cramp. She could feel her blood draining from her face, and she bit her lip viciously to keep from crying out with the pain.

"Well, good Lord," Daniel said snippily. "There's no need to look so pained at the idea." He tried to pull away. "I am going to change and go back on deck, make sure everything is all right."

"Nay," Valoree gasped, refusing to let him go. Seeing his building impatience, she felt her own snap. Suddenly she was furious at him, both for the pain she was suffering thanks to *his* child, and at the fact that he somehow hadn't yet grasped the situation. "I—*oh!*"

"Do not trouble yourself over my feelings. I shall be fine," he said icily, trying to disengage her from his shirt.

That only managed to make Valoree more furious. "Daniel!" she snapped as the labor pain finally eased.

"What?" he snapped back, though they were nose to nose.

Valoree glared at him briefly, then snarled, "Oh, for heaven's sake! I love you. All right? I love you! Are you happy?"

He stopped trying to remove her hands. "What?"

"What?" she repeated with a shriek as another spasm came. "Are you deaf now as well? You wanted me to say it, and I said it! Now—" She paused on an indrawn breath as another contraction struck. Groaning, she sank back down onto the bed. Rolling into a fetal position away from him, she faced the wall in misery, her concentration taken up by the pain.

Her husband immediately crawled onto the small bed behind her, molding himself to her spoon-style and wrapping his arms about her. He pressed a kiss to her neck. "I am satisfied. And I am sure someday you may even say that without sounding so angry about it. But for now, an angry admission will do." He whispered that by her ear, then nibbled gently at the lobe. Nudging himself against her, he said, "I cannot wait until this babe is born and we can make love again. It feels like forever since I have felt your warmth wrapped around me."

"Aye? Well, it won't be *much* too long," she said archly and felt him stiffen.

"Do you not miss my lovemaking?" he asked with a bit of pique.

"My lord, at this moment, I loathe your lovemaking."

He stiffened at that, his mouth dropping open. "You what?"

Reaching back, she grabbed his hand and pulled it around, pressing it flat to her stomach. Daniel went stiff as he felt her stomach shift and tighten.

"What is that? What—"

"I am in labor, my lord," she explained dryly.

*"What?"* He was off the bed in a heartbeat, and Valoree glanced over her shoulder at him with a pained laugh.

"It is a bit late for that, my lord," she pointed out. "You should have done a little more leaping out and a little less leaping in several months ago to avoid this."

Daniel gaped at her. "How long has this been going on?"

Sighing, she shook her head. "I felt a bit odd when I got up this morning, but thought it would go away. It didn't. It just got a little stronger and harder as time passed. But it didn't really set in until all the excitement was over."

"You mean you were in labor the whole time the pirates were . . ." He paused at her nod and stared around blankly for a moment, then shook his head.

"Well, make it stop. You cannot have the baby here on a ship with a bunch of pirates. We need a midwife and—"

"Oh, aye, of course," Valoree snapped, then peered down at her stomach. "Did you hear that, little Jermina? Your father says to stop now. You should wait till we reach Ainsley and he can find a midwife." She paused, cocking her head slightly, then nodded. "I see." Turning, she smiled at Daniel. "She says to sod off. She's coming now."

Daniel's eyes widened in the horror of a sudden realization. "Oh, God. I am going to have two of you on my hands!"

"Aye. Lucky you. Now do you think you could go call the women in here? Maybe one of them would be a bit more useful than yourself at the moment," she suggested.

Valoree's husband was out the door in a heartbeat, bare-arsed in his linen shirt, shrieking at the top of his lungs that she was in labor and for Meg to come quickly. There was a roar as the men and women all exclaimed in mingled excitement and horror, then the sound of a stampede as everyone raced across the deck, eager to be in on the action. There was no doubt in Valoree's mind that Henry and the rest of her men would insist on being in on this. Any why not, she thought. They had been a part of every other aspect of her life. No doubt they would all try to vote on what to name the babe, too.

Sighing, Valoree rubbed her belly soothingly. "You shall love your father, Jermina. Mayhap almost as much as I do." Then she laid her head on the bed and tried to relax as she awaited the arrival of the people who loved her. This was such a large family to replace the few she had lost, she thought. And with that, Valoree suddenly realized that sometimes curses created blessings.

# Fairest of Them All
## Josette Browning

A true stoic and a gentleman, Daniel Canty has worked furiously to achieve the high esteem of the English nobility. Therefore, it is more his reputation than the promise of wealth that compels him to accept the ninth earl of Hawkenge's challenge to turn an orphan wild child into a lady. But the girl who's been raised by animals in the African interior is hardly an orphan—and his wildly beautiful charge is hardly a child. Truly, Talitha is a woman—and the most compelling Daniel has ever seen. But the mute firebrand also poses the greatest threat he has ever faced. In the girl's soft kiss is the jeopardy which Daniel has fought all his life to avoid: the danger of losing his heart.

___4513-3                                    $5.50 US/$6.50 CAN

# Always
## Lynsay Sands

Bastard daughter to the king, Rosamunde is raised in a convent and wholly prepared to take the veil . . . until good King Henry shows up with a reluctant husband in tow for her. Suddenly, she finds herself promising to love, honor, and obey Aric . . . always. But Rosamunde's education has not covered a wedding night, and the stables are a poor example for an untried girl. Will Aric bite her neck like the animals do their mates? The virile warrior seems capable of such animal passion, but his eyes promise something sweeter. And Rosamunde soon learns that while she may have trouble with obeying him, it will not be hard to love her new husband forever.

___4736-5                                           $5.50 US/$6.50 CAN

**Dorchester Publishing Co., Inc.**
**P.O. Box 6640**
**Wayne, PA 19087-8640**

Please add $1.75 for shipping and handling for the first book and $.50 for each book thereafter. NY, NYC, and PA residents, please add appropriate sales tax. No cash, stamps, or C.O.D.s. All orders shipped within 6 weeks via postal service book rate. Canadian orders require $2.00 extra postage and must be paid in U.S. dollars through a U.S. banking facility.

Name_____
Address_____
City_____ State_____ Zip_____
I have enclosed $_____ in payment for the checked book(s).
Payment <u>must</u> accompany all orders. ❑ Please send a free catalog.
    CHECK OUT OUR WEBSITE! www.dorchesterpub.com

# Five Gold Rings

## Constance O'Banyon, Stobie Piel, Lynsay Sands, Flora Speer

In the Year of Our Lord, 1135, Menton Castle is the same as any other: It has nobles and minstrels, knights and servants. Yet from the great hall to the scullery there are signs that the house is in an uproar. This Yuletide season is to be one of passion and merriment. The master of the keep has returned. With him come several travelers, some weary with laughter, some tired of tears. But in all of their stories—whether lords a'leapin' or maids a'milkin'—there is one gift that their true loves give to them. And in the winter moonlight, each of the castle's inhabitants will soon see the magic of the season and the joy that can come from five gold rings.

___4612-1                                      $5.50 US/$6.50 CAN

# Sandra Brown

## Tomorrow's Promise

**MIRA BOOKS**

ISBN 1-55166-557-3

TOMORROW'S PROMISE